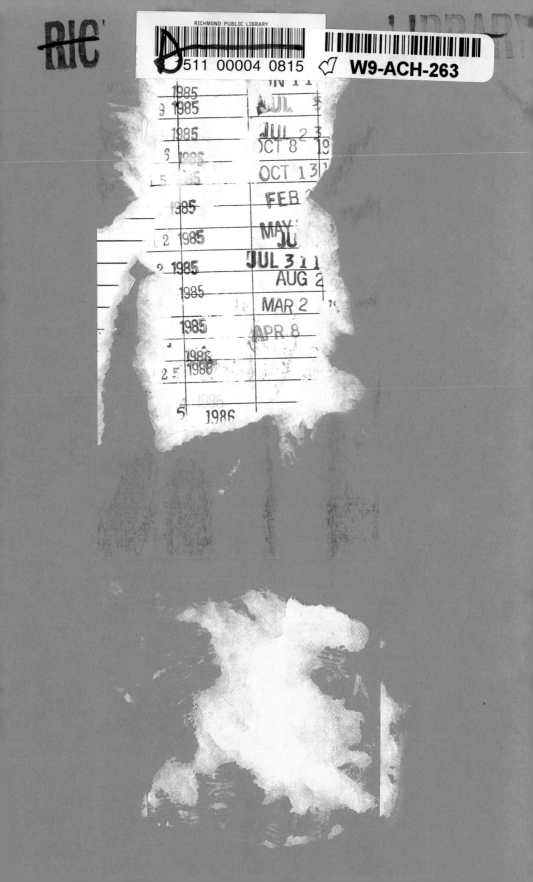

Limelight

Limehight

A NOVEL BY
TERENCE FEELY

WILLIAM MORROW AND COMPANY, INC.
NEW YORK

Library of Congress Cataloging in Publication Data

Feely, Terence.
Limelight.

I. Title.
PR6056.E35L5   1985   823'.914   84-22632
ISBN 0-688-04657-6

Printed in the United States of America

First U.S. Edition

1 2 3 4 5 6 7 8 9 10

BOOK DESIGN BY JAYE ZIMET

For my wife, Elizabeth,
with my love

1

May 8, 1973. *Liverpool Echo*. Stop Press. Security van stopped and robbed in Mersey Tunnel this afternoon. Believed £17,000,000 stolen.

September 25, 1980. Two o'clock in the morning. A big Honda motorcycle glided to a stop outside the barracks of the Alhambra Television Studios in Manchester. The blue-jeaned, helmeted rider had cut the engine twenty-five yards away.

The rider swung off the bike, stacked it, took off the visored helmet. Her blond hair tumbled out around her T-shirted shoulders. She shinned deftly up a drainpipe, took a jackknife from a side pocket of her jeans, examined the window carefully and loosened a well-concealed wire that ran round it. She slackened it sufficiently to make a loop. She put the jackknife away, took from another pocket a flat black object about the size of a cigarette packet. On it was a meter and two leads ending in shark-toothed clips. With great precision she clipped the sharks' teeth to the wire at two different points, puncturing the insulation at precisely the same moment. She looked at the dial. The needle shot up to maximum then down to zero.

Satisfied, she produced a slim jimmy from the spanner pocket of her jeans and forced the window. The opening was small, but she slipped through it like an oiled seal.

Inside, she made her way swiftly up the stairs to the third floor. At this time, the security man should be there. She heard his footsteps, saw the flash of his flashlight. She melted downstairs again, silent as a shadow.

On the ground floor she made her way confidently to the wire-cage Documentary Library where the cans of recorded documentary tape and film were kept, awaiting transmission. She picked the lock on the door with what looked like a tiny crochet hook and went in.

A pencil flashlight showed her the can she wanted, its title on the front and edges. The title was *Rape of a City*. She took the can, went out, relocked the door and merged with the darkness.

Four minutes later she slid back through the window, found her footholds and closed the window carefully. She removed the sharks' teeth from the wire, slid down the pipe. She swung back on the bike, tucked her hair back into her helmet and canoed herself silently down the street on her long legs before starting up and roaring into the night.

Her name was Tara Stewart. She was eighteen years old and for the first time she shivered, missing her riding suit. She had completed stage one of her plan. From now on it was going to be difficult; and dangerous.

Tara Stewart, blond hair tossed loosely about her face, was at her job next morning in the Mail Room of Alhambra Television. It wasn't much of a job. But on Merseyside to have any kind of a job at all at her age was remarkable. Terry Lewis, her cherry-red T-shirt vying with her cheeky auburn curls, and sleek, black-headed Jean Soong, leafing, as usual, through a computer magazine without yet understanding more than one word in ten, were next to her. Tara instinctively chose her friends for their native intelligence, an intelligence quite distinct from the abysmal education they had all shared.

"D'you gerrout at all last night, Tara? See any of the lads?" asked Terry.

"No, me auntie had one of her mullocks. Been on the bevvy again." Tara mimed the act of drinking. "I spent half the night keeping the furniture between us. She nearly had me with a broken bottle before she passed out. I told her I could see St. Theresa standing behind her." Tara laughed, a sudden dazzle of strong white teeth in the fine-boned face.

"I don't know why you don't just elbow her," said Terry, "get out of it."

"Don't be bloody daft. How would Len and Corby get on without me?"

"Well, they're both older than you for a start," Jean Soong chipped in, delicate Chinese face still buried in incomprehensible print about modems and interfaces.

"What difference does that make? Len's two years older, Corby's only one. It's not so long ago that I was bathing them both, washing their little thingies for them and everything. Listen, what is it with you and computers?" she went on. "You wouldn't recognize one if it came up and blew down your ear."

"I know," Jean admitted helplessly, "they just, like, get me."

"It's the men in the white coats who'll get you."

Tara liked to gossip, but this morning she had only half her heart in it. She was listening. She was not sure exactly what she was listening for, but she knew she would recognize it when she heard it.

She hadn't long to wait. Faintly at first, like the rumors of a tidal wave, then increasingly hectically, there came a jangle of noise. Feet running, voices raised, doors opening and slamming. Behind the wide-spaced, clear gray eyes of Tara a devil danced. She lowered her lids demurely. But the corners of her mobile mouth twitched.

In his office, Paul Cranmer, celebrated, hard-nosed documentary director and producer, was behaving like a child of three. It was a fearsome sight. At fifteen stone, little of it fat, he had once nearly knocked the studio head, Cyril Goldstein, over the gantry surrounding the control room in his anxiety to get down to the studio below.

"I'm sorry," he had said hurriedly to Goldstein, "they're screwing up my show down there."

"There are two ways of screwing up your show," Goldstein had replied, brushing down one of his twenty-five identical dark blue suits. "The first is the way they're doing it. The second is to splat me out over the studio floor like a pizza. Which, incidentally, would screw up everybody else's show, also."

It was true. Cyril Goldstein was the last of the great television entrepreneurs. He was both the water and the wheel it drove. He was Alhambra Studios. Without him, it was just a building that looked rather like the Lubjanka. Many people who had failed within its walls claimed it bore a closer resemblance to that institution than its looks.

At this moment Cranmer wouldn't really have cared if he'd knocked Cyril Goldstein off the top of the World Trade Center. His current show—and his current show was always his best show ever—had gone missing. And perhaps *Rape of a City* really was his best ever. It was a brutally brilliant exposure of the rapine that had been practiced on the once-beautiful neighboring city of Liverpool.

Always invisible when she wanted to be, Tara had slipped into the back of the viewing room one day while Cranmer was taking a look at his rough cut before making the final cut. Tara was a Liverpudlian born and bred. She knew not only its present but its matchless past. Poor people didn't go to university in Liverpool: not when they were as poor as she was. Had she been able to go she would have made a fastidious and sensitive historian. She was equipped to know the program was good. That was why she'd chosen it.

Paul Cranmer's office now looked as if a rifle grenade had hit it. Scripts, books, correspondence were tossed in every direction. His whole department looked as if some nameless catastrophe were heaving itself slowly over the horizon. People ran here and there down corridors, the four-minute-warning-look on their faces. Others poked in corners, closets, wastepaper baskets, drawers. One was even seen peering into a lavatory cistern. And over all, Cranmer lurched maniacally, a big, brown, balding bear, his voice, as if on some personal amplification system, booming into every crevice: "One doesn't just lose the finest bloody show of one's whole bloody life! Someone has to know where it is. Some monstrosity conceived in an unwashed test tube must know what they've done with it! If I don't get it back, I'll tell you now, I'll pound you all into bloody hamburgers and eat you raw!"

It was in this homicidal state of mind that he finally reached the Mail Room. It was his equivalent to poking about in a lavatory cistern. He crashed in, puce-faced.

"Did anyone in here dispatch any tapes yesterday?"

He answered himself. "No, of course they bloody didn't, where would they be bloody dispatching them to?" He turned in despair to go again.

Tara cleared her throat.

"Mr. Cranmer," she said, "I've gorran idea."

Cranmer, on his way to the door, jumped as if a fire bucket had spoken to him: "Eh? What's that? Who's that?"

Tara held up her hand like a schoolgirl.

"It's me, Mr. Cranmer," she admitted, as though confessing.

Cranmer put on his glasses. *In extremis,* which was how he felt now, he could be a bit of a bully. "Did I hear the word 'idea?' Did I understand you to say that you had an idea?"

Tara spoke rapidly and apologetically.

"Well, we can't help knowing what's up," she said, "and I just thought . . ." She faltered.

"You just thought . . . yes?" Cranmer encouraged her, menacingly.

"Well, your show's called *Rape of a City,*" she declared tentatively.

"I believe I remember the name of my own show."

Tara's colleagues were looking at her as if she were having some kind of seizure.

"Well . . . a couple of weeks ago, we showed a film, a movie, didn't we? . . . called *Rage in the City* . . ."

"Why, so we did!" said Cranmer, as he might to someone dangerous who had to be humored.

"Well, I just thought the cans might have got mixed up in the library . . ." she ended limply.

Cranmer indulged himself in the put-down he had been promising himself: "What a bloody silly idea! It makes the presumption that half the staff are illiterate and in case you didn't know, documentary and drama have separate libraries at opposite ends of the building, with their own separate staff, their own separate system, their . . . Oh, what's the use!"

He headed for the door, turned back briefly.

"Sorry, love," he said, "you were trying to help. No call to take it out on you."

Tara smiled wanly: "S'all right."

He went, his great shoulders slumping like a snowman melting.

He went and sat in his office, looking like a fall of rock. Five minutes went by. Then he leaped from his chair and tanked toward the Drama Library, spinning people around in their tracks, including, once more, Cyril Goldstein, who was sent cannoning back into an office he was just leaving. He sat carefully in a chair.

"I think I broke my left shoulder," he told the young executive he had been talking to. "I think I'm getting too old for this job."

The executive, overwhelmed by the sight of God being tossed back into his office like a rag doll, said nothing.

In the Drama Library Paul Cranmer rampaged along the racks: "R . . . R . . . . . Ra . . . . Ra . ; . . . . . . Rape! *Rape of a City!*" He grabbed the can and clasped it to his bosom like a child: "Got it, by God!"

"Then wh-where is *Rage of the City?*" quavered the librarian, who had been wallowing meekly in his wake.

"Who cares about crap like that?" boomed Cranmer, leaving like a gale. "What was lost is found and there shall be great rejoicing."

He thundered back down the corridor, spinning people anti-clockwise whom he had spun clockwise when he was going the other way. He erupted into the Mail Room, thrust a thick finger at Tara: "You! My office!"

He disappeared.

The faces of Tara's colleagues registered varying degrees of sorrow and dismay.

"What's he gonna do, Ta?" asked one of her friends, fearfully.

"He's gonna crunch my bones to make his bread, kiddo," said Tara, treading on light feet, supple as a willow, toward the door.

"How d'you know where the bugger's office is?"

"I know," Tara shouted back.

In his office, Paul Cranmer saw the tallish blonde with the large gray eyes and wide cheekbones stride through his door and wondered why he'd never noticed her before.

"You," he said, "are bright. You are bloody brilliant! I've got an office full of high-tech brains and graduates milling about like maggots in a bucket and you cracked it in one. Bless you!" He enveloped her in a bear hug, lifting her off her feet and kissed her juicily on both pale cheeks. "If you could only type, I'd make you my secretary."

He turned his back on her to clear a compost of papers from a chair so that he could sit down. The next moment he heard what sounded like machine-gun fire.

He wheeled to find Tara sitting behind the Olivetti golfball, firing off as though a thousand Chinese were coming at her through the wall. She looked like an emancipated angel in her T-shirt and bonded-on jeans—the cheapest she could find in what was still known in Liverpool as Paddy's Market, although Town Planner's garbage-speak had now dignified it with the title of St. John's Precinct.

"I say," said Paul, "where did you learn to type like that?"

"Oh, I'm fully secretarially trained, like," said Tara in her native, singsong accent which, treacherous to the unwary, made everything spoken in it sound naïve and childish. "Shorthand 140 words a minute, typing sixty, audio, copy-typing and word-processing as well." Silently, she blessed the two years of grind she'd spent at council-subsidized night school while her mates were out at discos, or having it off with spotty youths in the parks and entries.

Paul moved around behind her to see what she'd typed. On the paper was written: "Those who type letters should make a copy of everything they type. Those who make documentaries should do the same—even before final editing."

"What do you know about editing, you cheeky prawn?" asked Paul.

"I have been here two years," she said. "I'm not deaf and blind, you know." Again the lilt of the voice draining the offense from the words.

"No, and you're not exactly mute, either," said Paul, "are you?"

"I can speak up for myself if that's what you mean," said Tara. "I don't take no old buck from no one."

"I believe you," said Paul dryly, "and I think I can promise you that I shan't be giving you any buck, as you say, except in moments of extreme stress, when I've got to give some to someone or burst into tears. For a man of my size I think you would agree that would be unseemly."

"It would be bloody wet," said Tara.

"As you say," Paul agreed. Every instinct told him that he had found a gem of the purest water.

Tara Stewart, this morning a Mail Room gofer. Now secretary to one of the most prestigious producers in the business. Cranmer watched her, working out how to fly her desk, deftly, methodically. She was cool cream, that was certain.

Tara herself had no qualms about taking another girl's job. Paul Cranmer would promote his current secretary to his P.A. His current P.A. would be given a little program of her own, making her a mini-producer. This was how girls got promoted in television, the pressure from below pushing those further up the ladder higher still.

That day, Cranmer played with Tara as with some exquisite new toy. He fired off letters, memos, *pensées* that he'd been meaning to get down to for weeks, for the sheer joy of watching the slim fingers skimming over the notepad or the keys without hesitation or mistake. Her command of English, no matter what she did to it when she spoke it, was flawless. ("Good old Calcutta Corner," as they called the English class at night school, thought Tara.) There was one slight tremor which he didn't see and that was when he dictated to Personnel her own notification of appointment. At the mention of what her new salary was to be her pencil jerked upward like the needle on a lie detector. Outwardly, her cool smooth face gave no sign. Inwardly, her mind was racing.

This friendly bear of a man evidently had no conception of what riches he was conferring on her, nor of what it would mean to her family. Life was going to be altogether different. The reason she was not even more elated was that she had always meant it to be so. Once she had realized that she was going to learn practically nothing at her gigantic slum of a school with its terrorist gangs, broken teachers, mutilated books and urban guerrilla ethos she had decided she had to do it all herself.

Now it was beginning. And it was only the beginning. The gray eyes gazed luminously at the big man in the brown cashmere sweater opposite her and she wondered how he would react if he knew what was behind them. Stage two had started.

At roughly the same time a private Telex in a lavish office in London stuttered out the information that a girl called Stewart had been in the market for a sophisticated security-baffle device. It was not known what she had done with it.

At lunchtime Tara went to the Mail Room to collect her riding leathers—her most precious possession after her bike—and transfer them to her new office. She evaded with ferocity the ritual debagging, mandatory for anyone in the Mail Room, whether male or female, who got the slightest advancement. It was performed in fun by some, in malice by others. She poked Terry Lewis in both eyes, encouraging her to take her knee off her chest, twisted Jean Soong's right nipple until she let go of the belt of her jeans, kicked young and muscular Sid Molloy in the crotch, then went to the canteen, fully trousered, followed, utterly without resentment, by her former antagonists.

"How the bloody hell did you work it?" asked Terry, over their stewed tea, her poked eyes looking like peeled tomatoes.

"Where his lost tape was," confided Tara. "I guessed right."

"Yeah, but he wouldn't make you his secretary for that. Not just for that," objected Jean Soong cynically across the plastic table, wondering if her right nipple looked like it felt, a small Walnut Whip. "You must have done something else for him."

"Yeah, come on," nudged Sid Molloy, sitting very delicately on the edge of his chair, his friendly bruiser's face alive with interest. "What did you really do?"

"I gave him a blow-dry," said Tara, "and I don't mean his hair, either."

At that they laughed and were satisfied. Even if they didn't really believe it, it was close enough to what they could accept as the truth.

At the end of the day—the first anyone had ever known Paul Cranmer to spend exclusively in his office—Tara presented him with everything she had done interleaved in a blotter as she'd been taught, and handed it to him for signature.

"What about the stamps?" he asked.

"The Mail Room does all that," she explained, as to a child. "Where have you been all your life?"

"I'm just beginning to wonder," he said, dryly.

She started to climb into her leathers, the gleaming skins she hadn't wanted to ruin climbing through the window last night.

"Where d'you think you're going?" asked Cranmer.

"Home. I do have one, you know. I don't sleep under the desk."

With his physical size and his talent, Paul Cranmer had never been spoken to like this in all his adult life.

"I tell people in this department when they can take off," he warned.

" 'Take off 's' " really antique, you know that, Dad?" said Tara. "It's like from when I saw all them fuzzy pictures from the moon when I was just learning to walk." She laughed, a joyous phenomenon which lit up her face. "I thought that's how you walked—like they did it on the moon. I was trying to bounce around like that for days afterward."

She finished zipping up her leather suit. It glazed on her like a snake's skin. For the first time he became conscious of her body.

"I say," he began. He'd no idea what he was going to suggest. One could hardly ask her out to dinner. Besides, although he was only thirty-two, she'd made him feel bloody old with that "Dad" shaft. She picked up her visored helmet.

"Ta-ra," she said. "See you termorrer." And went, her glossy buttocks winking as she bounced out of the door.

He sat there silently. He hadn't felt so horny for a long time. Morosely, he wondered if he were becoming a leather fetishist.

Outside, Tara threw a leg over her bike and squeezed the motor up to maximum revs once or twice, feeling in her loins a sense of the joy the day's achievements had brought her. Then she turned the bike's nose toward home, half-witch, half-angel on her four-stroke broomstick.

The broomstick was her one luxury. She had got it for a fifth of its real price, which she was still paying off. It had turned up at a neighbor's home. A skillful file had already removed all traceable numbers from engine and chassis. For all practical purposes it was a stateless vehicle. The minute she saw it she had to have it. Speed under her most intimate control was one of her pleasures in life. Her leathers, of superb quality, had undoubtedly fallen off the back of a truck. Jack Harris, a muscular lad next door, seventeen but already the size of a big man, was in her English class at night school. He had asked her help to analyze a particularly prickly piece of John Donne. She had patiently taken him through it, making him see it for the first time as a piece of thought that had to do with his own life. He had felt a thrill as if a lock had been turned for him and he'd been left with the key. Two nights later there'd been a knock on her door. She had opened it and found a parcel on the doorstep. Inside it was the riding suit. She had rushed in and tried it on. It fitted her like a skin. He may have had trouble with John Donne, but Jack Harris thieved like an artist.

Now she lasered along in the fast lane of the M62 between

Manchester and Liverpool, her wheels singing her salary, her exhaust chorusing her sense of triumph. Cars got out of her way as her slim, skillful image arrowed toward them in their rear mirrors.

One car would not get out of her way. A red Lamborghini. Lean, tanned hands on the wheel, dark, richly fringed eyes watching her in the mirror. She flashed him. He simply increased speed. She taught him and flashed him again. Again he increased speed. Gradually, she slowed down, letting him think he was losing her. What she had seen was a glint of sun on the blue light of a police car lurking about a mile ahead. Mr. Lamborghini, intent on his rear mirror, didn't see it until he'd flashed past it at 120 miles an hour.

Tara slowed down and stopped at the animated discussion between the police and the Lamborghini. She heard a derisory remark from the police as she approached: "Seventy-five? The speed you were going, you needed a bloody heat shield!"

She shouted to one of the policemen, lifting her visor, wanting Mr. Lamborghini to know it was a girl who'd outwitted him: "Am I all right for the 'Pool straight on?"

"You're all right for anywhere in that gear," said the young copper. "How about my place, nine o'clock?"

"I'll be in bed by then with me granny shawl and a cup of cocoa," said Tara.

Swiftly, she leaned into the Lamborghini to meet the lean, beautiful, cruel face of Jason Planter. Black eyes confronted gray.

"You should practice on something easier, wack," she said, "like a supermarket trolley!" She revved up and was gone.

It was the first time she had met Jason Planter. It was not to be the last.

She crunched to a stop twenty-five minutes later outside the inner city hillbilly shack in the Toxteth area of Liverpool which she called home. Toxteth had once been splendid. The most uncluttered kind of Georgian, built by men of great discernment and sensibility on fortunes founded and sustained by the most vicious exploitation of man by man the modern world has seen. The slave trade was directed largely from there. From there the nightmare miasma of terror and misery spread out around the globe. There was a bitter irony about what it had now become, as if what had been planned and directed from there had left a stain, which could not but corrupt.

Now it was a crumbling perilous jungle of bed-sitters, squats, crash-pads. Homes built for a family of ten had thirty people or more crammed in. Toxteth was not an area into which a stranger would knowingly stray. A car left there by someone who did not know the form would be stripped within twenty minutes. But Tara was no stranger. Her wheels, her leathers, her confident body language, her history and her connections made her a person of respect. She was one of the few people in the neighborhood who could actually leave her bike outside the house, as she now did, leashing it with a token chain.

She did not see the red Lamborghini that prowled past the house a few minutes later before accelerating away. After his encounter with the police, Jason Planter had caught her up, but remained two cars behind. This kid with the eyes had insulted him. She also excited him. It was a combination Jason Planter found intriguing. Sooner or later, he had found, the wheel came around in this singular city. He drove on through it to his country estate, thinking that tomorrow he must be up early.

Tara bounded up the stairs to the top two rooms which she, her aunt and her two brothers—with the help of plasterboard partitions—managed to share.

Her brothers, Len and Corby, had heard her coming and were rushing around like an Indian restaurant with a panic on, trying to pretend they were halfway through getting the evening meal ready when they had, in fact, only just started when they heard her motorbike outside. They were both out of work, but they kept their self-respect by doing jobbing gardening around the posh houses of Calderstones Park and over the water in the Wirral. Their open-air life had made them ruddy, in contrast to Tara's ivory pallor, and the sky had found its way into their eyes. Big lads by courtesy of Mother Nature, certainly not because of any nourishment they'd ever had, they were both waiting to join the Marines.

They would make good soldiers; they attacked first.

"Warra you doing home at this time?" accused Len. "Skiving off while Buggerlugs, the Mail Room gaffer, wasn't watching? We haven't got the meal on yet."

"We're eating out!" cried Tara, joyously.

"You what?" asked Corby, his generous mouth hanging open.

"I'm raiding the gas money," said Tara, "and we're eating out." From its hiding place in which they kept it from the thieving hands of Aunt Rita, she seized the jam jar in which they dropped the odd coins which helped to pay the gas bill when it came in. "We're going to Kwok Fong's."

Kwok Fong had run "The Far East" restaurant in Great George Square as far back as anyone could remember. He was dead now, but not his memory. He'd been a distant great uncle of Jean Soong's.

"Have you gone bolo?" demanded Corby, grabbing the jar back. "One blow-out of chicken chow chollops or whatever they're called and then the Gas Board do a vasectomy on the gas pipes!"

"I'll put it back," explained Tara patiently.

"With what?" asked Len. "Buttons off your Sally Army uniform? Honestly, Tar, I'm surprised at you. You're the one who's always kept us in line . . ."

Tara could withhold it from them no longer. She leaped in the air and descended on them, sending all three crashing to the floor.

"I've got me stripes!" she yelled.

"You what?"

"I've been promoted!"

"You mean you make somebody else lick the envelopes?" The tangle of bodies thrashed about on the floor.

"No, you steaming great turd, this is the real McCoy—I've been made a secretary!" The thrashing suddenly stopped. To the boys a secretary was someone with nice legs and hair, floating sniffily around downtown during the lunch hour.

"On the level?" asked Len.

"Honest to God!"

"Oh Christ, Tar," said Corby.

"Well done, love," said Len. "God knows, you've worked for the bugger!"

"And you haven't heard the best of it yet," said Tara triumphantly. "My money goes up straight away to six and a half grand a year!"

"You what?"

"Six and a half thousand pounds? I mean . . . not bottle tops or Coke can rings?" asked Corby.

"The real mazoolahs," said Tara. "Three times what I'm getting now! Just think what we can do with it!" The joyous thrashing about, as they embraced and kissed and slapped each other on the floor, like three puppies in a basket, was interrupted by the abrupt arrival home of Aunt Rita. She stood swaying in the doorway, pissed as a newt that was also on Valium. She carried a stick, whose ostensible purpose was to aid her "bad leg." Its real function was to enable her to stay upright. The only thing wrong with her bad leg was that it was, like the good leg, usually full, from toe to crotch, of alcohol.

"So!" she shouted, executing a looping sway. "So this is what goes on when I'm not here. Goings on on the floor!" She staggered and inadvertently nearly joined them.

"Oh, don't be so thick," said Tara, "you fuddled old fart! Why don't you go and find a hole to fall down?"

Aunt Rita lurched forward, stick raised, forgetting that it constituted, together with her legs, the third part of a tripod, and promptly collapsed in a bibulous heap across them.

"Christ!" said Corby, "it's like having a brewery fall on you!"

Aunt Rita was a great rolling lard-tub of venom that they had had to learn, over the years, to deal with. When their father went away and their mother, Elspeth, knew that she was dying from his loss, she had realized that, for her children, it was a choice between council care, in which case they would inevitably be split up, and the tender mercies of her sister Rita.

She had no illusions about her sister. Rita was a disappointed woman. She felt that life had failed to give her the things to which she was entitled. True, she was big, but she was also beautiful. In another age she might have been a much-fêted artists' model, with her thundering curves and outrageous red hair. She had wanted a man and children of her own. But there was something about Rita that put men off, despite her lusciousness. It was the more frustrating in that it was impossible to define. The most one could say was that in the whole of that great, overblown peony of a woman there was not a trace of sex appeal. Therefore she became bitter, embraced the bottle instead of a man, and devoted her life to making that of those who fell into her power as miserable as possible. She became fat, eccentric and wicked.

When her sister Elspeth pleaded with her to take on the responsibility of looking after her children when she died, she caught Rita at a vulnerable moment. She had just been sacked, without a reference, from her job as cook-housekeeper to a rich, sugar-broker young bachelor up the coast at Hoylake.

Her employer, a George Taylor, had gone down to the cellar for a bottle of his favorite twelve-year-old malt, only to find that it was full of cold tea. Worse, further investigation had revealed that another two and a half cases were also full of cold tea. A red hot steel needle had been used to punch two holes in the bottom of the bottles and drain them. They had then been painstakingly refilled with the tea and the holes sealed with wax. Yet, such was the capacity for absorption of the woman's gross tissues that he had never once, in the year she had worked for him, suspected her of being drunk.

An equally bizarre discovery was to follow. Opening a small spare room in her quarters to find out what else she might have been up to, he was almost overwhelmed by an avalanche of dirty pots and pans. He subsequently discovered that she had given up washing dirty cooking utensils about six months previously. When they had become too disgusting, she had simply stuffed them in the little spare room and gone out and bought a fresh supply on her employer's charge account, to which she had access for household purposes. Being rich, young and busy running a string of girlfriends, he was not the type to scrutinize too closely accounts from hardware departments. He was to remember her sacking for years, combining, as it did on her part, cataracts of fat tears with overtones, he could have sworn, of attempted rape.

Unlikely to get another job, Rita settled for Social Security benefit and the child allowances she got for the kids. She also relished the prospect of the unhappiness she could inflict on them.

An expert at the great Liverpool "sexual guilt" game, she would porridge silently around the neighborhood like some great billowing bolster of suspicion, trying to "catch" them at something, preferably with each other, for she had a powerful faith in the prevalence of incest. She would also censor their reading of any scrap of newspaper that managed to find its way into that illiterate household. A picture of a man paddling in the sea with his trousers rolled up to the knee or of a well-endowed woman, even with her clothes on, was sufficient grounds for immediate confiscation and a stunning blow from a ham-like fist.

In being a surrogate mother she had absolutely no interest. While she cradled her bottles, Tara cooked, cleaned and brought up the family. She wore her bruises like badges of pride for, in her little woman's mind, she knew she was making a good job of the boys.

This was the hulk that was currently lying inert across them. They extricated themselves and laid her, already snoring, on her side—in case she was sick, which she frequently was.

Then they went to Kwok Fong's and blew the gas money.

The next day at Alhambra Television the jungle drums discreetly rataplanned out the news that Paul Cranmer had recruited a new secretary "from the Mail Room." All morning other secretaries made excuses to wander into her office and give her the secretarial mind-and-body scan from the soles of her feet to her scalp. They took away with them varying impressions. The silly ones giggled. The clever ones looked thoughtful. The silly ones noticed only that Tara made no attempt to adopt the refined version of the Liverpool accent, which she privately defined as sounding like a constipated duck.

The clever ones noticed the tidiness of her desk, the errorless perfection of the letters they saw on her blotter, the way she already had the switchboard eating out of her hand on difficult calls with her guileless, singsong requests for help. They could also see the understated shapeliness of the makeup-free face, which was only waiting for a whisper of shading to send it blazing into beauty. Most of them liked her. Jane Beaumont did not.

Jane Beaumont was secretary to a junior producer in the Documentary Department. She had had her eye on the secretaryship to Paul Cranmer for a long time. She'd been to Grammar School. She had fistfuls of "A" levels and "O" levels. She'd been to secretarial college. She detested this urchin who had materialized from the Mail Room and walked off with what she considered to be her job.

She had had her first jab at Tara in the canteen during lunchtime. Many of the secretaries ate together in their own favorite corner. Tara had been asked to join them. The exchange was listened to in fascinated silence by the other girls. Jane had an uncanny capacity for making one look a fool. She was feared. Jane waited until Tara had sat down: "I usually sit in that chair," she said.

"I'm not surprised," said Tara, who had sensed Jane's hostility from the start; "you can see everyone who comes in and goes out from here and who's talking to who and all like that. It's what I'd call a nosy parker's chair; I can see why you'd like it. Here, you'd better have it."

"I was just making a remark. I didn't say I wanted it," snapped Jane.

"Well never mind, you'd better sit somewhere; your scouse will be getting cold."

"It's casserole, actually," said Jane.

"Yeah, well where I come from we call it scouse."

"And where exactly," sneered Jane, "do you come from?"

"A couple of slum rooms in a slum flat in Toxteth," said Tara. "You know—where all the violence is. How about you?"

"Otterspool," replied Jane, triumphantly flourishing one of the residential jewels on the outskirts of the city.

"Oh yeah, we went there once," said Tara admiringly. "It was smashing. All the girls wore knickers. Until it got dark, like."

After that, nobody tangled with Tara. Jane did have one more try. She told her junior producer that Tara had called Paul Cranmer a big fat slob, knowing that it would get back to him. Cranmer, a sensitive soul despite his size, asked Tara if it were true.

"Is what true?" asked Tara; "that you're a big fat slob or that I said you were a big fat slob? The truth is that you are, but I never said so. Gorrit?" She smiled in a way that lit up the bald patch on Cranmer's head and disappeared into the Mail Room to talk to her mates. For the next two days, the whole of Jane's boss's mail was unaccountably dispatched to Saudi Arabia.

She had no more trouble with Jane.

The stories began to build up about her. She smiled wryly to herself at the smallness of her triumphs. She was after far bigger game than a reputation as the smartest girl in the pool.

She was learning all the time. How to make up a rough script from Paul's notes and jottings. How to turn that into a shooting script. How to time. How to get the thousand and one permissions a documentary director needed to film out on the streets, whom to speak to in order to get them, how to get the cooperation of the police in getting streets closed off if necessary. What traffic was about at dawn. Which officials in the A.C.T.T. union that controlled the technicians and the directors were bolshie and which were reasonable.

Paul's P.A., Mary, was a deceptive girl. She was thin and gave the impression of being hyperactive. She was, in fact, lazy, cloaking the fact by rapid speech and an obsessive attachment to trivial detail. The result was that she was happy to leave more and more to Tara so that Tara was, effectively, operating as a Production Assistant as well as a secretary. Now, in addition to what she already knew, she had to learn how big a crew Paul would need for a particular project. She had to learn what his editing ratio was—in other words, how much film or tape he customarily shot in order to edit it down to what was actually shown. She had to compete for space in the overloaded editing theaters for him, see he got them when he needed them, arrange the prompt arrival of the catering truck at locations, try to work out shooting schedules that would minimize overtime without antagonizing the crew. If there was traveling to be done, she was the one who had to make sure that the technicians went first class—according to the union agreement, including flights—even if no one else did. She had to keep the electricians, the most crucial element in any crew, sweet by throwing in an unnecessary hour here and there so that the Head Sparks would not be standing ostentatiously in view, stopwatch the size of a soup plate in hand, as break times like lunch approached.

All this she did without complaint, typing it up in immaculate dossiers for Mary, which Mary made her own.

Mary made one mistake.

She did not thank Tara. Worse, she pretended she didn't even realize it was happening. Tara could never be sure, later, how long she would have tolerated the situation. As it happened, her decision was triggered for her.

One day she had to go urgently to the editing theater with a message for Paul. In the theater with him as he sat at the controls watching the monitors was Mary. She was helping him to time the show, one function which she could not delegate to Tara without Paul knowing. She had to be there in person. Tara opened the door quietly so as not to interrupt at a crucial moment, slid in like a cat and waited at the back for an opportunity to break in. It was a program about municipal council corruption in local building. She watched, fascinated, as Paul's incisive interviews blew away smokescreen after smokescreen thrown up by successive officials. She noted how he always cut on the shot that told the whole story; the sigh of relief after the official line had duly been delivered; the handkerchief dabbed across the brow when the councillor thought he was out of camera. The sequence they were timing finished but, before she could speak, Paul did:

"Good stuff!" he said. "That's damn good stuff! It'll have the I.B.A. reaching for their tranquilizers, I know that." He clasped his hands behind his furry bear's head. "D'you know, I don't think I've ever worked so well in my life. It's since Tara came. That girl's a lucky mascot, I feel it in my water."

"She's a secretary," said Mary, shortly. "D'you want to go on to the interview with the Town Planning consultant—the one who claims he was offered a bribe?"

Tara slipped away as quietly as she had arrived. Paul never got his message.

His next assignment was an investigation into Rugby League football, the bone-crunching game in which it's rare still to have all your teeth by the time you're twenty-five and all your wits by the time you're thirty. He'd chosen Wigan as the club from whom he would ask cooperation, including the covering of training sessions and the revelation of one or two dirty tricks. Paul had a gift for inducing confession; rather like a large monk. For his purposes he needed the clubhouse, the pitch, the players and directors all to himself for one day. Mary Widgery dumped the whole problem on Tara's desk as usual and skittered off, quivering with ersatz energy and a large sheaf of papers in her hands.

"Ta, Mary," said Tara; "keeping you busy, are they?"

"I manage to cope," said the Widgery bird, as Tara had privately dubbed her.

Tara got down to her research. The club proved cooperative. What date did her producer have in mind?

"Well," said Tara, "you give me your most unsuitable dates and we'll work backward from there."

A few days later, Tara handed the Widgery her usual immaculate set of slim dossiers.

"Have a good time," said Tara.

"It's all work," said the Widgery.

Came the day of the shoot. The huge Outside Broadcast truck rumbled into the compound, followed by the retinue of the crew, some in their own cars (so they could drive back home at night while still claiming the overnight allowance), some in a coach.

On the pitch the local brass band was practicing drumming and marching. In the changing rooms were two girls' hockey teams in various stages of screeching undress, waiting for a friendly match. The sole occupant of the boardroom was an elderly cleaner with the only authentic bent cigarette Paul had ever seen drooping from under his moustache, and the catering truck was twenty-five miles away at a soccer field. As Paul slowly turned around in a complete circle three times, taking in the enormity of what had happened to him, a road-making machine the size of the *Queen Elizabeth,* followed by a steam-roller, came majestically around the corner, their drivers asking him kindly to get his whole bloody shooting match out of it since they had an urgent contract to resurface the compound. Paul turned slowly around one more time.

"Widgery!!!" he bellowed, in a voice that set every dog barking within three-quarters of a mile.

Mary Widgery was not to be found. The next day a doctor's note arrived on Paul Cranmer's desk, stating that she was suffering from nervous exhaustion and needed a week's rest.

The first person she came to see when she got back was Tara. She leaned forward over Tara's desk, bracing herself on her hands. She put no padding on her accusation: "You," she said, "fucked me up!"

Tara looked up, the gray eyes twinkling like the sun on a stream.

"How could I do that?" she asked, in her most innocent sing-song. "After all, Mr. Cranmer might think I'm his lucky mascot, but you and I know that I'm only a secretary, don't we?"

Mary Widgery put it together in a flash.

"You conniving bitch!" she said.

Tara gave her one of her special white smiles.

"You ungrateful cow," she said, without malice.

Mary Widgery put in for a transfer to another department. Paul granted it with relief. Despite his passion for his work and his temper, he hated putting people down. All the same, he was now without a P.A. What was worse, he didn't know of one with whom he would want to work. Two days after the Widgery had departed Tara went into his office with some letter and found him with that crumpled-factory-chimney look he always had about him when he was low.

"Whatsamarrer, boss?" she asked. She knew that he got a frisson out of the contrast between her efficiency and her excruciating diction, so she always exaggerated it.

"What the hell am I supposed to do without a P.A.?" he demanded. "That's the matter."

"Well . . . gerranother one," she shrugged; "there's plenty of them."

"But there aren't any I want to work with. I mean . . . I'm not that easy to get on with," he admitted.

"We gerron okay, don't we?"

"Well, yes, but, you see, you're not a P.A."

"What does a P.A. do?" she asked, innocently.

"Well, she organizes things . . . arranges . . . this sort of thing, I mean, here." He pointed to a hopeless muddle of pages half-filled with scrawled names and times and telephone numbers on which he'd been trying to construct his own schedule for another try at the Rugby League documentary. The brown eyes looked at her appealingly, hoping that she might say well that looked fine to her. She could have kissed the balding center of his nice head, he looked so helpless. Instead, she left the room. A second later she was back, with a sheaf of her slim dossiers.

"Sort of like this kind of thing, you mean?" she asked.

Like a man in a dream from which he was afraid he might awake, Paul went through the dossiers, page after immaculate page.

"But this is fantastic!" he exclaimed. It ought to be, reflected Tara. It was the one that idle, knocking, sour little bitch Widgery should have got instead of the little special she'd concocted for her.

"Where did you learn all this?" he demanded.

"Oh, keeping my eyes open, as usual, like," she said.

He rose from his seat and enfolded her in his bear hug.

"Are you for real or are you from Venus, or something?" he asked. "I've been looking for someone like you all my life."

He felt himself getting randy again. She felt it, too. She had a great warmth for him, but not in that way and she gently disengaged herself. She saw a momentary bruise in those soft brown eyes, but, after all, he couldn't have everything he wanted, could he? There was no resentment from him. He was a big man in every sense.

"I tell you what I'm going to do," he said. "I'm going to use this for this assignment. If it works, you're on as my P.A. Fair?"

"Cracking, chief."

It worked. Like a Rolls aero engine. It worked for two reasons. Firstly, because it was an excellent piece of organization. And secondly because everyone on the unit made sure it would work. They all liked this tough, friendly, long-legged wacker with the tow-colored hair spilling over her denim bomber jacket. She could give as good as she got to any razor-tongued grip or gaffer in the crew and she asked for no concessions.

At the pub party after the Rugby show, Paul lifted a brimming pint and announced her as his new P.A. and the sound was like that on those rare occasions when Manchester United manages to score against Liverpool.

Tara was lifted by the giant hand of euphoria. Every advancement took her one step further on her mission. She felt a surge of warmth for this great grizzly bear who kept giving her the things she needed to accomplish it, even though she was aware she had worked for them, had the talent for them and deserved them. But she knew many girls who had the same three qualifications in their spheres and who did not get what they wanted. She wanted to make him happy, too. But she knew that she must not do it in the way he wanted. She recognized his symptoms. He found himself being wound up higher and higher by this singular girl. The combination of brains, looks, guts and alley-cat street wisdom was a brew he found heady in the extreme. They were staying in the same hotel overnight.

"Have dinner with me later," he asked. It was practically a plea.

"You don't have to feed me, you know," she grinned; "I've been eating quite well since I got me raise." She thought of what else she had been able to do with it, too. Move them all into a decent flat near Sefton Park, which Aunt Rita was doing her best to turn into another slum. Get the first color T.V. they had ever had. Get their first record player, their first lavatory and bathroom of their own— one they didn't have to share with twenty other people. Best of all, buy some privacy. The families in that terrible Toxteth tenement mingled their sweat and secretions like blindworms sliding over each other in a burrow. Now, suddenly, there was the fresh, crisp, ozone tang of privacy.

The perceptive brown eyes that had made Paul one of the best documentarists in the business read a little of what she was thinking in her expressive face. He pressed his plea.

"Just dinner, that's all," he urged. She studied the kind, ruddy face:

"You're on," she said. "For dinner," she emphasized, adding, "you can teach me about all them irons they have in these posh-nosh pads."

"Irons?"

"All those knives and forks and spoons and things. You'd think they was going to war, not to dinner."

They had dinner in the French Bistro of their hotel, complete with a genuine French maître d' and genuine young French waiters, over in England to better themselves back home by learning the language, and totally unaware that they would be returning to France with a Lancashire accent you could cut with a wooden spoon. To Tara it was paradise, movies-time. They had their own alcove, with a pink candle on the table and pink napkins. The room had a lovely warm glow to it. The menus were wonderfully bewildering works of art. To honor the occasion she had put on new, expensive jeans, a simple white blouse with a stand-up collar, and knotted a blue silk scarf round her slim throat. The French waiters appreciated her economy of style. *"C'est chic, ça,"* they nodded.

Watching the candlelight do mystical things to the huge gray eyes and mold the contours of the smoothly modeled face, sensing the profound pleasure this great girl with her passion for life was getting out of a very ordinary restaurant, Paul felt as if someone had put his heart in a vise. However, he had not reached the age of thirty-two without learning one or two pieces of wisdom and he kept it casual.

"Would you like some wine?" he asked, after he had guided her through the menu. She had chosen steak and chips.

"Norrarf," she said. "No point in having French nosh without the fancy booze!"

He started with six snails, ordering Daube à la Provençale for himself, asking the waiter, in French, to have a little garlic butter smeared on Tara's steak, and went mad by ordering a bottle of Léo-ville-Poyferré '74, the first glass of which went a long way toward sedating Tara's incipient hysteria when she saw him winkle out and eat his first snail. He offered her nothing to drink before and no brandy or liqueur afterward. "The Cranmers have never been cads," he proudly told himself inwardly. To which a second interior voice instantly replied, "Why the hell not?" But he knew that if anything were to happen, her decision had to be made with a clear mind. He soon learnt how clear it was.

When they had finished they were mellow, comfortable in their friendship. He reached out and caught her hand. She did not try to pull it away. Instead, she talked, the play of expression flickering over her mobile face a delight to behold.

"I really do like you, Paul," she said, "but when I said just nosh, I did mean it. I may not seem like it, but I'm a bit of an old-fashioned bint that way. It's going to have to be more than 'like' and it's never going to be my boss, because that would change things. I'd start using it; I know I would. And so would you in another way and the whole thing would become a mess and what's a great team at the moment would go down the pan."

He held on to her hand for a moment longer, wanting her more than he'd ever wanted anyone in his life. Then he said: "I was just going to ask you if you'd like more coffee."

Her laugh rang around the room: "You rotten sod!"

Her wheels beat rhythmically over the regular, recurrent joins in the slabs of motorway as she spanked along the road home the next day, the countryside on either side of her a green and gold blur: "Production Assistant, Production Assistant, Production Assistant."

They beat out the message that rang in her brain. It meant more money, more power, more respect and prestige. One more step toward her goal. She couldn't believe it was happening to her. She swerved expertly past a traffic cop who was doing a sedate sixty, checking first that she was doing no more than seventy, and gave him a cheery wave as she went. Something in the sight of that svelte, happy figure, welded dexterously to her bike, lifted the rest of that policeman's morning.

Arrived back home, she jumped her front wheel on to the pavement and rode straight into the drive of the block of flats where they now lived. There was greenery in the road; there were French-pleated and ruched curtains at many of the windows. She knew these were small things, but she reveled in her disproportionate pleasure in them. She racked up her bike in a parking space, and went in. There was a lift, all burnished steel and winking lights, but Tara got a charge out of physical activity and she ignored it, raced up the stairs to their flat on the second floor and flung open the door.

It was her helmet that saved her. She hadn't bothered to take it off and as she came through the door she felt a tremendous bang on the side of it. She staggered, swung around and there she was—Auntie Rita, swaying, the jagged remains of the full cider bottle with which she'd hit her still in her hand, her eyes as malevolent as scorpions.

"Slut!" she screamed at Tara. "Whore! Trollop!" She struck out at her with the jagged bottle. Tara jumped back like a cat.

"What is it?" she asked. "What's up?"

"I'll tell you what's up, you filthy hussy," shouted Rita. "You were seen!"

Oh God, that dread phrase, known to every inhabitant of Liverpool, city of a million bright, unwinking eyes. Rita was still coming for her with the bottle. Tara dodged behind the sofa, praying for one of the boys. But she knew they wouldn't be coming. They had both been accepted for the Marines and were already away at training camp.

Rita came after her, her speed surprising for her size. Tara put a table between them.

"What the shit are you talking about? There was nothing to see."

Rita leered, flourishing the wicked-looking bottle slowly to and fro: "Ma McGovern is a washer-up in a certain hotel outside Wigan. Oh, very flash, she says it is! She saw you last night with your fancy man, paddling fingers and rubbing knees. She said he gave the impression he thought his dinner was up your bloody skirt!"

It was the sheer grubbiness of the accusation that did it for Tara. No doubt Maggie McGovern had seen her and Paul having dinner, but the rest of it had come from the cesspit of Rita's festering imagination, where a foul thought burst the surface roughly every half-minute, like a bubble in a mud geyser. The adrenalin surged in Tara's veins. She clamped down the visor of her helmet and instead of going backward went forward. Disconcerted by an experience that was new to her, Rita stopped in her tracks. Heartened by the remembered protection of her leather suit, Tara leaped forward, seizing Rita's bottle arm. She banged her aunt's wrist repeatedly against the wall with all the force generated by her hatred until the strength was numbed out of it and the bottle fell to the floor. Then she turned her so that a low coffee table was behind her. She shoved her, the coffee table took her behind the knees and Rita crashed backward to the floor, her gross bulk knocking all the breath out of her body. She lay there, breathing stertorously.

Tara stood over her: "Now listen to me, you sick-making tub of offal! I've had you. I've had your filthy stew of a mind, I've had your big, smelly, blubbery body, I've had your paralytic, piss-assed drunks and your vomit. It might have escaped your notice, but I'm not a minor any longer. I'm over eighteen. This flat is in my name and whoever stays in it is here because I want them here."

"You can't throw me out," gasped Rita.

"If I had a bleeding fork-lift truck I'd throw you out right now," said Tara, "through the bloody window!"

Rita made a feeble attempt to sit up. Tara pushed her back with her foot.

"I've got to go now," she said, "and when I get back tonight I want to see this place cleaned up, I want to be able to tell that you've had a bath and I want you to have clean clothes on. Gorrit?"

"Some hopes," muttered Rita, her spirit seeping back with her breath.

"You what?" asked Tara, her heel poised over Rita's face.

"Nothing," Rita mumbled.

"Great," said Tara. "And not that it's any of your garbage-minded business, but nothing happened last night. What did I just say?"

"Nothing happened last night," said Rita.

"Great again."

Tara went down into the communal, straggly garden at the back of the flats, sat with her back to the wall and took off her helmet. Then, for reasons which she would have been hard put to it to isolate, she sobbed as bitterly as she could ever remember.

Paul was in pain. His next program, after which he'd lusted for a long time, was to be an investigation into the fashion for illegal, bare-knuckle prize fights which had spread like a bloody rash across the North of England. They were held in fields and barns in remote parts of the countryside and the police rarely got to hear about them until afterward, if then. In popularity they had overtaken the equally illegal sport of cockfighting. The betting was big and the action slaughterous. There were no rules—at least not so that anyone would notice. The men who ran it were brutal and anonymous.

The problem for a documentarist was getting anywhere near it. Paul's network of contacts was one of his great strengths. But this time—nothing. "If the police can't find out anything, how do you expect me to?" asked his best researcher. "In any case," he added, "suppose they found out I was getting close to them—who's going to pay for my broken shins?"

Tara watched Paul sit and suffer. Or rather watched and listened to him suffer. Paul was no Job. When he hurt, the world knew about it—along corridors, down telephones and in the corner of his office from whence would issue, ever and anon, the kind of groan on which old-fashioned ghosts used to pride themselves. Suddenly, it came to her. She disappeared into the Mail Room again and sought out Sid Molloy.

"Sid," she opened, "your old man works for the scummiest bookie in town, doesn't he?"

"You always did have a lovely way with words, Ta," Sid answered, smiling the smile that made his face look like some great natural catastrophe.

"Shut your trap and listen," she said. He heard her out attentively, and sucked in his breath.

"I'll have to wait 'till he's pissed before I can ask him about that," he said, judiciously.

"I'd be more worried if you had to wait 'till he's sober," retorted Tara.

Paul suffered. Tara sat still and waited. When Sid came through with the goods, as she knew he would, she made a telephone call in her lunch hour.

The next evening, she and Paul had been working late. Unexpectedly, Tara had come in by train that day. Instead of her jeans she was wearing a simple white dress with an indefinable quality of "eye" about it. On someone else, it could have been ordinary. It was cinched by a thin, sandy suede belt. The long legs were gripped by soft gold suede boots and around her throat she had the blue silk scarf again. They had been there all day, finding only frustration. Paul emitted one last sigh like an elk in pain: "I vote for home," he said.

"Me, too," agreed Tara. She slipped her gold suede trenchcoat around her shoulders, turned casually: "Fancy a bevvy?" she asked him.

He looked up in surprise. It was not that he didn't understand the word—Tara had been gradually initiating him. It was just that she'd never suggested a drink before.

"I'd love a bevvy!" he said. "In fact, the main element missing from my life at this moment is a bevvy. Where shall we go?"

"There's a place down the docks in Liverpool that's a bit of a giggle," said Tara. "You wouldn't exactly find it in a Thomas Cook *Guide to Merseyside by Night,* but if you did, they'd definitely call it . . . kind of . . . picturesque."

"You crafty little devil," grinned Paul. "All you're after is a lift home because you haven't got the bike. Incidentally, why haven't you got the bike?"

Tara indicated her dress. "Can you imagine me flashing me tights all the way down the M62 in this?"

Paul's face took on a reflective look. "Yes, I can, actually," he said, musingly.

"Paul . . ." she said, warningly.

"Fantasizing . . . just fantasizing," he assured her, hastily. "Come on, the sooner we get into the old BMW the sooner we get our bevvy." He didn't mind being used to give her a lift home. It was on his way in any case. He lived on the other side of the Mersey in the creamy pastures of the Wirral peninsula, so that he had to pass through Liverpool to get home to his rich-young-executive-bachelor-penthouse.

The Cockpit pub turned out to be somewhat more than just picturesque. At first glance it reminded Paul of nothing so much as one of those foul and crumbling French inns where the Scarlet Pimpernel sits disguised as a toothless hag in the old movies, surrounded by heavies of almost unimaginable sinisterness. They caused a ripple as they went in, which magnified to waves of sensually hostile vibrations when Tara took off her expensive coat to reveal her virginal white dress. Paul, in his purple Russian shirt with the bishop's sleeves wasn't exactly the hit of the evening, either.

"I say," he whispered, doubtfully, "it's a bit off, isn't it?" He looked anxiously at some of the hard cases lounging at the coarse, plain, wooden bar. Asked previously, he would have said it was probably impossible to lounge aggressively. He was obliged to revise his opinion.

"What's up?" asked Tara. "Don't you like it?"

"Well, let's put it this way," he answered, "if it were a club, I'd pay a great deal not to have to join."

"Gerraway," she said. "Scared of the scarfaced Jimmies? And you an Oxford Boxing Blue—heavyweight!"

He looked at her, intrigued. "How do you know about my boxing blue?"

"Had a gander at your rap sheet, didn't I?"

"My what?"

"Your 'curriculum vitae.' " She said it slowly, syllable by syllable.

"Get you!" said Paul. "Into Latin now, are we?"

"Did I say it right?" she asked.

"Absolutely right. You even pronounced the 'ae' as 'eye' instead of 'ay'—very classy! Not to say pedantic."

"You what?"

"Never mind for now."

He ordered a double Scotch, neat, and Tara had a glass of red wine. As the drinks came up, a big, blond man in scuffed jeans came out of the lavatory. He looked hard enough to roller-skate on. He looked down the bar to where Tara and Paul sat on their rough wooden stools. His eye lighted on them with a kind of joy. He came down the bar, treading like an engine of war and made a dead set at Paul.

"You got my seat," he said to Paul.

"Oh, have I?" said Paul. "I'm terribly sorry. There you go." He shifted one along and the blond young man, who was about the same age, took Paul's seat. He also took Paul's drink, which was now sitting in front of him: "I forgot my Scotch, too," he said, swallowing it in one gulp. Paul blinked hard, then shrugged.

He gestured to the barman. "Another of those, please."

The barman poured another, without comment, and put it in front of Paul. But before Paul could get his hands on it, it had been engulfed by the blond man's great paw.

"That's very nice of you, wack," he said. "Ta!"

Again it went down in one, without touching the sides. He turned and looked at Paul hard, as everyone else in the pub had been doing since the incident began. There was a great silence. Paul turned to Tara, but she was staring embarrassedly down into her drink. He took a deep breath.

"Tell you what, barman," he said, cheerily, "make it two this time. One each. Seems to be the only way I'm going to get a drink!" He grinned, but he grinned alone.

The barman contemptuously poured another two large Scotches, set one down in front of Paul, the other in front of the blond man. The blond man scooped them both up, turned to another equally intimidating hulk along the bar. "Nice pouffy wacker here bought you a Scotch, Mick."

"Ta!" said Mick, dispatching it with a skill and celerity equal to that of his blond friend. The silence around the room was now a substance that could have been fashioned like fabric. Paul paused, his eyes downcast. Then he turned to Tara.

"Let's go," he said.

The blond man laid a hand on his arm. "Fair's fair, wack," he said, "let your little whore finish her drink first."

Paul paused. "What was that?"

"I said let your little whore . . ."

"That's what I thought you said," Paul answered. A sigh came up through him, as it were from the soles of his feet.

"How's the old ticker?" he asked in a cheery, conversational tone.

"Drive a bloody tank," said the other man. "What . . ."

"Any ulcers?" asked Paul, interrupting him.

"No, I haven't got any ulcers. Look . . ."

Paul took Tara's drink as if to put it back on the bar. Instead, he flung it in the blond man's face, some of it splashing back on to Tara's dress. Before his opponent could clear his eyes, Paul grabbed him by the shirt front, ripped him from the stool and slammed him against a wooden pillar behind him.

As the man sagged against the pillar, Paul smashed a right into his stomach. It was like hitting teak, but Paul had always punched his weight and Blondie buckled. But as Paul moved in to finish him off, his opponent surprised him by bringing his head forward and up in a fearsome butt. Paul's reflexes were still fast enough for him to deflect it with his forearms, but he realized he had been served notice that his antagonist was far from finished and that he had a nasty fight on his hands.

The man was a street fighter—hero, no doubt, of a hundred dockside brawls. However, Paul had always been a mixture of science and brawn: a boxer-fighter they would have called him in "the fancy" and he was fairly well equipped to deal with the knees and elbows, as well as the grenade-like fists that thundered in, seeking his vulnerable spots. He was quicker on his feet than the other man, too, and the fight swiftly resolved itself into an encounter between a trained technician and a slugger. The man was a heavy but inaccurate puncher. Paul found it easy to make him miss and even the blows that did land he found himself riding so that only a percentage of their energy reached him. On the other hand, he was delighted to find that his own punch had lost nothing since his university days. It was, if anything, heavier. Every time he hit the man, the fellow gasped. Every blow that connected with his head rocked it. The detached, director's part of Paul's mind couldn't help seeing the scene itself. It was like an old-fashioned Western movie saloon brawl, with tables and chairs crashing and knockdowns tending to do as much damage to the furniture as to the contestants.

Paul's superior skills were making themselves felt. He was hitting the blond man more or less at will now, increasingly astonished at the power of his own punching. The blond man went reeling against walls, crashed spectacularly over stools. It seemed as if Paul's fists were exploding against him rather than just making contact and the anger started to go out of Paul. One last right hook sent the man spinning backward over a chair, which splintered under his weight. He struggled to his feet, but his legs had gone and his coordination was a thing of disconnected nerve junctions. He swayed toward Paul once more, unable to accept that his reign as king of the pub had ended. Paul chose his shot with care and clipped him crisply on the side of the jaw.

His opponent went down in sections, the knees unhinging first. He turned on his side, tried to get up, fell back and rolled over on to his face.

The other customers took a last look at Paul then turned back to their drinks without comment. It was somehow clear that they did not expect to see much of the blond man after tonight. The deposed king groaned, dragged himself to his feet and made for the door without a backward glance. He paused only to rest in the doorway, big hands grasping the lintels on either side before lurching out into the night.

Paul walked slowly back to the bar, his breath coming in deep heaves. Tara was waiting for him in her wine-bloodied dress.

"Hey!" she said, admiringly, "they teach you great at Oxford, don't they?"

"That's as may be," answered Paul, surveying his rapidly swelling knuckles, "but unless you'd like another glass of red wine, which may end up down your throat or down your dress again, my taste for the picturesque has been fully satisfied for one night and I'd be quite happy to go."

"Okay," she said. "Give us a mo' to go to the Ladies to see if I can stop this stain setting with cold water and we'll go." She disappeared into the Ladies. A man with the expressionless face—and probably, thought Paul, the lovable disposition—of an Easter Island statue, approached Paul.

"Like to buy yer a drink," he said, in a particularly thick Liverpool accent.

"Thanks," said Paul, "but I'm just finishing this one and then we're off."

"Ration the bevvy, do you? Keep in shape?"

"I'm driving," Paul answered. "By the way," he asked, "who was that?"

"Never seen him before," replied Stoneface. "Came in here tonight, started some aggro with three real useful lads, put all three of dem away—then you come in." He nodded at Paul's fists. "You're pretty useful with dem. You're not the usual type, neither."

"What type would that be?" asked Paul, beginning to wonder if this were going to build into a situation where he was going to have to do it all over again.

"Well . . . you know . . . the way you talk, like."

"Yes, well, I'm sorry about that, but there's nothing much I can do about it. They brainwashed me at an early age."

Stoneface's features developed a hairline crack, which could have been interpreted as a smile: "Bit of a card, too, aren't you?"

"If you say so," said Paul, wondering where the hell Tara had got to.

"It's the punters," said Stoneface; "they like cards."

"Punters?"

"Ever heard of 'The Circuit'?"

Paul's pulses jumped. Indeed he had heard of "The Circuit," known by some as "The Knuckle Circuit." It was the insiders' name for the organization that controlled the bare-knuckled butchery he was looking to expose.

"What is it?" he asked, as casually as he could manage.

"It's what you might call a loose association of gentlemen of the fancy," said Stoneface, quoting, Paul felt sure, from somebody else. "A few of the lads up and down the country, who like to see real boxing—without gloves. Someone like you, a bit different, like, with a hell of a dig in both hands, could divvy up a lot of bread. What d'you do now?"

"Teacher," replied Paul. "Physical training."

Stoneface snorted. "You could make five, ten times that kind of money—and in your spare time." He studied Paul's face. "What d'you say?"

"In the first place," Paul answered, "it's illegal. Secondly, I've never seen you before in my life—you could be a policeman acting as an *agent provocateur*."

"You what?" The first signs of animation rippled across his face as his mind reeled around the phrase.

"You might be trying to get me at it," Paul translated, patiently.

"Do I look like a scuffer to you?" asked Stoneface.

"Look," Paul explained, "I'm a cautious sort of chap. That's why I took up boxing in the first place. Before I get involved, I want to go to one of your fights. I want to see how well organized they are. I want to meet the promoters. I want to know from them exactly how much I'll be paid, win or lose, I want to know the rules and see precisely how they're administered, and I want to size up the opposition."

"Get stuffed," said Stoneface, economically.

"That's exactly what I'm trying to avoid," said Paul. He turned away, dismissively, to see Tara coming toward him.

"Ah, there you are," he said. "Let's go."

"Look," said Stoneface, hastily, "I'll see what I can do. Here's a card. You can get me at that number. Give me a couple of days and then call me."

Paul was already on his way to the door, guiding Tara by the elbow. He took the card almost as an afterthought. "Fine, I might do that," he said as he and Tara disappeared through the door.

Paul waited until they'd got five yards from the pub. Then he grabbed Tara and hoisted her a foot in the air.

"You," he cried, "are a witch!"

He did his Bogart, something in which he indulged only in moments of great elation. "Of all the pubs on all the waterfronts in all the North, you had to take me into this one!" He dropped the Bogart. "D'you know what you just did? You just cracked 'The Circuit'—the bare-knuckle story!"

"You're pleased? You're really pleased?" asked Tara.

"Come on!" answered Paul, "what do you think?"

Tara shouted into the darkness: "Ben!"

Out of the shadows, tinged by the pub's red neon sign, a figure emerged. It was big and blond in a dark blue T-shirt.

"Oh, no!" breathed Paul.

Blondie came forward like an amiable tank, grinning. It crossed Paul's mind that he looked inappropriately handsome for someone who had just taken a beating. He had his right hand outstretched. Paul met his grip cautiously.

"Ben Maitland's the name," said the blond man. "Know who you are. Pleased to meet you."

For the first time, Paul recognized the accent as Australian.

Ben grinned.

"I'll take the hundred quid now," he said.

"You'll take what?" asked Paul.

"He was fantastic, Paul," said Tara. "Worth every penny."

Ben grinned again at Paul: "You're good, sport. But not as good as I made you look. I did help you just a bit in there, you know."

Paul looked at Ben and then at Tara, then back at Ben.

"Into the bloody car," he said. "Let's find a civilized bloody pub and then somebody can bloody tell me what's been going on."

Twenty-five minutes later, on Paul's driving, they were in another world. They were in the snug of The Childe of Hale, in the parish of the same name, in what Whitehall fondly believes to be Cheshire, but which every sane person knows to be Lancashire. Its almost Disneyesque, thatched prettiness surrounded them outside and Paul was booming, in what he fondly believed to be a quiet whisper, into Tara's ear: "You set me up! Why didn't you let me in on it, you tow-haired little swine?"

"Because," Tara whispered back, "you wouldn't have bloody done it, that's why. I know you, you rotten great slab of middle-class respectability. If I'd put it to you as an idea, you'd have rolled yourself up into a naffing great ball and stuffed yourself in a cupboard until I went away."

It emerged, in the course of a convivial evening, that what she had done was to invent a scenario. She had found out that The Cockpit was one of the pubs frequented by talent scouts for The Circuit, and had then asked Ben Maitland a favor. She'd known him since she was a kid of ten when he had first come over from Australia. There was a bond between them almost as strong as the one she had with her brothers, except that in Ben Maitland's case it was he who was the protector.

He had once been a professional boxer, but was now a stuntman, in the front rank of his profession. His first meeting with Tara had been bizarre. He was twenty-two; she was ten. He had been fighting, middle of the bill, at Liverpool Stadium. He had stopped his man in four rounds and was walking back to his small hotel. It was raining. Passing a tumble of cardboard boxes in an alleyway he had heard a rustle. Inside one of the boxes he found this solemn, damp, dirty-faced little mudlark. He'd hoisted her out with one hand. The minute he looked into those steadily luminous gray eyes, he was lost.

"What you doing in there, sport?" he'd asked.

"It's too late to go 'ome," she'd said. "I'll get me ass tanned by Aunt Rita."

"What's your name?" he'd asked.

"Tara," she'd said.

"Well, you just show me where you live, Tara sport—and leave Auntie Rita to Ben." He held out his big paw and Tara, who would normally have bitten any stranger who touched her, instantly put her little hand into it and he walked her home.

After that, whenever he fought in Liverpool, which was often— he was a favorite in that boxing city—he'd seek her out. They'd walk hand in hand to the Pier Head. He'd tell her about Australia, about the Sydney orphanage in which he'd been raised. She'd tell him horror stories about school—except that she didn't realize they were horror stories. They'd have tea and a doorstep sandwich in a dockers' café. He was the first friend she ever had. He'd been in love with her ever since he plucked her like a little frog from that soggy box. To watch her grow up had been both a miracle and a heartbreak. For something had inevitably been built into their relationship—a paternalism—that stood in the way of any sexual development of it. Instead, he took refuge in jokes—and heartfast loyalty. He had driven up from London on the strength of a simple request from Tara. And he had played his part superbly in the scenario she had invented.

"I thought there was something weird about the magic punch I'd suddenly developed," muttered Paul, looking discomfited.

"Oh, you can punch all right," said Ben. "You parked a few on me I wasn't quick enough to dodge, but mostly I was riding them, just making them look like bombs. It's easier, of course, when the other guy's a stuntman, too, and you can fake angles with the camera. Still, I think we made a fair old job of it between us."

"Your reflexes must be extraordinary," said Paul.

"They're not bad," Ben answered. To prove his point, he stacked four coins on the back of his hand, flipped them in the air and caught them all, one by one, before they hit the floor. Some of the men at the bar saw him do it and within minutes the place was a maelstrom of small change rolling about on the carpet.

In the fun that ensued, nobody thought to ask Tara how she knew where the talent scouts for "The Circuit" trawled. Nor did she volunteer the information. She was keeping her Mail Room gang under cover for the moment.

She had a great deal on her mind. The way Paul had conducted himself in The Cockpit, his willingness to submit to insult and humiliation because—and this was something she knew instinctively—he didn't want to involve her in a brawl; his ultimate decision that he must fight, not for his honor, but for hers, all this had started a curious chemistry inside her. She had always liked Paul. She had always admired him, even in the Mail Room, as a tough, hard-nosed investigative journalist. Since she had worked for him her admiration had increased a hundredfold. Yet there had been nothing that turned that secret little switch. Until tonight. Tonight she had realized that he was young, gallant and yes, all right, knightly. And the little switch had made its soundless move. Maybe it always happened when a man fought for you; all she knew was that her nipples were sensitive, that she had a warmth between her thighs and that she wanted that warmth around Paul Cranmer. For the first time she found it hard to look at him in case she gave something away.

She needn't have worried. He already knew. There isn't a man on earth more psychic than one who longs for a woman the way Paul yearned for Tara. After she, bloody young urchin, had laid down the terms of their relationship, he had scrupulously observed them. It had made no difference at all, however, to the way he felt about her, nor to his sensitivity to her emanations, both mental and physical. What was it? Was it scent? Body language? Was it telepathy? Paul didn't know and he didn't give a damn. All he did know was that he had the furnace stoked up for his beloved, clever Tara and hers, tonight, miraculously, was on a high number for him.

The third factor in the equation was Ben. Ben wasn't too familiar with the role of chaperone, but the macho exterior cloaked a sensitivity that was equal to Paul's and it had come to him that chaperone was the role in which he had currently been cast. He finished his drink, raised a big paw to the barman: "Can you get me a taxi, sport?"

"Oh, look here," protested Paul, as enthusiastically as he could, "I can easily run you back to your hotel."

"No hassle," said Ben. "I'm just going to check out, pick up my car and drive back to London. No point in you putting yourself about. Thanks to both of you for the evening—it's been kind of different!" He grinned his big white grin, kissed Tara and was gone.

Paul reached across the table and grasped Tara's hand.

"Yes," she said, simply.

2

Paul Cranmer's program on the savagery of modern bare-knuckle fighting has since become legend—as has the method of its achievement.

One fine summer evening in the golden air of a green meadow, remotely cradled in the Lancashire dales, the gentlemen of "the fancy," a mixture comprised of criminals, near-criminals, farmers, rich businessmen and gentlemen of leisure, foregathered in their Range Rovers, Land Rovers, farm trucks, Mercedes and BMWs to watch six pairs of men beat each other senseless in fights that simply went on until one man could no longer get to his feet no matter how long he was given to do it. Some, mostly bookies, had come in horse boxes, from which they conducted their business.

There was one horse box, however, where no bookie hawked his odds, where no champagne corks popped and no lobster was consumed. For the horse box was a Trojan horse box, a hide from which man, instead of observing animals, was observing man. Through holes in the sides, miniaturized silicon-chip cameras with long-Tom lenses traversed in the deadly gunnery of crusading television. The pictures came up on little monitors inside the horse box. Through other slits, marksmen sound experts aimed acoustic rifles to pick up and record conversations, sometimes hundreds of yards away, and the thud and crunch of knuckles on bone and cartilage.

Down among "the fancy," accompanied by Stoneface, was Paul, playing the innocent, lavish in his questioning, a radio mike under his shirt relaying every word back to the spinning tapes in the horse box. On the tiny screens in the horse box were the faces of "the fancy," caught in close shot, ruddy, rough, pale, refined, all with the unbuttoned, unguarded ugliness of beings abandoned to a primitive lust.

Watching the pictures, Tara suddenly caught her breath. It was a face that would have seized her eyes anyway. Unlike the others, it was enjoying the brutal spectacle without any outward show of emotion. Perhaps the eyes were narrowed, but that was all. Pale, narrow, cut with precision, capped and framed by the immaculate black hair, it was the face of a Renaissance prince. It was the face of Jason Planter.

Tara could not have explained the sudden sense of panic that swept over her at the sight of those sardonic features, but a second later she had real cause for it. For Planter, as though by some mysterious communication with the monitor, suddenly seemed to be looking directly at her. What had happened was that the last rays of the sun, spraying over the top of one of the surrounding crags, had caught the lens of one of the cameras and Planter had seen the telltale flash. The picture started to move off Planter as the cameraman looked for fresh targets.

"Stay on him!" hissed Tara, quite unconscious that she was whispering.

Fascinated, she watched the puzzlement grow on Jason Planter's face and then turn slowly into suspicion. She turned to the cameraman to whom she had just spoken: "Bert, I think we've been sussed." She nodded to the monitor carrying Planter's image and Bert followed him with his camera as he crossed and spoke to one of the more malignant-looking of the organizers and jerked his head toward the horse box.

"Someone had better get Paul out of there," said Tara, urgently. "I'd go myself but I'm the only bird here and I'd stick out like Dolly Parton's tits."

"I'll get him," said Bert. He slipped out of the back of the horse box and made his way through the crowd to where Paul stood with Stoneface. He saw that Stoneface was absorbed in the ferocious fight in progress.

"Tell him you're going for a pee," he muttered to Paul; "we've been rumbled."

By this time Jason Planter and his malign partner had been joined by a third man with a face to spread panic in the streets. They were all looking toward the horse box. Paul made his excuses to Stoneface and, with Bert wandering behind, strolled back to the horse box as slowly as he could bring himself to do. By this time Jason Planter and his two companions were also on their way toward it.

Paul scrambled in with Bert. Jock, the dour Scots driver of minimal words, was already in the driving seat with the engine running.

"Right, Jock!" ordered Paul, and the vehicle started to roll over the tussocky grass and small flinty boulders of the rough ground.

"Strap the equipment down," shouted Paul as they gathered

speed. The three cameramen and two sound men began to secure their precious cargo. They were Paul's regular crew, had used this improvised, undercover Outside Broadcast van before and had developed their own technique for dealing with this kind of emergency. Central to it was Jock, of whom it was said that he could drive a furniture van around the Nurburgring racetrack and probably come in the first fifteen. As the horse box reared and bounced across the field toward the road, they could see, behind them, men running for their cars. As they reached the road, powerful engines were being kicked into life.

Jock reached the road, his foot went down and the slab-sided transporter started to sway and bucket down the flinty country lane. The first of the pursuing cars was not yet in sight. Nobody was under any illusions as to what would happen to them if they got caught. Out here in the dales they were a million miles away from civilization. Paul and, traditionally, the technicians would give a good account of themselves, but their equipment and their program would be smashed— and so would they.

As they screeched around a bend, the first of the pursuers appeared about three-quarters of a mile behind them. It was a Range Rover with a massive cow-catcher grille on the front.

"Oh Christ," muttered Paul, "it would be!" He leaned forward to Jock: "D'you think you can reach the village, Jock?" There was a police station in the village.

"Nae," said Jock, one eye on his rearview mirror. The Range Rover, with its superior ride, was gaining on them quickly. Jock's throttle foot went down further. Tara gasped as their rear wheels came within a millimeter of an escarpment with a 200-foot drop the other side.

The cavalcade of snarling cars, headed by the Range Rover, was gaining faster now. She could see the set face of the leading driver. Jock drove like a demon, throwing the horse box round bends it was never meant to face, the vehicle rocking from side to side, its left side threatening to topple over the escarpment, its right side in danger of hitting a wall of rock. Three hair-raising minutes went by and then what Paul had feared, happened. The Range Rover caught up and rammed the back of them with its cow-catcher. Jock wrestled with the wheel as the horse box rocked and swerved. The Range Rover pulled back to take another run at them, then charged again. They were now in a kind of canyon with rock walls on either side. Jock clipped both walls as he fought to keep control. Again the Range Rover pulled back and again it roared forward and the shuddering jolt rippled through the horse box. Equipment started to shake loose. Jock, all his energy concentrated on holding a line, said nothing. Tara leaned forward to him.

"Jock, next time he pulls back, can you go like hell and give us a hundred yards?" Jock nodded.

Tara took the crate of beer without which no crew would ever come on an expedition like this and distributed a bottle to each man.

"You can't do that!" protested Paul. "You could kill them!"

"What the fuck d'you think they're trying to do to us?" asked Tara.

"Yes, but all the same," muttered Paul.

"Look," asked Tara, "d'you want the best program you've ever done destroyed or not? D'you want your ribs and your teeth or not? D'you want an odds-on chance of crashing and being crunched or not?"

Paul was silent. This kid had a way of seeing life in fundamental terms with which you couldn't argue.

The Range Rover had pulled back again and Jock had miraculously managed to give her 200 yards. Now the Range Rover, looking like some strange-tusked monster, started to come at them again. Tara watched.

"Bit closer, wack, bit closer," she breathed.

As the monster closed to within seventy yards she shouted, "Now!"

The bottles of beer exploded on the road behind them, covering it with a jagged, foaming carpet into which the Range Rover plunged helplessly, all four tires exploding practically simultaneously. The car bounced rendingly off the rocky walls of the canyon. There was a domino effect as succeeding cars cannoned first into the chewed-up Range Rover and then into each other, some of their tires splurting very satisfactorily too. The narrow, enclosed road was totally blocked by a knotted tumult of painfully expensive garbage.

Jock glanced briefly in his mirror again: "It'll take them five hours to clear that lot."

A shotgun blasted at them from one of the piled-up cars, but they were well out of range and they disappeared around the next bend, cheering offensively.

That night, Jason Planter awoke screaming. His houseman was there with a half-tumbler of neat Scotch almost before he realized he was awake. He poured it down. It was the only thing that helped when the dream came. He wouldn't sleep again that night, but the whiskey dimmed the dream's immediacy.

"Thank you, Bowman," he said, handing the glass back with a hand that still trembled.

Bowman went without a word. Anything he might have said would have sounded like a comment. A comment is a kind of judgment. Mr. Planter did not care to be judged.

The dream was always the same in every detail. There was just enough light to see his skin. It was black. He was a slave in the hold of a slave ship. He had been torn away from his family and children by white men who had broken into his hut in the middle of the night. In the sight of his family they had held him down and clamped strange metal contraptions on him that rendered him as helpless as a trussed boar. Then they had carried him off. He knew that he was being carried to an alien world; that his wife and family would be deprived of his protection for ever, that they wouldn't even know where he'd gone. It was a kind of death-in-life with all the consequences of death. Yet he could do nothing a man can usually try to do about his fate. He was utterly helpless; his bondage had been scientifically calculated. The head room in the hold of the ship was four and a half feet; this he knew precisely. There were more than a hundred of them down there in a space that was not suitable even for thirty. The trick had been achieved by the building of two shelves along each side of the hold, one above the other.

On these shelves they had been stacked neatly, chained together in threes, lying on their backs. There was no question of movement. The heat was at least one hundred degrees and the air was moist filth. Soon the other slaves would awaken from the solace of oblivion and, rediscovering their situation, would begin to howl like dogs. He was the middle one of three. The thing chained to his right wrist and ankle was a corpse. He had been dead for ten hours and in that environment decomposition had set in almost immediately. On his left he was chained to a screaming woman. She was screaming because she was giving birth, the baby's head was coming out and, manacled as she was, she could do nothing to help herself. He could do nothing to help either, so he screamed too. It was the screaming that always awakened him.

The dream, which had become rarer of late, was a sign that Jason Planter was currently a very agitated man. He was a deeply private person whose privacy was about to be invaded. The obsession with privacy was an ingrained habit of mind, burned into his genes by generations of Planters.

It began about 130 years ago when the family suddenly learned to be discreet about the foundations of its colossal riches. The Planters were not alone in their sudden discovery of the virtues of discretion in an increasingly hypocritical age. Prime Minister Gladstone and his family also found it convenient to forget that they had grown fat on the slave trade. It was just that the Planters had, perhaps, more good reason for discretion than anyone else. For they had been the undisputed emperors of that diabolical business. They had had the business acumen to go in for what today would be called vertical integration. Unlike most slavers, they not only built or owned the ships that carried the slaves, but the slaves they carried were their own. They bought or kidnapped them on the west coast of Africa and sold them in Antigua in the West Indies or in Charleston, South Carolina. They made money at each point in the hideous chain of transactions. The four Planter brothers eventually owned and ran fifteen of the ninety slave ships that sailed regularly out of Liverpool, specifically designed as people-containers; people as cargo.

Jason Planter, the last of his line, had burned most of the family records relating to the period; and in the course of it had unleashed another incubus to plague his mind. For in one of the papers there was the unmistakable possibility that he could be descended from a black female slave. He kept the thought constantly locked away, but it could spring out at him at any time. Three times it had brought him off his own horse when well placed in the Grand National. Twice it had cost him the British squash championship.

He could burn the papers, but he couldn't burn out the inherited guilt and fear of his forebears. He tried. He employed black labor whenever he could. His houseman, John Bowman, was black. Three of his gardeners were. One of his maids was Creole. He gave generously to black charities. He had set up trusts in the West Indies and the American South, known as BLADE, Black People's Aid, Development and Education, into which he had poured money. Through it all, he retained the knack of remaining a private person.

At one time, his obsession had nearly bankrupted him. Then he had learned to use other people's money. Currently BLADE was funded half by himself and half by an *arriviste* multimillionaire of dubious origins who gave for self-glorification and social advancement. Jason Planter didn't care. Money was money and his own motive was selfish, too. He hoped to exorcize his demon. So far he had hoped in vain.

This was the complex man who sat brooding now in his paneled dressing room overlooking the dawn-flushed velvet lawns and the sweep of the home park beyond, wearing a high-collared, full-skirted silk dressing gown that made him look more like a Regency rake than a modern man.

Unless he did something quickly he was about to be seen on television across the nation in the company of thugs and *nouveaux riches,* watching a brutal and illegal sport.

He had one advantage. Unlike anyone else attending that meeting of "The Circuit," he, at least, had a clue as to which television company had recorded them. His Land Rover, now a total write-off, had been fifth in the pack pursuing the horse box. Just before the beer bottles had cascaded out of the back, a twist in the road had given him a clear view of those about to throw them. He saw one face. The low sun had shone straight into an unforgettable pair of eyes.

There was no possibility of a mistake. His encounter with Tara on the motorway had imprinted those eyes on his mind. After he had followed her home that evening he had been up early the next morning and had driven into Liverpool. He had parked 200 yards down the street and waited for her lithe figure to come out, vault on to her motorbike and roar off. Then, as discreetly as the previous night, he had followed her. And he had confirmed that she worked at Alhambra T.V. He had plans for that intriguing young madam. Jason Planter was a man who wove webs. Sooner or later, he would weave one around her. Now, however, it looked as if she were helping to weave one around him.

He considered going to Cyril Goldstein—they met at the Garrick a couple of times a month in London, Goldstein up on business, Planter about his own devices—but dismissed the thought instantly. The man's integrity was almost painful. There was no known instance of his ever intervening in the work of any producer or director employed by him. Planter had, in fact, once sounded him out on behalf of a friend who had got himself mixed up in some reinsurance mess which was to be the subject of an Alhambra program. Goldstein had gone into his "divine fool" routine: "Planter, my boy, I can't even spell reinsurance. You want I should get into an argument with a minion who can outspell me?"

Jason Planter had known better than to push it. He, was aware that behind the innocent Yiddish routine there was a steely morality that was not to be breached.

Dawn was almost fully flushed before the inkling of an idea began to shape itself in Jason Planter's mind.

At Alhambra that morning Documentary were jubilant. They had been trying to crack "The Circuit" for so long and now they'd finally done it. Tara's role as the blond female Svengali behind it all lost nothing in Paul's retelling of it, nor did Tara's description of Paul's epic encounter in the pub become any less exciting every time she told it.

"You mean you bloody set up your own bleeding boss for a bleeding punch-up in a docky pub?" they asked her incredulously in the Mail Room, where she was a constant visitor.

"He couldn't lose, could he?" was Tara's reply. "The other feller was going in the lavatory bowl, wasn't he!"

"Yeah, but what if he'd lost his temper?"

"Paul can handle himself," said Tara, "don't get your jockstrap in a knot about that."

"Oh aye . . . ?" The Liverpool instinct for sexual involvement rippled around the room. "And what else does he handle, Tara?"

"Sid," said Tara, advancing on her interrogator, "do you like your balls the way they are or would you prefer them mashed—you know, as in potatoes; very small potatoes."

"All right, Ta, only kidding, only kidding—honest," said Sid, retreating rapidly to the other side of a table.

The other secretaries and P.A.s looked at Tara with even more intense speculation. She hadn't been out of the Mail Room for more than six, seven months, yet already she was transforming the image of what they thought their job was. It was as if she thought within a completely different sphere of values. Now that she had more money, her innate taste was beginning to shape her, too. It was not that she was buying a lot of clothes; just a few good things: a Jan Vanvelden dress in yellow and white silk in which she looked like sunshine, a slinky off-white gabardine suit with a tunic collar—she wore her hair pulled back with that one. She bought a romantic Gina Fratini in pale blue, all puffed frilled sleeves and neckline, two pairs of suede boots—and her beloved bomber jacket and jeans would now sometimes be soft glove leather rather than denim.

She wore her good things sparingly, out of an instinct for thrift and because she had to use the train instead of her motorbike if she was dressed in them. When she did wear them, there was a long-stemmed, tomboyish rhythm to her walk which endowed them with a difference. Whether she was in denim, silk or leather her hair always shone an immaculate white gold; she was beginning to brush in the underlying shape of her face. She seemed to be able to hint at any color she liked in her unfathomable eyes according to what she did to them. She was becoming a traffic-stopper.

The Circuit assignment had been on the Saturday. It was now Monday, a North-Western Monday in July with the sun cracking glass and Tara dreaming of cool water around her body as she came out to lunch. She was grateful for the cool simplicity of her white cotton dress. Her long, tanned legs were bare, she wore thonged gold sandals and a gold belt. Her hair swung behind her in a ponytail.

Parked across the pavement from the front doors was a red Lamborghini Countach. An electronic window hissed down and the face of a Renaissance prince was framed in the opening.

"I've been practicing on a supermarket trolley and I'm now quite safe," said Jason Planter. "Moreover, I have a blinding chef and an excessively sparkling, crystal, cool blue pool."

His offer so exactly matched her thought that she was temporarily blocked for words. But only for a millisecond, which he wouldn't even have noticed.

"Are you talking to me, chewing a brick or picking a winkle?" Tara inquired politely. Her basic street backchat was such an ideal weapon for puncturing Planter's smoothness that he choked momentarily. But he hadn't been a gladiator in the sexual lists since he was thirteen for nothing. A response was a response. If she'd ignored him—that would have been trouble.

"I'm talking to you, Rapunzel," he said.

"Rap who?"

"She was a girl in a fairy story. She had hair just like yours. Get in and I'll tell you about her."

"Get in for a fairy story!" said Tara scornfully. "At least I should be allowed a chocolate or a candy and one call to the bleeding police!"

She noted a tightening of the muscles in the lean face. He was beginning to lose his temper. That was fifteen-love to her. She decided she could afford to give a little.

"Would you like to come to lunch with me or not?" he demanded, avoiding snapping it out only by great self-control.

"Good idea," she said, "why didn't you say that in the first place?"

She bounced around the car and slid like a cat into the passenger seat which enforced an almost recumbent position on its occupant.

"Well, that's one way to get a girl to lie down," she said, in her guileless lilt, fastening her safety belt.

"I'm sorry. Aren't you comfortable?" he asked, gravely.

"I'm a bit too bloody comfortable, thanks," said Tara.

He reached over his right hand. "I'm Jason Planter."

"Tara Stewart." She shook the brown, sinewy hand, which knew exactly how hard to squeeze a girl's to show sincerity without crushing her. He had on a creaseless pale blue safari-type suit with epaulets. He looked like a millionaire mercenary. Outside of the movies, she thought, she had never seen a man who was quite so good-looking.

The car surged away from the studios in a smoothly rising graph of power and within minutes they were curving along the Mancunian Way, flying them high over the city and into the big-skied Lancashire countryside. The car's ride was so effortless, Planter's handling of it so sure, his small talk so elegantly practiced that the miles melted away without her noticing. She realized with a start that they were already in the Forest of Rossendale, its soft greenness reflected in the mirror-like red of the car's finish.

"Here," she said, "you did say lunch, not a week's holiday."

"Not far now," he said, as they breathed past ancient bridle paths and poplar-paraded drives, at the end of which Tara sometimes glimpsed some magnificent Tudor or Jacobean manor, its lawns like velvet in the sunshine that slotted down through the trees.

They wound around the side of a wooded russet hill and confronted, without warning, a massive Norman tower at the end of a golden drive running between box hedges fashioned by a topiarist into the shapes of mythical beasts.

"Keld Castle," said Jason Planter, briefly. "We've lived here for 700 years."

"Moving's always a nuisance," said Tara, amiably. "Bloody 'ell!" she thought.

They drove over a drawbridge and into the courtyard of what had obviously been the final battle redoubt of the castle. There was something about the scale or detail of its architecture that gave one a feeling of security. Bowman appeared from nowhere to help Tara out of the car. He was wearing a striped waistcoat and black trousers, his white shirt immaculate against his handsome black skin.

"I thought butlers went out with maids in frilly aprons and no backs to their skirts," Tara murmured quietly.

"He's not my butler, he's my houseman," answered Planter, his refusal to call Bowman a butler being his one protest against pretentiousness. He omitted to add that he did have a number of maids about the place, together with a housekeeper who was Bowman's wife, four gardeners and the chef he had already mentioned.

The interior of Keld Castle was a lived-in palace. Tara had a bewildering impression of paneling, huge, dazzling pictures, gilt, and the scent of cherished wood, roses and cigars. Every surface shone. She freshened up in a powder room the size of a small drawing room, in which she could quite happily have lived.

One room, of which she only got a glimpse, was full of complex equipment. She had seen something like it before, in one of Jean Soong's magazines. Jean had told her it was something called a mainframe computer, of prodigious power, the kind that big companies operated.

"What d'you use that for?" she asked.

"To run the estate," he answered.

"Gerraway! You could run an empire with one of them things."

"Perhaps I do that, too," he grinned. "Maybe one day we could run it together."

Was she being proposed to? She played it safe: "You and me against the world, babe!" she exclaimed, doing her Edward Whatever-his-initial-was Robinson.

"Something like that," he smiled. "Anyway, what do you know about computers?"

"I know nothing," she said. "But my mate knows a lot."

"Yes," he said, scanning her thoughtfully, "you would have knowledgeable friends."

"With a mainframe, who needs friends?" she retorted. She made a mental note to get every contact she had working on Planter; there was something more to him than he allowed to appear. She did—and still was never to find out anything about him until he was ready to let her.

Luncheon was laid out on a terrace overlooking a rolling park at the rear, studded with copper beeches, glossy bays and enormous oaks. The satin-smooth greensward sloped down to a lake surrounded by a lacy mist of willows.

The table was laid for two, the linen was starched snow, held down against the light breeze by clips, and the sun glittered on silver. As she appeared from the powder room, Jason was lifting a bottle of champagne from a bucket that looked an inch thick. There was a cold salad, salmon and strawberries on a side table, with which Bowman was occupying himself.

"Hey, it's all right here, innit?" remarked Tara as she approached. "Be nice when it's finished."

Planter, unsure whether he was having his leg pulled or not, held out a glass to her.

"Champagne?" he offered.

"Great," said Tara, "it's the next best thing to a cold lager on a day like this." Bowman's knife slipped as he prepared the salmon.

Planter realized that, for once in his life, he was being kept off balance, whether deliberately or not he couldn't tell. Normally the combination of his looks, his presence, his charm and confidence and the splendor of his background would have melted the iciest of cool cats by now. But this extraordinary creature appeared to be totally and genuinely unimpressed. Actually, she was not unimpressed at all; she was having a hell of a time. It was just that, like most Liverpool girls, she had a capacity for undemonstrative appreciation that could be disconcerting. Jason Planter was disconcerted. He decided to bide his time and look for a different point of attack. As it happened, the play was taken away from him by Tara.

She opened up on him the minute he had sat her down and taken his seat facing her.

"What d'you want from me, Mr. Planter?" she asked, watching how he tackled his salmon and copying him.

He looked at her warily with his heavily fringed black eyes: "What makes you think I want anything?"

"You took the trouble to find out where I worked. I'd quite like to know how that little trick was done, by the way."

"You said it yourself. I took trouble."

"Look," said Tara, "I'm not just off the boat, you know; let's not mess about. I'd probably never have laid eyes on you again after our ding-dong on the motorway if I hadn't happened to see you at that bare-knuckle punch-up last Saturday."

"Don't be too sure about that," said Planter.

"And I certainly wouldn't be getting the Prince Charming treatment in the fairy castle if you hadn't somehow found out I was there."

"Thank you for the compliment and don't be too sure of that, either," he said. He found himself wishing he could revert to his plan of gentle seduction. The vibrations this girl gave off were getting through to him again, just as they had on the motorway.

"I am sure of it, and I'm a working girl and I haven't got all day," she said, "so let's have it."

In fact, she had got all day. Paul would be cocooned in the editing suite and nothing was likely to happen outside it that couldn't be handled by the secretary.

"Come on," she said, encouragingly; "on Saturday you and your mates were trying to kill me. Now I'm suddenly Queen of the May. It doesn't take bleeding Einstein to see a connection."

"Very well," answered Planter, understanding her directness at last, "it's very simple. I want out of your program. How do I go about it?"

"In the first place there's no way you can go about it and in the second place you've come to the wrong party," answered Tara. "It's not my program. It's Paul Cranmer's program. I'm just his gofer."

"A Production Assistant's a little more than that," he observed.

"Been doing a bit of research, I see."

More than you know, he thought. She'd be surprised to learn how far back his initial interest in her went and what had triggered it, long before their first encounter on the motorway.

"Correct intelligence is the basis of most success, someone once told me," she added.

"Only if you know what to do with it," he said.

"Exactly. And if you want to mess with the media and their rights you don't come to a P.A.," she said. He was refilling her glass yet again. It didn't worry her. She had inherited her father's head. Jason Planter might just as well be pouring lemonade down her. She looked again at the stupefying view from the terrace. All his. How could anyone so impregnable get so uptight about being shown at the fights?

"Mr. Cranmer is a dedicated man," he went on. "At least, that is what I'm told. He wouldn't understand what on earth I'm talking about. You, on the other hand, are, I think, an opportunist . . ."

"Thanks a bunch," Tara interrupted amiably.

"I am telling you that I do not wish my face to be shown in that program and I'm willing to pay to see that it doesn't." They were now on to the strawberries soaked in Cointreau.

"Ah!" said Tara.

"Have I reached you?" asked Planter, wishing urgently that he could reach her in quite another sense.

"Oh, you've reached me all right," said Tara, "and I'm thinking about it. It's just when you say 'pay' . . . well, there are all kinds of ways of paying for things, aren't there?"

"I don't under—"

"Well, you can pay with money, or you can pay with services. Or," she went on, "you can repay a favor with a favor." The spectacular eyes flashed. Gunsmoke, he thought. It was almost as if she'd been stalking him rather than the reverse. He paused; his spoon tinkled on his crystal bowl.

"What kind of favor did you have in mind?" he asked eventually.

"Yes," she said, "what do I? Well now, you've got to remember that I'm only a gofer—I did explain that to you." Her tone was deliberately patronizing. Planter's only response was a skeptical smile.

"But I am involved," Tara admitted, "up to my hairline." Up to your delectable hairline, thought Planter, designed by Nature as a perfect frame for those bones.

"What Paul wants, I want," she went on, aware of, but remorselessly ignoring, his unspoken thoughts. "And I do know that Paul Cranmer is obsessed with exposing the 'house-bouncers.' "

"The what?" queried Jason Planter.

"You prob'ly don't know them by that monicker," she explained, indulgently.

"That what?"

"Name, thickhead." God, thought Jason, if I had you on a wide bed right now! But she was lilting on again.

"They're the vultures who lend people money to buy their rented council houses. The only trouble is the people they lend it to can't afford to borrow it—that's why they haven't been able to get it from anyone else. Naturally, they get in trouble with the repayments and the vultures jump on them."

"They foreclose on the mortgage," said Planter.

"Then they throw them out" she went on, "tart the houses up with a bit of paint, plastic and nylon carpets and flog them for a packet. Meanwhile, the poor buggers who fell for it are homeless."

"You're breaking my heart," said Planter, "but what's this got to do with me? I'm not a . . . what? . . . a 'house-bouncer.' "

"No, but I'll bet you know who the pig at the top of the racket is."

"How d'you arrive at this surprising conclusion?"

"Just who you are, what you are. You're the big bread . . . and land and . . . class—going back all them hundreds of years. You're the kind of man that kind of man wants to know." She said it without any sense of admiration; it was evident that none of it cut any ice with her. "Especially the kind of ratface I'm talking about," she went on, "whoever he is. He'd be the sort of crud who'd go to that bareknuckle filth partly because he likes it, but mostly because you go."

"Supposing I did know him," said Planter, hiding the sting he felt, "what then?"

"Then," said Tara, slowly, sensing the breakthrough, "you tell me his name and I see to it that your face is cut out of the fights program."

"How can I be sure of that?"

"You look to me like the kind of geezer who's learned who he can trust."

He was silent for a pause. She was right. He did know the man she was talking about. He was a loud-mouthed bully and boor who'd been trying to break through into a circle that despised him for years. He constantly accosted Planter noisily in public as an old friend, despite Planter's having already inflicted on him the death of a thousand cuts. Planter would have been quite happy to drop him in it without any inducement of the kind he was now being offered. He hesitated because he couldn't yet quite come to terms with how he had been effortlessly manipulated by this slip of a girl who couldn't even speak the Queen's English. He had had the initiative, it was his game on his own ground and yet he was being beaten out of sight.

"Just when did you think all this up?" he asked, a genuine curiosity in his face.

"On the way here," she told him frankly, "while you was rabbiting away."

"Thank you very much," he said, his shapely eyebrows raised.

His irony was lost on her.

"You see, it was obvious there was something you wanted from me—and I had a pretty good idea it was to do with Saturday. Well, where I come from, for family, friends . . . it's all free. Everything's free—doesn't matter what. But for strangers, nothing is for nothing. So when I worked out what you likely wanted from me, I got to wondering what you was best placed to do for me. Well, Paul and me have been working for weeks trying to find out who the Mr. Bigballs behind this rotten caper is and we come up with a big zero. But then it sort of came to me it was prob'ly the kind of thing you just would know as simple as what day of the week it was. D'you cotton?"

"Oh yes," he answered, heavily, "I cotton." He had thought he was going to amuse himself toying with this girl. Instead, the boot was on the other foot. He sat, studying her evenly. She smiled at him suddenly, like a flash of lightning lighting up her face. Where in God's name had a kid who'd been fed on the diet she'd probably had as a child got teeth like that? But there was another quality to the smile: it was one of total, unfettered openness. This girl could, if she chose, be a formidable friend.

He made up his mind.

"The man's name is Ed Friendly," he said. "He hides behind a cluster of companies, but the key company is Lizter Holdings. Now come and have a look at the park before I drive you back."

They got as far as the lake. The air was very still, as though waiting for something. The lake was a ripple-free glass, mirroring the sky, blue, printed with splashes of cottony white and the veil of pale willows.

He took her by the elbow, gently, and stopped her inside the latticed tent of a willow. They seemed out of the day and out of time in a cool, mesmeric dimension of green and gold as the sun and the leaves wove a fabric around them. Through the leaves was the serene blue face of the lake saying I was here before you came and I will be here long after you have gone; your span is so short, don't waste it. The psychic tension between Tara and Jason had been building all the way to the lake. He cradled her chin in his palm and tilted her head. He pressed his lips on her lips. And the meeting of flesh on flesh which he had desired increasingly all afternoon had begun.

Tara responded at first like a child offered a treat it had been lusting for and grabbing it. Her mouth and tongue were as active and vivid in the encounter as his, if less experienced. His hands started to work on the supple smoothness of her body. Instantly she knew that she would go no further. In her way, she was a curiously puritanical girl. She had to have emotional involvement, as she had with her big, vulnerable teddy bear, Paul. All she shared with this lean, hard man today, rippling with sexuality, was a lust which she felt was forbidden to her at this moment. Perhaps it was too obvious, too expected. She understood the agony of suspension she was imposing on him. She justified it with the reflection that she was imposing it equally upon herself. There might come a time, if they continued to know each other, but it was not now.

"You're a strange girl," he said, trying to fathom her eyes as he sensed her drawing away from him.

"I'm just a kid from Slum Valley," she said. "Don't take me so seriously."

"I'll try not to," he promised, "but you make it difficult. What do you want, Tara Stewart? What d'you want, really?"

"That," replied Tara, "would be telling, wack."

He drove her back as effortlessly as they had come—not to the studios, it was too late for that—but to her flat. He dropped her outside and sped off. It was only as she was opening the front door that she had a slight sense of having made a mistake in laying open to him her new address.

"No, no, bloody no!" Paul roared next morning. "No bloody deals! Not with animals who support obscenities like The Circuit!"

"Great!" said Tara. "Fine! Forget it!" She started to walk out of the office.

"Just a minute!" he called after her. "The name. The name of the house-bouncer operator; what's his name?"

"I thought I'd explained," she said. "I gave my word. We'd take him out if he supplied the name. He's come across with the name; now we take him out."

"Your word?" shouted Paul, the decibels rising again. "Your word doesn't mean anything when you give it to a sod like that!"

"My word doesn't change according to who I give it to," said Tara.

"Look," said Paul, "you needn't have anything to do with it. You don't even need to know. Just give me the name and I'll do the show on my own. You can be on holiday."

She was ashamed for him.

"Sometimes, Paul, you can be pathetic," she said. "I'm going to forget I heard you say that."

His color boiled up. He grabbed her, his great hands on her arms like clamps, and started to shake her. He was actually hurting her, her gentle Paul.

"Gerroff!" she yelled, "you big fucking rubber duck! If you don't want a knee in the goolies get your Mickey Mouse hands off me!"

She made a threatening move with her knee and the steel grabs left her arms and she stepped back. To say he was surprised would be an understatement. Since Tara had become his P.A. his life as a producer had become one of the keenest bliss. He had come to think of her as his white witch. Even before last Saturday's coup she had set precious gifts before him. Did he yearn for six dockers to come forward and speak openly and freely about corrupt practices on the waterfront? Tara went out and got them. No matter that one of the six was Terry Lewis's uncle and that they were all pushing for redundancy payoffs anyway; Paul and the nation got a fascinating program, which at least made them wiser than before, although not as wise as Tara. Did he wish a program depicting the latest methods of "fencing" stolen household goods? Tara produced a burglar with his own traveling "shop"—a van, the side of which let down to reveal a dazzling array of televisions, radios, videos, record players, electric kettles, blankets, one or two washing machines, bicycles, sets of cutlery, mixers and electric carving knives. The man would tour the van around the poorer areas, both inner city and suburban, and he had one unwavering rule, of which he was proud. He outlined it in his false-naïve Liverpool singsong: "If you see anyt'ing dat belongs to you, like—you gerrit back for nut'n."

What the public didn't know and what it wasn't felt necessary to tell them was that the burglar in question had already done time for the offense he was demonstrating, and what they were watching was, in fact, a reconstruction of his operation, so that he was in no danger from the police. What the police didn't know was that he had already recommenced operations on the other side of the river, in

Birkenhead. And what nobody at all knew—not even Paul—was that the man was a drinking friend of Jean Soong's brother. The only one with the whole picture was Tara and she wasn't telling.

"Where the devil did you find him?" Paul had asked, delightedly.

"He's an old friend of the family," Tara had said, straight-faced, and he really hadn't been able to tell whether she was joking or not. Nor did her manner encourage further probing. For someone so apparently open she talked very little about herself or how she went about achieving her miracles. He had a shrewd idea that she was running some kind of private Mafia and that those villains in the Mail Room were part of it. It had also crossed his mind that she might have some vague criminal connections herself. But all he really knew was that in everything she did she was a winner; and she won for him. Even in the constant battle between department and department and producer and producer for facilities and technicians that goes on in every television company, she always got him the best, when he wanted it and where he wanted it.

"How d'you do it?" he'd once asked her.

"I take all the boys behind a shed once a week and show them me navel," she'd said.

All this ran through his mind as he let go of her arms, felt the blood draining back from his face into his system and achieved a certain amount of calm. It was their first fight and he was grieved by it. He sat down heavily and was aware of a sense of loss. His great shoulders slumped in a way that never ceased to touch Tara. She had never believed in confrontation unless there was no other answer, and as her adrenalin ebbed, she found that it had left the answer on the beach behind it. It had come to her that Paul had never seen Jason Planter. When Planter's image was on the monitors in the horse box, Paul had been down in the field, so that he hadn't the faintest idea what the man she was asking him to cut out looked like. He rectified that omission now. He was a split second too late. She already had her plan.

"What does this swine look like, anyway?" he asked, sullenly.

"Fat, red-faced, carroty hair," said Tara, promptly. "Look," she went on, conciliatorily, "we might not have had him in camera at all. This could all be a row about nothing. Why don't we go and see?"

"Well, I suppose we could do that," he grumbled, wondering why the hell he hadn't suggested this kind of intelligent initiative instead of leaving it to this willow-witch half his age.

"Give me five minutes," she said, "you've messed me up a bit."
She went, leaving him feeling guilty, which was precisely her intention.

In the shadowy, glowing editing suite, buttoned with bright screens and winking red and yellow plastic switches, it was as she had hoped: Paul's program was still twenty minutes over length. Jason Planter was shown, in bits, for a total of twenty-five seconds on the stopwatch she surreptitiously punched under the console. Unfortunately, because of his looks, the camera tended to go in for close shots of him.

A picture came up of the fat, red-faced, carrot-haired man she had described.

"That the fellow?" asked Paul.

"Can't remember," said Tara, with pretended stubbornness.

"See if we've got any more stuff on him, Jack, would you?" he asked his editor, vindictively.

"We're already twenty minutes over, Paul," said Jack.

"I know, I know," said Paul, "but there's bags we can get rid of. Trust me, we'll be down to 53/50 before you know it."

"If you say so, boss," said Jack. At which point Paul was called away, as Tara had arranged when she was supposed to be repairing the damage that she said he'd inflicted on her. Tara was left alone with Jack.

"Jack, can you punch up the good-looker?"

Jack manipulated his controls like a concert pianist.

"I take it that's the feller you had in mind?" he asked, as a picture of Jason Planter came up on screen and Jack froze frame.

"The same," said Tara.

"What about him?"

"You've got twenty-five seconds of him," she said, tapping her stopwatch. "You're twenty minutes over. Paul listens to you. I'd take it as a favor if the twenty minutes you lost included the twenty-five seconds of old black-eyes there. D'you think you can manage it?"

"Personal, Tara?"

"Personal, Jack."

Jack looked at the lean, handsome face on the monitor.

"He just would be your type," he grinned.

Tara shook her head: "Not that kind of personal."

"Consider it done, love," he said. She kissed him quickly on the nose and went.

And so it was that Jason Planter disappeared from *The Circuit* by Paul Cranmer and an obscure fat farmer with a red face and carroty hair found himself, to his bewilderment, an overnight celebrity as his bucolic features flashed across the screen again and again in the course of the program, showing him at a savagely primitive rite on an evening his wife thought he was playing bowls.

When Paul had returned to the editing suite after what he considered a mysteriously pointless errand, he found Tara had gone to lunch. But she had left him a contrite little note in his office. It was deliberately not a complete surrender, which she knew would have made him suspicious: "Maybe you're right. I still don't think so. But I want Mr. House-Bouncer as much as you do. Let's go and get him!" And get him they did. Mr. Ed Friendly of Lizter Holdings became the object of their every waking thought.

They set him up with great care. "This one," said Paul, "we can't rush. We lay it down and then we let it mature."

In the end it was Jean Soong, in the Mail Room, who delivered the perfect bait for Ed Friendly. It was a council house on a corner site in Liverpool's West Derby village, not far from the 300-year-old courthouse. Its previous occupants had smothered the facade in roses. It lent itself perfectly to the kind of cheap gentrification in which Ed Friendly specialized. Best of all, it was currently rented by two old schoolfriends of Jean—Johnny and Sheila Madden—who agreed instantly to cooperate. They had a year-old baby.

Tara filled in Friendly's newspaper advertisement and it was she, holding the baby, who answered the door when he called three nights later. She wore a crumpled polyester cream blouse and creased brown skirt and her hair was tangled around her face.

Friendly's success with his clients was based on his intimidating size and his total lack of compassion. So far as his competitors in his dirty business were concerned, he had wiped them all out by simple, ruthless violence. As Tara opened the door to him, he seemed to block out the light. She noted that his forehead was totally flat and his thick, black, lifeless hair was dyed.

"Oh yes, go through," she said, meekly, adapting herself to the role she sensed that girls were supposed to play opposite him. As she followed him, conscious of the delicious composition it was going to make for the cameras, she kicked off her high heels in order to make the contrast between them even more grotesque.

Tara was counting on Big Ed to be good, and he was. She and Johnny were maddeningly ignorant and indecisive. Against their vacillations he brought a whole battery of weapons into play. There was the barely-reined-in-explosion-of-temper trick, designed to make the victims feel they were sitting in the shadow of a volcano reaching critical pressure. There was the laying of the huge hand, like a bunch of bananas, on a slim feminine arm—a very primitive image of violence. There was the outrageous lie ploy. He told them three during the course of the evening. Firstly, that the council planned to evict all the tenants in their row and turn it into an old folks' home. Only those who owned their own houses would be safe. Secondly, that he was engaged in negotiations to buy the block from the council himself and he would be reselling them for three times what they were going for now. And thirdly, that the council would be putting up their own selling price any minute so they'd better act quickly.

Tara and Johnny, the bewildered youngsters, constantly and obsequiously refreshed the ritual tea which Friendly absorbed in mega-quantities, his fist making the cup look like a thimble, as he gradually wore them down.

There was only one anxious moment when Friendly, sensing the battle was won, asked to see around the rest of the house. "No," said Tara, "it's a mess with the baby and everything." Once Friendly got upstairs he'd walk into it all—the cameras, the peepholes, the microphones, the tapes; the whole apparatus of a setup, including the not-inconsiderable presence of Paul.

"Messes never worry me, love," said Friendly cheerfully. "None of us live in Buckingham Palace, do we?" He made to brush her aside like a cobweb, as he did with most obstacles, but he found her planted before him, blocking his way. Her eyes, which he could have sworn were gray, now seemed to be a kind of glinting blue. He felt as though he were looking down two shotgun barrels.

"I said no," she repeated; "this is my house, even if you are lending us the money to buy it, and when I say no, I mean no. I don't want it seen. All right?"

Jesus! he thought, we've got a temper here and no mistake. Unpredictable, this one. Better get it sewn up before her big temper changes her tiny mind.

"Whatever you say, love," he conceded. "Much better spend time getting the old paperwork done, anyway."

It was at this point that Johnny threw in the question in which she'd coached him. Pen poised, at the point of commitment, he asked: "Er . . . like . . . what happens if I lose me job? Get laid off, like . . . you know, out of work. I won't be able to pay, will I?"

"Don't you worry about that, sunshine," said Friendly. "We're not heartless monsters. We'll see you all right until you're on your feet again. Just sign here, lad."

Johnny looked at Tara, as if for support. Tara, eyes shining, but not for the reason Friendly thought, nodded. Johnny signed. Friendly was out of the house within two minutes and suddenly the living room was full of excited technicians and Paul was hugging Tara.

She went back with Paul to his flat across the water that night. She had stayed with him several times now. Her reasons were complex. She wasn't in love with him, but he made love exquisitely and to be with him in bed or on the furry soft rug in front of the fire was like being with him at one of the concerts he had started taking her to; like the music that she was beginning to understand. Like it, beyond it in some way, less than it in others. She realized that she was just beginning to explore the more delicate tissues of her being. Up to now it had been simple survival. That she had learned and she was very good at it. But it wasn't enough for what she had to do. Now, perhaps, she could move on to something else. Was the something else Paul? How could she decide when the alternative, so far as where to spend the night was concerned, was with a slobbering, sadistic old drunk of an aunt, whom she would probably have to scrape up off the floor and put to bed if she went home? How could Paul not be preferable? Tonight she was in for a surprise.

Paul's flat was a typical, rich young executive's apartment. Open plan, clever lighting, expensive modular furniture, one good Lowry and several Hockney lithos on the walls and an exquisite Lucy Lyons sculpture of a girl gymnast in flight. The usual rich young executive's toys were strewn around, the cameras, the mini-recorders, hi-fi system, slim microcomputer, the scuba diving equipment and skis fastened, like *trouvailles,* to the wall. Tonight, as Paul and Tara came through the door they were immediately aware that something else was strewn around—right across the long, lovely sofa that snaked in a semicircle around the centrally sited fireplace. She was brown-eyed, lily-skinned and her glossy black hair spread over the yellow cushions like exotic plumage. Trouble seemed to be written all over her. From the smug security of her Givenchy silk harem-suit she took in Tara, in her cheap little blouse and skirt, bought specially for her encounter with Ed Friendly. She brought off the trick of throwing Tara away with her eyes then turned their luster on Paul.

"Well, husband of mine?" she said. "Been at your charitable works again? Going to give her a bowl of nourishing soup and a bed for the night, were you?"

Paul looked shattered. He was utterly lost for words. Tara was not. She turned on Paul, consciously thickened her accent.

" 'Ere," she said, "you didn't tell me you was married"—which, indeed, he had not, but she'd made it her business to know, and to whom—"what about the baby, then? And I'm up the stick again, according to the doctor. You bleeding promised we was going to be man and wife. And what about the house you've bought me? And the car? If you think you're getting the bleeding Mercedes back, you've got another think coming. As for you tar-nut," she went on, turning to the black-haired beauty on the sofa, "you've got nothing coming, 'cos by the time I've finished with your ever-loving all he'll have left to give you will be the pair of shoes of yours I found in here one night. 'Ere," she added chattily, "haven't you got big feet?"

"And you," answered Black Beauty, "have got a big mouth."

Paul's mouth opened and shut like that of a goldfish. Bella Cranmer slid to her feet, her eyes like gun slits.

"Oh, I'm glad I came tonight; very glad," she told Paul. "When we separated, the allowance you agreed to pay me was just about enough to keep a cat on."

"Seems very suitable," commented Tara.

"Tara, please," said Paul.

"Now," Bella carried on, "we're slinging around houses and Mercedeses like rice at a wedding."

"Look," said Paul, "in the first place you left me, so I didn't really have to give you anything at all; it was just to feel I still had some sort of connection with you. And in the second place, can't you see she's pulling your leg? Can't you see that? Tara is my Production Assistant. Yes, we have got a relationship, but there are no houses, no Mercedeses and no babies, either here or on the way. And even if there were, it would be no concern of yours. Our two years is nearly up and you've got your tycoon anyway, so why would you be concerned?"

Tara gazed solemnly at Bella with her big gray eyes, then her face broke into a wide urchin grin. It was infectious. Bella made a heroic effort to resist and then had to give in, grinning back.

"You," she said to Tara, "are a wicked little bitch."

Tara dropped her a little curtsy, which this time drew outright laughter from both Bella and Paul.

"You always did know how to pick them," said Bella to Paul.

"Including you," he answered. "Bella, what did you come here for tonight?"

Bella sat down suddenly.

"May I have a drink, please?" she asked. Paul brought her a large vodka with a bubble of tonic in it.

"You haven't forgotten," she smiled faintly, taking her first familiar sip. Then she took a gulp.

"My tycoon," she said, "has thrown me out on my ear."

"What?!"

Bella shrugged: "Found someone with even more blue in her pretty black hair than I have."

"I always told you Shaun Patterson was a bastard," said Paul. "You thought it was just natural bitterness on my part. It wasn't. It was just something I felt about him. Yes, I know all the good works he's done, but d'you never get the feeling that it could all be done a great deal more quietly? As it is by other people. 'Do good by stealth and blush to find it fame'—that's my idea of a philanthropist."

They had been so engrossed that neither of them had been watching Tara. Had they been, they would have seen an odd expression, quickly covered up, cross her face. When they did look at her the marbled features were as calm as ever.

"Take him to the cleaners," she told Bella, "and shake the loose change out of his pockets first."

"I haven't got a prayer," said Bella. "How can I prove I've materially contributed to the welfare of a man who had millions before I met him? And I've only been with him two years."

"That's his game," said Tara, "can't you see it? Sorry, love, but it's turn 'em in for the new model every two years and save on the palimony. Haven't you got anything on him at all?"

Paul looked at Tara, surprised. He had never seen her as a vindictive person and yet here she was, encouraging Bella to behave like a gold-digging dragon. He wondered what sort of Tara he would see if their relationship finished. A relatively indifferent one, he felt, sadly. He knew that there was no more than a sweet, friendly commitment on her side.

"What are you going to do?" he asked Bella. "Have you got any plans?"

"I'll have to find a job, I've got to find somewhere to live. I suppose I imagined you living some kind of monastic existence down here and I thought I could seduce you into giving me house room. But I can see you've got your own Goldilocks—no offense—and neither of you want Mamma Bear prowling about the flat."

"No, it's not like that," Tara assured her, rather taking the play away from Paul. "I'm not a live-in." She smiled her dazzling urchin smile again. "I'm an interlude of occasional ecstasy."

"Quite true," confirmed Paul. "There's absolutely no reason why you shouldn't stay here until you make other arrangements. We'd have to be careful, of course, not to invalidate the divorce proceedings."

"Oh, I hadn't thought of that," said Tara, the music of her voice making her sound seven years old.

"We'd have to be discreet about it," said Paul.

"Of course," added Bella.

Tara looked at them as if she couldn't believe her ears.

"I take it that neither of you are native-born scouses," she said. "If you were, you'd know that we are the nosiest people on the face of this earth. You can't switch to a cheaper brand of toilet paper without everyone knowing about it the next day. Your neighbors would have you sussed out within forty-eight hours. I've got a much better idea. Why don't you stay with me for a couple of weeks? It's a biggish flat and my two brothers are away in the Marines. The only thing you'd have to put up with would be my piss-artist stroke religious maniac aunt. Sure as fate she'd peg us for a couple of lesbians and shout Sodom and Gomorrah through your keyhole every five minutes, but if you could handle that, you're laughing."

Bella looked at her solemnly.

"You are, without doubt, a very remarkable kid," she said. "And I accept, gratefully."

She was to stay with Tara a great deal longer than two weeks and their lives were to be entwined in a more complex spiral than she could have dreamed of, but just then, as Paul drove them back to Liverpool to Tara's flat, she was conscious only of how remarkably good people can be to each other.

For the next seven months the scenario schemed out by Paul and Tara in the Ed Friendly operation was followed meticulously. The monthly payments, provided for the Maddens by Alhambra, were sent to Lizter Holdings according to a strict schedule worked out by Paul and Tara. The first repayment was made promptly. The second was a week late. The third one was over two weeks late. The fourth one wasn't sent until the fifth one was due. Then Johnny wrote to say they were already in difficulties about the fifth payment and now he'd lost his job. There was no answer from Lizter Holdings. The fifth payment was made about seven weeks late. The Maddens defaulted on the sixth payment completely. Johnny wrote again—all recorded on camera—his lips moving as the pen covered the paper, frightened, insecure, pleading for time. Again there was no answer.

On the second default, in keeping with the microscopically small print on the agreement the Maddens had signed, Ed Friendly's legal machine swung into action. Foreclosure, writs delivered, possession within thirty days, eviction otherwise. And still the cameras turned.

At this point, Tara went into action again. Visits to Ed Friendly's office, where she was barred entry. Waiting outside all day for Friendly to come out. When he finally did come out being knocked sprawling on to the pavement by an arm like a battering ram before he climbed into his large and lovely motor car. And still the cameras went thrum-thrum and the mikes tweeted in the canvas-covered "hide" truck parked outside. Coming back the next day, cradling Tracy's baby. This time, Friendly left by the back door, which Paul had also thoughtfully covered with another hidden camera.

The final stage was to find out where Mr. Friendly lived. To their delight, it turned out to be a fine, detached house at Aintree, on the green outskirts of Liverpool, with a swimming pool and a two-car garage.

All three of them, Tara, Johnny and child turned up this time, looking tired and dusty and defeated on the long trek from the nearest bus stop, wheeling the baby in the collapsible pram, tracked ever by the crawling, canvas-topped camera-hide. With her usual, uncanny intelligence work Tara had suggested to Paul an evening when, she had discovered, Friendly, craving acceptance, had invited some of his posher neighbors for an *al fresco* buffet supper.

When he opened the front door and saw the two ragamuffins, plus infant, straight out of Dickens, Tara thought she was going to die with joy at the look on his face. The supper party was at eight and it was now a carefully calculated twenty minutes to the hour. Tara raised her voice. She pleaded, she argued, she scolded. "Where are we gonna go? Warra we gonna do?" was her repeated refrain. "Please, mister, you've got so much and we've got nut'n!" She blushed, later, as they played back that shameless corn. She made a great deal of noise. The increasingly disoriented Friendly imagined that he could hear windows being quietly raised nearby. She finished with her hands clutching his great arms, sobbing.

To the delight of Paul and the whole hidden crew, Friendly responded by wrenching himself from her, sending her falling across the baby, who obligingly started howling, and fetching two huge, hell-black Doberman pinschers, straining on choke-chains.

"You get the fuck out of here *now*," he growled, "or I let go of these two!"

Tara waited just long enough for the cameras to gobble up the full luxury of the shot and then she turned and fled, with the baby, followed by Johnny. The last shot was of their backs as they trailed down the long, comfortless road to . . . where?

The show was too controversial, broke too much new ground

in technique and attitude—especially in Tara's impersonation of the wife—to go through on the nod. The Program Controller, when he saw it, was disturbed. He took it to the Managing Director, who was also disturbed. The Managing Director took it to Cyril G., the Chairman, who took it to the Independent Broadcasting Authority. They were the most disturbed of all. They spoke of "entrapment," they talked of "balance." Paul and Tara started to despair. They could see their explosive destruction of a vile man being watered down into an acceptable gruel that could offend nobody. They had not reckoned on Cyril Goldstein.

He had taken the program to the Independent Broadcasting Authority, not because he was disturbed by it, but because he simply wished to follow the proper channels. When he heard of their disapproval, he demanded a full meeting of the Authority. With the full weight of his universally admitted integrity behind him he rose in rarely seen wrath: "Entrapment?" he boomed, "How else do you catch a rat? As for balance, I will give this Friendly a whole hour on my station to explain himself to the people he has thrown on to the streets. We'll have them all in the studio to be sure they hear him. Gentlemen, come hell or high water or a plague of boils, I am putting out this program on this unspeakable person. If you don't like it, you can take away my license next time around."

The program took the public by storm. Normally a high-rating program anyway, this time *Ranger,* the generic title of Paul's show, went through the top of the graph. The public responded with a scream of rage against friendly Ed Friendly, there were questions in the House of Commons, the Government promised to consider legislation to stamp out the Friendlys of this world.

The show got swept up in the bitter winds of controversy. Half of the critics took the view that this kind of spectacular "television *vérité,*" as *The Spectator* and *The Listener* called it, was the way forward for Paul's kind of rugged documentary.

Others, like the *Express,* the *Mail, The Sunday Times* and the *Observer* were more cautious. They admitted that the show had performed a valuable public service but they questioned the manner in which it had done it. They called it a dangerous mixture of fact and contrivance; they asked if it was the job of television to act as *agent provocateur.* It became a celebrated issue, which spilled over into the correspondence columns of *The Times.* On the question of Tara Stewart, critics were at one with the people: here was a star.

Her "performance," as it was accurately described by most commentators, had been stunning. In the first place, it had become obvious during the first viewing of the material that the camera adored her. Although she and Paul had insisted that the makeup department should not lay a brush or a blusher upon her, all the beauty that was latent in her face had been drawn out by the lens. With her calculatedly cheap little dresses, her undressed blond hair, her bare feet and her vulnerability in the hands of the gigantic Ed Friendly, she had the appeal of a Chaplinesque flower-seller. In the second place, she had turned out to be a natural actress. She had triumphantly vindicated Paul's theory that she could negotiate the hazards of the scenes with Friendly better than the real wife. Where the real Sheila Madden would undoubtedly have fumbled and blown out in difficult situations, Tara had risen to them like a Bernhardt. In the third place, whether it was the face, the eyes, the acting or a genuinely unmeretricious quality it was difficult to say, but there was something about her that touched the heart. She looked like a child that had known sadness at an age when sadness should be a stranger. Men wanted to embrace her; women wanted to be her friend.

Two men looked at her and at the show in completely different ways. Ed Friendly came home on the night of the show, having spent a highly rewarding and personally gratifying day. To put it crudely, he had ground two more faces of the poor into the dust and it had been hinted to him that he might well be up for membership of the local Rotary Club. His mother—Ed Friendly had never felt the need for a wife; why lock yourself to a slave from outside when you had one already in the family?—handed him his Bacardi and Coca-Cola as he walked through the door and he flopped into his specially strengthened armchair to watch his favorite pre-dinner program, which was customarily some poor, ignorant sod, who didn't know enough to come in out of the rain, getting his from this right bastard Paul Cranmer in this show *Ranger*.

Twenty minutes later his mother warbled "Dinner, sweetheart" through the hatch, to be greeted by a roar like an elephant caught by the testicles and a brief vision of her beloved son's face, which looked like nothing so much as a heavily veined purple mango. She closed the hatch hastily.

Thirty-odd minutes after that she heard him heave himself from the chair and smash the television screen—so there went *Dallas* for tonight.

Next day there was a minor earthquake at Alhambra as a medium-sized hillock, draped in a suit, walked through everyone and everything—including Cyril Goldstein, who was on his way out—in its search for Paul Cranmer and Tara Stewart.

Ed Friendly found Tara first.

"You lousy, rotten, stinking, buggering, sow-faced bitch," he remarked, for openers, to Tara.

"Pleased to meet you, I'm sure," Tara answered, in her naïvest melody. "Can I help you at all?"

"The question is," retorted Friendly, reverting instinctively to the very physical foundations of his success, "is anybody going to be able to help you after I'm done with you?"

He slammed and locked the door of her office. He picked up the heavy electronic typewriter and threw it against a wall. The door to Paul's office opened and Paul emerged.

"Was there something, old man?" he queried mildly. "My name is Paul Cranmer." His arms hung loosely by his sides and he shook his hands slightly, the fingers rippling. Friendly recognized the signs of an athlete relaxing himself for action. He stopped all movement and took stock. Cranmer was a big man, but Friendly could still give him, maybe, fifty pounds in weight, and three, four inches in height. On the other hand, Cranmer was about fifteen years younger, looked hard as carbon fiber and had the body language of a man who knew what it was all about. On the other hand again, this was the bastard shitehawk who had cut him down, destroyed him as surely as if he'd put a chain saw to his legs. Maybe a surprise attack, really dirty . . .

Tara watched everything that was going on in that walnut-sized yet cunning brain, as if Friendly's small rhinoceros eyes had been tiny digital display units. At the split second Friendly tensed himself for the first kick, Tara leaned forward and spoke quietly into the pen-holder on her desk:

"You okay for sound, Harry?" she said. "Tell cameras to roll VTR."

She knew she was dealing with a man who, for an hour the night before, had been forced to swallow, with increasing rage and wonderment, the incredible fact that for God knew how long practically his every act had been watched and filmed, his every word listened to and recorded, without his having been aware of a thing. He was ripe for a bluff like Tara's. He jumped as if he'd been jabbed by a cattle spike, spun like a huge, ungainly top as he peered into the unlikeliest corners of the room for hidden cameras. Then, with a strangled, inarticulate roar, he turned, unlocked the door and lurched away down the corridor. Cyril Goldstein, who was on his way back in to find out what was happening, with three security guards behind him, just managed to find sanctuary in an open door before Friendly swept past, carrying the security men, like debris, before him.

He did not stop, according to Paul's and Tara's later intelligence, until he reached the island of Jersey. A long time later a cuttings service sent them a clipping from a local St. Helier newspaper with a very short account of a large man who had been fined for unaccountably going around smashing inoffensive tourists' movie cameras.

The second man who had been overwhelmingly impressed by Tara was Cyril Goldstein. If there was one thing Cyril G. knew when he saw it, it was a star. This dashingly courageous Liverpudlian Garbo was the most impressive creature he'd seen on camera for a very long time. As was his habit with anything really important, he put everything aside to think about how best both to do her justice and to stop anyone else from pinching her from him. A week later, her internal telephone buzzed, and five minutes after that she was in the austere luxury of his penthouse office. "Space, sparse and greenery" had been his instructions to his decorator and that is what he had superbly got. As Tara was ushered in by a plump little homebody, who looked as if she should have been patting pastry but who could see through skulls, he was spraying a large, glossy rubber plant with window polish.

"They like it," he confided to her. "I don't tell many people."

"No, I wouldn't if I was you," advised Tara. "What d'you clean your windows with—plant food?"

"Sit down, please," he said. "What can I get you—coffee, tea, a cigar?" After all, he had to keep the Sam Goldwyn image that caused people to underestimate him.

"I wouldn't mind a pipe of Old Shag," said Tara.

Cyril G. put up a battle, but in the end a laugh split the bland, sphinx-like face from small ear to small ear.

"Listen to me, little girl," he said, "you and I are too old to play games. I am too old in years. God knows how you got too old." As Tara remained silent, he went on, "And I can see you're not going to tell me."

"My dad used to say life's the wrong way round," said Tara. "We should start as ignorant, weak old people and grow into wise, strong young ones."

"Your father is a philosopher," said Cyril G. "He's still alive, yes?"

"He left us," said Tara, shortly.

"Yes, my father left us, too," he said. He'd known there was something. "But we are not here to indulge in maudlin family reminiscences, are we?"

"I don't know, boss," said Tara. "It was your phone call."

Again he laughed, this time without trying to restrain himself. "You must know you're a natural," he said.

Tara thought for a second.

"I saw myself on the playbacks of that last show," she said, "and yeah, I think I am. I mean . . . whatever I am, the camera gets it. I know it's me up there. And it certainly does wonders for the physog, too."

"The . . . ?"

"Physog . . . face. I liked the look of myself."

"That's how you do look," said Goldstein. "Now that you've realized it, that's the way you'll look all the time—on camera or off it. But for God's sake don't think about it, just forget it."

He didn't know much about women, thought Tara.

"Oh yes, I do know about women," exclaimed Cyril G., "don't you make any mistake about that!" A lot of people thought he was psychic; he wasn't, he just read faces, especially ones as delicately open as Tara's. As Tara's jaw dropped in astonishment, he privately chalked himself up his first point against this fascinating challenger.

"All I'm saying is," he went on, "don't get conscious about it."

"No," she said, "I won't," keeping it short in the hope of bringing him to the point.

"All right," said Goldstein, again shaking her, "I'll come to the point. Where do you want to go from here?"

"I want to go on working with Paul. He's not only the best there is, but he's the best teacher there is. Just to watch him is to learn, like . . . d'you know what I mean?"

"You're sure you're not saying that because you make love with him?"

"Christ!" exclaimed Tara. "What are you—the K.G.B.?"

"Success . . ." he began.

"Yeah, I know," she interrupted, "is based on good intelligence."

"Where the hell did you learn that?" he snapped.

"You wouldn't believe me if I told you," she said.

"Try me," he challenged her.

"Not until I know you better," she answered.

God! Hit me with a thunderbolt! he thought. This was his company, yet here was this urchin, this stray elf, laying down the ground rules. He decided he had to reassert himself and with the laser-sharp brain which enabled him to see quality equal to his own, he realized that the only way he could do it with this one-off extraterrestrial was to articulate her own thoughts.

"Very well," he said, "I'll tell you what we're going to do with you. You stay with Cranmer for now, but not as his P.A. I want you in front of the camera, not behind it. If you like the digging and the research and all, fine—carry on. But from here onward, I want you to front and present the show. Do you understand?"

"Yes, chief," said Tara, outwardly calm, but her heart thudding with excitement. This was beginning to be it. "But what about Paul, what does he think? I mean, like, it's his show."

"Paul Cranmer was on his way to see me about the idea at the same time my secretary was trying to find him for me. And in any case, even though he does bounce me around my own corridors like a rubber ball, I do happen to be the boss. All right?"

"Great!" shouted Tara, resisting the temptation to fling her arms around his neck and hug him.

"Why resist?" asked Cyril Goldstein, grinning at the startled look on her face. At least his command of physiognomy gave him something with which to astonish this extraordinary child.

Downstairs again, she did hug Paul. He swung her around and around, hanging from his neck like a rag doll. "Now!" he said. "Now we'll bloody well show 'em!"

"You've been showing 'em for years," she responded.

"Maybe," said Paul, "but with that particular quality of yours . . . God, we can get away with murder! Nobody's safe!" He never, thought Tara, spoke a truer word.

There was yet another man, who had also watched and been impressed by the show. It was in his office that the Telex had tom-tommed the news many months ago that the Stewart girl had borrowed an alarm bypass. His reflections, more personally felt, were roughly the same as Paul's. But he had learned to be still—until stillness was no longer enough.

Hurtling along the motorway that evening, a familiar sight by now that the motorway police looked forward to—she was always bang on the seventy button, never a mile an hour more—she reflected on what had happened to her in the fourteen months since she had got out of the Mail Room. It couldn't really be called a fairy tale; too much hard work and planning had gone into it for that. Not just in the past year, but in all the years before that, ever since she had recognized, at school, that if she left it to society and the system, she could end up like a piece of the rotting flotsam you saw swilling against the quaysides at the Pier Head. And if she let that happen, she would never be in a position to do what had to be done.

She was a mini-star, newborn. She was now earning, according to what Cyril Goldstein had offered her that day, £22,000 a year. It was a figure she couldn't really comprehend just yet, even though her street sense told her she could have got more. She didn't want more. Let her find out what £22,000 meant and did for her life and her loved ones before getting tough.

She wasn't going straight home. She had a meeting at the maximum security Walton Gaol just outside of Liverpool. She patted the breast pocket of her riding suit to make sure she had the permit.

Ahead of her, with a sense of shock she couldn't quite analyze, she saw the red Lamborghini Countach. It was doing a sedate sixty-five. She had a curious hesitation about drawing close to it. Eventually, she thought "Sod it, he's only another motorist" and closed down on him, flashing her headlight. The Lamborghini meekly pulled over to allow her to pass. As she approached, a brown hand emerged from the driver's window and gave her the courteous, old-fashioned "Please pass" signal. As she thundered by, the lean beauty of Jason Planter grinned at her. He gave her the thumbs-up sign, then blew her a kiss. It was the first acknowledgment she had had from him since their meeting eight months ago that their pact had been fulfilled. She'd taken him out of *The Circuit* and she had now duly slaughtered the sacrifice he had offered her in exchange. She had the feeling that he was not on the motorway at that time, that particular night, by chance. He was discreet, this Jason Planter, but the fact that he'd gone to this kind of trouble, warmed her. Life, she thought, was coming good. After all that she had gone through earlier, it was now beginning to shine. She had a warm glow in her stomach and around where she thought her heart was.

It was the fatal lapse in concentration due to her euphoria that caused her to misjudge her braking time as the truck in front slowed down.

Jason Planter saved her life. Appalled, he watched her smash into the back of the truck. He swooped down in the Lamborghini and broke all the rules for handling maimed bodies by gathering her up and laying her along the backseat. Then he cut a swath through the evening traffic to get her to hospital. The surgeons told him later that he'd delivered Tara to them with roughly twenty minutes to spare.

3

For some days she dreamed, as the intensive care unit fought for her. Her helmet had preserved her face and head, but she had internal injuries that put her very near to the closing credits. She dreamed of her very early childhood among horses and green meadows and paddocks. Which was strange, for Tara Stewart came from one of the oldest criminal families on Merseyside. Jason Planter might be able to trace his antecedents back seven centuries, but Tara could go back at least two hundred. Known, collectively, as "The Mystery," there were dynasties of crime on Merseyside that were respected in criminal fraternities throughout the country. They had their links with Glasgow and the East End of London and certain enclaves in Derbyshire and the Midlands but it was largely a question of to each his own. Territorial rights were respected, though sanctuary was readily offered to outsiders if the pursuit had become too hot on their own patch.

The Stewarts were among the aristocrats of the hierarchy of The Mystery. They had been responsible for the premature retirement of several thief-takers in the eighteenth century, before the term "nervous breakdown" was known, as well as a number of Detective Chief Superintendents in the twentieth, when it was. They had never committed a murder nor an assault, except on one of their own, or perhaps a member of another family who had overstrayed his boundary. Every young policeman was told about them in terms approaching something like strangled awe. And no Stewart had ever been in jail. Until Tara's father. He was in for thirty years.

Jed Stewart had been the best of the line. Educated, blindingly quick-minded, swift to anticipate developments in technology and society, he had moved into what was known as "white-collar crime." Rather than people, he corrupted machines—computers, telephone cable clusters, input terminals. There was the famous occasion when Merseyside had a total electrical blackout and every policeman within a radius of forty miles said, "Christ, it's Stewart!"

He had married Elspeth, a delicate, sweet-moving girl with almost transparent skin and white-blond hair, from within the fraternity but somehow, he by degrees discovered, not of it. She was too feminine and too much of her time to say anything; to her, her man was king. But Jed Stewart could not have been as good as he was at what he did had he been an insensitive man, and he felt the vibrations.

He managed to ignore them, exploiting his chauvinist ascendancy, as long as he could. He would talk about it to his principal partner, Sean Pattison, a man always more inclined to the physical aspects of thievery than Jed. Sean would reassure him that he got the same kind of loving, silent disapproval from his own wife.

"It's women," he'd say, "they're all the same. They'd make you think you're bruising them by lighting a cigar!"

Jed held out through the births of the children, Corby, Len and Tara, and through their early years, until it became obvious that the kids had not inherited the criminal Stewart gene. Nobody but a born criminal would have noticed, just as nobody but a virtuoso musician knows very early that his child hasn't got the magic. Stewart knew. His wife's genes had triumphed. A great line had come to an end.

He had always been a pragmatist and a fair man—except in respect of the honest whom he held, by tradition, to be "Mugs," the unimaginative criminal word for the rest of the population, who provide the bread. He held a large party at an exquisite small hotel in Morecambe Bay. It was exquisite, that is to say, to members of The Mystery, who kept it fully occupied all year round. It was run by a former member of the fraternity and was "safe." Those who were not of The Mystery and happened to stray into it were discouraged from coming back. Not by anything so crude as intimidation; but sandwiches really do taste awful if the knife that's spread the butter has been previously used to slice onions; and tomato soup spilled on anything is very hard to get out; and repeated wrong numbers, purporting to come from Los Angeles throughout the night, are not conducive to sleep.

Jed Stewart threw his big party and made a speech announcing his retirement. It turned many a squashed nose pink and many a little piggy eye moist. But he neglected to tell his partner, Sean Pattison, first. The fact that it would have been rather hard to do so, since Pattison was hiding from the constabulary in South America, was not taken in extenuation by Pattison. The minute he had straightened the detectives sent out to fetch him from Rio and returned to Britain in a kind of convenient legal air bubble, he sought out Jed.

"You screwed me," he shouted. "To tell the bloody world that you were getting out while I had my bleeding head down in Rio was as good as saying I was fucking finished."

"Don't be thick," Jed answered. "They were watching me like old men at a stripshow. If I'd tried to get in touch with you they'd have known where you were in five minutes—and you weren't ready for them."

All might still have been well had it not been for the site Pattison chose for the confrontation. It was a famous thieves' pub across the river near the pretty, middle-class village of Eastham. And every word the two former associates had uttered had been drunk in by a silent, absorbed audience.

"You bloody dumped me," accused Pattison. "You waited until I was in bother then you pulled the chain on me. What did you want, my piece of the park?"

Jed, slow to anger, was getting irritated: "Your piece . . . ? Listen, Einstein, I've been carrying you for years! Why did you get into bother in the first place? Because you decided to go it alone on a caper I told you was bad fish to start with. Your piece of the action? If I'd wanted that I could have taken it while you were blowing your nose, you stupid git!"

Sean Pattison was not a stupid man. He had always felt for Jed the resentment that a clever man feels against a cleverer man. Jed's thrust went in where it hurt most and Pattison's reaction was straight from the nursery.

"You big-headed prick!" he said—and chucked his drink in Jed's face. The inevitable fight followed. It was long and bloody and Jed had the misfortune to win it. A fight, if it's a close-run thing, can have one of two effects. It can make friends of enemies; or it can make enemies of friends. In the case of friends, the one who becomes inimical is the loser. As Sean Pattison dragged himself into a corner to recover before he could get to his feet, he silently swore a swift and terrible vendetta against Jed Stewart. Jed got the strength of it when he strode across and held out a hand to help Pattison to his feet. Pattison spat on it. Jed shrugged, walked out and drove home. And he made one of the rare mistakes of his life. He forgot about Sean Pattison.

"Oh, Jed!" Elspeth cried, when she saw his ill-used, battered face.

"Not to worry, princess," he grinned, "you should see the other six fellers!"

"Please don't let the children see you like that," begged Elspeth and he had respected her wishes. But one child did see him. Toddler Tara, as always somewhere where she'd no right to be, peered through the banisters at the top of the stairs and went back to bed and cried. Her father, wide and flat like a big mahogany door, with his lovely face with the cracks and creases in it and the bluey-gray eyes, she didn't think anyone was strong enough to hurt him. Yet there were cuts and dark bruises on his face and the knuckles of his hands were angry and purple. He was such a lovely father, who would want to do that to him? Elspeth cried, too, as she tried to bathe his cuts despite his impatience. But she cried not for the cuts. She cried because she knew that whatever he'd gone through, was going through, was for them. He'd enjoyed being a villain and if she was glad that he'd given up The Mystery, it was not from any moral disapproval of it—she was too steeped in its traditions for that—but because she could at last be free of the constant, haunting fear that he might get caught and taken away from her.

Tara's earliest recollection had been a big house at Aigburth with a large garden at the back and around the sides and at the front. A house, Tara realized later, which it would be very difficult to approach without being seen. They moved now to a bigger, rambly house near Southport, low-built and crusty like a warm cottage loaf. It was in the middle of fields, with its own paddocks and meadows and Daddy went into the business of importing horses from Ireland, bringing them on and then selling them.

Tara was five when they moved there and the next five years were sunny with pleasure, as they were for Len and Corby and their mother. Jed was good with horses, a gift he'd got from his father, but didn't know about, and he made a remarkably good living, a little to his surprise.

"I thought the only things on four legs I'd ever be interested in would be two birds on the beach at Benidorm," he told Elspeth.

"Randy devil!" said Elspeth, not entirely without supporting evidence. Country life seemed to turn up his flame; not that it had ever been particularly low. Only last evening she had gone out to the stables to remind him to telephone Ireland, as he had asked her to do. Passing a barn, she had been scooped up from behind and deposited inside where Jed had pretended to take her against her will. The smell of hay and horses and wood, Jed's firmness with her, the extraordinary length of time he had stayed in her before they had both shuddered out their pleasure, had been intoxicating to her, a kind of renewal. The hay hadn't even prickled, as she had been told it did, because Jed had had the foresight to lay down a big, clean horse blanket in advance. Which caused her to wonder, briefly, when the glow had subsided, if he'd had previous experience of barns . . .

Elspeth had felt like a puppet with its strings snipped the first time she had seen Jed, with his tall lean body and the curiously graceful walk it imposed on him, at her father's house. He was the new thing, the young man from a family with long connections to her own, who was going to take The Mystery into the new realms. Their marriage had been dynastic. But it had been a deep love-match, too. Her knees had buckled as she came into the church and saw him waiting for her at the top of the aisle and he still had the same effect on her now. To have him around all day and yet not under her feet, to see him passing windows, perhaps driving a tractor, or carrying hay, or with a shovel over his shoulder, wearing string around his knees and a preposterous hat that looked as if it had been woven out of mud and straw, coming in for coffee at eleven, all this was profoundly pleasurable for her. The jolly, jokey, relaxed men who worked for him and with him, they were all so different, too, from the men that both of them had been used to associating with all their lives. They had been jolly enough and jokey, too, but they had dead eyes and hearts like a swinging brick. It wasn't that she had been shocked or shaken by them—all the men in her own family had been fired in the same oven. It was simply that she had now realized what life could be like under another sky.

Jed taught them all to ride, as his father had taught him. Tara and her brothers spent every available hour, before and after school, on horseback.

Jed was a subscriber to the theory that sea water toughened horses' feet and legs and some of Tara's most wonderful rides were through the surf along the firm golden sands of Southport's incomparable beach where, later, the local wonder horse Red Rum was to train for his triumphant runaways at the Grand National. The horses loved it. They would throw their heads up and flail their manes at the smell of the sea and cruise through the lacy, sparkling water in a mist of spray, ears pricked and tails flying. Tara would scream with the sheer joy of living as her "girl-horse," an amber bay, blond-maned filly called "Angel" trumpeted her own delight.

It was a gilded time. And it lasted five years. Elspeth's bad dreams had finally gone away. She had never told Jed about them. In them, faceless policemen came and pointed swords and guns at Jed and politely requested him to accompany them to some hellish oblivion. Although they had no faces, they were smiling. She never made any noise, quiet in her nightmares as in everything, just woke up, sweat streaming down between her breasts and reached out a hand to touch the solid, steadily breathing figure beside her. More often than not he would be unaware of the touch. Sometimes it would stroke a key in his brain and, still asleep as he was, he would lurch over and cover her face and breasts with quick, small kisses before relapsing on to his back, completely unconscious that anything had happened. Then she would get the giggles until she drifted off to sleep again.

Sean Pattison had been waiting, cherishing his hatred. When the Mersey Tunnel caper came up, he knew it was the one. The "Big Lift," as the fraternity called it, was the regular shifting of overused banknotes from banks throughout the Wirral peninsula to a special, London-bound train at Lime Street, Liverpool. It was the dream target of villains both Northern and Southern. The Southerners looked to intercept the consignment between King's Cross station in London and the Bank of England in the City, where the destruction of the notes would be supervised. The Northern brothers knew that their best chance was while the van was in the tunnel under the River Mersey and out of radio contact. Their trouble was the same as that of their fraternal rivals in London: the dates when the money was moved, the time of day, the type of van used, the particular van of that type, the route taken, the crew manning the van, were all worked out by computer. The day before, the computer was fed with typical traffic profiles for every twenty-minute segment of the day on every conceivable route, with a mix of vans, a tumbled combination of crews and then asked to come up with random alternatives. This it did, one hour before the shipment was made the next day. Didn't give one a chance. "Bloody suspicious bastards!" grumbled the villains. There was great rivalry between North and South as to who would come up with the answer first.

It was Sean Pattison who cracked it. He remembered an old adage: "When faced with a machine, go for the man." Up against an impregnable bank vault, all you had to remember was that the bank manager had the key. Up against a computer, he looked for and pinpointed the man who programmed it. After that it got a little sordid. The programmer, who worked for a firm of independent consultants, was a young man called John, with a young family, a loving, very pregnant young wife and a normally high sex drive for his age. He thought it was his birthday when a lovely redhead, hot enough to start a Number One Priority Fire Alert, picked him up in his normal lunchtime wine bar in Dale Street in Liverpool.

"What time you got to be back?" she asked, drinking her glass of white in a way you wouldn't have believed if you hadn't seen it.

"Half past."

"You really keen to finish that salad?"

"No," he said, his voice quavering a little.

"I only live round the corner," she said.

She did, too, very temporarily, in a nice, very newly decorated flat. Parts of it looked still unfinished, but the bedroom was a work of art, with mirrors everywhere but the floor. By the time Red had finished with John, he didn't get restless with his ballooning darling for at least two weeks. Perhaps it was giving too much to Red to attribute his newfound continence entirely to her: by this time he had problems on his mind.

They had to do with this fellow he'd met a couple of days after Red had comprehensively dismantled his warhead. He'd approached him in the same wine bar. Tall, tough, lean, very distinctive haircut, dark glasses. Name of "Jed." Sean and Jed had always looked sufficiently alike to be called "the terrible twins." All it needed was Jed's old-fashioned neat haircut and the dark shades. "Jed" suggested to young John that he might like to fill in his lunch hour with a movie. John said he didn't think so, but this fellow "Jed" said he thought it might be in his interest and John began to get, like, some sort of message.

He got the full printout five minutes later in the same flat where it had happened with Red. It happened again, only this time on film and he was the star!

"I wouldn't let Robert Redford get to hear about you," said "Jed," after it was over and John sat there in a suit that looked as if he'd just walked through a car wash, "he'd put out a contract on you!"

After that, things followed a fairly predictable course. No, his darling little wife didn't like home movies. No, bloody especially not that kind. "You what?"

Was it possible, repeated "Jed," patiently, to "access"—talk to— a computer without the joker that owned it knowing anything about it?

Well, of course it was. All you needed was a compatible computer, a code and both computers plugged in, through a modem, to a phone.

Was the computer he programmed for these security blokes on the phone?

Well, of course it was; it had to send out orders, didn't it, to branches and all like that! He'd got the full profile now and all he wanted was to get it over with. "Let's have the negative first." Sean handed it over. He didn't even have a copy. This time he wanted it that way. After that, John came across with the lot. Type of computer, code and instructions.

From then on it was almost boring. Buying the right computer—Sean was glad he'd let Jed bore him all those years about them—monitoring the pegheads' computer for a couple of minutes a day, and finally getting the drop on the next "Big Lift." The heist itself was textbook stuff. Car breaking down in the tunnel in front of the security van just opposite a turnoff to the docks, electric chain saw to gut the van like a sardine can while the guards very sensibly, in view of the two sawn-offs pointing at their windshield, sat in their cab with a dead radio, then down the turnoff to the docks ten minutes before Traffic Control arrived to try and sort out the biggest traffic jam the Tunnel had seen in years.

By the time C.I.D. had been called in, seventeen million pounds, less expenses—the girl, decoration of flat, cameras, cameraman, computer, sawn-offs, muscle—was on its way to Rotterdam for temporary safekeeping.

It had to have been an inside job, said the underworld—even the Woodentops must see that. The Woodentops did. They also saw that the key to it was the computer. It took a couple of days before they got around to young John at his computer consultancy and the minute they walked in he started to cough so hard they were afraid they had a case of terminal bronchitis on their hands. He hadn't watched television since he was eighteen months old for nothing. In return for immunity and a promise that his wife would hear nothing of his film debut with Red, which the police insisted on seeing and much enjoyed, he offered them the lot.

They took him down to Mulcahy's nick, the main Bridewell off Dale Street, and showed him the photographs. There was no one in any of the books who looked anything like the man in the wine bar. Then they took him upstairs to the Photofit lads. It took them twelve minutes of sliding in eyes and noses, chins, ears and hairlines and then John said "That's him." And every man in the room leaned forward and said "Christ! It's Jed Stewart!" Although Stewart had never been inside, nor even charged with so much as a motoring offense, everyone knew that he'd been behind most of the clever jobs for years and everyone had his face engraved on their memory. They'd have thought of him from the start had it not been for the shotguns—not his style—and the physical nature of the heist; not his style, either. With Stewart, banks didn't usually know they'd been robbed until the end of the year when technologically-trained auditors climbed inside their clients' computers and started looking for answers. Also, he had undoubtedly been straight for five years. Nevertheless, there was a computer involvement here and a bang-up identification of Stewart.

Aware of Jed Stewart's habit of living in houses which commanded all approaches, making him a difficult man to surprise, the police arrived just before dawn the next day. Tara would never forget that dread descent on them. She was ten years old and cradled in the sweet, untroubled sleep of her age. She was dreaming her favorite dream of the secret garden where she could fly. She had chanced upon the door to it in a hedge she had passed a thousand times at the edge of Friars' Meadow. Then, without warning, there was thunder and the thunder forced her out of the sunny buoyant air, tumbling to the ground. She woke up and it seemed that there was thunder at every door in the house simultaneously.

She rushed out on to the landing to collide with her brothers Len and Corby, who were staggering about, bumping into each other, rubbing the sleep out of their eyes. She got them organized and marshaled them toward their parents' room. But Jed was already on his way down one side of the double staircase into the hall, wrapping a toweling robe around him and issuing a stream of harsh words that Tara had never heard before. Her mother was standing at the top of the stairs, trembling, unable to move, her nightmare starting to come true. Tara instinctively rushed into her parents' bedroom and grabbed her Mummy's wrap. She gave it to Len, who was the tallest, to reach up and put around Elspeth's shoulders. Absently, her eyes fixed on the front door, Elspeth drew it around her without comment.

Tara watched her father look through the spyhole in the front door: "Oh, for Chrissake!" he said, more in amusement than in anger. Then he opened the front door. In walked the muscle-corseted big belly of Detective Chief Superintendent Mulcahy, followed by Mulcahy himself, who had escaped the statutory nervous breakdown Jed Stewart had always traditionally imposed on his opponents in the past because his brain was as musclebound as his belly. Mulcahy and his belly were followed by a number of other men, some in uniform, but mostly not, who stared at her father like rabbits hypnotized by a stoat. Mulcahy had held them spellbound, in the pub across the road from the Bullring, with stories of this supercriminal whom he had made it his life's work to bring to book. He'd had about as much chance as a mouse on a cat farm until a loving deity had dropped this one into his lap.

"Mulcahy!" grinned Jed. "Shouldn't you say 'Ello, 'Ello, 'Ello?" he queried. "Come in, you thick old sodbuster. I suppose you've got a little bit of paper?"

Mulcahy waved the warrant at him: "You'll be laughing on the other side of your face, presently," he said, his Cork accent as strong as ever.

"I have reason to believe," said Mulcahy, whose strength was that he knew the book backward and therefore never gave defense lawyers the chance to fault him on procedure, "that you can help us with our inquiries into the theft of seventeen million pounds in the Mersey Tunnel."

"Oh, be your age, Mulcahy," said Jed. "You know I've been out of it for five years or more. D'you think I'd be mixed up in a crude can-opener caper like that?"

"I have reason to believe . . ." repeated Mulcahy, doggedly.

"Listen, if you're going to stand about repeating yourself," said Jed, "you may as well do it in here. At least we can all sit down." He opened the door to his den, which was to one side of the hall, and Mulcahy and the other four men trooped in after him. Len and Corby crept down the stairs. Tara stayed with her mother on the landing. Her mother seemed paralyzed. Tara cuddled her. "It's all right, Mum," she said, "it'll be all right. Honest! We all know Dad's been here all the time."

She was a bright kid and from the age of seven her father had adopted a policy with her, as he had with the boys, of disguising nothing from her. He had told her the family history and the family business. He had told her his reasons for getting out of it. He had told her all the old tales and legends of deeds done by ancestors and strokes pulled by himself and his contemporaries, so that she had a family anecdotal record as rich, in its way, as that of any aristocrat, a class he described as being in the same game, except that they got into it five hundred years before anyone else.

Dawn was breaking and it was getting light, making it easier for the squad Mulcahy had outside, searching the outbuildings and even the stables. He had, naturally, come mob-handed, with a squad of thirty men, larger than he'd used on many a murder inquiry. Murder, of course, remained the most heinous crime, he supposed, technically; but to steal the mind-bending sum of seventeen million pounds was to offend against the laws of Nature. Nobody had ever heard anything like it and let it not be said that Mike Mulcahy let a villain he had bang to rights get away for want of some size twelve foot-power.

It was in one of the stables that a bright young constable found the computer. Sean Pattison had done his work well. It was just where Jed would have hidden something if he'd wanted to; under a pile of straw in the stall of a vile-tempered young stallion who wanted either a sweet mare right now, or someone to kick to death. The young constable, whose imagination would undoubtedly be a drawback to him in his future career, put himself in what he thought was Jed's place and—being a farmer's son—enticed out the stallion with the aid of a jolly little filly from another stall and went pokeabout among the straw.

By this time, Tara had coaxed Elspeth into the den with the boys and her father, who seemed to be enjoying the whole thing: "Would you like a whiskey, Mulcahy?" he had just asked, "or are you over the limit already?" When they brought the computer in, Tara saw some of the gorgeous high color drain from her father's face and the blue overtones start to seep from the gray eyes, to be replaced by the shadows of furious thought.

The Scene-of-the-Crime officer, the civilian technician covering the scientific aspects of the exercise, took a brief look at it.

"Yes," he said, "it's compatible with the one the security firm used. In fact, it's the same model."

Mulcahy's face glowed into a smile that would have melted titanium. "Now what would you want a computer for in a stallion's stable?" he asked. "To let him work out when he was due for his next . . . ?" He remembered the presence of the children and desisted.

When a detective sergeant walked in with a plastic sack filled with well-used banknotes, Mulcahy's smile glowed so warmly that he seemed in danger of nuclear fission. The sergeant had found the sack, well-sealed, suspended on a well-disguised string in a cesspit on the outskirts of the property. He had thoughtfully hosed it down before bringing it before his Chief's delighted gaze.

"Well," said Mulcahy, enjoying himself as he couldn't remember doing for a long time, "they do say that where there's muck there's money."

Jed, usually a quick man with a comeback, was silent. He could feel the jacket of a superbly tailored fit-up being buttoned about him as he sat there. Who and why? Who and why? was the refrain chasing itself around his head as, now, Tara watched all the blood being pulled away from his beautiful hard-rock face and she and her brothers saw nightmare stalk into their mother's eyes even though she was wide awake.

"Jed Stewart," intoned Mulcahy, going by the book as always, "I'm charging you . . . must ask you to accompany me . . . must warn you that anything you may say . . ."

"Shut it," said Jed, now a gray man of stone. "I want to call my brief."

"When we get down to the station," said Mulcahy. He was in the driving seat now and by God he meant to enjoy it.

"Look," said Jed, "you can either let me make the call now, or have one of my family make it when you leave."

"I'm afraid we won't all be leaving," said Mulcahy with a self-indulgent grin. "Some of my fellows will be staying to poke around a bit more. I don't think they'll take kindly to telephone calls being made."

"You know that's against the law?" asked Jed.

Mulcahy laughed until his lungs wheezed. "You're telling me what's against the law?"

Tara realized they had to act; so did Len and Corby. With the split second timing of the Red Arrows aerobatic team, they did a starburst, each lighting out simultaneously in a different direction. Mulcahy's men, taken completely by surprise, snatched at phantoms as the kids vanished at three different points of the compass. Even Mulcahy had enough self-consciousness not to have his men playing hide-and-seek with three kids slippery as eels in their own house. Instead, he took the receiver off the hook in the room where they were: "They can't dial out now anyway," he said.

"Wrong," said Jed. "We've got five lines. That's only one of them."

Tara knew where her father kept his book of very private telephone numbers. She got his solicitor, Sir Jonathan, out of bed and was so clear and explicit that he was waiting for Jed at the Bridewell in Liverpool when he was escorted in. That—and the reputation of Sir Jonathan—was the kind of thing that impressed Mulcahy.

"We've a tiger by the tail here," he muttered to his men; "watch it!"

Tigers they might be, both Jed and Sir Jonathan, but there was nothing they could do against so skillful a fit-up.

"What in God's name have you been up to?" was silver-haired Sir Jonathan's first question at their private interview in the cells.

"Nothing," said Jed, flatly. The two men knew each other like brothers and Sir Jonathan knew it was the truth. Aware of the initial strength of the case against his client it was the last kind of answer he wanted to hear.

"Oh, Christ!" he said.

The identity parades confirmed his despair. He managed to make objections to the first three—in each of which the little computer programmer, John, had unhesitatingly fingered Jed—but the fourth clinched it. Mulcahy had assembled a line of men who, with their dark shades on, could almost have been clones. Little immunity-protected John unhesitatingly tapped Jed on the shoulder.

From Sir Jonathan's point of view, it was the worst kind of fix in which a client could have found himself. Had Jed really stolen the seventeen million pounds he would, strangely, have been in a strong position. Everyone wants seventeen million pounds back and if Jed had had it to give back, Sir Jonathan could have arranged a little exercise in plea-bargaining that would have had Jed out in two years, maximum. The trouble was that Jed didn't do it and hadn't got it. He therefore found himself listening to a judge who said:

"Jed Terence Stewart, you have been found guilty of stealing, by considerable cunning and the threat of physical violence, if not death, the sum of seventeen million pounds. You have shown no inclination to reimburse, to those from whom you stole it, that enormous sum. It is my duty to impose upon you a sentence that will debar you from ever enjoying the fruits of your ill-gotten gains. I therefore sentence you to imprisonment for life and I strongly recommend that parole not be considered until a period of thirty years has elapsed."

Which was when Elspeth, in the public gallery, despite all the efforts of little Tara and Len and Corby and big Sir Jonathan to prevent her being there, had fainted, in a kind of awful, solid, final way that had the St. John's Ambulance voluntary attendants who were present, looking solemn.

Given her temperament, she had put up a remarkable fight against the black horror that had overpainted her days since they had taken Jed away. There, as she had watched, that first morning, wide awake, was her nightmare coming true. It had been right, her nightmare; the policemen had no faces, yet they were smiling. And they were taking her heart's only love away with them into black, impenetrable night. It was in vain that Jed had kissed her jauntily on the forehead, saying, "Elspeth, love, see you in time for tea."

She knew. Her dream life had always been a more reliable forecaster than her waking hours. The dread realization that it had come true, just when she had begun to think she had somehow slipped through the mesh of Fate, seemed to cut her will to live. She had always been a frail beauty, full of life, but soon burning out and going quietly away to rest. Jed was her life force and so long as she had him she could draw without limit on his energy and his rejuvenating love. Now that he was gone, the ventricular disease of the heart, which that strong love seemed to have been holding off, advanced rapidly. She hung on during the Appeal, which Sir Jonathan put in automatically, but without hope. He knew, as did Jed, that Jed had been framed as neatly as a Rembrandt. He knew, too, as Jed did, who had probably done it. But there was no conceivable way of introducing the name of Sean Pattison into the case. Naturally, his inquiry agents had checked Pattison's recent activities, only to find, as expected, that he had an interlocking chain of alibis. Pattison had exacted a sweet and terrible revenge: he had not only virtually closed the case of the missing seventeen million, he had put his enemy away for life.

When the Appeal was inevitably brushed aside, the life started visibly to go from Elspeth. She had never been able to cope with complications on her own. Jed had always handled everything. The banks and insurance companies started restitution proceedings against Jed for the recovery of any scraps they might squeeze from his estate. It was a purely cosmetic and vengeful exercise, as Sir Jonathan forcefully pointed out to the courts. Nevertheless, he could not deny that they had both the law and moral justice on their side and they bankrupted Jed. The house and stables were sold over their heads and they were given a month to get out.

"Elspeth," said Sir Jonathan, gently, the brilliant blue eyes for once hazed with gentleness, "I don't quite know how to put this; but hasn't Jed got something put by, something not in a bank, perhaps being held for him somewhere, or hidden?"

"I saw Jed in prison last week," she said faintly. "He reminded me who I was to go to if anything like this ever happened . . . I made inquiries. The man's in Wakefield Gaol. All I've got is this." She produced a brown envelope. It had two thousand pounds in it. "Jed called it his float." Then she fainted for the second time.

The doctor whom Sir Jonathan called wanted to put her straight into hospital in Southport. She refused to go. "Who's going to look after the children?" she asked.

"Surely you have . . . friends?" asked Sir Jonathan tactfully. He was supposed to know nothing about the underground web of interlocked relationships in the fraternity.

"I don't want them mixed up with anyone like that," said Elspeth, who was aware that he knew all about them. "I've had them away from all that for five years; they're not going back to it now."

Every day a little more strength ebbed away from her and she became aware that she was not going to last. Little Tara took over the housework, the cooking and the looking after of the boys. The boys looked after the horses until they were sold by the Receiver, and Sir Jonathan handled the dismantling of the rest of the estate.

As day merged into day, each one a little fainter in its outline, the problem resolved itself. Elspeth's sister, fat Rita, turned up on the doorstep. All right, so she was a slob and a drunk and they had never had much in common, but at least she had come, unasked, and at least she shared Elspeth's antipathy to the great kingdom of crime. She had followed the case in the newspapers, she knew her dim-witted sister wouldn't be able to cope and—what the hell!—she'd just been fired herself. To be fair to her, she'd have come anyway. Inside that great gut there was a steel core of family solidarity that Rita would have died rather than admit. Maybe Elspeth always had been her father's favorite and maybe that had bent Rita toward other forms of solace, but this was her sister and she was in trouble and there was an end to it.

It was what Elspeth asked that shook her. Rita had never liked kids. Couldn't stand their racketing, illogical, ungrateful, gobbling natures nor their sometimes filthy habits—and she wasn't thinking about a reluctance to wash. But here was Elspeth, looking about the size of a white-faced doll in the big bed she used to share with her beloved Jed, asking her to take on the kids.

"I've got to the age of forty," she told her younger sister, "without having to have much to do with kids. Why the bloody hell should I land myself with three of them now?"

"Because I'm dying!" hissed Elspeth, with a sudden access of passion drawn from somewhere. "And if you don't take them the council will and that means they'll be split up and as God's my witness, if that happens, I'll come back and haunt you, Rita."

Rita, who was superstitious, paled.

"You're not dying," was all she could think, lamely, to say.

"I imagine I'd know," answered Elspeth, wearily.

"I dunno," said Rita, shuffling uneasily her gargantuan bottom, which was uncomfortably overflowing the little bedroom chair on which she was seated. Elspeth reached underneath one of the big, lacy pillows against which Jed had liked to see her fragile beauty and brought out the brown envelope.

"There's two thousand pounds there," she said. "What with that and social security and child allowance, you should be able to look after my children properly."

Rita's quite striking navy-blue eyes seemed to lighten a whole octave with greed.

"Well," she said, trying to conceal a complete U-turn by making it very long and shallow, "taking it all in all, everything being considered, it might be possible." She took the brown envelope the way she took a glass of spirits whenever she was offered one—with an exaggerated gentility, little finger cocked, intended to suggest she really didn't want it, but a lady should always be polite.

Elspeth died, as she had lived, delicately and considerately, at the civilized hour of three o'clock in the afternoon two weeks later. The foreclosure proceedings by the Official Receiver were respectfully postponed until they could get the body and the children out of the house. Told about it in the maximum security wing of Walton Gaol, Jed maintained a rocky exterior in the face of his informant, the Governor, and didn't weep until two o'clock the next morning when there was nobody awake in the cells around him to hear. He applied, on compassionate grounds, for leave to attend his wife's funeral. It was denied. He was surrounded by an aura of superstitious awe on the part of his jailers. They all knew of his miraculous unpunished exploits in the past and were afraid that, if he were once allowed beyond the prison gates, he might vanish in a puff of smoke.

A less well-balanced man, in the face of such frustration, might have gone out of his mind. That was not an option Jed allowed himself. He worked, instead, on escape plans, clever pieces of thinking, any one of which could have succeeded for a lesser figure. The trouble was that Jed's charisma meant that the screws were unable to leave him alone. When they weren't searching his cell, which he shared with no one, they were finding some excuse to come by for a chat, with hopes of beefing up, with the magic of his name, the mind-numbingly boring memoirs on which they were all working. What helped him during those years, too, was the knowledge of the unremitting efforts of Sir Jonathan and his firm to prove that there had been a massive miscarriage of justice, and a philosophical turn of mind, which told him that there was an ironic balance between all the strokes he had got away with and being done for a caper he hadn't pulled. The thing that helped him most of all, however, was the reinforcement he got from the regular visits of his kids, who were brought conscientiously by Aunt Rita, whether drunk or sober. Monster she may have been in many ways—which Tara impressed on the boys that Jed should never be informed about—but her sense of family could not be faulted.

It was during one of these visits, when Tara came without the boys, who both had flu, that Jed sensed a quality in Tara which answered something in his own soul. It was a wisp of larceny, an imp of rebellion, or sideways-thinking, certainly not criminality, but a way of looking at the world that was decidedly not conventional. Tara was thirteen years old, already with that elusive hint of beauty in her face. In the gruesome visiting room of two-tone cream and clover-green gloss paint on top of bare brick, Aunt Rita had gone to sleep. Tara fixed her enormous gray eyes on her father, disconcertingly.

"Dad," she said, "tell us who done it to you."

He was distressed by the change in her speech over the last three years—she was beginning to talk like a real slum kid—but struck very hard by the blue shadows of a particular intelligence behind the gray of those eyes. He began to fence with her, testing her out.

"What makes you think anyone did anything to me?" he asked.

"Because I've been thinking about it every night in bed," she said, "for years. If you'd done it, you wouldn't have hidden the computer thing; you'd have dumped it in the Mersey, or smashed it into little pieces and let them dribble out the back of the car one night on a long drive miles away. And you wouldn't have had none of the money, 'cos you didn't need it; and when you conned that twit in the wine bar you wouldn't have looked so much like yourself; you'd have messed yourself round, like."

Sweet Jesus! She thought like a villain! He felt a guilty flush of triumph that she had inherited something from his genes after all; and an immediately compensating sense of relief that she had no drive to use it against society.

In the small hours of every morning in jail one particular crab of anxiety had always fastened itself into his guts: the knowledge that he was never going to be able to do anything for his kids. He was never to be able to pass anything on to them, have them profit by all the things he knew, make them that gift of experience or skill which it was every father's joy to donate. He knew now he could do just that!

From then on, every visit was a tutorial. While Rita boozily snoozed and the boys scuffled and fidgeted, Jed would talk quietly and steadily to Tara, passing on the arcane knowledge of The Mystery, of locks and keys—and keys could be people, not just pieces of metal—of safe houses and the surprising facilities of storm drains and sewers, of where lists of combinations could be found and the blueprints of the latest electronic devices and who was developing what. He found she had an astonishing memory and he gave her lists of names and telephone numbers. He told her the histories of the families and the capers they had got up to centuries ago. Above all, he taught her two things: everything he had learned about human nature and human venality; and the vital importance, in whatever you were doing, of accurate information.

On and on he talked, visit after visit, and Tara soaked it up. It was the best pupil-teacher relationship there could be. She had always loved her father. She came to love him more as she saw him locked up, like some superb animal taken out of the world, trying to adjust to what had happened to him.

Tara Stewart got her qualifications at night classes, her physical fearlessness in the corridors and playground of the urban guerrilla training ground they called a Comprehensive Day School, and her education in the Visiting Room of Walton Gaol. The one question her father would not answer was the one that had set it all off. He would not tell Tara who had framed him. He was in no position to prove it and he didn't want her doing anything silly or sharing the seething fury and frustration that was, despite his strong will, building steadily inside him year by year.

The shock of moving from green meadows, big skies and glossy horseflesh to the mean and filthy confinement of a two up, two down hovel in the inner city of Liverpool, which Aunt Rita rented to start with, having no bathroom and an outside lavatory, was shattering for Tara and her brothers.

"Aren't there ever going to be any fields again?" asked Tara, bewildered.

"No, there aren't going to be any sodding fields," answered Rita, "stinking, damp, draughty places."

This was accompanied, like most of Rita's pronouncements, by a thump from a thick hand that had the same alarming impact as a sock full of wet sand. Rita seemed to be incapable of speaking without hitting at the same time. The first time she sent Tara sprawling in this fashion, Len and Corby jumped on her, clinging like its infant progeny to a female gorilla, trying to find something that would hurt that thunderhead of dense and wobbling flesh. There followed the kind of battle that social workers and sociologists never hear about. Rita knew that her only chance was to throw the three of them down—for Tara was now involved—and overlie them like a soggy balloon. But she could not shake them off and Len and Corby had found that her vulnerable points were the insides of her upper arms, which they pinched mercilessly. In the end her only salvation was to lumber, shrieking, into the back yard with the three of them still clinging to her like mollusks to a whale and scrape them off by banging herself against the walls.

This episode did much to establish them favorably in the eyes of their neighbors, who had not known quite what to expect from the newcomers and who had been put off by the initial neatness of the children. They were reassured.

There was no Aunt Rita, however, to help them make their bones at school. They had been to a good little school at Aintree, where some of the teachers wore gowns. Their clothes were still good—Aunt Rita had not yet started to pawn them—and their accents, although singsong, were nothing like so thick as their schoolfellows'. They became the instant target of the various gangs of school bullies, both in and out of class. Their hair was ripped out, they were tripped up and trampled on in corridors, stinging pieces of chalk caught them in the face during class.

However, their outdoor life had made them harder than their tormentors realized. Children used to pitting their growing young muscles against the natural willfulness and weight of the odd ton of horseflesh were not overimpressed by creatures their own size, however vicious. Nevertheless, there came a point where something had to be done. Big Harry, the godfather to whom all the other organizations bowed, got Tara on her own in the lavatories one day, together with two of his colleagues, Billy and Banjo, and at the point of three flick-knives, extorted from her her school dinner-money, then held her head-first in a lavatory bowl and flushed it.

When Len and Corby found out, they went berserk. They were big lads for their age and they were all for a frontal assault on Big Harry, Billy and Banjo. By this time Tara had started her tutorials with her father and she counseled cool thinking. "Be first, be ruthless, but get it right" was her father's dictum in matters of this kind. She worked it out like a small female Duke of Wellington.

"What does Big Harry care about most?" she asked her brothers.

"His hair and being cock of the walk," said Len.

"His bike," said Corby.

Both were right. The expensive bicycle which he had bought from the profits of his extortion of other kids' dinner-money was the pride of his life. His hair was an exotic pompadour, dressed with a disgusting mixture of brilliantine and dried soapy water.

"Right," said Tara, and started to make her dispositions. Quick-drying clear varnish was the first war supply she got hold of, two hacksaws the second. There were a number of other supplies she also assembled.

At the end of the second period three days later, the teacher left the minute the bell sounded, as all the teachers did. The object was to reach the Common Room as quickly as possible without being roughed up, robbed or near-raped. Len had put up his hand and asked to be excused earlier.

As the teacher disappeared, Tara and Corby walked swiftly up to Billy and Banjo and each smacked a thin paper bag filled with tomato sauce into their faces. Billy and Banjo leaped to their feet, enraged, to find their threadbare trousers ripped from their loins by the invisible varnish on which they'd been sitting. Neither was wearing any underpants. Sinister ascendancy vanished in a gale of laughter, never to be reestablished.

Meanwhile Big Harry, who was in a higher form, made his way to the shed where the fuel for the central heating was kept. It was his gang headquarters. Today, as he opened the door and walked into the dimness, he was hit in the face with the flat of a coal shovel. By the time Tara and Corby had got there, Len had almost finished tying him into the wheelbarrow used for carrying the fuel to the boiler.

Big Harry's head started to clear as Tara and Corby walked in. Tara was carrying two hacksaws, a pair of scissors and the razor Aunt Rita used to shave her legs. Corby was wheeling Big Harry's bicycle.

Tara, Len, Corby, and Big Harry were all absent from the afternoon's classes. But when school finished for the day, everyone streamed past a sight which they would never forget. Outside the gates was Big Harry tied into the wheelbarrow. One side of his head had been shaved as smooth as a peeled egg. On it had been scrawled, with a purple felt pen, "Big Harry is just a little shit." And in front of him his bicycle had been arrayed, neatly sawn into fifteen separate pieces. Of Tara and her brothers there was no sign. But everyone knew who had done it. A move gathered momentum to promote the Stewarts to Chief Terrorists. They refused the honor as politely as the language they were obliged to use would allow them and thenceforth were left severely alone.

There was one sequel. Later that night Big Harry's large stevedore father, who had been obliged to go and retrieve his desecrated offspring from where he had, by universal consent, been left, came around to the house, looking for a man to fight. He was stunned to be confronted by two hundred pounds of enraged and drunken Rita, who opened negotiations by smashing her English ironstone beer jug over his head and finished them by kicking him very accurately where he would have preferred it least. She then went back indoors and inquired what it was all about by the simple expedient of swinging her ham fists indiscriminately at anyone who came within range until they told her. Whereupon she collapsed into a chair and quivered with laughter like a malarial blancmange. The laughter changed to an enraged bellow the next day when she tried to shave the spreading, larded acres of her legs with a razor as blunt as a butter pat, but by that time Tara and the boys were back at school, being treated as persons of respect.

It took Rita about twenty-five months to get through the two thousand pounds Elspeth had given her to look after the children. Then it was a steady descent into the pits of the city until finally, in Toxteth, Tara, Len and Corby looked back from their two rooms, shared kitchen and shared lavatory to the dreadful little house in Anfield with positive nostalgia.

Jed, in Walton Gaol, had noted helplessly the steady deterioration in speech, dress and manners of his children. He had only two reasons for hope. Len and Corby were too straight-up and—he had to face it—square, to be much affected by their environment. They had the easy toughness of Labradors. They were growing, like him, into brick blockhouses, but without too much going on up top. They were army material. Tara, on the other hand, was wickedly bright. There was very little she couldn't work out for herself. He found himself becoming more and more careful now about what he said.

One visit she took him between wind and water. Without warning, she said: "Dad, it was Sean Pattison, wasn't it?"

"You what?" he said, playing for time.

"It was Sean Pattison who carved your overcoat," she said.

Jed looked at her little pale face steadily. She was fifteen now and it was getting hard to read her. "Where are you picking up language like that?" he demanded. "You're not still mixing with kids from the old crowd, are you?"

"No," she lied. Bonds between children are not broken as easily as that. She had a gift for friendship and a magnetism that drew her old friends to her. The gang would meet in Sefton Park in the "fairy glen," whose muttering brook and blazing rhododendrons brought briefly back to her the surroundings of her early childhood. Mail Room Sid and Terry Lewis and Jean Soong were founder members. There was no formal agreement to meet, simply an unspoken understanding that if you were to go along there in the evenings or at weekends, there would always be someone around whom you knew and could chat to, idly, plucking the odd blade of grass, fidgeting around. Others would turn up; gradual accretions to the group would sometimes make it as large as fifty. Nothing happened. It was like an open air club. The foundations of several marriages were laid there.

More importantly, to Tara, now that she was out of "The Mystery," it was a source of intelligence for her about what was going on and who was doing what. She was pretty sure her father wouldn't approve, which was why she lied to him. He now lied to her. "No," he said, "it had nothing to do with Sean." He deliberately used the friendly first name to mislead her. He looked at her curiously. "What made you think it was?"

"I heard it was him you had the big punch-up with that time I saw you all bruised." He looked up at her sharply. "I saw you through the banisters," she explained, apologetically. "Then you had nothing to do with each other for years. Then just after the seventeen million was lifted, he went straight and now he's the big 'I Am,' dead rich and respectable, like, in London. He's even changed how he spells his name; he's Shaun Patterson now, if you don't mind. Also you went down on a cast-iron identification, as well as the rest, like, the computer and that—and he's always tried to look like you."

My God, this kid can think her way through things! thought Jed. What strokes couldn't we have pulled together when she grew up! It was a fleeting thought, instantly suppressed. He lied again, therefore, comprehensively and with all the ersatz sincerity of which any member of The Mystery had to be a master.

"Sean Pattison had nothing to do with fitting me up, nothing to do with that job, nothing to do with nothing," he said. "Put him out of your mind and get on with school!"

Sean Pattison, alias Shaun Patterson, was sitting in London in his quietly elegant suite of penthouse offices overlooking Hyde Park. In a corner stood the Telex on which he had learned that a Stewart scion had made an unexpected move. He knew it was stupid but he had an almost superstitious awe of the Stewart genes. Just now he could afford to relax; she was in hospital. But when she came out he wasn't going to take his eyes off the bitch.

He was having his hair cut by a shimmering blonde from Vidal Sassoon. She was not only a sensational hairdresser, but she had a pair of breasts that cradled a man's head from behind like a Chinese pillow. The baby-blue nylon coverall that he wore for the operation unfortunately covered his thousand-pound Huntsman suit, his fifty-pound Turnbull and Asser shirt and his thirty-pound Gianni Vecci tie. On the other hand, it merged very conveniently with the shift of the same material and color that his hairdresser was wearing, so that it was impossible to tell where one began and the other ended. In his left hand he held a Monte Cristo Number One. His right hand was not in view. From the look of smug complicity on the blonde's face, however, it was not too hard to envisage where it was.

Pattison had been very clever in the way he had manipulated his big score. He had laundered the money in Holland, losing only three percent of it in the process, and while he was doing it, he had watched the London property market collapse in a welter of greedy dreams. He waited until he calculated it had reached bottom and then he started to buy, so cautiously and tentatively that the big boys, who watched everybody, laughingly nicknamed him "Scouse Fried Chicken." He didn't mind. He played the country boy, who had made his little pile in the sticks and now wanted to join the big boys, and he bought small prime sites; nothing too big, but always in a superb situation. Small office blocks, houses, boutiques, every one of them choice.

The market was slow to recover, but he didn't care, he was in no hurry. When it did recover, the market realized how cheaply Pattison had been getting his bargains. And when the Arabs moved in, they weren't interested in merely good. They wanted prime property and Pattison was the man who had it. They multiplied his original stake almost as fast as the oil price hike had multiplied theirs. And the joke about Pattison—or Patterson as he was called by now—changed. They called him the first oil multimillionaire who didn't own an oil well.

Money on the scale on which Patterson now had it acquires a momentum of its own. Conservative as he continued to be—after all, he had thieved hard for it and he wasn't going to throw it all away now—it seemed to roll over twice a day and end up fatter than it was in the morning.

Where other *arrivistes* bought racehorses, Patterson was smarter. He bought goodwill. He started a parallel career as a philanthropist. With the help of the most celebrated—if not necessarily the best—legal firm around, he started the Patterson Trust. Its object was in a small and quiet, but not too quiet, way to find worthy causes that needed a little help. An Oxford college library here, a hospital that needed a body-scanner there, a charity somewhere else; this last in conjunction with the type of fellow he never ceased to resent, an aristocrat who dominated him totally without conscious effort.

As soon as Patterson's son came back from America, where he had sent him at seventeen for his further education, he was put in charge of the Trust, an undertaking very much to his liking. He, too, had been born without the criminal gene and the faster he could give away the illegally founded fortune his father had made, the better he liked it.

It was his son who saw the paragraph in the papers about the motorbike crash of Alhambra's coming young star Tara Stewart.

It was Shaun who sent the flowers.

It was his first mistake.

4

Tara was on the mend. At last she was allowed visitors. While she was in intensive care she was allowed none at all. Len and Corby, on compassionate leave, sat in an anteroom, taking turns, with soldierly precision, to keep a family presence near their beloved girl, feeling, rightly, that in a mysterious way it helped her. Aunt Rita, being drunk as a benchful of lords, was initially refused entrance to the hospital.

"You are the bleeding servants of the sodding public," she cried, reeling around the lobby, "and I have a niece in here nigh unto sodding death!" Her phraseology always took a biblical turn in moments of high stress. "I am here to do one of the corporal sodding works of mercy and this is good in the eyes of the Lord!"

She floored two porters with her handbag which, as always, was the size and weight of a workman's toolkit, staggered backward, tripped over a low magazine table, reducing it to rubble, and ended up flat on her back, like a massively obese turtle, quite unable to get up. Reinforcements were hastily summoned and four porters heroically got her to her feet and escorted her out, locking the glass doors behind her. She went with surprising meekness, thus gaining the advantage of surprise for, five seconds later, having taken a run at it, she came crashing backward through the splintering doors like an enraged rhino and almost made it to the lifts, staff bouncing off her like pinballs hitting a huge spring. This time she was jumped on by everyone in sight. She stood there for a few seconds, like Samson festooned with midgets, before finally going down and being given a sedative injection.

Nobody knew what it cost her, but when she woke up she went home and stayed off liquor for one whole week before presenting herself at the hospital again and joining Len and Corby in their vigil.

In the women's surgical ward, Tara's stream of visitors began. She sat up, a little like a wan fairy princess in a bower of flowers from well-wishers, and touched the romantic heart of every woman in the ward. They appointed themselves her unofficial guardians. If she looked distressed or started to cough—which was extremely painful—or spilled a glass, half a dozen bells would immediately be rung, calling the nurses' attention.

"You're like bloody royalty," said Aunt Rita on her first visit, as she furtively slipped a bottle of stout under Tara's pillow. "That's the stuff to give the troops," she whispered. Absent-mindedly, a quarter of an hour later, she removed it, opened it and drank it herself.

Len and Corby caused a buzz when they marched in, in step, in their Marines' uniforms, big, hard and handsome. They treated their sister like spun sugar, holding her frail shoulders with big calloused hands as gentle as a mother's, while they kissed the pale heart-shaped face. "Ah . . ." went the sigh, to their acute embarrassment, around the ward.

An early visitor was Paul. He brought a massive bowl of fruit and a beautiful framed blown-up color photograph of Tara, which she didn't even know had been taken, her face shadowed by leaves. He did his Bogart; sure proof that he was concealing emotion: "Of all the trucks on all the motorways in all the world, you had to run into that one!"

"I'm sorry, Paul, I let you down," she said.

"Let me down—balls!" said Paul, his language sounding, as always, strange in that beautifully modulated voice. "Who d'you think you are, anyway? I can get along without you, you know, missy!" He leaned over and kissed her softly on her pale hospital lips: "But not for very long," he murmured. Again the "ah . . ." wafted around the ward. Paul, great ham that he was, caused further delight by standing up and taking a bow. He left in his customary tornado fashion, sending reeling Cyril Goldstein, who had the misfortune to meet him in the doorway as he was coming in.

"Move over," said Cyril, as he reached Tara's bed, massaging his collarbone, "I think I'll join you. How are they on fractured clavicles here?"

Tara was overwhelmed by Goldstein's visit. After all, God didn't often descend to minister to little idiots who had cracked themselves up like any lame-brained Hell's Angel. He took one look around the crowded ward: "Listen," he said, "I'm going to get you a private room—telephone, television, special menu . . ." He was already on his feet, looking for someone with whom to organize it.

"No . . . Mr. Goldstein . . ."

"Please . . . Cyril," he corrected her.

"Well, anyway, please don't. It's great in here. It's a big family. We all look after each other and there's always something going on.

I mean, it's just like a telly serial watching the comings and goings and the crises and watching other people's visitors and all like that. You put me in a private room and I'd prob'ly die of boredom or from ringing my bell all day and nobody coming, like."

"Whatever pleases you," said Cyril, "but why don't I send in a side of smoked salmon just for a few snacks between meals?"

"No, honest, thanks all the same, Mr. Gold . . ."

"Cyril."

"Cyril, sorry . . . burra don't like smoked salmon."

"You will, child," he predicted with a smile, "you will. How are the medical standards in here?" he went on. "You'd like a second opinion? I know some of the finest brains in . . ."

"They're just great in here, thanks, Mr. Go . . . Cyril," she said. "They really seem to know their stuff, like, you know?"

"So long as you're happy," he said. "Happy is healing and I want you out of here as soon as possible. You know what I mean? We haven't got so much talent we can allow it to lie around in bed; you know what I mean? I'll bring you some smoked salmon next time," he added; "just a quarter."

The evening of the same day the Mail Room mob, Terry and Sid and Jean Soong, computer magazine in her hand, arrived. They were led warily up the ward by Sid, his mashed face looking as if he expected an ambush. Hospitals qualified in his book as officialdom, which he didn't reckon. The three of them carried bags of bruised peaches and weeping grapes. Tara's heart rose at the sight of her mates. At last her own personal cavalry had arrived.

"Dey wouldn't lerrus in, like," complained Sid, "and I'd purra clean shirt on, special."

"We've had this fruit for days," Terry explained.

Jean Soong's doll-like Chinese face split into a big grin. "They're liars," she said; "we've just gorrit on the cheap in Paddy's Market."

Underneath the chat their eyes surveyed her with an anxious expertise beyond their years. They weren't reassured. Something was chewing on their friend. Nobody else had noticed.

"What is it, Ta?" asked Sid, bluntly.

"Yeah," said Terry and Jean in unison.

Tara let free a long sigh of relief. "God, I'm glad you've come," she responded. "I couldn't tell anybody else. When I had the accident—I was on my way to see my old man."

"In Walton?" said Sid. "Oh, Christ!"

These three were among the tiny number, outside her family, who knew where her father was.

"He'll have heard all about the crash," said Terry.

"But I'll bet the bastards haven't told him you're okay," added Jean.

"Right," confirmed Tara. "He'll be going through hell-and-all."

"No problem," said Sid. "My cousin Frank's doing a stretch in Walton—thieving from the docks."

"My brother-in-law's in there, too," added Terry. "G.B.H. He caught my sister with her fancy man."

"We'll get word to your Dad that you're all right," said Sid. "And we'll get The Mystery to give him a regular bulletin, like. Don't worry about it no more."

"Right?" asked Jean.

"Right?" asked Terry.

"Great!" answered Tara.

That night Tara slept right through for the first time in three weeks. The next night, she knew, her father would be doing the same. She might have been tempted to lie back and luxuriate in the ebbing away of her tension. Her next visitors put an end to that.

The first, typically well before visiting hours, was Jason Planter at eight o'clock in the morning. In an off-white oiled wool sweater a quarter of an inch thick and a tan as deep as a brown shoe he looked as if he'd just come off a ski slope which, indeed, he had. His host in Aspen, Colorado, had programmed his telephone to call this obscure British hospital once a day, every day, to ask when Miss Taransay Stewart would be receiving visitors. He was straight off the plane and jet-lagged yet he still looked good, as the buzz in the ward confirmed. Tara was glad that she had on a delicate lacy pink bedjacket Bella had brought in for her and that Maureen, a little Irish nurse who was devoted to her, had already at this hour brushed her hair until it shone.

She sensed that Jason was embarrassed by the fact that he had saved her life and filled with terror that she might mention it. Therefore she didn't.

"Who should be driving a supermarket trolley now, then?" he opened, laying on the wheeled table that bridged her bed a deceptively small-looking box of chocolate truffles. She smiled at him with affection.

"That's right," she said, "kiçk a girl when she's down."

He shot off at a tangent. "D'you have to do this television thing?" he demanded.

"What's that got to do with anything?" she asked. "It wasn't my work that put me up the back of that truck."

"No, I know," he said, his dark eyes probing hers and flicking away.

"Well, then," she prompted, as he hesitated.

"I just thought you might like to work for me," he said. "Girl Friday, partner—whatever you want to be. It might be less hectic . . . I mean . . . it would be a different rhythm."

Tara studied the lean, tanned face.

"Jason," she said, "you don't do anything. Why d'you need someone to help?"

"I'm a great deal busier than you think," he persisted, "you wouldn't be bored."

She paused. "Jason, I'd love to work for you and with you, even if you do only play . . ."

"Wrong!" he interrupted with a hint of irritation. "And I'd pay you triple whatever Alhambra gives you."

"But," she went on, "I have . . ." She nearly said "a mission," but caught herself in time. "I'm ambitious," she said. "I want to amount to something in my own right. I couldn't do that working for you. Thanks all the same. I'm flattered."

He took the turndown with his usual grace of manner.

"You've got plenty of time to come to your senses," he smiled. "And I don't give up easily."

His face set. "At least do one thing for me. Give up your broomstick. You're a big girl now. You have to put away childish things."

"I need it," she said. "I'm a girl in a hurry."

The brilliant dark eyes looked at her as if he knew something she didn't.

"To where?" he asked, almost sadly. Then he kissed her quickly on her forehead and was gone. She felt melancholy and guilty. He had saved her life and now he'd flown in from God knows how far away just to see her and all she'd done was to send him away without what he wanted. Yet she couldn't be diverted now. She did have a mission. And nothing could be allowed to divert her from it. And she'd lost time.

It took Ben Maitland to make her realize just how much.

Ben came in that afternoon, his royal blue eyes and clean blond hair stirring up the hormones of the women's surgical ward like an electric mixer. As always, he wore the stuntman's uniform of jeans and T-shirt, none of it hiding anything. He'd come up from London the minute he'd heard about Tara's accident and he'd been sitting in the Adelphi Hotel in Liverpool ever since, waiting for word that he could come and see her.

"I've warned you before, Tara sport," was his opening salvo, "leave the stunts to the professionals. What were you trying to do with that truck—jump over it?"

"Oh, Ben . . . Ben," was all she could say at first, as he hugged her as carefully as if she were a butterfly. Ben, who calculatedly laid his health and his life on the line every day of his professional life, had the gentlest quality of all. He knew how frail the human temple was.

"D'you have to ride that thing?" he asked.

"You've got a nerve," she said. "I've seen you ride one upside down in midair through a blazing warehouse."

"I'd worked it all out first on me calculator, hadn't I?" said Ben. "Plus I was wearing fireproof knickers."

Ben always had been able to make her laugh. Now, as she doubled over with the pain of it, she begged: "Please Ben, don't make me laugh. I can't afford it."

"All right, then," he said, "I'll tell you something that'll wipe the smile off your face."

It did, too. With his show biz background Ben had learned the ground rules. He saw the vulnerability of Tara's situation. You were only as good and as memorable as your last show. And her last show was beginning to be a long time ago. With the lead time in television as long as it was from inception of an idea to completion to showing, it was getting to be too long since Tara had made her impact. This was what Ben told her. In vain she argued that her mail from viewers, which was being forwarded to her, was as lively as ever, that Cyril Goldstein was as attentive as ever; none of it impressed him.

"You need a new show like now," he said brutally, "or the water will close over your head."

For all her outward chirpiness the crash had splintered her confidence. She had felt, up to then, that she was invulnerable. The sudden, outrageous intimation of her own mortality had shocked her. She was fretting to get back into battle but for the first time she was aware that she could lose. She resisted the jolt of energy which Ben was trying to inject.

"And what sort of show d'you suggest I do lying here," she demanded; "a cross between *Angels* and *Emergency Ward Whatsisname?* 'Will Nurse Jones get the bedpan to Mrs. Smith in time?! Will Dr. Evans be discovered trapped in the Matron?! Watch tomorrow's exciting . . .' "

"All right, all right," grinned Ben. "There've been soap operas about hospitals, there've been comedy shows about hospitals. But who's ever done a straightforward look in depth at a general surgical ward in action while she's actually getting a sore bum lying in one?"

"We'd never get permission."

"That's just low vitality talking. Look, kiddo, you're talking to someone who's already been where you are right now—and not just once. Last time I'd just been offered a real acting job. A big part, big series—you know the kind of thing, fast, macho, physical . . ."

"You'd have been great!"

"Just after I'd been offered the part, I smashed both legs doing a stunt I'd never have tried if I hadn't been so high. Instead of fighting, I lay there and died. It took me twice as long to knit together as it should have done—and by the time I was ready, they'd found a star instead: George Peppard."

"Oh, Ben love, how bloody awful. I'm sorry."

"We're talking about you, not me. That was, like, by way of illustration, so don't try and sidetrack me."

"The cameras!" she pounced. "What about the cameras? They'd be in everybody's way. We couldn't hide them and everyone would be self-conscious."

"You've seen Roger Graef's documentaries," insisted Ben. "He's proved once and for all that people get used to the camera and after that they just forget it's there. One or two hand-helds in here, cutting to you and your own problems now and then, following your progress, hearing you rabbit on about it all—great!"

"This is a women's ward," she objected, fighting all the way, "full of birds being poked about in rude places. They don't want hairy great cameramen gawping at them."

"Then get a camera-bloody-woman, woman!" said Ben. "There are some ace ones around!"

Which is what did it. For Tara, for Paul, to whom she instantly put it on his next visit, it was the instinct for the difference a woman behind the camera in a women's ward would make that finally fired them.

"I'll get Pam Johnston!" cried Paul, all instant excitement. "We'll shoot it on film. We'll rig the best remote-sound we can get . . ."

"Permissions," she interrupted. "Paul, can you get the permissions?"

"Permissions?" he roared, "I didn't go to school with half the boils who run the United bloody Kingdom for nothing. I did all right for permissions before you waltzed into my life, missy. The only ones I can't swing are those of the women in the ward—that's down to you, honey-child." And he rose and left, smiling hugely at the women on either side, leaving them with the delicious impression that next time he might well pluck them out of bed and eat them on the way home.

After he'd gone, Tara called for attention of the ward. She told them who he was and reminded them of the programs he'd done, both before she'd joined him and afterward. Ordinary viewers to the last woman, they recognized integrity when they saw it and they'd seen it in what Paul had put on the screen. She outlined the intention of the program to them and what it would entail.

"Now then," she shouted, "are we all agreed to show our bare bums on the telly?"

"Yeah!" roared the ward.

The filming was utterly uncompromising. It showed, with all its imperfections, the great machine of a modern hospital in unsentimental action, not helped by a visionless bureaucracy. No blinds were drawn. Even when little peaky-faced Jean, who had come in with massively general peritonitis and whose bed had always been positioned scarily near the exit door, died, Pam Johnston kept filming as the sheeted bed was wheeled discreetly out. When Tara herself was wheeled down to X-ray by a white porter at the head of her trolley and a black one at the bottom and they came to blows in a corridor over one of them not pulling or pushing his weight, there was the miraculously invisible Pam Johnston, camera turning, catching every expression, especially those of the terrified Tara. And when, as a result of the row, Tara was left unattended in a draughty corridor, lying helplessly on her trolley for two hours, she got that, too.

One unscheduled bonus was a visit from Aunt Rita, majestically bottled as usual. She got out only three words as she came through the door into the ward.

"Hello, our Tara . . ." she said. Then her uncertain footing skidded on the mirror-like floor and she shot forward, with all the kinetic energy of two hundred pounds behind her, grabbed at the tea trolley, and she and the trolley, on which she retained a grip of drunken desperation, careered the length of the ward, between the beds in a ruler-straight line, ending with a smash of stupefying proportions against the far wall.

It became a classic clip, repeated in television anthologies for years. It could have led to a whole new career for Aunt Rita. For the first few days afterward she was inundated by calls from comedy producers, wanting to exploit her and her undoubted talents—some of the angles, panicked contortions and configurations of her massive legs as she fought against the headlong flight toward inevitable catastrophe had strong men weeping. She disposed of them very quickly. "I was drunk, you stupid little fart!" she would yell down the telephone. "When I'm sober I'm a very retiring person!"

To be working again, even from a hospital bed, was the tonic

Tara needed. Her progress back to health had been disquietingly slow. Her height and shapeliness were deceiving. Nearly ten years of malnutrition at the hands of feckless Aunt Rita had had their effect. She hadn't the physical reserves a well-nourished middle-class girl of her age would have had. Her strength started to build from the first muted whine of Pam Johnston's camera. By that time, too, a number of interlinked puzzles had engaged her mind.

The first started the morning after Ben's visit when a very large and tasteful arrangement of flowers arrived. They were not cut flowers, but growing plants—miniature azaleas and pelargoniums and fern, set in soil in a boat-shaped holder made of bark. There was no message, but on the bottom corner of the card accompanying them there was a fancy monogram with the initials T.C.D. The initials meant nothing to Tara. The only other information she gleaned from the card was that the flowers had been delivered by a fashionable London firm. Not telephoned through by Interflora, but actually delivered. That, reasoned Tara, argued clout of a very high order.

That afternoon Bella Cranmer solved the mystery and created another one in the process. Bella was still living in Tara's flat. The two had struck up the kind of comfortable, livable relationship that can be shared only by two women who have enjoyed the same man, without the highest passion, and each knows roughly where the other is at. Bella was working for one of the partners of an old-established firm of Liverpool stockbrokers. She had an M.A. in Economics and a weird theory about share index charts and market cycles fully shared by her boss. He was a happily married Catholic with nine children, but in Bella he had found a business wife without the faintest tremor of sex ruffling the surface. Tara's only comment when she heard about him had been: "If he's as good at working out his charts as he's been at working out his wife's safe periods, the firm's in trouble!"

Bella arrived in her magnolia-skinned, raven-haired splendor, causing a young house doctor, who was taking a rectal temperature reading, to insert his thermometer some centimeters shy of its true location, to the mixed confusion and interest of his patient. She took one look at the card on Tara's latest offering of flowers: "I didn't know you knew Shaun Patterson."

Tara stiffened: "I don't."

"Well, that's the logo of one of his companies." Bella pointed to the card. "T.C.D.—Town and Country Design."

"Are you sure?"

"I should be. That's my logo. I drew it." Tara's mind revved furiously. Why should Shaun Patterson send her flowers? A bluff? A tiny act of reparation? A genuine reflection of his confidence that she didn't know he was her father's betrayer?

Bella watched the face of her flatmate and wondered what was going on behind those spectacular gray eyes. She knew there were areas in her friend's life about which she knew nothing and she was too wise a girl to probe. But the Patterson connection . . . she couldn't help but be intrigued. Tara could see it and she took the opportunity now to do something she had never been able to do before without arousing Bella's curiosity and that was to probe her about her ex-lover.

"I don't get it," she said. "I wouldn't know him if he came up and stuck his finger up me nose. What sort of man is he? I mean, is he one of those wallies who get stuck on a face on television? You've never talked much about him. Is he a star-screwer or what? He must know a thousand people in London who are famous. Why pick on me?"

"Well, he does like being around show business people," said Bella. "But he also collects politicians, high flyers in the Civil Service, merchant bankers—you know the sort of people I mean."

"The fixers," Tara answered. "If you run a launderette, you need to know a good plumber. If you're in Patterson's game, you need that lot."

"No, listen," said Bella, "naturally I hate the bastard's guts after what he did to me, but I can't say I ever caught him at anything actually illegal."

Tara, realizing that she had betrayed more of her feelings about Patterson than she had intended, backtracked hastily.

"No, I didn't mean he's Godfather Mark Three or anything like that," she explained. "It's just that if you're on his kind of roller coaster, it's just as well to know the wackers who pull the switches and look after the track; know what I mean?"

"Yes, I do," said Bella, "but from the little he let me know about his affairs, I got the impression that he was so well stacked he was practically living off the interest on his interest."

"Well, he's certainly using his lolly in the right way," responded Tara, fishing. "I mean this Merseyside Trust and everything. He's doing more for the 'Pool than Michael Heavyshine or whatever his name was ever did. I mean, what did *he* do? Came up and flashed his big head and his tiny little mouth around, blubbed a few dead embarrassing tears then pissed off to play toy soldiers at the Ministry of Defense. I'll tell you something; if that blister does as much for Defense as he did for Liverpool, we'd better start learning Russian now."

She was deliberately widening the scope of the conversation in order to disguise her interest in Patterson.

"It's true, you know," said Bella. "Patterson does have this thing about Liverpool and Merseyside. It's a fixation with him."

"Well," offered Tara, "he's obviously a do-gooder—he's probably the kind who's always on about prison reform and let's treat them nicely and all that."

"No, he's not like that," said Bella, "not a bit. He's all for coming down hard on crooks and layabouts, you know the kind of thing. He's in favor of capital punishment—he's even against parole. He says if a man gets twenty or thirty years for breaking the law, that's exactly how long he should stay in jail."

I'll bet he bloody well does, thought Tara. If Mister fucking Patterson has nightmares—and I devoutly hope he does—one of them must star my father walking out of Walton Gaol with his eyes pointing like lasers toward London and Shaun Patterson. In a way it was a nightmare she shared. Although one part of her dearly wanted to see her father beat Shaun Patterson into a pancake and stuff him down a sewer, the other half shuddered at the thought of the violence and at the realization that all it would mean would be her father back behind the bars that she knew were driving him very, very slowly mad.

"It's amazing how well he's done, though, for a local lad," she prompted Bella. "I wonder how he got his start?"

"He said he started by buying and selling a couple of houses around here, suddenly saw how easy it all was if you knew what you were doing and never looked back from there."

Plausible, thought Tara. Plausible sod. He always had been. Even when, as a child, she'd caught him in the kitchen, with his arms around Elspeth, her mother. Her mother was thrashing like a wild bird in a snare and Patterson had abruptly let her go when Tara walked in, looking for an ice cream.

"That's what I want," Patterson had said, "and your Mum won't let me have one. Let's both ask her nicely, then perhaps we'll both get one."

Quick, plausible bastard. Child though she was, she knew she was being lied to in some way, but a kind of mute pleading in her mother's face convinced her to take things at face value and file the incident away as one of those things one will understand when one's much older. Plausible glib bastard. Smiling, damned villain. The Osiris Players had done *Hamlet* at the school and Claudius was the character she'd really related to because she identified him instantly with "Uncle" Sean.

"I'll bet he's a bit of a soft touch, all the same," she pushed Bella, "anyone from the old days with a hard luck story."

She wanted to know if they were still putting the bite on him.

She knew that for every big, successful crime there was a price to be paid. All the components suppliers, as it were, who helped to put that particular engine of crime together, became your pensioners for life. In Patterson's case, the driver, the muscle, right down to the Dutch sea captain, the Rotterdam connections and the man who supplied the chain saw, plus, sometimes, people who'd simply learned things by listening to others, friends or relatives. Whenever any of them were short of the folding stuff, they went to the cupboard. And the cupboard in this case was Shaun Patterson. At least, she hoped it was.

Bella confirmed her hopes.

"God, yes," she said. "Some of the people he helps you wouldn't believe. They're as rough as an elephant's elbow."

Patterson had been wise, thought Tara, to put his loot to work for him. He could afford the payoffs. There had been others, in the past, who had been bled dry. Still, it was good to know he was still under that kind of pressure, even after all this time. It could force him to make a mistake. In the fullness of time, it might be that he could be stampeded.

She was about to pump Bella more when the earth suddenly wobbled on its axis. Into the ward walked a tall young man in a pale gray suit, which had the kind of throwaway grace that costs a thousand pounds. He had glossy brown hair, strong bones and a great mouth. And he wore heavy-rimmed tortoiseshell glasses behind which were the bluest eyes Tara had ever seen. He was deep in conversation with one of the hospital administrators. He glanced casually at Tara and Bella as he passed. Tara found herself feeling sorry she was in her tatty linen hospital gown.

She beckoned to Maureen, the little Irish nurse.

"Who was *that?!*" she whispered.

"Have you not seen him before?" Glad, as always, to be passing on knowledge, Maureen's manner became spritely and conspiratorial at the same time. "Sure, that's Mr. Michael."

"And what does Mr. Michael do?" asked Bella, who had not been insusceptible to his powerful presence herself.

"Is he a consultant or what?" asked Tara. "If so, what's he a consultant in, because whatever it is, I've got it!"

Maureen giggled. "Don't you go wishing things on yourself," she said reprovingly. "Anyway, he's not a consultant nor nothing like that. He's from London. He's to do with the new wing."

"What new wing?" asked Tara.

"It's for research. You wouldn't think so to look at some of the senior doctors, but this is a teaching hospital, you know."

"So what is he, the architect or a boffin or what?" asked Tara.

"No, he's to do with the money side of it," Maureen explained.

"Money," exclaimed Bella, "that's the word I couldn't think of."

"Think of when?"

"The minute I laid eyes on him. He could be towing a kite with it written in six-foot letters."

"Oh, I don't think it's *his* money," said Maureen. "It's like he's just in charge of it, sort of thing."

"Darling," said Bella, "allow me to know about money. Whether it's his or he looks after it, he uses a dilute form of the stuff for after-shave."

"Would you like to meet him?" Maureen asked Tara, the born matchmaker coming out in her.

For the first time, Tara knew what it was to blush. Because she had come late to it, she came hot and strong to it. The blood started to mantle her skin somewhere around about her navel, then rose steadily all the way up to her hairline. It was a spectacle to which one could have sold tickets. Bella and Maureen, with the unrepentant cruelty of feminine curiosity, watched in fascination.

"Bloody of course not," cried Tara, trying to brazen it out. "I was just having a joke. Why should I want to meet him?"

"We really don't know," said Bella, glancing with exaggerated, wide-eyed innocence at Maureen. "Perhaps it's got something to do with the fact that you're sitting there looking like a beetroot that's having a hot flush."

"Perhaps you've forgotten," Tara spat, "but I'm not well. Ill people do go funny colors."

"Of course they do, darling," agreed Bella, soothingly. "Just try not putting on the *Son et Lumière* show the next time he passes or he might think you're choking on a fishbone and call Emergency."

Tara lay and simmered. Here she was, the original, air-conditioned cool cat and she'd made a bloody exhibition of herself. She'd been taken totally by surprise. She'd never been affected by a man like that before; she hadn't known it was possible. One glance and bingo! It was damned ridiculous. And blast Bella and Maureen, sitting there like a couple of Buddhas, looking smug. Meet him? She was damned if she wanted to meet him now. She'd show them. She was Tara Stewart, the chew 'em up and spit 'em out menace to mankind at large. See if she'd meet him!

She met him two days later and she seriously thought she was going to die. When she found out she wasn't going to, she hoped she might. She was glad she was wearing a new delivery from Bella, a bed-jacket in foaming yellow chiffon. She was with Paul at the time, who was visiting. She was asking Paul how he felt about the footage he had so far. Paul was busy telling her how it was going to be the best show he had ever done in his life when a look of alarm leaped into his eye. Although she wasn't eating at the time, Tara appeared to have swallowed something the wrong way. She was suddenly choking and spluttering and had turned a bright crimson from the neck upward. She had just seen Mr. Michael walk through the door. What was even more petrifying, he appeared to be heading purposefully in her direction. It was the ever-watchful little Maureen who was her savior. She'd seen Mr. Michael before Tara had and she'd observed her pathetic attempt at camouflage. She hurried over with a glass of water and a jug.

"Here, drink this," she said. Tara gulped it down, peering over the rim of the glass at the steadily advancing figure. Maureen turned to Paul accusingly.

"It can happen at any time, you know," she reproved him.

"Wha-what can?" he asked, bewilderedly.

"This," explained Maureen, with unassailable logic.

"But I mean, I never—that is . . . it's never happened before."

"You're working the poor girl too hard and too soon," said Maureen, severely. "You must realize she's been very, very ill."

"But it was her idea," said Paul, flustered. Maureen, who had the kind of timing one can't learn, gave Tara a savage thump on the back just as Mr. Michael, in all his fully realized, twenty-seven-year-old, beautifully designed manhood, reached her bed. Leaving Tara puce, but excusably so, she turned to Mr. Michael.

"Were you wanting to see Miss Stewart?" she asked, with something of the manner of a rather grand maid.

"I would like a word if it's possible," he said, his richly modulated voice precipitating another bout of coughing on Tara's part and another, this time slightly irritated, thump on the back from Maureen.

"She'll be free to see you in a minute," she announced, as if Tara were upstairs, heavily engaged in the yellow drawing room, "but I must ask you not to keep her long. She's already had an exhausting morning." This with a stem glance at Paul, who once again looked bemused.

"I'll be as brief as I can," he said. Maureen took in Tara quickly out of the corner of her eye and noted that she was as composed as she was ever going to be. She turned to her as if she'd just swept down a gracefully curving staircase: "Miss Tara, there's Mr. Michael here to see you."

Tara was pretty good from then on, considering, thought Maureen, whose Killarney-green eyes weren't going to miss a microsecond of it.

"Oh . . . yeah," said Tara, "you're the money-bod or something. Pleased to meet you."

"Well, it's the first time I've been described like that, but I suppose that's about what I am," he replied. He smiled, nearly undoing all Tara's hard-won composure with a strong white smile that went right into the corners of his mouth, as hers did.

"Well, I know about the new wing and everything," said Tara.

"Yes, but the point is it's being built entirely with private money," he explained. "We're not going to the Government for a cent of it and although we think we've got enough, well, what with costs creeping up on one all the time . . ."

How could brown hair be so alive, wondered Tara. It was as shimmering and rich as a clipped bay horse in sunlight.

"And the thing is," he was going on, "the more help we can get from the public, the better."

"Oh, dead right, dead right," said Tara, desperately picking up the thread. "We all need Joe Public."

"It's just that I hear you're doing a program on television about this hospital," he continued, "and I wondered if you might be able to slip in a mention of the project."

"Oh, well, you'd have to speak to Mr. Cranmer about that," said Tara, indicating Paul. "Mr. Cranmer's the producer and he decides what goes into the program."

The two men shook hands and d'you doed automatically while making instant computer-appraisals of each other. They knew at once, Tara realized, that they came out of the same educational drawer, which meant that they could speak in a kind of shorthand.

"I just thought . . ." said blue eyes.

"Don't see why not," answered Paul. "Good cause. Interesting. Might be able to work in, say, twenty seconds."

"That would be tremendous." He took off his glasses and looked at Tara in a laser-blast of blue that had Maureen slapping her heartily on the back again.

"Er, I don't know how these things are managed, but you do, as they say, present the program, don't you, Miss Stewart?"

"Yes," she croaked.

"It's just that you have a certain quality to which people react." Maureen gave her what she considered to be a surreptitious wink, for which Tara could have killed her. "And if you were to be able to mention it yourself, it would do us so much more good."

"Producer . . ." croaked Tara, waving feebly in Paul's direction and hating herself for being such a wimp.

Like many big men, Paul bitterly resented the way his perceptiveness was consistently underestimated. Just because one was built like an ox, that's what they thought one was. He had just dialed in to the wavelength rippling between Tara and this Michael chap, had played back his mental tape of her reactions from the moment the four-eyed bugger had walked in and had penetrated the fellow's game plan. It was simply an up-market version of "haven't I seen you somewhere before?" Fine; he could play games, too. What was more, in this one he was not only a contestant, he was in the umpire's chair as well.

"You don't have to worry your head"—skillfully, he made it sound like "little head"—"about that," he said to khaki hair. "Television's a tricky game. We'll work out how best to put over your message; always supposing," he added, putting the boot right in, "always supposing we do manage to work it in at all." He sat back with a sense of a job well done.

The blue eyes looked at him through the becoming spectacles with a new hatred and respect. Why hadn't he waited until this Nazi was out of the way before making his pitch? Naturally Paul Cranmer—had he got the name right?—naturally he must feel the same way about this huge-eyed, pain-planed waif as he did himself the minute he'd walked in two days ago and set eyes on her. He had, however studied his Wellington and made it a point never to defend an untenable position. Withdraw, regroup and wait until this heap with the brain as well as the muscles had gone. He rose.

"It's very good of you to consider it," he said. "I'll have my people get out a paper on it that will give you all the details." He put out his hand to meet hers—he just absolutely had to touch her. The contact seemed to run right up to his shoulder.

"Goodbye, Miss Stewart, goodbye, Mr. Cranmer."

For the first time they both noticed that his accent was a faint Bostonian American.

Paul was a realist. He'd always known that he had all too short a lease of Tara; but the pain as he realized the chemical pull this other man, from out of nowhere, exerted on her was none the less for that.

"Bloody fund-raisers!" he said to Tara as the Michael fellow disappeared; "they think all we've got to do is to do their work for them."

"But it is a good cause, Paul," she said.

"The world's full of good causes," Paul riposted, now getting thoroughly aggravated. "If we gave all of them time on T.V., there'd be no room for anything else."

"Well, maybe there's nothing else that's as important," replied Tara. It was developing into one of those intensely logical arguments, she realized, which were never about what they were supposed to be about.

"So you put them all on T.V., everyone switches off out of sheer boredom and nobody sees any of the good causes anyway," replied Paul, feeling ridiculous.

"Oh, don't be so bloody daft," said Tara, echoing his thought. "Anyway, why didn't you tell him all this? Why tell me?"

"It's just that you seemed to be a distinctly interested party."

"What's that supposed to mean?"

"I should have thought it was pretty clear." He was doing this all wrong, he knew; he should be on the same side as she, blunting coconut head's sting by not making him forbidden fruit or attacking him. But he couldn't help himself.

"Yeah, well I never have been able to talk in riddles," said Tara. "You'd better go and pal up to a sphinx."

"Listen to me, Goldilocks," he heard himself saying, to his amazement and dismay, "nobody's indispensable, you know. I can always get someone else to front my programs."

"Front them!?" she exploded. "I sodding invented half of them!" She was horrified as she listened to herself, too, but she had been brought up in a tradition that you never lost a roughhouse of any kind, if you could help it.

"You invented them!" roared Paul. "I was in this business while you were still pissing in your carrycot!"

Guardian angel Maureen, who had been listening tactfully from a distance, decided it was time for intervention. She bustled over officiously with a screen, which she proceeded to erect around the bed.

"Time for your what-d'you-call-'ems, Miss Stewart," she said, briskly.

Paul, who had a superstitious horror of hospital procedures, especially those involving the opposite sex, was on his feet and moving with the speed of a rabbit that's just seen a stoat.

"I was just going. We'll talk about this again, Miss Taransay Stewart," he said, giving her the full name of the Scottish island after which she'd been christened. It was a signal between them that he was in his paternal mode, disposed to be indulgent and not to take too seriously anything that had been said previously. Good director that he was, he completed it with a fatherly kiss on her forehead and left, with a nod in the grand seigneurial style he simply couldn't help, to Maureen.

"He's jealous," said Maureen, triumphantly, settling down for a cozy old chat behind the screen.

"Don't be a nit," answered Tara. "What's he got to be jealous about?"

Maureen went into a spasm of derisive laughter. Tara hit her with a pillow.

"Listen," said Maureen, "don't you be thumping me. With two fellow-me-lads like that with their horns locked over you, you're going to need all the help you can get."

Late into the night, as the ward quieted down and Rene, to her left, started to twitch into her dreams, Tara lay and marveled. His handshake, for God's sake!—she could still feel it. She'd swear she could still smell the aftershave he had patted on his face with that hand. The world was now a magic place because he was in it. Yet she was Tara the tough, impervious to distractions, dedicated to her one implacable objective: the destruction of Shaun Patterson and the rescue of her father. It was absurd, but just the thought of being seen walking about the streets in Mr. Michael's company made her stomach twang.

He came to see her again the next day. He had pulled rank and arrived outside of normal visiting hours. She had, mercifully, been dozing; so that when Maureen, with a wink that made her eyelid look as if it had been glued down, shook her awake to tell her she had a visitor, she had a good cover for her confusion. This time she was in cornflower blue, another present from Bella, and the color reflected in her eyes. It was silk and utterly impractical, but she looked like a song of delight.

She looked up and felt a fist tighten around her heart. She experienced again a phenomenon she had noticed the first time. So great was the turbulence he aroused in her that she really couldn't see him properly. It dazed her to be near him and she couldn't make sense or think straight. It came through to her that he was saying something about their knowing each other, but she couldn't take it in. The encounter had some of the quality of an hallucination. He gave her his dazzling smile and left her with the document he had promised. It was almost a relief when he had gone. She lay back on her pillow, gauzed with sweat.

Presently, she looked at the paper he had left with the details on it, and the room reeled. It was headed "The Shaun Patterson Foundation" and it was signed "Michael Patterson."

Feverishly, she signaled to Maureen, who was just coming into the ward. She came forward, her eyes shining with complicity.

"What did he have to say?" she asked.

Tara countered with a desperate question of her own: "His name—what's his name? You've been calling him Mr. Michael." She had a frantic hope that the paper had been signed by someone else.

"That's right," said Maureen, "Mr. Michael Patterson. We just call him Mr. Michael. He has that sort of grand thing about him."

Her professional eye noted Tara's deathly pallor.

"Here," she said, "are you all right? It's not good to get over-excited. We don't want you having a relapse." Automatically, she reached for Tara's pulse and consulted the little watch pinned to her tunic pocket.

"I'm fine," said Tara. "Just a bit tired."

"Your pulse is nice and strong, anyway," said Maureen. "Now, tell us everything he said. Every word, mind." Tara was saved by the Ward Sister calling Maureen away.

"Later," she promised her, then tumbled back into the black waters of her agony. She had fallen hopelessly in love with the son of her father's bitterest enemy, the man she had sworn an oath to destroy.

The things he had talked about began to come back to her and started to make sense. He had said something about knowing her as a little girl, but he had been much older than she. Yes, that was it; it had seemed so strange. The last time he had seen her, he said, she'd been about nine or ten and a funny little thing. It was only her eyes that had brought the sudden realization that it was the same Tara Stewart. He'd been seventeen and had been just about to go to America to some school there. He'd been there ever since until recently.

So he came, this cultured, grave, authoritative, old-money-looking young gentleman, from as deeply and historically criminal a background as her own and his father was the biggest thief and the foulest swine in the world.

But did he know? That was the question that now obsessed her. Obviously he must know his own ancestry, but did he know what his father had done? During the whole day and most of the night her mind tumbled and turned it ceaselessly. Did he know that his father had stolen seventeen million pounds and framed her father for the crime? Condemned her father to a living death while he lived like an emperor? Did he know? If he knew, how could the guilt he must feel allow him to be in the same room with her, much less come and make a play for her in his quietly commanding way. Maybe he was a monster; it could be as simple as that. Either the capacity for shame had been left out of him or he got a perverse pleasure out of romancing her. She had to know, had to know.

On into the hours of the night she turned and thrashed, listening to the night noises of the other women. The little moans. The sighs. The sudden endearments of men's names thrown, in a dream, into the dark.

By morning, she looked terrible. The hollows in her cheeks had gone past the point of beauty and the circles beneath her eyes were the color of thunderclouds. When Maureen saw her, she was shocked.

"What the devil's happened to you?" she demanded as she grabbed Tara's wrist, shook and inserted the thermometer and consulted her watch, all, seemingly, at the same time. The results reassured her as she marked up the chart at the end of the bed.

"You've no fever," she said; "you must be in love." It was an old joke, thought Tara, but this time it was more bitterly funny than Maureen could ever have dreamed.

"I didn't get much sleep," said Tara.

"I dare say," commented Maureen, drily. "You still haven't told me what he said yesterday."

"He just talked about what he wants me to put in the program," said Tara. "About the new wing and that."

"And the rest," said Maureen, skeptically.

"Honest," said Tara.

"I believe you, millions wouldn't," said Maureen. "When's he coming to see you again?"

"I don't know. He didn't say."

In fact, he came again that afternoon. By that time Tara had decided on her tactics. A frontal attack, but leaving out certain vital areas.

He arrived again out of visiting hours, like a young king, in another superb suit, dark blue, deepening the eyes behind the amber-framed glasses. The hands of every woman in the ward, no matter what her age, flurtered up to her hair. He sat down by her bed.

"Well," he said, indicating the document that was on her bedside table, "what do you think?"

She came at him straight out of the sun.

"Your father's a thief," she said.

His reaction took her breath away.

"Yes, I know," he answered, casually, "so is yours. The only difference is that yours got caught and mine didn't. Is there some point here I'm missing?"

"I just wanted to be sure you knew," she said.

The central issue she had decided to leave out, for her tactical plan, was his father's treachery to hers.

"Why wouldn't I know?" he asked. "I was born into The Mystery, as you were. In a way we go back two hundred and fifty years or more, you and I. I thought we both understood that the other day."

There was a calm ruthlessness about his honesty that defied argument.

"I wasn't very well the other day," she told him, "and for your information, now that I've got my marbles back, I want to tell you that I'm out of all that."

There was one thing the shock of her discovery of his identity had done, she reflected. It had burned away the charismatic aura that had so unbuckled her at first. She was still profoundly attracted to him, but at least she could function.

"I'm out of it, too," he said.

"How can you say that?" she challenged him. "Your old man nicked seventeen million quid. That's what you're living on."

"What I'm doing," he said, always calmly, "is administering the fortune my father built on what he stole, so that the greater part of it goes to other people. My father is among the great entrepreneurs. The only difference is that he got his start-up money by stealing it directly instead of indirectly, like some of the others. Moreover, by this time the Patterson Foundation has undoubtedly given away a very great deal more than my father stole in the first place. Looking at it that way, he's not a thief at all, he's a public benefactor. And just for the record, it wasn't seventeen million he got; it was eight and a half. Your father got the other eight and a half. Unfortunately, he left some of the loose change lying around at home and got taken, that's all."

So that's what he'd been told, thought Tara. He didn't know! A flood of relief washed through her, so intense it felt like a physical tide. That explained the flowers, too. They were Shaun Patterson's way of showing, in his son's eyes, loyalty to an old colleague.

"What did he do with it, by the way?" Michael asked. "Stick it in a Swiss bank where only he can get at the account, no good even giving you the number?"

"Something like that," she said.

"Pity. We could have been making it work for you. After all, he paid enough for it."

Tara knew now how she was going to play her game. She would apparently accept the version Michael had been told of what had happened. There was nothing to be gained by challenging it with the truth. He would simply not believe it. She would love him, but it would be a complex, treacherous love. For she would mine Michael for every detail that might help to bring his father down.

That she did love him on the immediate level there was no doubt. She had also no doubt that he was equally disturbed by her. He had more command, more control and experience than she, but anyone who could read eyes couldn't help but know how he felt about her.

"When are they letting you out?" he asked, as if they hadn't just had a conversation which most people would have regarded as, to say the least, mildly exceptional.

"In a couple of days, they tell me."

"It can't stop here, you know."

"I know that."

He put his hand on hers and they both felt the jolt.

But visiting hours had started and Aunt Rita came in. Spectacularly, as always. She crashed through the swing doors at the end of the ward and measured her length on the polished floor, the swinging dangle of bags and carriers, without which she was constitutionally incapable of going anywhere, scattering their contents all over. They included a police truncheon, a Bible, half a loaf green with mold, an alarm clock and a large bottle of cider, wrapped in several cardigans which, fortunately, prevented it from breaking. Five strong nurses winched her to her feet to the accompaniment of loud, if blurred threats of lawsuits over the state of the hospital's floors. She did not seem to have come to any harm. Tara had seen Aunt Rita tumble, like a gigantic sackful of foam rubber, down a flight of stairs and get up and carry on to wherever she was going, without comment. She bore down on them, peering hazily at Michael.

"I know you," she said, "you're that Patterson brat. Wot ther hell you doing here?"

She stood swaying, like an avenging custard. Tara was terrified. This was something she had not foreseen. Aunt Rita shared the family view of what Shaun Patterson had done to Jed and if she revealed it now to Michael, Tara's whole plan of campaign would be blown.

"Put your glasses on," she muttered to Michael. Puzzled, he did so.

"Aunt Rita," she said, as if she hadn't heard the remark, "I'd like you to meet my specialist, Dr. Conran. Doctor, this is my Aunt Rita."

She looked at Rita hard, as if accusing her of something.

"She's a bit fond of the bevvy," she continued, "so she doesn't always see too well. Would you say, looking at her eyes, that it was beginning to affect her liver?"

Michael took his cue beautifully. He adjusted his glasses, reached over to Aunt Rita and before she could stop him, gently pulled down one of her bottom eyelids.

"Ay!" she protested, "gerroff! You'll have me flaming eye hanging out of me head!"

"I think you might need a little treatment," he said. "If you'd like to come in for observation for a few days . . ."

Tara, who was well aware of Aunt Rita's dislike of hospitals, particularly when they threatened her drinking habits, watched her blanch.

"Not bloody likely," she said. "I don't want anyone farting about with my liver. It'd probably end up getting fried with onions in the Nurses' Home!"

All she wanted to do now was to get away.

"I just came to bring you this," she said. She reached into one of her capacious bags and brought out a newspaper cutting from the *Liverpool Echo*. It had a little paragraph on Tara's progress.

"I'm glad you're better," she said. "Ta-ra, doctor, I can't say it's been a pleasure 'cos it hasn't. And you do look like that bastard Patterson kid."

She weaved out. As she got through the glass doors they saw her lean against the wall and stay her shaken nerves with a massive draught of cider. She then went from sight, the only further evidence of her progress toward the exit being another mega-crash, the echoes of which dimly reached them.

"What was all that about?" asked Michael.

"She can't forgive your father for getting away with it when my father didn't," she told him.

"Ah," he said, in a tone which indicated that there was nothing he could do about that. But Tara had had a fright. She understood now that she was sailing in tricky waters.

She was discharged next day with some tears and many shouts of "Good luck, love! We'll be looking out for you!"

"Look out for yourselves, too," she shouted back. "You might see yourselves on the show with your curlers in!"

5

The hospital program set standards of reality, accuracy and honesty which became the benchmark for documentary for years. It confirmed Paul's preeminence in his field and it consolidated Tara as an undoubted star of the first brilliance. Her courage in the face of great pain, her candor in letting herself be photographed looking at her most wretched, and the shrewd intelligence of her reporting all proclaimed a personality that had found its time, its place and its medium.

Above all, the range of her face, from the huge-eyed waif and the wickedly funny sprite with a smile to crack concrete to the acid-tongued castigator with danger behind her eyes, every shade of meaning was covered and caught by Pam's inspired camerawork. The critics shoved each other aside in their rush for the choicest adjectives. A week later the preliminary ratings came in. They were not only toweringly high, but the minute-by-minute graphs showed that viewer attention had been unwavering from beginning to end.

Paul studied them silently and solidly, region by region, for ten minutes at his desk. Then he rose, picked up Tara in her tiny leather skirt, lifted her high in the air and planted her on top of a tall cupboard against the wall. He fell solemnly to his knees and joined his palms in an attitude of prayer.

"Oh, goddess of the box . . ." he began.

"Get me down off here, you daft bugger!" yelled the goddess of the box.

"Pray grant a humble mortal to worship thee," he continued, "and the absolutely fantastic view I'm getting of your thighs from here."

"I'm warning you . . ." she said.

"Furthermore . . ." he added, at which point she launched herself from her perch and landed on his massive figure as confidently as she'd have vaulted on to a horse. He tumbled sideways and they did an Aunt Rita, collapsing on the carpet in a tangle of arms and legs. Which was how Cyril Goldstein found them when he walked in a second later.

"Is this a Union orgy," he asked, "or can Management join in?"
They scrambled to their feet.

"We're working on a new show." said Tara; "The Kiddies'
Guide to the Kamasutra."

"Don't joke about such things," said Goldstein. "You make me
nervous. Already I hear there are questions down in the House of
Commons for the Health Minister."

"So there should be," said Tara; "everything we said in that
show about what hospitals have to put up with from Whitehall is true."

"I'm sure it is, my dear," said Cyril G., "but you're not having
dinner with a big banana in the Government tomorrow night. Well,
it's not so much him, it's his wife; she's got delusions of mediocrity.
But that's not what I wanted to talk about. I've had a green telephone
this morning from the chief of every network in the country. They
all want to know two things: when's your next show and what's it
going to be about. I pretended to be secretive. I wasn't going to admit
I didn't know. So do you think you could make an old man happy
by telling him?"

"The fact is," said Paul, we honestly don't know. We haven't
even had time to think about it."

"Well, instead of wrestling around on my carpets, d'you think
you could do that in your own time and give the question a little
thought in mine?"

"We will," said Paul. "Meanwhile, I did rather want to have a
word with you about something else. Shall I come to your office?"

"What's wrong with here?"

"Well, it is rather a private matter."

"He's going to ask me for more money," said Cyril G. to the
world at large. "So why don't we go into your office?" He indicated
Paul's private office, which led off the one they were in.

"Yes, fine," said Paul, a little reluctantly, Tara felt.

They went into Paul's office for their private conversation. For
Tara, as for most people, private conversations were for listening to.
Not everyone, however, was as well-informed as Tara. She had long
ago discovered the remarkable acoustic properties of inside, non-load-
bearing walls, particularly about halfway up. She settled herself comfortably in a chair near the spot and tuned in.

The opening sentence turned her white with shock. It was Paul's
voice: "I can't work with Tara Stewart anymore." That was what
he said, straight out, no mistaking it.

He obviously hadn't forgiven her, after all, for the episode in
the hospital. For all his play-acting just now and since she had come

back to work, he had been nursing his terrible grudge. And she had thought that she knew something about human duplicity and hypocrisy.

Her thoughts raced so fast that her ears picked up the subsequent exchanges without her brain immediately interpreting them. It was Cyril Goldstein's voice:

"I'd like to know your reasons."

Paul paused and Tara held her breath. Her whole life could go down the pan right now.

"To be honest," said Paul, "I think she's outgrown me."

"You're one of the greatest documentary producers this business of ours has ever produced."

Tara listened, with increasing incredulity as Paul went on: "Tara Stewart has a fire inside her. I've got nothing more to give her. From now on I'd be holding her back. At first, I tried not to let her see I was teaching her. Then I realized she had a talent that was soaking it up just about as fast as I could pour it out."

Cyril Goldstein was testing the issue to destruction, as was his habit.

"You've done superb things together," he said. "The breaking of that shyster Ed Friendly—a great piece of crusading journalism."

"She broke him."

"The exposure of The Circuit—the bare-knuckle boys . . ."

"Set up by her. I'd never have got near them without her." He would, the big, darling, generous dope, thought Tara—it would have just taken him a bit longer.

"I don't know where she gets her contacts," said Paul, "but they're unique in my experience."

"This last hospital show," Goldstein was saying. "A classic of our time."

"Her idea entirely," insisted Paul. "She had to talk me into it, worked out how it could be done, got me enthused. I mean to say, there's this kid lying smashed up in a hospital bed and all she's thinking about is coming up with the kind of show we've just seen!"

It was Ben who got her motivated about that, remembered Tara.

"And you—you give her nothing . . . ?" asked Cyril G.

"Oh, I've given her the grammar, the 'Cranmer style'; I've given her a sense of tempo, the feeling of size."

"So you're a team. Teams have been a part of show business since the beginning."

"It's not show business to her."

"It's all show business," Goldstein insisted. "Just because it's not legs and tits doesn't mean it's not show business. The Ten O'Clock News is show business, the *Times* newspaper is show business. What's so different about our little girl?"

"I don't know," Paul answered, musingly. "I just know that something is."

"So what do you suggest we do with her?"

Tara held her breath.

"She's much more than a presenter," answered Paul, "she's a producer. Make her a producer and give her her own show. And what's more, give her a free hand."

Goldstein studied the big man steadily: "You must be very fond of this girl. What you just did for her a person doesn't do for everybody. Won't you miss her working with you?"

"It'll be hellish," said Paul, simply. "Coming in to work every day with the certainty of knowing I was going to see her and be with her, it's been like spring all year round for me."

Outside, Tara felt a tear prick her eye. She also felt like a totally despicable bitch. She also knew that she really loved Paul. Oh, not because he was being so good to her—that came into it, but it was more than that. She loved his goodness and his kindness and his bigness of heart. It was a different emotion from the great electric arc that sizzled between her and Michael, but it was just as real in its way.

As her mind spinned, she was listening to Cyril Goldstein again.

"You may see her more than you think," he was saying. "How would you like to be Head of Documentary?"

"Thank you," said Paul, "but no . . ."

"That's a little word I won't take for an answer," said Goldstein. "Any man who thinks as clearly as you do, and as unselfishly, and can spot talent like you do, I want in one of the driving seats of this crazy coach we're all in. I wouldn't expect you to give up your own programs, and you could keep a helpful eye on our little girl."

"And I really could go on producing?"

"Am I such a fool as to turn a top-rating producer into a bureaucrat?"

"No, I suppose not," admitted Paul.

"Thank you for the qualified vote of confidence," said Cyril G. "Then you accept?"

"Tara Stewart gets her own show?" asked Paul.

"At once."

"Then I accept most gratefully," said Paul.

"Don't worry me by getting grateful," said Cyril G. "It's out of character for a creative person."

They sat and faced each other, the small, wise, always tanned little man and the big, brown bear, also wise.

"One of us has to tell her a thing," said Goldstein. "Someone has to tell her that she is now a star; to make her understand what that means. Is she tough, this fairy child of yours—I mean really tough where it counts?"

"As old boots," said Paul. "Don't you worry about her. And I think you should tell her."

"Thank you very much," said Cyril G., drily.

When Paul went out to find Tara and tell her that Cyril Goldstein wanted to see her, she was in the Ladies down the corridor, throwing up. She came back, pale and shriven, to discover Paul waiting for her.

"God's waiting to see you," he said. "I think he wants to take you to lunch."

Later in her career, Tara was to feel that she never acted so well nor behaved so badly in her life. She had to play out the charade now or everyone would look foolish and the whole thing would be poisoned, but she was disgusted with herself for every minute of it.

"What for?" she asked.

"I don't know. Maybe he wants to make passionate love to you under the table." God, I certainly do, he thought!

"But Cyril Goldstein . . ." she said.

"Just be your impudent, irreverent, bloody-minded scouse self," said Paul. "After all, that's the combination you pulled me with; why shouldn't it work on him?"

What she wanted to do was to hug Paul, to kiss him hotly on the mouth, to pleasure him. That a man could do what he'd just done for her without even giving a hint of it—well, that was outside her experience.

"When?" she asked. "I'm not dressed right."

"I don't know," he said, deliberately unfeelingly. "I mean, he might only be taking you to the corner pub, what are you worried about? What do you need to eat a pie and chips, a satin ball gown?"

"Thanks, Paul." she said, marveling at the smoothness of his performance, "you really are the most terrific help."

In the event, Cyril G. took her next day to a club on the river at Egremont, across the Mersey from Liverpool. It was called simply "The Club." It wasn't where one would expect to find it and it was known to not more than one hundred rich men in the Merseyside area. The essential qualification was that one had to be one's own millionaire. No senior directors, no astronomically salaried super salesmen, no chief executives. One had to have baked one's own bread or at least to own the bakery. The subscription was astronomical which, together with the prices of the exquisite food, made it an economically sound proposition for the land-poor younger son of a local family and his Carrier-trained Sloane Ranger wife.

Cyril Goldstein was as childish in one respect as most men. He enjoyed the imperceptible ripple that ran through the stream-bisected, marble-floored garden ambience of the dining room as they crossed to their table overlooking the glittering summer river. Everyone knew that Cyril had a wife who looked like a combine harvester, to whom he had been irreproachably devoted for thirty-five years and that he often brought famous and beautiful actresses to The Club when he was trying to romance them into doing this or that series for his company at a price at which everyone could make money. But this gray-eyed, siren-faced Garbo was a different thing altogether. In her short, body-hugging hyacinth dress, her eyes as deep and mysterious as fjords, her hair glittering, she drifted across on Cyril's arm like one of Tolkien's elf-princesses, looking at once vulnerable, yet capable of who knew what terrible magic.

Never one to waste time, Cyril plunged in the minute the streaked-blond young maître d', who Tara sensed fancied her despite the fact that he was gay, had impeccably seated them.

"Now then, young lady, you and I have got to have a serious talk," he said, for openers, spreading a lump of butter on his melba toast that should have closed his arteries for good.

"Yeah, well that's great, because that's just what I'd like," she replied.

"What is it you would like to say to me?" he asked.

"No, you first," she countered, "after all, you're buying lunch."

Goldstein was beginning to get the flavor of this girl. He had never been a man to demand servility, but he knew that many people, simply because of who he was and what he'd done, couldn't help being a bit in awe of him. Not this Tara Stewart. It wasn't that she was impudent or insulting to him, just that she was completely at her ease in his company. What he didn't know was that she had her favorite secret weapon holstered away in her mind—information. She knew exactly what the lunch was about. There was none of the unsettling element of uncertainty the situation usually carried.

They were interrupted by a waiter. Would they care for an aperitif before lunch?

"Yeah, I'd like half a pint of light ale," said Tara, cheerfully. Goldstein blinked just noticeably.

"We'll be having wine with lunch, of course," he told her.

"Oh great—I'll just be ready for it by then," she said.

Goldstein decided it was as good a place as any to start.

"That's one of the things I wanted to talk to you about," he said. "There are certain things people do and certain things they don't do. For a girl in your position, knocking back half a pint of beer before lunch is one of the latter."

"What the heck is my position, if I have to kick beer into touch?"

"Your position, dear girl, is that I am about to make you a star. That means putting a certain investment in you, building your publicity, paying for your wardrobe, maybe hiring an agency to shape your image. Listen, I'm not talking about the old Hollywood movie days or any of that, when your life wasn't your own. But the public is a funny animal. It can make you or break you. And if you step out of the mold it's made for you, it'll break you."

Tara, watched fascinatedly by every man in the money-scented room, drained her beer in one steady tilt before answering.

She replaced her glass on the table—he followed it, mesmerized, with his eyes—then turned to her host.

"Mr. Goldstein, can I get something lined up straight in my head?"

"That seems like a very reasonable idea," he grinned, looking more like a twinkling brown gnome than ever.

"Well . . . you're going to make me a star—right?"

"Right."

"And the reason you're going to make me a star is that people seem to like me."

"They respond to you."

"I don't know quite what that means, but, okay, they 'respond' to me and to how Paul's presented me to them."

"Yes—and I'm glad you recognize your debt to Paul Cranmer."

"Oh, listen, without Paul I'd be nothing; I know that. But if that's what being a star means—and the critics and the high ratings and everything, well amn't I a star already and why do you have to start mucking about with me and changing my image and all that?"

Cyril Goldstein started using his fingers to check off his points; a sure sign that he knew he was in a fight.

"Firstly," he said, "nobody is going to muck about with you, simply enhance what you've already got. Secondly, critics and high ratings are all very well, but people are going to start writing pieces about you in magazines, the gossip columns are going to start getting interested in you. It's no longer just your work that you're going to be judged on, it's your whole life."

"My life's my own," she said, watching how he cracked his lobster tails and doing the same.

"I'm afraid it isn't, dear girl," he said. "If you were in Light Entertainment it might be different. But you're not. You've set yourself up as a conscience of the nation. People trust you; believe in you. Let me give you an example. Years ago, long before your time, there was a man who got a reputation as a champion of the people. Knight on a white charger, all that. He was terrific television. Then a nosy reporter found out that he owned three streets of slum houses in Liverpool and that he was the kind of landlord who wouldn't even stick a piece of chewing gum over a hole in the roof. It destroyed him overnight. He was still as good a pro as ever he'd been, but he'd lost his credibility, d'you see what I mean?"

The conversation was momentarily interrupted by a waiter bringing a single, exquisitely scented long-stemmed gray-and-pink rose to the table with a note. It read: "From an electrified fan."

The waiter nodded to a far corner table, shaded by the branches of one of the trees that grew up through the dimmed glass ceiling of the dining room. Jason Planter, alone at a table, gracefully inclined his head and raised his glass to her.

"Would you excuse me a mo, Mr. Goldstein?" she asked, and slipped gracefully out of her chair without waiting for an answer.

She threaded her way through the tables, her route strewn, like rose petals, with admiring glances from men who were expert at putting a price tag on everything, but found it impossible to put one on her. As she reached Jason's table he stood up, elegant, dark and flashing.

"Fairy Queen," he said, "may I offer you a glass of champagne?"

"No, ta," she said, "but I like your style." She wafted the rose he had sent gently beneath her nostrils. "You always seem to be where I am. What are you doing here?"

He smiled with gentle malice.

"I'm having an excellent meal in surroundings where a man can be fairly sure nobody's going to ask him what he's doing here," he said.

"Sorry about that, love," she grinned, "but us louts get in everywhere now."

"How about dinner tonight?" he queried.

"Sorry," she said. "Booked up. How about tomorrow?"

He grimaced: "Tomorrow I'm off on my travels again."

"Where?"

"Oh, all over. Come with me!" He'd lost the slight self-consciousness she'd sensed in him at the hospital. He'd realized she knew he would want no dutiful sense of commitment to him.

"Jason, I'm a working girl!"

He sighed again: "I suppose I'd gathered that from the sight of your host. You're going back to being Joan of Arc."

"D'you know Cyril Goldstein, then?" she asked.

He grinned.

"I know everyone," he said. "You'll realize that once I've recruited you."

"Ring me when you get back," she asked.

"You can bet on it," he said. "By the way," he added, "my ancestors were among those who burned her."

"Who?"

"Joan of Arc."

He bowed slightly and she went back to her table. She had a growing conviction that there was a great deal more to Jason than the playboy image he projected. There was something . . . what was it? . . . almost dangerous about the vibes he emitted.

When she got back to Cyril Goldstein it was to find him looking slightly at a loss, not a characteristic expression of his.

"How do you know Jason Planter?" he asked.

"It's a long story," she said. "Started on a motorway. Why?"

She was touched to hear him clear his throat, a little bit flustered.

"He hasn't got a very good reputation with women," he muttered.

"Thank you for telling me, Mr. Goldstein," she said, her face as sincere and solemn as she could make it; "I appreciate it, I really do."

His brown eyes flashed.

"Don't you patronize me, young lady," he snapped.

"I wouldn't even know how to spell it, Mr. Goldstein," she said. "Ask anyone."

He mopped his brow with his napkin. No wonder that goddamned bastard Paul Cranmer had landed him with this assignment. It was somehow all getting away from him.

"Anyway, to get back to what we were talking about. Let me tell you what I'm prepared to do for you . . ."

Tara interrupted: "Mr. Goldstein, I don't want to be a big head, but don't you think it would be easier for me to tell you what I want?"

Cyril G. took a long sip of Perrier water, followed by a good mouthful of wine. He had always found it a splendid specific for getting back his equilibrium. How old was this child, for the love of God? That was a damn silly question, he knew how old she was. She was twenty-one. Then where did she get a negotiating technique aged about a sixty-five-year-old top lawyer? What did it matter where she got it? She'd got it and he was in the ring with it and he was going to have to keep the left jab pumping out and his chin tucked in. Listen, he'd mixed it in his time with Bette Davis, Lauren Bacall, Raquel Welch, Bo Derek and her husband John; he couldn't handle this kid?

He leaned across warmly.

"So tell me what you want," he said, with as much sincerity as he'd have used toward a crocodile with his foot in its mouth.

She started by asking for the things she knew he already wanted to give her.

"First of all I want my own show," she said. "Something like *Tara Stewart—Public Eye*. I know it's nicking from that marvelous old series by Richard Bates and from Peter whatsisname, the playwright, before him, but it's what I am."

"It's got potential," he said, noncommittally.

"Second, I want to be my own producer."

"Could be a practical idea," he agreed.

"Third, since I'd be doing two jobs instead of one, I'd want double the money I'm getting now."

"Anything's negotiable," he countered blandly. So far it wasn't too bad. In fact, it could have been worse. To tell the truth, he was within a whisper of being a happy man.

"Fourth, I want my own team. None of this business of being lumbered with people just because they're on the strength and have to be paid anyway."

There's no fool like an old fool, he reflected bitterly. He should have known it was too good to last. He could see it all looming ahead—trouble with the A.C.T.T. Properly speaking, they were a technicians' union, but because they had got clout they had swept up a lot of people who weren't technicians into their net. They had clout because, with their allies the electricians' union, they controlled the hardware and the juice; it was as simple as that. All they had to do was pull out the plugs. Black screens across the nation. Advertisers wanting their money back. Interrupted continuity of series. The B.B.C. happily picking up viewers. This kid probably wanted her sisters, straight out of school, no ticket, no nothing, straight on the show's staff. What was this she was saying now?

"You don't have to worry," she was adding, "the people I'm thinking of have all got their A.C.T.T. tickets."

He was definitely getting too old for this business, he decided.

This kid had him on a switchback, down one minute, up the next. He tried Perrier with the wine chaser again. It didn't help.

"Point five?" he gargled.

"I get a free hand. Nobody bangs the drum on what I have to do or haven't got to do, but I can call on Paul Cranmer to hold my hand if I get out of my depth."

"I've just appointed Paul Cranmer your departmental head, so that's automatic," he said, childishly pleased to have been, at last, one step ahead of her.

"Have you finished?" he inquired, politely.

"Yeah," she grinned, "but I'm afraid I've got behind with me lunch." She began to eat her ragout of lamb with relish.

"Terrific!" she pronounced. "Just like scouse!"

Her remark was passed on by the eavesdropping waiters to the internationally famous chef in the kitchens.

"She's dead right," said the chef, who had learned his French in his birthplace—a French enclave in Chiswell Street, Liverpool—and his cooking in Arles in France, "it is scouse—with garlic. You lot know nut'n."

"Then let me now give you my terms," said Cyril G., courteously. "Your own show, producership, granted. More money . . ."

"Double," she mumbled, her mouth full.

"Don't worry, we'll agree," he said. "Have you got an agent?"

"No."

"You should get one."

"Why?"

"It's embarrassing dealing with you directly."

"Don't be embarrassed," she said, soothingly, "just give me what I want." She had become, over this luncheon, very fond of this brown, twinkling little man. But she didn't underestimate him. She remembered that a famous actress had applied Hitler's remark about Franco to him: that rather than negotiate with him again, she would prefer to have all her teeth pulled without anaesthetic.

"And you're going to read all the fine print yourself?" he asked.

"Why not? You wouldn't screw a poor little scouser, would you, Mr. Goldstein?" she asked, with such a hypocritically pathetic grimace that he couldn't help a smile squeezing through.

"As for the completely free hand," he went on, "we'll have to see. Nobody in this business has a completely free hand. There's the Independent Broadcasting Authority, the advertisers, the viewers, the Government, M.P.s trying to make a name for themselves, catch their boss's eye; then there's Mary Whitehouse . . ."

"We had a different name for her at school," said Tara.

"Don't tell me," said Goldstein, hastily. "But, off the record, so do I."

They grinned at each other, the elvish quality in each finding a friend.

"We'll row and fight," he warned.

"And I'll always win," she said.

"No, you won't," he promised.

They smiled at each other again, raised and touched glasses.

"Here's to a long and exhausting relationship."

"It needn't be exhausting, Mr. Goldstein," she said. "Just lie back and enjoy it."

He allowed another smile to sneak through.

"There is one last thing," he said, "but it can wait."

"What is it?" she asked, anxiously.

"No," he said, "let's enjoy our lunch. Afterwards we can have our first row."

They had coffee in the rose garden, cloistered by fragrant hedges, so that the only sound was the curiously muted conversation of people at other tables. It was one of those spots where, usually by accident, there has been created a tiny space outside of time, so that ambition, worries, resentments fell away as fleshly irrelevancies. It occurred to her that Cyril G. hadn't chosen The Club by accident for their first encounter. As they sipped their coffee—Goldstein with his inevitable Perrier on the side—he asked about her background. She gave him Aunt Rita and the slums as if it were the whole story. She never lost sight, even in this lotus-land, of the fact that all this was simply an aid to her mission and that about that nobody must know. She didn't yet appreciate that her genial cynic of a boss never took anyone's word for anything as being the whole truth.

They left by the back way, a golden driveway fading into hazed vistas of green and russet, created by a pupil of Capability Brown.

It was at this point that Cyril G. sprang his surprise and started their first row, as he had predicted. On the drive, against the distant mists of the trees, sat a glowing amber two-seater Jaguar XJS sports coupé with burgundy leather seats, looking as if it had been designed by Fabergé. Around it was tied a pink satin ribbon with a huge bow on the top. Glowing like a mechanical jewel, it took Tara totally with its beauty and its sense of the speed which had always intoxicated her.

"How d'you like her?" asked Cyril G.

"She's the most fantastic thing on four wheels I've ever seen," said Tara. She still wouldn't allow herself to believe what she thought it was all about.

"She's yours," he said. "Present from the company."

"But I . . . I mean . . . But . . ."

"There's one condition," he said.

"Oh?" warily.

"You give up your motorbike."

"No!" It was a cry of shock.

"You don't give up the motorbike, you don't get the car," he said.

"Stick the . . ." she began, petering out into ". . . what?"

"Listen," he said, gently. "Motorbikes . . . you were a kid then. You're grown-up now. Look what just happened to you with the bike. You're a documentarist—look at the statistics. Also, look at it from my point of view. The company has a big investment in you. We have to protect that investment."

Tara looked at him in a way to break a man's heart.

"I've become a property," she said, sadly.

"I've never called anyone a property in my life," Goldstein replied, "but the meaning of what you say—yes, you've got it right. But it's more than that." Gently, he took her arm. "In this life we're lucky to get one warning. You've had yours. Personally I would take it very hard to see a lovely, clever young girl like you throw away all her promise in some stupid, godless accident. Take the car," he pleaded. "Take the deal. Throw the bike in the river."

She stood motionless for a moment, then her wonderful smile ignited. Paul had already sat with her while she taught herself to drive. She had her license. She turned to Cyril G.

"Like a lift back?" she asked.

She drove Cyril G. back to Manchester with such sheer exuberance, luxuriating in the power of the machine she controlled, that at first he wondered if she wouldn't be better off with the motorbike after all. Then, as he began to appreciate the sureness of her touch and the speed of her reflexes, he relaxed, smiling to himself as he watched, in the nearside mirror, his chauffeur's determination to keep up in the Rolls.

She got back to the office, slotted the Jaguar into a new, personalized parking place which had been prepared in her absence and which her passenger pointed out to her and ran upstairs to play out an elaborate charade with Paul, she bursting with the news, he apparently staggered by it.

The only thing that was missing was that she couldn't thank him. But she had plans for that. It was Friday afternoon.

"Doing anything at the weekend?" she asked him, casually.

"Thought I'd play a spot of golf and squash," he said.

"Anyone you can't put off?" she asked.

"I suppose not, really. Why?"

"I thought you might like to help me put the XJS through its paces."

"What an absolutely splendid idea!" he answered. "Will you bring the crash helmets or shall I?"

"Sarky git!" she said.

That evening she purred home along the motorway in the Jaguar, her stomach twanging with the knowledge that she was finally on stream toward her sworn vocation. She had gathered into her hands the weapons with which she proposed to free her father and cut down his enemy. She hoped that her imagination and her will would not fail her in the battles she saw ahead.

At the flat she slid her gleaming new cat up the drive and raced indoors to give the news to Bella, who had seen the car already through a twitch of the curtains, a form of intelligence-gathering shared by most of their neighbors and known locally as CURTINT. As Tara told her her news they fell into each other's arms and hugged and kissed like schoolgirls. It was on this scene of licentious abandon that Aunt Rita opened her door from her afternoon's sleeping-off of the morning's excesses, preparatory to the evening's bacchanalia. It was as she'd always suspected, although she'd never been able to catch them at it; the brilliant blond head and the lustrous black one, nuzzling and kissing each other. She was on them before they knew it, her fat, bare, pillowy feet giving no warning of her approach. The first they knew was that they were being belabored by one of the omnipresent plastic bags, which Rita hung about her, even in the flat. This, from the feel of it, was filled with custard.

"Daughters of darkness!" she cried, for openers. "Depraved disciples of Baal! Filthy, sick, abandoned spawn of decadence!" She was getting very satisfactorily excited; she'd always known it would be as good as this if ever she could get among the real thing instead of merely her fantasies of it. She'd got a good swing going on the bag and the words were flowing well.

"Catamites of the pit! May ye descend to the fiery, stinking stews from which ye came!"

"Ye" was strong, she thought; "ye" was very powerful. She was really getting into her stride. She'd never hit a "ye" before. It was her excitement that was her undoing. She failed to notice that, presently, she was larruping only one fiendish catamite of the pit instead of two. Then Tara came silently out of the kitchen behind her, an ice bucket brimming with cubes in her hands. She gently pulled the neckline of Rita's dress and tipped the whole floe of ice cubes down her back. There, unable to escape past the belt of Rita's tent-like dress, they slithered and clinked around the mountainous landscape of her body. It was as if a valve had shut off her breath. Her mouth opened and shut soundlessly like a goldfish in a bowl and her eyes rolled in her head as she tried to work out what had happened to her. She had a ghastly feeling that she might have sobered up. Taking advantage of the temporary cessation of meaningful activity in Rita's central nervous system, Tara swung her gently around by her massive shoulders, like turning a large revolving door and led her, a tug with an oil tanker, toward her room. It was a haven to which Rita was nothing loath to go, it being her store of essential supplies.

Once she'd closed the door behind the strangely subdued leviathan, Tara turned to her friend.

"Bella, how much are you making with your stockbroker?"

"Nine thousand eight hundred," said Bella.

"How d'you like to make seventeen?"

"What?!"

"That's what being a television researcher pays these days. I wouldn't half love to have you on my team."

Bella clapped her hands like a child.

"I'd love to be on your team!" she cried. "I've always fancied getting back into television."

Tara knew that Bella had been Paul's P.A. when she married him.

"Have you still got your A.C.T.T. card?"

"I never let that go," Bella smiled.

"Then we're in business!" Tara yelled, embracing her excitedly again. Bella was by now a fast friend and Tara would have wanted her on her team anyway, but she couldn't help the private reflection that Bella's knowledge of Patterson would not exactly be a drawback.

Next, Tara telephoned Ben Maitland in London.

"How are your ribs, collarbones, tibias, fibias, knee cartilages and all like that?" she asked the stuntman.

"Fine," he said. "I calculate my risks, remember—more to the point, how are yours?"

"I'm great," she said; "I've just got my own show."

"Fantastic!" he said.

"I'd like to talk to you about it. I'll come up to you. How are you fixed next Monday?"

"Clean card," he said.

"I'll be there about six. Can you give me a bed?"

"I can even put something in it for you."

"Knock it off, Ben."

"Exactly," he said.

"Goodbye, Benjamin," said Tara.

Later that evening she paid her regular visit to her father in Walton Gaol. As she was led into the Visiting Room her heart went out in despair to the mind behind the hard, proud face, which she felt fighting with all its power against being institutionalized and sapped, but which steadfastly refused to allow any of its loved ones to become entangled in his despair.

"I saw," he said. "The bastards made sure I saw the newspapers about your crash. But d'you think they'd allow me a compassionate visit?"

Tara remembered her oath about what she would do for this beloved father, but said nothing for fear of his wrath. But it was more than a compassionate visit they were going to have to grant him by the time she'd finished.

"I got word, though—that you were going to pull through, I mean."

"How come?" she asked, fishing.

"I've still got *some* friends on the outside, evidently," he said. And that's all he would say, so determined was he to preserve his lily-pure daughter from any contact with the old world he gave up for her sake. She prayed that he would forgive her if he ever discovered that the word that had come down to him about her progress had come to him through her friends.

She told him about getting her own show, about being a star, about the lunch with Goldstein and the gorgeous car. His eyes lit up for her.

"That's the kind of thing I wanted for you, kiddo," he said. "It's what you deserve. I wish your ma had been around to see it."

"So do I, Dad," she said. "But you're around and you know and that's good enough for me." She wanted to inject purpose into him. "And so long as I know you are around, I know I'll be able to make it. Just knowing you're there—you know what I mean?"

"You're barmy," he said, "you don't need me."

It wasn't until the visit was over that either of them allowed their composure to crack.

Next morning Paul's pulses leaped as he heard the sonorous greeting of the XJS in the courtyard below his penthouse. He threw his bag in the back, slid his fifteen stones effortlessly into the passenger seat and kissed Tara quickly on the mouth.

"Definitely a better class of broomstick," he said.

He strapped himself in, the Jaguar growled discreetly out, all amber and burgundy and shining blond hair; and a bachelor vice-president of the Wirral-side arm of an American oil multinational nearly fell off his balcony opposite as he leaned out, wondering why nothing that spectacular ever happened to him.

Tara drove Paul like the gilded morning breeze high up into and over the rugged Pennine ridge, following the high lemon sun over the dangerous, clean crags from Lancashire down into the great, green rival county of Yorkshire. Hard men peopled both, although Tara had heard it said that Lancashire men would drink only Yorkshire beer before a funeral because they wouldn't want to be caught at a graveside with alcohol on their breath. As she dropped down skillfully through the passes, hugging the rocky curves, her eyes slid for a split second toward Paul, relaxed, securely strapped in; and the gunsmoke drifted behind the gray as she savored the feeling of having the big, amiable animal in her gentle power.

Across the broad acres of the historic Ridings they raced—appellations now abolished by Whitehall in favor of computer-speak compass points—leaving a wake behind them across heather and scrub-strewn moors that could have altered very little in a million years, wildernesses as wide and brooding and savage and mystical as any biblical desert, capable of striking inexplicable terror into the hearts of the timid, exhilarating to the bold. This was country that Tara's father had brought them to often as children. It answered the temper of his mind. The thought of the wild-flying spirit now crabbed and confined stabbed Tara momentarily from chest through to spine. Then she pushed it resolutely away. Nothing must spoil this weekend for Paul.

They stripped the miles away like peeling off bands of cellophane tape. They had lunch at the quietly pretty Crooked Man inn outside Middleton-One-Row, a village with the air of everlastingly expecting Henry the Eighth to drop in on its line of cottages and remark how little they had changed. Then they dropped on down toward Richmond, her father's favorite location in all Yorkshire, a town of perfect understanding between man and nature: a velvet green bowl, necklaced by streams, girdled by oak and ash, beech and elm, bays and conifers, crowned by a castle, graced by the most perfectly preserved little Georgian theater in the United Kingdom and studded in the center with honey-streaked stone houses that looked as if they had grown out of the ground.

They drew up outside the luxurious little hotel, set like a gem in the square, ordered dinner for nine o'clock and went straight upstairs to the room Tara had booked in the names of Mr. Aramis Maunkberry-Clutton and Mrs. Miranda Atalanta-fforbes, a fact she didn't impart to the profoundly, conventionally hypocritical Paul until they were walking up the front steps of the hotel, preceded by the porter. She watched him, the silent hilarity growing inside her, as the pen shook while he signed his patently adulterous *nom de guerre* beneath hers, under the sparklingly clear blue eye of the Yorkshire beauty at the Reception desk.

"I must say, those names were a bit much," he protested, as the door of their room finally closed behind them at five o'clock, the sun streaming through their balconied windows.

They were the last fully articulate words he spoke for three and a half hours. The moment the lock clicked, she attacked his giant frame like a fury, tearing off his clothes first, discarding hers as and when she needed to. She clambered around him like an ivy around an oak, she thrust him back on the bed and bestrode his face as if she would swallow him. She kissed him, licked him, rode under, over and around him with no thought but for his pleasure. She played his magnificent body like some great responsive instrument, every time it flagged with fatigue finding some new artifice to bring it rearing and roaring to life again. And she discovered something. That to make someone moan with pleasure as she made this big man moan was in itself a trip of a kind she had not experienced before. Each of his spasms triggered off a shudder in her until she didn't know whether she was being generous or a glutton.

At nine o'clock on the dot she made him drag his ruined body down to dinner among a collection in the dining room of Yorkshire's finest—and shrewdest. Tara looked as if she had just stepped from behind some cool and magic waterfall. One look at Paul and you knew exactly what he'd been up to. And all through dinner, demure, gray-eyed, with her fairy-tale hair and her tranquil face, she quietly kept up a stream of the most lubricious, inspirationally pornographic conversation he had ever heard—and that included those at his Rugby Club dinners. He didn't dare lift his eyes from his food. His muttered "steady-ons" and "hold the mustards" had absolutely no effect on the shocking, unstoppable flow, and by the time they had finished their Chateaubriands and a bottle of Rausan-Ségla '69, he was as mad as a hornet and as horny as a stag all over again. She wouldn't allow him any port or brandy, but led him back upstairs, slipped off her dress to reveal the whole black corselet, stockings and suspenders heavy drama she had streaked into before dinner and let him take her comprehensively apart, nerve by nerve.

As Saturday had gone, so went Sunday. They had breakfast and lunch in their room, each served, quite unnecessarily, by three waiters, for the word had gone around the hotel and everyone wanted a look at Britain's Olympic sexual decathletes. On Sunday night she dexterously drove him back home and kissed him a passionate goodnight in the car—nearly occasioning the final, fatal precipitation to the courtyard below of the balconied oil executive across the way. She watched Paul walk slowly and satedly indoors, carrying his bag, not as he normally did—as if he were unaware he had anything in his hand—but as if it were loaded with bars of lead.

He could not remember being so relaxed and blissfully tired in his life. Only two questions exercised him. He knew what he had done to deserve it, but how did she? And was there just a faintly valedictory minor chord in the melody?

Michael Patterson had been trying to reach her all weekend. He was too fresh from America to have found his own roots yet in London and was content for the moment with the bachelor *pied-à-terre* he inhabited, leading off his father's enormous Belgravia flat in Eaton Square. He'd told his father he had met Tara in hospital and it had started a tremendous row.

"You damn fool!" Shaun exclaimed. "What d'you want to go and do that for?"

"What are you talking about?" Michael hit back. "Who sent her the flowers?"

"Sending her flowers is one thing—that's the least one can do for the daughter of an old mate—an unlucky old mate."

"And the least you could do is exactly what you would do, isn't it?" retorted Michael.

"Meaning what?" demanded Shaun.

"Sending flowers with just a company logo on them seems kind of weird to me—the absolutely minimal kind of gesture a man could make."

"What's she been saying about me?" asked his father, tensing himself for the answer he was sure was coming. It was not the one he expected. It took him a second or two to realize that he shouldn't be feeling relief, that it was even worse.

"She didn't say anything about you. She was only a kid when it was all going on. She doesn't remember much about it except that her father made a mistake and got caught."

Which was the historic moment when Shaun Patterson realized, with a shock that went right down to his toenails, that Tara Stewart was a very dangerous little lady indeed. She must have known, as all the Stewarts knew, how he had set her father up. Yet she had said nothing to his son. She had pretended to accept the Patterson version of events, as told by him to Michael. He didn't like it; the more so since she was rapidly becoming a lady with real shoulder power. He had watched her demolish that shrewd and ruthless old operator Ed Friendly and the blood had perceptibly cooled in his veins. She had what her father had always had—and which he had always corrosively envied—the kiss of star quality on a foundation of rippingly sharp intelligence. And now she had evidently ensnared his son. He didn't like it one little bit. Why in God's name had he not foreseen, after keeping him out of it for all that time in the States, that Michael might meet her on one of his trips to the 'Pool? Because he didn't expect her ever to rise above the gutter to which he'd devoutly hoped he'd sent the whole family.

It had been walking into his son's apartment and finding him once again trying to get through to Tara Stewart that had lit his flare. Now it was too late to turn back and he was strapped by being unable to tell the truth. He knew Michael. Michael had recognized his origins and decisively rejected them. In fact, since he'd felt it safe to bring him back and he'd been administering the Foundation, he'd been handing out money so fast you'd think he was trying to drive his father back to crime. Once let him get a whiff of the filthy thing he'd done to Jed Stewart and he'd lost the boy for good. And he loved him dearly. He loved the look of him, the bone in him, the quality in him. He was a man among men. He commanded. And he didn't know what he'd ever done to deserve siring him.

"Look," he appealed to Michael, "I know Cabinet ministers, ambassadors, big bankers. How's it going to look if you're clocked having it off with a tart whose father's in the nick?"

"You're a snob!" cried Michael delightedly. He loved his father, even when they were rowing; a man's man, with curiously endearing gaps in his sensibilities. But he did find him funny. "You should be in jail yourself fifteen times over, yet now you're too respectable to have your son associate . . . Any more and I'll piss myself laughing. Look, just let me call my girl and . . ."

"Oh, she's your girl now, is she?"

"Just a figure of speech. Nothing over which to have a coronary."

" 'Over which'!" mimicked Shaun. "If ever I do have a coronary, I hope I can have it with that kind of class!"

"Besides," his son carried on, unflurried, "if you're going to look at it like a snob, she's not just a girl with a father inside, she's a television celebrity and she's a damn sight more likely to end up at a Buckingham Palace luncheon than you are."

"I don't know why I ever sent you to America," said Shaun. "All they did was turn you into a bloody smart ass."

"Why did you send me?"

"Because I didn't want you soft, like the pansies they turn out here."

It was an evasion, Michael knew. His father was too bright to believe that. But at what the reason was, he could only guess and his guesses fell far short of the target. The truth was that by some warp of irony, Michael had been born straight, like the Stewart kids, and Shaun knew that Michael wasn't about to sit still for what he planned to do to Jed Stewart. He'd shipped him off to America and the boy had done him proud. He'd been a prep school and university football star, he'd shone at Choate, got into Harvard and taken a degree in law and a doctorate in philosophy. His thesis for his Ph.D. had been "The Corporate Structure and Strategy of the Mafia." His tutors had been astonished that any young Englishman could understand so instinctively the infrastructure of American organized crime and Michael had marveled at the universal uniformity of the workings of the criminal mind.

Shaun had hoped that, by the time the boy got back, the whole Mersey Tunnel *cause célèbre* would have been yellowed and dry. And so it would have been, but for this bloody tart. Something would have to be done about her. Michael had called him a snob. Well, perhaps Michael was another kind of snob—an achievement snob; he was interested in her as a somebody who had made it. What, he speculated, would his reaction be to her as a nobody?

"I don't believe you're as dense as that," said Michael, referring to the "turning out soft" remark. "I think you realized I was beginning to see how badly you treated my mother and you knew I was getting old enough to create merry hell about it."

"I treated your mother like the Queen of England!"

"Oh, surely, she had all the fur coats, jewels, cars, holidays, a woman could want. She also had to swallow a succession of whores passing through your life—and hers—that everyone knew about. You weren't satisfied with one; you had to have three or four on the go at once. Lunch with this one, dinner with that one, hours in the bathroom poncing and primping and scenting yourself up for your next date." He remembered his mother's face. She'd been a quiet woman, rather like Elspeth Stewart, with hazel eyes that showed the inner bruises.

"You arrogant young sod!" Shaun Patterson was pierced by the accuracy of Michael's recollected observation. "I don't answer to anyone for the way I live my life!"

"You got it in one," said Michael. "Neither do I." He picked up the telephone again, which he had put down when the row started. "Now if you don't mind, this is kind of private."

"Ah, piss off!" replied the nationally renowned Father Christmas, kicking a hole in an expensive glass coffee table on his way out.

Michael was wasting his time on the telephone. Tara, girl with a mission, was already about her business. She didn't want anything as emotionally heavy as Michael on her mind just now. She was rifling down the motorway to London on her way to see Ben Maitland.

She'd never been to London before; but she had an apache's eye for topography and a map to her was like reading a well-written postcard. Just before six in the evening she drew up in the courtyard of Ben's block of modern luxury apartments on the Thames at Westminster. A young porter parked her car and nearly bent it, torn as he was between the thrill of being behind the wheel of the latest XJS and the desire to watch her incredible legs as she swung through the front door in her suede skirt.

Ben, in his immaculate and inevitable blue denims and T-shirt, faded to within a wavelength of the precise shade of his eyes, met her out of the lift. It had delivered her directly into his living room, with one huge window looking across to the Houses of Parliament the other side of the river and the barges and police launches plowing through the white-veined, choppy waters under Westminster Bridge. She took in the whole, extraordinary bustle and thrash of London's river as if it were a living mural there in Ben's living room—she could even, peering around the corner, see the Tower and St. Paul's. She drank it in in all its curiously monochrome tracery, then she turned to Ben delightedly.

"You're sick," she said, "you're living in a bloody movie!"

They hugged and kissed and he swung her around, her arms around his neck.

"It's good to see you, Tara, love," he said. "You look fantastic! I don't mind telling you I was dead worried about you when you were in that hospital."

"I was never in trouble, Ben," she laughed.

"Don't you believe it," Ben contradicted; "I used to ring up every night . . ."

"Nobody ever told me that!" she interrupted, indignantly.

"No, I asked them not to," he said. "But you were sailing a lot closer to the wind than you knew—you take it from your Uncle Ben."

Ben was a man who lived on fine edges. She had to accept that he knew. So how had she pulled through?

"Constitution, love," he said. "It's either in you, or it isn't."

Ben had survived one of the most savage orphanages in Sidney to grow up into the granite Adonis he was now.

Like a number of the men she knew, he was a superb cook. As a matter of fact, they made her a bit annoyed. There were few things she liked less than being made to feel, by a man, like a spare prick at a party in a kitchen. And Ben, in particular, did it all in a muscly, flat-footed sort of way that should have spelled disaster, except that she had forgotten his timing and his reflexes.

That night, after a cheese soufflé that visited her mouth like a cloud and an Aylesbury duckling that fell off the bone, its skin as crisp and brown as a seventy-year-old film producer's at the Cannes Film Festival, with black cherries and *mange-tout,* overlooking the now illuminated river, all its buildings floodlit against a benignly blue-black London sky wearing its jewels, she felt at a distinct disadvantage. After all, she was the one who was supposed to be pulling him. No wonder he had the reputation of bringing down any woman he aimed at.

As he was pouring her coffee, with a whisper of Delamain in her glass, she cleared her throat.

He got in first.

"All right," he said, "let's have it."

"You what?" she exclaimed, taken by surprise.

"You really will have to stop saying that, you know," he said. "It's dead common."

"Listen, Ben Maitland," she snapped back, "I've seen you with your ass hanging out your pants, so don't you come it with me . . ."

She saw the delighted smile break out on the rugged film-star face and realized she'd been had.

"Bastard!" she answered, instantly relaxing.

She set out her stall. "Look, Ben, as I told you, I've been given my own show. I can do whatever I want and I can pick my own team."

He sat watching her, his extraordinary blue eyes on her face. He'd always adored this kid, but there'd been nothing he'd been able to do about it. When the kid's ten and you're twenty-two, what the hell can you do? But when the kid suddenly blossoms into twenty-one and you're thirty-three, well then, that's a different story, as the baldy old sod in the fairy tale said.

"I know you earn enough to live like a prince," she was saying, "and I know you're probably better with your dukes"—looking at his scarred fists—"than your brain box . . ."

"Bollocks!" he exclaimed. "I'll lay odds I know my way around a computer keyboard better than you do. How d'you think I'm still around in my game?"

"Sorry," she said, grinning at having got her revenge, "but what I wanted to say is that I need a personal assistant. Someone who knows me and my background. Someone with contacts as good as mine, who knows how to dig and where and can put himself about because he's got respect. And someone"—the gray eyes met the blue full on—"who can look after me."

"Christ!" he said, softly. "It's as tight as that?"

He didn't know much about television. He knew there were areas in Light Entertainment where a certain brother had built up a heavy mob, which offered the stars protection whether they needed it or not. It was all done on the most tactful possible basis, of course, and he'd noticed that the brother was now even getting guest spots on the star's shows, buttressed by crawling compliments from his hosts. But that was Light Entertainment; he'd never heard of anything like that in the more serious areas of television that our Tara was in.

"No, not generally," said Tara, "it's just where I might be going."

It never even occurred to Ben to ask what her destination might be. He had taken it as it came all his life as far as his mates were concerned. If they were mates then, *ipso facto*, their credentials were good and any enterprise in which they were involved was automatically all right.

"I don't know what you make a year, Ben," she said, "except, looking at this place, it must be pretty horrendous. But I've got a bit of shoulder where I am and I think I could have a fair bash at matching it."

"They've got it, I'm worth it, but we both know they won't pay it, love," said Ben. "You just get as close to sixty grand as you can and I'll let 'em slide for the rest. I'm with you in any case, but don't let's tell 'em that, ay?"

He engulfed her hands in his.

"It's going to be a real pleasure working for you, love, the real gear," he said.

Gently, she withdrew her hands. This relationship had always walked a very fine line. If she let it happen, she and Ben could end up very complicated indeed.

"The accent is going to be on the work, Ben," she said.

"I know that," he said indignantly, "all I'm looking for is human warmth, contact, a bit of a cuddle now and then."

Tara laughed out loud.

"The thought of you going short of a bit of human warmth," she said. "Ben, you're breaking my heart."

He grinned ruefully. "I've always fancied you, you know that—and sooner or later . . ."

He had a hell of a smile, thought Tara.

"And now, I've got an early start back tomorrow," she said.

"Some people don't know when they're on to a good thing. Come with me," he said, holding out his hand to her as to a child. He led her to a bedroom which he had prepared for her. When she saw it, her reaction was a mixture of a squeal of delight and tender laughter. He had tried, in his masculine way, to create a girl's bedroom in forty-eight hours. He had bought a flounced and frilly bedspread, put up French-pleated curtains, suitable for a cathouse in New Orleans. But, most touching of all, half of him obviously still thought of her as ten years old, for he had covered the bed with Snoopy dogs, toy tigers, fluffy pandas and teddy bears. These reached her at a level at which he couldn't have guessed, for they were the kind of toys of which she'd been deprived since the disaster at the age of ten.

She threw her arms around his neck impulsively.

"Oh Ben, love," she cried, "you really are a love!"

He glowed with pleasure. "You really like it?"

"It's knockout—and that's the truth," she told him.

They kissed, just enough to be pleasant and close, not enough to start anything, then went separately to bed. Ben had to be up at dawn to dive off Tower Bridge and Tara was up at the same time for the drive back North.

She slept that night feeling enclosed and comforted in a way she hadn't experienced for years. In the morning they met hastily over the coffee percolator in the "fly me" kitchen, then went their separate ways.

Michael Patterson, telephoning Alhambra again, was frustrated to find that she had been in London, but was now on her way back.

In Manchester, Tara's first move was to raid the Mail Room. She grabbed Terry and Sid and Jean Soong and took them off to the canteen. She explained to the enraged supervisor that she was doing "a study in depth of the clerical worker in a technological society."

In the canteen she told the open-mouthed trio her plans for them.

Their initial reaction was shock. To them researchers were god-like intelligences moving on a different plane.

"Don't be bloody daft!" said Sid. "We can't do research— libraries and writing stuff down and all that."

"That's not the kind of research I want, thickhead," Tara explained patiently. "I want people who know the streets, the back alleys. I want operators, who know who's who and who's doing what. I want people like me."

"Yeah, but . . ." started Terry.

Tara interrupted ruthlessly: "Up to now, when I've had a real problem—I mean, for instance, like finding out about the bare-knuckle fights—who did I come to? You lot! Every top researcher in the building had tried to crack that one and hadn't got anywhere. Who did I come to to crunch Ed Friendly? You lot. The fence with his traveling van? You lot!"

"Ah, well . . . that's just because we happened to have the contacts," said Sid.

"And that's what research is all about," insisted Tara. "It's contacts. It's knowing the ground, knowing how to fix things, where to find out, having mates in useful places. My show is going to be rough. The ordinary researcher would be about as much use to me as a nun in a wrestling ring. You're what I need."

She pressed home her advantage as she saw their diffidence wavering.

"Listen," she said, "don't you give me a hard time. I'm going to have enough trouble selling you to everyone else. Well, I mean, I'm not worried about the bosses—Cyril Goldstein's given me a free hand. The hardest part will be getting you your union cards."

"How are you going to do that?" asked Terry, her screwed auburn curls gleaming. "The A.C.T.T. are tighter than a cow's ass in flytime about letting anyone in."

"And the researchers who are already in are going to nut us," added Jean.

"Don't you worry about that," said Tara, "that's my problem. Just get your nit-sized minds sorted out for doing some real work."

Tara went to see the A.C.T.T. shop steward. He was a craggy Aberdonian called Macrae. She wore a cheeky tartan skirt and waistcoat with a white stock spilling down the front of her blouse. Unfortunately, he was the kind of man who only became more awkward if he thought a girl had gone to trouble. He was brusque to the point of rudeness.

"Not a chance," he said. "We've got more than enough A.C.T.T.

researchers here; you should be able to find some of those to suit you. Paul Cranmer seems to do all right."

"Paul had me, you jug-eared pisspot," said Tara, storming out.

She sought out Sid and Terry and Jean.

"Spot of practice for you," she said. "I want everything you can find out about Macrae. You've got two days."

From the mass of material they produced—proving to herself that she had been right about them all along—she picked out two salient facts: his wife was a dragon and he was having a bit on the side with Jilly Pringle from the typing pool.

The next night she telephoned him where he was most vulnerable—at home. Mrs. Macrae answered and asked who wanted him. Tara pointedly ignored the question and asked again for her husband, deliberating stirring up the aggro. Macrae came to the telephone.

"Oh hello," she said, innocently, but loudly. "Jilly Pringle"—she pronounced the name with emphasis—"she told me you were so much nicer out of the office so I thought I'd try you again about those cards. It's three I want."

She didn't need to speak again. Macrae's scalp itched madly as the hot blood rose up and suffused it.

"I'll talk to the branch committee," he said gruffly and rang off, desperately preparing a bland face with which to meet his wife's interrogation.

At the other end Tara put down the telephone in the knowledge that she had got her heavy mob into the union.

The first thing she did next day was to throw Jean Soong in at the deep end. She bought her, on the company, a microcomputer and an account with Dialog, a powerful information-retrieval service. As ever, she held fast to the knowledge that information was power. And she knew that Jean Soong's untutored logical intelligence and computers were made for each other.

"Listen . . ." said Jean, her little face aghast with mingled delight and fear.

"You've always wanted one," said Tara, shortly. "Now get on with it. I want you up and running inside four weeks."

Tara wanted one last player on her team. A coolly elegant, upper-class girl called Suzy Blond-Hackett. She was Benenden and Somerville with all the trimmings and her father was with the Ministry of Defense in Paris. Since his family went back to the Crusades he was possibly the only DI6 man in the service the poor old Foreign Office could trust. She had an incisive mind with a cutting edge as sharp as Tara's and she was a universally respected researcher as well as a chiseled beauty. She wore tailored suits and feminine blouses. Her taste in men ran to very clean, handsome country boys.

Tara telephoned her internal number with a little trepidation.

"Hello, Miss Blond-Hackett," she began.

"You're that riotous Tara Stewart," Suzy interrupted. "I'd heard you were recruiting. I do hope you're ringing to ask me," she said in her smoked-crystal voice.

They met for lunch at a little bistro down the road, all red-checked tablecloths and red-cheeked waiters, competing to serve this double-blaze of blond beauty.

"What made you think I'd be asking you, then?" queried Tara, bluntly.

"Because you'd be hopeless with snobs and you know it," said Suzy, with equal candor. "To look at—fantastic: a Plantagenet at least. With people who are sure of their status, no problem. But the minute you open your mouth to a social climber, it's goodbye Charlie. Whereas I'd have them eating dog biscuits out of my shoe."

"That's what I reckoned," said Tara, relaxing in her chair. "You're in, then?"

"I should be very disappointed if I weren't."

A week later, Tara assembled her team in her new office. Ben, Suzy, Bella, her three old friends from the Mail Room, and Pam Johnston, who had got permission to second herself as permanent camerawoman to Tara's team, sat waiting expectantly.

Tara hadn't got a desk. She'd sweethearted a designer in Drama to do the room over as a kind of salon, with sumptuous easy chairs and sofas and coffee tables and concealed drinks cabinets and stereo. She'd got it all from some old Rock Hudson, Doris Day movie she'd seen on television and the designer had tactfully prevented it from going over the top.

"We're going to make Attila the bloody Hun look like a social worker," Tara opened up. "When we walk down streets I want to see villains tremble. That's what we're going to concentrate on—thugs, crooks, villains of every rotten variety. All the feeding maggots. There's more crime going on in this country than there is legitimate business; and there's more brainpower going into it, too. We can't actually put anyone inside ourselves, but if every program doesn't result in the scuffers taking action, or someone running like hell for the exits, I'm going to be disappointed. We're going to use craft, guile, tricks of every imaginable kind. We're going to play dirty. Now then, who wants to know what?"

"Is there likely to be violence?" asked Suzy, crisply.

"There could be," admitted Tara, "but not if we're clever. Why, does it worry you?"

"No," said Suzy, easily, "I just wondered if I should brush up on my judo."

"I'll give you a couple of refreshers on the mat if you like," grinned Ben.

"Then afterward we could practice some judo," said Suzy, laughing back. The drums were already beating there, noted Tara.

"Tara," said Sid, his crumpled face even more distorted with worry, "a lot of my mates are villains."

"And so are a lot of mine," she answered. "What we do is run the supergrass system. So long as they help us to nail the really nasty bastards, they get immunity—from us, that is. We obviously can't guarantee to keep the police off their backs. Mind you, if we do pick up a whisper the scuffers are getting interested in anyone who's helped us, we'll give him the office, so's he can get out of town for a while."

"We're going to start off small," Tara continued, "small but rotten—like Ed Friendly. Then we'll gradually build up; we don't want to startle the horses. And the two things we all have to remember is that what we need, all the time, is information, griff, travel, the inside track, and that it's not going to be like any documentary program you ever saw before."

"That," said Suzy, with dry relish, "is very, very true."

6

As the meeting broke up and Tara went out into Reception, she saw his back. He was talking urgently to Sheena, one of the girls on the desk. The shock wave hit her just as it had that first time in the hospital. The jolt in the stomach, the feeling that everyone must be able to hear her heart, the sense of alienation, as if she were wading through some strange medium, through which she couldn't see properly and which impaired the usual sharpness of her mind and her reactions. Above all, the sheer terror of showing her embarrassment to him. And there was no Maureen this time to slap her on the back. This was why she had deliberately kept away from him while she was setting up the project of her life.

Instinctively, she turned to run, but Sheena had spotted her.

"Oh, Miss Stewart," she called enviously, "there's someone here asking for you."

Sheena obviously hadn't even inquired his name. If he'd said Hitler, you could tell it would have made no difference to Sheena.

"Michael!" said Tara, with casual pleasure, wishing there was something she could hold on to and thinking she deserved a bloody Oscar, "Great! What brings you down this way?"

The blue blazed out at her furiously from behind the glasses.

"You know damned well what I'm doing here. I'm looking for you. What the devil have you been up to? You've been scuttling about the countryside like a manic squirrel!"

Just as the discovery of who he was had sobered her up last time, so did his use of the word squirrel this time. She called something else her squirrel. She amazed herself by almost giggling. "I've had things to do," she said, marveling at the ridge that ran all the way around his lips, "they've given me . . ."

"Your own show," he interrupted, impatiently. "I know. I must have read it a hundred times. Look, when can we meet? How about dinner tonight?"

No point in messing around now it had happened.

"That would be the gear," she said.

"I'll pick you up at nine," he said, making swiftly for the exit.

"You don't know my add—"

"Yes I do." And he was gone. Like a tall, tawny, impatient professor-god, who only came down to earth now and then when he fancied a bit of spare. In one way she wished it were so. It would make the ambivalent role she had to play easier. But she knew very surely that it was not so. She knew that what she felt for him, he felt for her; but because he was in the hunter's role, it made it easier for him to be more relaxed about it.

At nine o'clock sharp that evening, Bella, who had her own date at half past, peered out through the curtains at the car which had just pulled into the communal drive. It was the strangest-looking vehicle she had ever seen.

"He's here," she yelled to Tara in the bathroom. "I don't think much of his car."

Then Michael got out and Bella whistled.

"Oh, all right," she said, "I'd forgotten he looked like that!"

Tara hurtled out of the bathroom.

"Let him come up and collect you, that's my motto," said Bella.

"I don't want him to bounce off Rita," said Tara, nodding toward her aunt's room. "Being belted around the nut with a bagful of custard somehow doesn't seem to get an evening off to the right start."

She met him at the front door at his fourth ring on the entry-phone. The third one had been answered by Bella in an absurd stage-maid's voice, telling him that Miss Stewart would be down in a moment.

"Who the hell was that?" he asked, looking bewildered, as he greeted Tara.

"My bleeding maid, who else?" she answered scanning his face anxiously for a trace of a smile.

There was none. Was this an incomplete god? she wondered. Had they left out a sense of humor? It wasn't the first time she had wondered about it. He was always so earnest, so straight, the eyes unwavering.

He ushered her into the car, which was a great deal more luxurious inside than one would have suspected from the outside, and got in himself.

"You've got two choices," he said. "We can go to the French Restaurant at the Adelphi where I've booked a table which they'll hold indefinitely. Or we can go to a little place I've got over the water."

After all his time in America, she noted, he still used the local term for the Wirral Peninsula. The choice was obvious—short night or long one . . . very long one?

"If you'd prefer my place, my housekeeper has got everything prepared," he said, as if reading her thoughts. His housekeeper, she reflected. Such a nice, old-fashioned, safe ring to it. His housekeeper was probably a deaf-mute Vietnamese, who went to bed at eight-thirty.

"Your place," she heard herself saying.

Accidentally, he touched her knee as he slipped into "drive" and the shiver ran all the way up her thigh to her breasts. The car slid through the warm evening, Michael driving with what she would call, from her horsey days, "good hands." A new moon rose ahead through the windshield. She turned some money over in her purse.

"Mad money?" he inquired.

"Try finding a taxi in this lot," she shrugged, indicating the leafy lanes in which they were now embedded. "No, I'm superstitious, that's all," she explained.

"About us?"

"No," she said. She had misgivings about them, forebodings. But all she said was no.

His "little place" turned out to be the sort of unbelievable cottage, thought Tara, that you only ever saw advertised in *Country Life*. Nobody ever actually bought or sold them; they just advertised them in *Country Life* to see how nice they looked. Thatch flowed like amber down to and across the tops of the dormer windows; and roses, celandines and columbines looked as if their ambition was to throw a net around the rough-cast white walls and carry the place off. It had a well and a swimming pool and on its skyline were the sternly handsome Roman walls of Chester.

Michael had won it in a poker game at Harvard from Raymond Schlitzz, heir to one of the big old movie fortunes. His producer-father, flying over it once in his location-seeking helicopter, had decided, with tears in his eyes, that this was the place where he wanted to end his days, given orders there and then over the R.T. for its purchase and refurbishment and five minutes later had forgotten all about it in contemplation of a set of stills of his new Italian movie queen, her flesh as glossy as a peeled egg. When the papers came through a few months later, he strove to recapture the first fine foolish rapture, failed, and made it over to his son, Joe. Joe needed it just once: when he was deep in the hole to the Computer Kid, as they called Michael in the poker school. Michael took the pot and the cottage. Given a choice, he would have picked something less fero-ciously pretty, but he detested hotels, needed a base for his frequent trips to the Northwest administering the Foundation, and found it still in immaculate order and well-sited.

He parked under the great oak that sat in the middle of the greensward like a majestic, gnarled parasol and they walked to the door under an adolescent moon now so rich and creamy, hanging down over the thatch, that Tara felt she could have reached out and plucked a piece of it. She wondered idly if Michael had consulted the lunar calendar before choosing this date to come and make a dead set at her.

Her cogitation was overtaken by the sight of Mrs. Truscott, who opened the door to Michael's ringing. She was a lusciously rounded forty-five, honey-skinned and auburn-haired with a look in her brown eyes that spoke of a deeply romantic soul and a dedicated discipleship to Pan and all country matters, including those mentioned by Hamlet. She and Michael? No, not his type. But Tara knew that one look from those rich brown eyes had told her how it was between Michael and her and she sparkled with the delighted complicity of Juliet's nurse.

"Come in, my dears," she said, in her succulent Cheshire accent; "everything's ready for you."

"Thank you, Mrs. Truscott," said Michael. "This is Miss Stew-art. I think she might like to freshen up."

"Oh, I know Miss Tara Stewart, sir," she said. "I've seen every-thing you've ever done, m'dear, and I'm so much with you. You keep on giving 'em thunder, that's what I say."

"Thank you very much," said Tara, giving her one of those smiles that fastened people to her.

Tara freshened up in a powder room decorated by someone who had obviously been devoted to Beatrix Potter, then joined Michael in the sitting room. It was glowing with gold and russet fabrics and gleaming woods, with touches of crimson, a perfect foil for Michael's coloring. It was as if the whole ambience had been chosen to set him off, except that she knew he wouldn't bother. Nevertheless, as he leaned against the mantelpiece over a quietly chuntering log fire—even in this weather it struck a little chill in Cheshire at night—she thought how well judged was the glowing Lawrence Isherwood against which his handsome head was contoured. He had a whiskey, straight. That was right for him, too. Amber. She had a grenadine. She didn't drink much at night.

Michael was straight out with it.

"You know what happened to us back there in the hospital, don't you?" he demanded.

"You tell me," she said.

"The thunderbolt," he said. "That's what the Sicilians call it. The Victorians called it love at first sight. I've never believed in it. Until now."

"Yeah . . . well . . . that's as may be," she countered, eloquently. They were now in the dining room over some holy table—she couldn't remember which monks had eaten from it. "What about all them American birds?" she asked, over the Dublin Bay prawns, presented to them like an *objet d'art*, around a huge plate, by Mrs. Truscott, who promptly disappeared. "All those blond cheerleaders with the legs that meet over the top of their heads and the disposable knickers?"

"I never went in for cheerleaders myself," he said solemnly. "They had to spend too much time practicing."

Over the *carré d'agneau* with tiny roast potatoes and petit pois and all the mint sauce and red currant jelly—she always had both—her idiosyncratic palate could desire, he turn the tables on her.

"What about you?" he asked. "Child of the slums, target for every thrusting libido in sight—social workers, school friends, school friends' uncles. Your own uncles! Your own aunts! Sisters, nieces, stepbrothers, grandfathers, my God, girl, the mind boggles!"

It was the first sign of humor she'd seen in him. She hoped to God it was humor!

"To be honest," she said, "my brothers used to tell me they agreed with our Dad that I wasn't half as good value as our Mum."

The laugh started deep inside him and caused him to choke on his food.

"You're not pulling my fizzer with that one," he finally spluttered; "I've heard something like it before."

"Well, you were having a go at me," she said.

"I was doing it for a different reason," he said. "I took a short summer course at Harvard—how to get information out of people."

"You wasted your time," she told him. "Everything they taught you I've known since I was three. So has every kid in Liverpool. So has every kid in the Bronx. So did you, for God's sake, before they got hold of you and hygienized you and sent you back in a plastic packet—'Use before end of September 1989.' "

He absorbed the insult without visible damage and helped her to pudding: Cointreau-marinated poached peaches, glazed with caramel. Mrs. Truscott had left it on a side table with a pot of coffee made with fresh spring water before excusing herself and going to bed. Tara had a passing insight that it wasn't often a lonely bed.

"You still think I'm overhygienized?" he asked, forty minutes later. He had just "keeked" her, an action known well to them both since their youth, but which they would not have found easy to describe, with any degree of style, to interested third parties. They were rolling naked, in a state of semi-suffocation, in a billowing snowdrift of a down-filled, fresh-air-smelling four-poster bed with the curtains drawn.

They had got there by stages less than subtle. The charge which had originated the minute they saw each other had continued to build in their thoughts even while they were apart. It got a whole fresh input when they met that day and it had been like a reactor running wild ever since. Each time they had brushed each other in the car it had been like two bare wires shorting. Some day, thought Michael, the boffins would break down the phenomenon into its chemistry— or would it prove to be physics? And then we could forget all about oil, coal and nuclear fuel and run the world on it.

The tension had continued to build during the beautifully presented dinner. Tara had only the haziest idea afterward of what they had actually talked about. She remembered the bits when Michael had talked about his father, how he had the impression Shaun Patterson felt he had some kind of debt to pay to his place of origin. She remembered Michael's enthusiasm for the good he thought he was going to do with the Foundation's money. But all the time the real conversation was going on underneath, blood to blood, pheromones to pheromones, or whatever they were; she could hardly bear to touch her own skin and he began to think he was about to invent a new form of table-rapping—from underneath.

By the time they got up from the dining table it was after midnight. Michael and Tara looked at one another.

"It's late," he said.

"Yeah," said Tara, glancing at her watch.

"It's quite a long drive back," he said.

"Yeah," she answered. For the second time in her life she felt shy. This time she held down the blush.

"I had Mrs. Truscott prepare a room for you just in case. Would you like to see it? It's a pretty room. It's worth seeing, even if you decide not to stay."

"All right, then," she agreed.

They went up the curved and polished staircase to a landing over the hall. He showed her into a delicious small bedroom, all white wood and cabbage rose wallpaper with a lattice window and exquisite porcelain figurines in the deep embrasure.

"Wow! It's the gear!" she said.

"My bedroom's at the other end of the gallery," he said. "Would you like to see that?"

"Yeah, I wouldn't mind."

It was in Michael's room that the four-poster was. When Tara saw it, she laughed with delight, ran over and bounced on it. Michael came and sat next to her.

"I tell you what," suggested Tara. "I'll sleep in this one and you can have mine!"

"I've got a better idea," he said, quietly, "why can't we both sleep in this one?" and kissed her with great and deliberate ripeness on the mouth. From that moment on it was like two children let loose in a sweetshop. All the dammed-up weight of their need for each other exploded.

The first naked touch of their fine skins burned and their first coming together was almost childish in its haste. There was no time for finesse. They were both ready and had been for two hours and his flesh slid into hers like a homecoming. He was long and solid and he moved in with a majestic sureness, in and in and in and she could have sworn she heard something like a sigh from him as she tightened her muscles and embraced the powerful presence that now inhabited her. Their orgasm was like the first there ever was. Tara felt it radiate from the middle of her, right out to the edges of her body, to the cushions of her toes, to every hair in her scalp. That was the first time. They lay back, gasping from the fulfillment of a sensual dream. They talked nonsensical things about each other's faces and bodies; their fingers flickered about each other like flames, his along her polished thighs, hers counting the muscled ridges on his stomach, and soon there were intimations, stirrings; he suddenly doubled and squirmed like a serpent, his head suddenly where his hand had been a second before, his tongue flickering like a salamander's, and then he squirmed again and was within her again, this time differently, with one of her legs over his side, and he was reaching a different, shudderingly sensitive corner of her.

They sported for hours, leaping over each other like slippery dolphins, squealing and laughing, stifling each other's screams in the snowy sheets. And it was here that she learned for certain that he had a sense of humor. No man without a sense of humor could even have thought of some of the things he had done to her. And it was here, as she looked down at the tawny head pillowed on her marble-smooth stomach, that she knew that the love between them was rare and real.

In the knowledge there was dismay.

Tara's first program was *Skyway Robbery*. It opened with Tara's luminous screen presence.

"The program you are about to see is not a reconstruction," she said. "It was filmed as it actually happened. We'll be giving you one or two inside peeps on how we did it, but not everything. Anyway, you're all so fly these days, you probably know anyway."

The famous smile. A dissolve.

On screen appear two strapping young men in their middle twenties. They lounge outside a Post Office in Wavertree, Liverpool. It is Friday, Pensions Day. The two young men watch the old people coming out of the Post Office. Tara appears briefly on the screen.

"Going to mug them for their pensions money?" she asks. "Oh, no, they're after bigger bread than that."

Resume the two louts on the screen. They pick out an old lady with a bent back, follow her at a discreet distance. They reach a little huddle of mean houses. The louts look cheerful. They glimpse at the rundown houses as they pass. The old lady reaches the front door of her house, knocks the knocker. The louts linger on the other side of the street. A man of their own age opens the door and lets the old lady in. Disappointed, the louts move off swiftly. Tara: "The mark wasn't suitable. Back to the drawing board."

The louts lounge again outside the Post Office, each with one leg bent at the knee, foot flat against the wall. A few more pensioners stride out briskly, and then another likely candidate emerges—an old lady, obviously arthritic, one of her knobbly old hands on a stick. Looking more cheerful, the louts stroll off after her, chewing gum, hands suspended in the pockets of their bomber jackets. They stay well back, so as not to alarm her. She makes her way to a shabby little street, not unlike the first. She knocks at a door. It is opened by a little, spent old man of about her own seventy-five years. A zoom in to a close shot of the two louts shows them to be well-satisfied. They go from shot. Tara appears on screen.

"A digression," she says.

She puts up an inset picture of a roof. It's in very good order.

"This," says Tara, "is the old couple's roof—their name is Morgan, by the way. We took it just after the two louts went away. And here"—a bespectacled, tweed-suited man walks into shot—"is Mr. Anderson, a well-known chartered surveyor." She turns to him: "You inspected that roof at our request, did you, Mr. Anderson?"

"I did," said Anderson.

"And what did you think?"

"It was in very good condition indeed—remarkable. Perhaps a bit of pointing around the chimney wouldn't harm"—a grin—"but I'm a perfectionist: it's not really necessary."

"How much for the pointing—supposing they had it done?"

"Oh . . . thirty-five pounds, maximum."

"Thank you, Mr. Anderson." Big smile from Tara. She goes on: "And now, two hours later that same day."

We are back in the Morgans' little street. A battered white van draws into shot. On the side it bears the simple legend "Roofs." Whatever other lettering there has been has apparently been washed away with time. Louts one and two get out, dressed in well-worn dungarees, hammers professionally slung from their leg loops. They knock at the door of the old folks' house. Old Mrs. Morgan opens the door and steps out into the street. An anonymous, canvas-topped little van is parked across the way.

Again the film stops and again Tara intervenes.

"You're going to get sick of me," she says, "but we've got to go back a bit here. You see, when those two cowboys went away, we not only had a gander at the old folks' roof, we had a word with them and told them a little white lie. We told them we were doing a radio show about the life of an ordinary street and the kind of people who come to call. Mrs. Morgan agreed to take part and not to tell anyone about it—not even her husband. So we stuck a radio mike up her jumper and told her to forget about it, which she very soon did, as you'll see. We didn't tell her what we were really up to because there's a school of thought in physics, you know, that says you can't ever know the truth because you alter what you're examining by the very fact that you're examining it. Well, I think it's just the same in television—specially the kind I do. Anyway, watch on! As I said, two hours later . . ."

Tara disappears, the film resumes with Mrs. Morgan coming to the door and right out on to the pavement, as she has been told to do, "for the sound." It's really for the benefit of Pam Johnston, shooting from her canvas-topped truck.

"Hello, love. I'm Jack, this is Tom; we're from the roofing."

"You what?"

"The roofing, love," Tom takes it up. "We do all the roofs around here."

"Oh aye."

"We've had a look at yours, it's in a grotty old state, love. Practically illegal under the Health."

"It's what?"

"Oooh, it's horrible, the whole thing's rotten—wood, battens, slates . . . everything. I'm surprised it hasn't been down before this. Has the Inspector seen it?"

"What inspector?"

"And the chimney's in a shocking state. It's shot. Leaning right over."

Mrs. Morgan has started to fiddle nervously with the neckline of her dress, which is sending the sound man in Pam's truck crazy.

"The chimney?"

"It could come crashing straight through the roof at any time, without any warning, straight through your bedroom ceiling, fall on you and kill you while you're lying in bed; they weigh a lot, do chimneys, you know."

Mrs. Morgan has forgotten all about the "radio documentary," is getting more and more agitated.

"I'll have to go and speak to Mr. Morgan," she says, dithering.

She goes indoors. We stay on "Jack" and "Tom."

"I reckon we're in here," says Jack.

"You reckon?"

"Got her buzzing like a blue-assed fly. She'll want us up on that roof faster than bleeding Superman."

"How much you reckon we can take her for?"

"These old gits, they been stuffing it away in the Post Office for bloody centuries. We'll ask for eight hundred, let 'em beat us down to seven fifty."

Meanwhile, the sound man is going ape. He's got an acoustic rifle trained on Jack and Tom, a fiendishly temperamental piece of equipment in the first place, while he's trying to get a level on the radio-miked conversation going on inside the house, which he's got rolling on another tape.

The viewers, of course, know none of this. What they hear is the viciously heartless conversation of Tom and Jack and the ago-nized conference that's going on inside the Morgans' house, cleverly intercut.

"Chimney pot through the roof? That could go right through the house," Mr. Morgan is saying.

"That's what they said," Mrs. Morgan answered, "and then there's the Health—they say they could come down on us for it. They said it was like a rotten apple up there, ready just to collapse in on us any time."

"I thought Joe done it all for us," said Mr. Morgan, "before he went to Canada. He was a good man at all that, our Joe."

"That's a long time ago," said Mrs. Morgan, "things can happen. I'm worried sick, George."

"Well, I can't get up there and have a look," said her husband with a bitter helplessness. His voice trembles with fright and panic. "How much they say it's going to be?"

"I don't know, but Maggie—her who used to live in Bootle— she reckoned her daughter's cost her a thousand pound."

"That's over half our life's savings!" You could hear the anguish despite the rustling of the radio-mike.

"I know. But what if the roof falls in on us? Where are we then?"

There's a silence. All the time, the camera is on the cocky louts outside.

Finally: "You'd better go and talk to them," says Mr. Morgan.

Mrs. Morgan comes out through the front door: "He says how much?"

"Well normally," says Tom, "a new roof, which is what you've got to have, well on a house like yours, would run you fifteen hundred quid."

Pam's camera doesn't miss the zoom-in on Mrs. Morgan's gnarled old hand, grabbing at the window sill for support.

"But," Tom goes on smoothly, "we're quick workers, so we can do it for less, say a thousand."

"And," adds Jack, "wink, wink, if it's cash, then we forget the V.A.T. and make it eight fifty."

"Look," says Tom, "you're a nice lady. Let's forget the fifty and make it eight hundred."

"Seven hundred," says Mrs. Morgan, promptly, her distress momentarily forgotten in the instinctive challenge of bargaining.

"Seven fifty," says Tom.

"Done," says Mrs. Morgan.

"By hell, you know how to drive a hard bargain," says Tom, admiringly. He scribbles on a pad. "If you could just sign that, agreeing to the price."

Mrs. Morgan peers at it and signs.

"We'll start first thing tomorrow," says Jack. "It's roofing weather."

The louts drive off in their van and Mrs. Morgan rushes indoors to recount her triumph to the still-shaking Mr. Morgan.

Dissolve and Tara reappears.

"And that's where we came back in," she said. "I immediately called on the Morgans, explained how they were being had, showed them pictures of their perfect roof and the surveyor's report and asked if they'd play along with us. From then on, they were tigers. Watch on! It's next morning."

Tara dissolves. The film resumes and the white van drives into shot. Since they're only two-up, two-down little houses, the louts don't need scaffolding or cradles. They use ladders. Up go buckets of slates and wooden battens and a good deal of other "flash," watched by Mrs. Morgan from her front room window. Then for the next day and a half, watched by Pam's pellucidly sharp camera from a roof across the street—facility fee to householder £100—Tom and Jack play cards, smoke endless cigarettes, listen to their transistor and occasionally make hammering noises with their free hands while reckoning the odds against three nines as opposed to a possible full house.

The end of the second day they come down, knock at the door.

"There you go, love, all done," says Tom. "Take an Exocet missile to get through that lot now. Best roof outside of St. George's Hall. Got the money, love?"

"Oh, no," says Mrs. Morgan, blithely.

Tom looks at Jack, then back at Mrs. Morgan: "You what?"

"Well, you see," says Mrs. Morgan, "it's in the old 'Buildy,' isn't it—the Building Society. And they need fourteen days' notice before they'll shell out."

"Fourteen days!" yells Tom. "Listen, we've got commitments. You'll have to come up with it some other way!"

"Can't be done, love," says Mrs. Morgan. "That's all we've got."

"Listen," says Tom, "we can just as easily bash that sodding roof down again, you know—no trouble at all, so don't you try and play tricks with me, you crafty old bitch."

"I'm not playing no tricks and what's more, I object to your bleeding language," says Mrs. Morgan. "Now piss off and come back in a fortnight when I've got the money." .

"You'd better have it, sow-face," snarls Tom, "if you want a house left, never mind a roof!" They both kick the wall of the house with their steel-capped boots, slam into their van and roar out of shot.

Tara's first show was programmed for the Sunday after next, in prime time. The nation had been psyched up by heavy promotion to watch. Tom and Jack were in their local pub, high on anticipation, precelebrating the seven hundred and fifty pounds they were due to collect the next day from Mrs. Morgan, when the program hit the air on the screen at the back of the bar. They did not at first recognize themselves, which is commonly the case.

Then Tom slowly changed color. Jack, an inveterate leaner on bars, eased himself off and sat down slowly, feeling behind him for a chair as his eyes remained glued to the screen. The customers watched, fascinated, their eyes flicking between the screen and the sickly faces of Tom and Jack. When the show ended, there was a full half-minute's silence while the credits rolled. Everyone desperately fought down a giggle; you didn't mess with Tom and Jack. Then Tom smashed his glass against the bar, Jack kicked over his chair as he got up and they barged out without a word. Halfway down the street they heard the gale of laughter that blew out of the pub doors after them.

First thing next morning, the doorman at Alhambra was smashed to one side as he asked the two bomber-jacketed thugs their business and a terrified receptionist was held off her feet against a wall until she told them where they could find Tara Stewart. They burst open the door with her name on it and found themselves facing a terrified secretary in an outer office:

"Where's that cow Tara Stewart?" demanded Tom.

"She's not in yet," said the frightened girl, "but I can get you her P.A."

"She'll do for now," said Jack.

The girl pressed a buzzer and out of another door came this block of concrete in blue jeans and a blue T-shirt and there was something about the way he moved that put a kink in your colon.

"I'm Ben Maitland, Miss Stewart's P.A.," he said. "What can I do for you gentlemen?"

Physical aggro was clearly out. Admittedly, they were two to one, but you could break your knuckles on this joker, besides which he was holding a heavy round ebony rule in his right hand and slapping it into his leather-like left palm.

"Why pick on us, you bastards?" the one called Tom demanded.

Ben spoke in a reasoned tone of voice.

"Because you are filth," he said. "You pick on the old and the weak. You pick on people who are crippled. You pick on people who are confused and frightened. You're a pair of turds. That's why we picked on you."

Tom made an instinctive forward lurch. It was the fact that Ben didn't even move, as well as his own second thoughts, that stopped him.

"Who shopped us?" demanded Jack.

"Nobody shopped you," said Ben. "You two have been at it a long time. We do our homework. We heard about you and we found you. And I'll tell you another thing: you're not only filth, you're stupid. You should have run for it last night. The minute you muscled your way in here someone would have called the police. You two shitehawks are about to get nicked."

As though on cue, the door opened behind them and a sergeant and two constables came in. The constables put armlocks on the two louts and started to hustle them out.

"All right then," said the sergeant, "let's be having you."

" 'Ere, bloody gerroff," shouted the one called Tom. "What's the charge?"

"We'll talk about all that down the nick," said the sergeant. He touched his hat to Ben. "Morning, sir," he said solemnly.

"Morning, sergeant," replied Ben, with equal gravity.

As they were propelled, struggling and cursing, down the corridor, they met Tara, on her way in, coming the other way. Tom spat in her face. Tara, with a snake-strike speed learned at school, unzipped his jeans and ripped open the retaining stud at the top. He was bundled the rest of the way out with his trousers round his knees.

"I'll have you for this, you slag!" he screamed as he went through the final swing doors, the policemen using him as a kind of ram with which to open them.

"I think you'll find it's the other way round," murmured Tara to herself as she went into her office, wiping the spittle from her face.

They went down for attempting to obtain money under false pretenses from Mr. and Mrs. Morgan. They asked for forty other offenses of the same nature to be taken into consideration. They got four years. Tara was in court. After they had been taken down to the cells, she quietly asked the senior policeman present if she could have a word with the one called Tom.

"Since you did our job for us," he grinned, "I don't see how I can very well say no. But what d'you want him for?"

"It's just something he might be able to tell me that he wouldn't tell you," she said, only half lying.

A constable unlocked the cell door in the dank block beneath the court.

"If you want any help, miss," he said, "I'll be right outside."

"Not too close," said Tara, "it could put him off." She carefully avoided specifying off what it might put him.

Tom was scrunched up against the graffiti-spattered green and cream painted brickwork of the far wall. As she entered in clinging leather breeches, glossy boots and a green silk shirt, he rose and hawked, as if to summon up another packet of offensiveness to launch into her face.

"You do," she warned "and I'll give you a kick in the balls that'll put two bumps on the top of your head!"

The gunsmoke was drifting in her eyes and Tom was an expert reader of body language. He swallowed.

"I know who you are now," he said. "You're Jed Stewart's stinking little prawn and I want to tell you something: I'm fucking glad he was fitted up. I'll do a bit over two years with remission and parole. Your old man's in for good! I couldn't be more bloody chuffed. I hope he rots away like a stranded fucking whale!"

The look on Tara's face made his bowels turn over. He realized that her coming here like this had been a deliberate provocation and that he had fallen into some sort of trap. Her answer was deadly in its quietness. She ignored the rhetoric and went straight to the simple question.

"How do you know my old man was fitted up?" she asked.

He saw instantly what the trap had been and he dived straight into every thick-headed villan's funk-hole.

"I don't know nothing," he said.

"That won't do, you stupid berk," she countered. "You just told me."

"I just said it to get you mad."

"Listen, po-head," she told him, patiently, "I didn't shoot you down by accident. I know you had something to do with framing my father. I *know* it, freak-face!"

"You're off your trolley," he said, trying to summon up a derisive laugh.

The reason she knew it, which she was not about to tell this insect, was that ever since Michael had told her about the odd people who came to ask his father for a handout, she had paid an all-female private detection agency, Security Sheilas, in London, out of her own income, which was now considerable, to photograph anyone going into Shaun Patterson's Belgravia flat who didn't look right in those surroundings and send her regular batches of pictures. She then put Sid and Terry and Jean, under Ben Maitland, on to looking for the faces in the right pubs, clubs, gyms and boxing halls they all knew so well and finding out what their particular line of business was at the moment. Tom had had the misfortune to be the first one they'd nailed. Of course, Tom could have been putting his little bites on Patterson in respect of services in some other connection, but he wasn't, because he'd just given away the fact that he knew about her father's framing. She could have shattered his defenses completely by telling him she knew about his connection with Patterson, but that would have been bound to get back to Patterson and her strategy didn't allow for Patterson being sure she was gunning for him quite so soon. She decided to use intimidation.

"Listen," she said, "you've got a choice. You can either tell me, or you can tell my Dad. You'll be going to Walton Gaol. My Dad's in Walton Gaol. Let me tell you about my Dad. He was a hard man when he went in. And he's been getting harder every hour. He pumps iron every day of his life and there's hatred in every press of the weights. When you go in there I'm going to tell him who you are and what I think you know. Either you tell him, or he'll put his fist through your head like a hammer going through a melon. Or you can tell me now. If you tell me, you've got my word that I won't even mention you to him."

He was silent. Then he asked: "How do I know what your bloody word's worth?"

"I mix with a lot of your sort in my job," she said. "If it once got around that I don't keep my word, I'd be finished."

Again, he was silent, his dilemma churning in his head. He made up his mind: "Just before the Mersey Tunnel job this wacker comes up to me in a pub. He wants a delivery made. It's this computer thing. I've got to hide it in a barn on this farm Aintree-way, at night, and nobody's got to know. There's two hundred quid in it for me. Well, soon as I read the evidence about how they'd found the computer on Stewart's farm and it connected him up to the job, I knew he'd been set up."

"Who set him up?" She knew he wouldn't tell her and she didn't need him to, anyway, but she knew he'd expect her to ask.

"I don't know. Honest to God, I don't."

"What did he look like?"

"A big fellow with a broken nose."

She knew him, from the photographs. He was one of Patterson's pensioners, too.

"Fine," she said. She rose abruptly from the table where they'd been sitting. He got slowly to his feet, too.

"Is that all you want to know?"

"That's all," she said. For now, she thought.

"And you won't tell your old man nothing about me."

"You have my word," said Tara.

"If you ever quote me," he said, "I'll deny every word of it."

"I know you will," she said.

As she went, she capped the tiny microphone encapsulated in one of the locks of her slim executive briefcase and used the knob on the other lock to switch off the tape recorder inside.

She went back to her office and brooded again over the latest batch of pictures from her detective agency, Security Sheilas. There was something puzzling her. In two of the last three batches there had been a strangely nebulous figure. It seemed, bizarrely, to have no face. Admittedly, it always appeared at night, but the Sheila girls used light enhancement techniques for their night shots. They brought up faces sixty percent as clearly as daylight. This face eluded their technology. Under the shadow of the wide, old-fashioned hoodlum hat there was . . . what? She had a teasing notion just beyond reach that she ought to know and that if she could only fill in the spectral outlines which were all the camera could catch, much else would be made clear. She made a note to ask the Sheilas to concentrate on the mysterious visitor—without getting too close and being rumbled; then she locked the photographs away and drove home in her XJS. She was conscious that with what she had got on tape today she had started to break through toward her walled-up father.

It was when Paul asked Tara what she had in mind for her next assignment that the trouble started.

"We're laying for a right villainous bastard who should be dropped in the Mersey with lead boots on . . ." she began, enthusiastically.

"Hey, wait a minute," Paul said, "crime again?"

"Yeah," said Tara, brightly, "I'm going to specialize in it."

"Over my dead bloody body you are!" exclaimed Paul. "I didn't train you into the finest documentarist we've got to throw you away on thugs. I blame myself. I should have known when I heard the kind of research team you were putting together—Ben Maitland, the Mail Room Mafia, my piranha-type ex-wife. What kind of a research unit is that?"

They were sitting in his cozy untidy office, which filled her with a nostalgia for their early days together. She bit it back behind her teeth. Nostalgia doesn't win battles and she had a feeling she was in one.

"The same kind I was to you," she snapped. "They know things that other people don't. They can get things done that other people can't. They've got contacts other researchers aren't usually expected to have. They're the kind I need for the job I want to do."

"Oh, come on, Tara, I want this department to reflect the whole of life, not just one murky corner of it."

"It won't just be one corner!" she cried. "You've got other documentarists doing other things. I'm just one!"

"You're my star!" yelled Paul. "I can't waste you on sordid crime."

"Oh, yes, it's sordid when I do it—what about when you did it? What about Ed Friendly? What about the bare-knuckle Circuit? It wasn't sordid then, it was bloody exciting, wasn't it!" she shouted back.

"And come to think of it," said Paul, bouncing up and down in his chair like some huge, furry toy, "it was you who steered me into those programs. You look like an angel, but what you really like is getting down and rolling in the gutter!"

"You said those were the best programs you'd ever made, you great bald ponce!"

"I say every program I do is the best I've ever made!" he roared, with a sudden surge of insight. "Anyway, I'm not having my star spending every program rolling in the mud."

"I'd have thought you'd have liked that—hippopotamuses do!"

"Hippopotami!"

"And hippopota-fucking-you!" she cried, storming out and slamming the door.

It went up to the Program Controller, Peter Casey, a stocky, black-eyed, black-haired, gray-suited former director with a talent for diplomacy and, like Paul, fundamentally a gentleman. He took the ultimate responsibility for the output of the whole station. He had a spare, elegant office in chrome, suede, and what Tara called knitted porridge walls with one Lowry and one Sutherland. He spoke quietly and persuasively.

"You say crime, perversity, the violation of society is what you do best, Miss Stewart," he opened, as she sipped her coffee. "Yet the program which has, perhaps, made most impact of all was the one you made lying on your back in hospital, showing the more compassionate and supportive side of human nature."

Oh, smooth, thought Tara, and clever—too clever to be taken in by her false-naïve act. She'd have to meet him on his own ground, but she'd have to break that soothing rhythm, too.

"Oh, come on, Mr. Casey," she said. "Daz-white nurses and godlike doctors and pale little girls with dark circles under their eyes, looking brave—you could put that on opposite *Emmanuelle Joins the Cistercians* and get a rating. Besides, it wasn't all compassion and supportiveness, if you remember. In some respects I took that hospital apart—remember the fist fight over my trolley? There was an investigation afterward by the Department of Health; it wasn't the little tranquilizer you seem to remember it as."

Hello, thought Peter Casey, he'd been careful not to underestimate this dashing young lady opposite him and now he found that's exactly what he'd done. He was in the ring with something to be reckoned with here.

"Perhaps the precise reasons are open to debate, but the fact of the impact of that program is undeniable," he countered, "and it certainly wasn't about crime."

"Aren't we confusing two things here, like?" asked Tara. "I'd like to know what you mean when you say 'impact.' If you mean it's that program that got me this job, yes, that's true. But if by 'impact' you mean ratings—and that's what I bet you generally do mean—then the show on Ed Friendly beat it by three points."

And she'd done her homework, too. He was beginning to see what was behind that glowing presence on the screen. He'd suspected her words and her thinking were done for her by her researchers, and when Cyril G. had first told him he was going to star her, he had had his doubts. Glamour, in its true sense, which was what she had, finally wears thin on television if there has to be a puppet master behind it, working it. There had been enough examples of T.V. lovelies beginning to believe their own publicity, deciding to go out on their own without backup and falling flat on their smooth little faces. But it had become obvious to him in the last five minutes that what one saw on the screen with this girl was the whole person with a twelve cylinder personality informing and powering the image. There was no way of conning this person. He was going to have to rely on the ultimate, most horrible weapon of all. Honesty.

"Miss Stewart," he said, "I'm going to be frank with you." Uh-oh, thought Tara, here it comes: the biggest lie since Ananias went out of business. It was a miscalculation that was nearly her undoing because it caught her with her guns pointing the wrong way.

"You are a very beautiful girl; I'm not trying to flatter you or woo you, we both know it to be a fact," he said.

You speak for yourself, thought Tara.

"Now the simple truth is that we want to exploit that beauty by making you a kind of angel of the screen—by associating you with the tranquil, uplifting, heartwarming aspects of life. Having you deal with people who have conquered great adversity, or created great loveliness, or given great help to their fellow man. We want you to create a haven from the ugliness of life, its grittiness, grottiness, spleen, anger, worry, stink—a segment every week where people can slip into a kind of paradise. That, Miss Stewart, is what we want."

Taking her by surprise, as he did, her heart nearly went out to him—until she caught it and dragged it back. Here was a man who was not afraid to sound like Billy Graham on a bad day. She admired him. He had told her the truth. It was up to her to do the same in return.

"Mr. Casey," she said, "I am not into the business of providing fallout shelters from life for people to crawl into. I want them to know about life. I want them to know the things that can come out of the woodwork at them. I want them to learn how to protect themselves against the shits out there, not teach them to curl up into a bundle and pull the pillow over their head. Most of all, I want to use this fantastic weapon we've got in our hands to blast those bastards who feed off the rest of us out of existence. If you want a tube of electronic Valium, Mr. Casey, you'd better get yourself another girl."

She put down her coffee and walked out. Casey, still adjusting to someone meeting honesty with honesty, could think only of how exactly the sway of her hips could be explained anatomically.

Now, to Cyril Goldstein's disgust, the dispute had reached Board level. Cyril G. might be God, but he still had his Principalities and Powers, his angels and archangels to carry with him. He often sighed, thinking of the old days when he used to run the place like the corner shop, with one errand boy and a bike. Now he had peers and admirals (retired) and, worst of all, lawyers and chartered accountants, quacking around him like a paddle of ducks, honking about shareholders' rights and Public Accountability around the handsomely gleaming, boat-shaped boardroom table. He generally managed to do exactly what he wanted, but it was an expenditure of energy and time which he could well do without. Today, on the Tara Stewart affair, he sensed that something was different. The matter had been brought up independently by one of the damned accountants, John Pannter, and Goldstein could tell he had been lobbying in advance of the meeting.

At the moment Admiral Pucey was on the air in the blue-carpeted, walnut-paneled room, his crimson cheeks attributable to the dedicated ingestion of port rather than to anger.

"I understand that this girl has issued some kind of ultimatum," he said. "Well, we can't have that kind of thing."

"Can't have the lunatics running the asylum, what?" contributed the attenuated Lord Broga. He looked like an El Greco and was under the impression he was a wag.

"When I gave Tara Stewart the status she now has," said Cyril, "I promised her a free hand."

"But was that wise?" asked Pannter. He always asked his most barbed questions with a cherubic smile on his pink, plump cheeks. "A girl of very limited experience?"

"What's more," asked Pewrry Lucas, a heavy-bellied lawyer—member of many boards—"had you the right, without consultation?"

"My rights I don't get wrong," said Goldstein. "I am the chief executive, chairman and principal shareholder in this company. I don't have to consult this Board every time I buy a paper clip."

"It's rather more than buying a paper clip, isn't it?" said Pannter. "I understand that this girl . . ."

"Miss Stewart," said Goldstein.

" . . . this Miss Stewart has set herself up as a kind of one-woman vigilante squad on a crusade against crime. We have a police force for that. It is no part of the duty of television to act as a law enforcement agency."

"Miss Stewart," said Goldstein, "as a documentary reporter, has decided to make crime her special study. There is nothing extraordinary about that. She is not taking the place of the police force. She is infringing nobody's rights."

"I understand," said Lord Broga, "that there was a prosecution as a result of her last program."

"There was, indeed," said Goldstein. "Two very nasty specimens were put away."

"It doesn't feel right," said Broga, "it's turning television into something it was never meant to be."

He'd forgotten that when television itself was first mooted as a possibility he had been of the opinion that it was never meant to be, either. It was the mention of the kind of director's fee he might expect as a member of this Board that had magically changed his mind.

"Her viewpoint, her methods, the consequences," said Pannter, "they're all so radical I don't think we can let them go through just on the nod. I think we need a working party on this. We need a paper presented to us examining all the implications before we can make a decision."

There was a murmur of agreement around the table. Goldstein felt the weight of conservatism on the board swinging against him. He knew that once Pannter's suggestion was adopted, that was the end of Tara's show. It would be lost in a sea of paper. He sighed as he started to arm his ultimate weapon.

"It's beginning to seep through all the words, words, words," he said, "that I am beginning to lose the confidence of this Board . . ."

At which point the double doors at the end of the room burst open and Tara stalked in. She was wearing a white silk Valentino shirt, skintight plum velvet jeans, a matching belt and delicate calf-length boots in the same color. Her hair was a torrent of polished gold and around her throat flew her blue silk scarf. She looked like a lithe young Garbo striding on to a film set. Goldstein grinned inside himself. Only someone who looked like that could get away with this, but how the hell had she got around the old dragon who guarded those doors, he wondered. He looked at the Board as their collective jaw dropped, their collective eye bugged and their collective Old Adam stirred. She stopped at the vacant end of the half-filled table where everyone could see her. The heads were all pointing toward her like minnows in a stream.

"Gentlemen," she said, "I understand you're talking about me."

Pannter was the first to recover.

"How do you know what we've been talking about?" he challenged.

"I'm an investigative journalist," she responded. "I wouldn't be much good if I didn't know that. Also, I was listening outside the door."

While they caught their outraged breath, she pressed on: "Every eleven minutes in this city someone is burgled. Every nine minutes someone is mugged. Every half hour someone is conned. Every twenty minutes a car is nicked. Once every forty-eight hours a bank is knocked over. And that's just the petty stuff. It's the same everywhere. The police can't cope; they need all the help they can get. It's time the victims, which is the population at large, stood up and provided that help. Television is the most powerful tool for exposing villainy anyone ever invented. I'm using it to do just that."

There was a pause. The Board members, men of wide experience, were recovering their sangfroid. Pannter turned away from the mesmerizing image of Tara toward his colleagues.

"Miss Stewart has said it all," he pointed out. "She talks as if she's some self-appointed avenging angel. I repeat that it's the police's job to deal with crime. We can't have everyone going about playing cops and robbers. That's the way to anarchy."

There was a murmur of assent.

But Tara hadn't walked into the confrontation empty-handed. As soon as she'd got wind of the meeting of the Board she'd had her whole team, including Jean Soong on-line with her micro to "Dialog," turning over every member of it, supplying her with everything from descriptions of personal appearance to intimate biographies. She turned now to Pannter.

"Mr. Pannter, you're an accountant, aren't you?" she asked; "chartered eighteen years ago?" That brought his head around to her again with a snap.

She knew him by sight, she knew what he did, she knew when he'd been chartered. What the hell else did she know? Someone who did her research that thoroughly was more than the plausible talking doll he'd taken her for.

"In all that time," she said, "have you never done what you call the police's job? What about Smith and Smith in 1979 when you audited the books and found that one of the partners had had it away with nine hundred thousand quid? Didn't somebody go to jail over that? Did anyone criticize you for playing cops and robbers?"

She turned to the stringy Lord Broga, his turkey neck flushing slightly as the level gray eyes appraised him.

"And what about you, Lord Broga? Put me right if I've got it wrong, but didn't your gamekeepers catch a total of nine poachers on your estate in Leicestershire in the last year? And weren't they all handed over to the police? Isn't that a kind of private police force?"

The Board members started to shuffle about in their seats. Whom was she going to pick on next? What else did she know and about whom and what kind of thing?

"Don't get me wrong," Tara went on. "I'm not knocking anyone. I think it's great that people are prepared to act on the side of the law. I mean, they're doing a public service, aren't they? Well, I was always told that television is a public service, maybe the most powerful of them all. It's a weapon the criminal fears and hates and if you're going to deprive Joe Public of its use against crime, then this station won't be a public service, it'll be a public disgrace."

She had watched the Admiral turning more and more magenta in the face. Now he bawled down the table: "You've got a confounded nerve, whoever you are—I've never seen your damned program anyway—coming in here and lecturing us like a bunch of raw recruits on our duty. Who the devil d'you think you are? We know our duty, I hope, without being told it by the likes of you!"

"Oh, I know you personally know your duty all right, Admiral," said Tara. "Wasn't it you who court-martialed his own brother and had him thrown out of the service? And didn't an inquiry later prove him innocent?" She paused just long enough. "That was after he died in a car crash while he was drunk."

The Admiral's color subsided to the shade of the white blotter in front of him. Tara swung around and left the room: "Good day, gentlemen."

There was no further discussion. A dense and embarrassed silence was broken by Cyril Goldstein moving "Any other business." There was none and the meeting broke up.

Five minutes later Cyril G. came into Tara's office, where she was sitting quite still.

"You shouldn't have done that to the Admiral, you know," he said, gently.

"I know!" she groaned. "But I sensed that he could turn them around again—against me. I couldn't afford to lose. I couldn't!"

"Don't be too hard on yourself," he said. "We've all had to be street fighters in our time. Anyway, half of us already knew that story about him. I won't ask how the devil you came to have it up your sleeve."

One viewer who had watched *Skyway Robbery* with the most avid interest was Shaun Patterson. He'd shot up in his chair the minute he'd seen Tommy Lane. Had Tara Stewart picked on him by chance or did she know something? He couldn't believe it was chance. But the one thing he could not do was put out any feelers. The world of crime was the most notorious caldron of gossip. The word would be out in five minutes and, if he had Tara Stewart pegged correctly, she would be aware within ten. The safest thing would be to assume the worst, but neutralize her respectably. He'd finally rung someone he owned, an accountant called Pannter, member of the Alhambra board. He'd instructed him, without giving him reasons, to see if he could mount a boardroom coup against the bitch.

She had bushwhacked Pannter, wiped him out, almost as if she'd been waiting for him. Had she been waiting? Did she have some inside source of information? Michael? But Michael didn't know anything. Did he? He'd ground away at the problem all night after getting Pannter's report.

This morning, in vivid golf gear of yellow trousers, pink sweater and purple shirt to promote the mood, he was trying to practice his putting in his fifty-foot drawing room in preparation for the Pro-Am Celebrity Golf Tournament. It was no use. He threw down his putter on the smooth Chinese gold carpet and strode along the corridors that led to Michael's *pied-à-terre*, rang his bell. Michael came to the door in the tracksuit that was his work-at-home outfit.

"Are you still seeing that slag Tara Stewart?" Shaun asked abruptly. He had used the offensive noun deliberately. He wanted to read Michael's face.

"I don't know what the hell it's got to do with you," replied Michael, "but no, as a matter of fact, I'm not."

Shaun was glad to see that not a muscle flickered on his face nor did his pupils enlarge by so much as a micro-millimeter.

"And if you want to talk," Michael went on, "don't stand out there in the hall, looking like a bad sunset. Come in."

Shaun grinned. Christ, he loved this cool son-of-a-bitch of his! How often he'd ached to tell him how he'd fixed that bighead Jed Stewart, to garner the approbation of that finely tuned mind for a clever coup. But he knew that was the surest way to lose him for good.

"No, I won't interrupt," he said, hearing the sound of typing in the background. "It was just one of those things, you know."

He grinned again and went. Michael returned indoors thoughtfully. What his father had forgotten in his plan to read Michael's face was that he was dealing with the undisputed poker champion of Harvard. For the fact was that he had, indeed, been seeing Tara Stewart; except that "seeing" was a totally inadequate word to describe the experience of being with Tara. He was besotted with her, bewitched as if by some psychedelic scent she gave off. Every weekend he would arrow up the motorway in his Lagonda to her spectacular new flat at Ainsdale, overlooking the National Nature Reserve, where Bella and Aunt Rita still lived with her. He had bought Aunt Rita's soul by taking up with him each time a bottle of Jim Beam sour mash Bourbon. It was eighty-six percent proof. The first time she tasted it, she made the mistake of doing so after a hard day's work on the ordinary stuff. She poured herself her usual four-finger slug and downed it as if she were pouring it into a bucket. Her eyes seemed to revolve in their sockets. "Now there," she proclaimed, ". . . there is a blurry drink a blurry woman can feel in her belly!" Upon which her right knee suddenly gave way as if someone had kicked it from behind and she subsided gracefully sideways to the floor, smiled beatifically, twitched once, then rolled over on to her back and lay there like a twenty-two-stone beanbag. Which was exactly the view taken by Bella's King Charles spaniel, who scrabbled on to her, found a particularly comfortable fold of flesh and joined her blissfully in sleep.

In his electronically wondrous Lagonda Michael transported Tara to some of the most beautiful places on earth. And in each of them they loved each other.

He introduced her to the Lake District, which must have been, he said, where God sat, in a bubble outside of time and space, while he wondered whether to create a world. And the first time she saw The Tarns, near Coniston, one lake that used to be three, on a still day, the water like a blue-green sapphire, and felt an almost dread, hushed serenity she thought that he was right.

He pointed out the mountains, the Red Screes, the Langdale Pikes, the Helvellyns. They brooded like thunder turned into stone. He told her that a poet called Wordsworth, needing a father, had made them into father-totems for himself in his poetry—tall, brooding, terrible yet tender. Tara reasoned secretly to herself that if he'd had a father like Jed Stewart, he mightn't have needed the mountains; mightn't even have written his poetry. But when Michael quoted long passages of it to her, she was glad that he did write it. And she became achingly conscious of just how much she had missed in that killing ground they called a school.

They stripped naked and plunged into The Tarns. They tried to make love in its clear waters, but however much she coiled her round and slippery limbs around his slim body, the deadly chill of the water tamed Toby, as he called his usually all-conquering penis, into something you might find in a prawn cocktail. They had to wait until they climbed out and took shelter under a pavilion of trees.

"I think it's frost-bitten!" he cried, recalling David Niven's famous skiing story.

"Massage is the only thing for frostbite," she said, decisively. And went on to apply it vigorously.

Toby was soon restored to his flushed and roving lustiness and drawing invisible patterns with his tip around and between her breasts down to her navel, which he investigated like an inquisitive animal, then down to the glinting golden fur and through and in, while the mountains looked down like gods on an ancient ritual. Not appreciating that they were on a slope, they rolled back, locked together in orgasm, into the icy water.

"Hey!" said Tara, delightedly, as they surfaced.

"Yes!" gasped Michael. "The shock. It heightens it."

So they did it again.

That night they spent in a tiny inn in the village of Sawrey on the west side of Lake Windermere where Beatrix Potter created her immortal animals. Tara had never heard of *The Tale of Peter Rabbit* or *Appley Dapply's Nursery Rhymes*, nor seen the exquisite fairy-tale world of the illustrations. Michael bought her some of the books, and that night, on a rug by a log fire, under a sloping ceiling, she caught a fragment of the kind of childhood that had been denied her. She looked up from studying the incredible magical draftsmanship of a Beatrix Potter mouse to find his eyes fixed on her as he lay on his stomach beside her, his chin resting on his clasped hands. He was not wearing his glasses and his eyes were radiant.

"I love you," he said. "From the first minute. It's as if I've always loved you. In some parallel world or something. You're the most beautiful person I've ever known. I don't mean just outside."

She kissed him delicately.

"I've never loved anyone before," she said. "It's weird, love, isn't it? It kind of takes you over. And it changes everything else. It's as if someone had turned on another light in the sky. I mean, all the ordinary things you do become great, too, don't they? It's not just sex; it's the whole, kind of mingling, with another person. It's not Tara and Michael anymore; it's Taramichael, or Michaeltara."

Now he kissed her gently.

"And it's time for Taramichael to go to bed. To sleep. It's an early start in the morning."

They went to bed in the billowing sheets with the glowing play of the fire on the ceiling. Michael went to sleep almost instantly, his face buried in her neck. She lay awake for a long time, trying to reconcile her love with her treachery. For she most assuredly knew that anything she might learn from Michael that she could use against his father, she would use. She cried before she slept.

Creaming silently through the countryside in the blade-slim Lagonda next morning, she was given a perfect example of her dilemma. He was talking, with critical fondness, about his father.

"He's a celebrity-snob you know," he said. "Especially show business. Members of the Variety Club, the Water Rats, all that. The one person he wants to meet in the whole world is Frank Sinatra. I'll tell you what he's like: you know how dead set he is against you and me? Well, despite that, he's started to tape your programs. It's to do with you being the biggest thing around on the box at the moment, I suppose."

Is it hell, thought Tara, reflecting once again on the importance of information. Patterson was no fool. He'd obviously been watching the direction in which she'd been moving. The last show, in which she'd put the arm on Tom Lane, would have had his antennae twitching. Was she beginning to move toward him? That was what he'd be thinking. She'd have to try to put him off the scent. If her next show was also about someone connected with her father's framing, Patterson's alarm klaxons would really start blaring.

That morning, at Alhambra, she stood her Monday morning conference on its head. They had been working on Iron Jack Thomson, the man Tom Lane had named as giving him his instructions about hiding the computer on Jed Stewart's land. She'd changed her mind.

"But me and Terry and Jean have got him all set up," said Sid, his squashed-eggplant face drenched in disappointment; "he's running this protection scam . . ."

"He'll still be there when we want him," answered Tara. "It's just that I want to keep the mix sort of random—so that the viewers never know what to expect. I don't want every show to be about a plug-ugly, d'you know what I mean? Suzy, Bella, what sort of shape are you in on 'Smooth Reggie'?"

"Smooth Reggie" was a ruthless, very classy crook, whose speciality was rich widows. He plucked them straight from the graveside while they were still disoriented and vulnerable. His pose was that of an investment adviser.

"We've got pictures of him and we've identified his favorite crematorium," answered Suzy. She handed over a file of photographs. Smooth Reggie looked very smooth indeed. Devastatingly handsome, black-haired, just silvering at the temples, Savile Row-suited, a ravishing sympathetic smile.

"Yummy . . ." said Tara. "What d'you mean about his favorite crematorium?"

"He waits in a hired Rolls-Royce outside the most expensive crematorium around here for miles," explained Bella, "unerringly picks out the richest widow of the day and discreetly follows her until he's found out where she lives. He finds out her name in a number of ways, usually from a neighbor, not too close."

"Next day he arrives in his Rolls-Royce," Suzy took it up, "says he was a great business friend of the lady's late husband and he'll never forgive himself for not being able to turn up to the funeral—he was at a business meeting in New York. Johnny always made him swear—yes, he's got the late husband's name, too—that if ever anything happened to him, he'd give his wife any help she needed. He knows Johnny has already got her well-invested, but he would remind her that there's a packet coming in life insurance and he's anxious she shouldn't make any mistakes. By this time, Reggie's dazzling charm, acting on the woman's current instability, has got her in a spin."

"It so happens that he's an investment adviser," said Bella, ". . . if she'd like to put the money in his care, he'd regard it as a tribute to a former colleague to handle it for her without any commission. He looks at his watch: 'Good heavens, is that the time?' He's got a meeting, won't have time to get to the bank, then he's got a restaurant date. He'd hardly like to leave his briefcase in a men's room, considering what's in it. Look, here's his card. Would she terribly mind if he left the case here and picked it up tomorrow when he calls to see what she's decided?

" 'Of course not,' says the woman. Off he goes and the woman, being a woman, naturally opens the briefcase. Inside is £50,000 in twenties and fifties. Deeply flattered by being so readily trusted, when Reggie calls the next day she writes out a check to the company on his card for generally not less than £150,000, which she never sees again, much less Reggie."

"Great!" said Tara. "Just what we need. Contrast! Bella, you'd better be the widow . . ."

"Oh, hey, just a minute . . ." Bella expostulated.

"Well, it can't be Suzy," said Tara. "I mean, look at her. Dolls with cut-glass faces like hers know more about money than the Treasury—not that that's hard, mind you. Smooth Reggie would never have a go at her. Whereas you, if you don't mind me saying so, Bella, look like the kind of brainless beauty that's never given a thought to money in her life, so long as it's been there in flour sacks."

"Thanks a bunch!" said Bella.

And so it came to pass on the show. Tara explained what Reggie's racket was, then they rolled film. Bella came out of the crematorium in a chinchilla that could have financed a new aircraft carrier, stepped into a Rolls-Royce Silver Spirit and was whisked away to a house in Millionaire's Row between the University's playing fields on the edge of Liverpool and five hundred acres of parkland and Botanic Gardens. Reggie followed. Pam already had her hidden cameras set up and even the sound man was satisfied. All went as the girls had described it—Smooth Reggie turned out to be a star turn—until he returned the day after the funeral to collect his hostage £50,000 and the massive check.

At this point, Tara intervened with a giggle that went to the funny bone of the nation.

"For God's sake, don't stop watching now," she said.

Dissolve.

Reggie sweeps up in his hired Rolls. The house has a "For Sale" sign outside which he hadn't noticed before. People like Reggie have an instinct and he walks up to the front door like a cat treading on tacks. The front door is open. He pushes it wide to discover an empty house. No furniture, no carpet, no curtains. Stripped. Just a large cardboard notice that reads "Watch TARA STEWART—PUBLIC EYE, nine o'clock, Wednesday." Pam's lens doesn't miss one muscle spasm of that handsome face. The picture goes out on a close shot of Reggie. Tara reappears on the screen.

"Hope you enjoyed the show, Reggie," she says. She turns as if to go, then comes back.

"Oh," she says, "your fifty thousand quid is quite safe. Any time you'd like to come and collect it . . ."

The show was a smash and she'd made a fatal error. Precisely the one she was trying to avoid. It hit her as she watched the program again at home on the Wednesday night. She had wanted not to alarm Shaun Patterson. And she'd only shown him that his ex-girlfriend was working for her.

7

As the Tara Stewart show opened that Wednesday, Shaun Patterson was standing in front of his enormous, flat-screen television set in his Eaton Square flat in London. He was tense. If the victim this week was again someone connected to him, she was definitely on her way toward him. As Tara introduced the tale of Smooth Reggie he exhaled—he hadn't realized he'd been holding his breath—and went and stretched out in the luxurious leather tip-up chair from which he normally watched television when he was in. He was getting paranoid in his old age. And chicken. Scared of a kid of . . . what? Twenty-one? Twenty-two? He reached out a lazy hand. His man, Cullen, had put a silver tray with a decanter of whiskey and a glass beside it. "His man!" He grinned. He'd been butler to some of the finest in the land. The trouble was they kept finding their pictures out of their frames and hidden under Cullen's bed. Cullen knew that if he nicked so much as a collar stud from Patterson, he'd end up with both his shins broken.

Patterson settled back to enjoy the discomfiture of Smooth Reggie. He had nothing against the man. It was true that he wasn't of The Mystery; he'd come to his calling from The Wrekin, a minor public school in the North. He was good at what he did and Patterson knew of him and liked him. However, as Confucius or someone of the same name had said: "Most pleasant to see best friend fall off roof."

Bella Cranmer emerged from the crematorium, in her shimmering chinchilla, as "the mark," and the adrenalin hit him like a shock wave. His drink slopped over as he put it down and stared in disbelief at the screen. Jesus Christ, the Stewart bitch had his latest ex-girlfriend on the payroll! As he watched the program, his mind raced backward like a computer on search and find. What did the Cranmer girl know? What could she have found out that he didn't know she'd found out? One thing was obvious. She'd have to be given a little warning. Whatever she knew, whatever she'd learned in that damnable way women had of ferreting out secrets, she'd have to be discouraged from talking about it. Or, if she'd already talked, encouraged to deny what she'd said.

But right there he was in trouble. He'd cut loose from The Mystery. He couldn't call on their heavy mob without adding to the list of blackmailing bastards who were already fastened on to him like leeches. The Mystery, like everything else, was not what it was. That was the trouble with the world. Standards were falling all over.

On Tara Stewart he couldn't lay a finger—yet. With the power she now had, it was as if she had a force field around her. Force fields could be broken, but it would take time and intelligence. The intelligence, he had. About the time he wasn't so sure. But Bella was a different thing. Bella could be shut up—and he'd just thought of the man to do it.

Through his close connections with show business, Patterson knew that show biz had a heavy mob of its own, organized by a man called Johnny Evans. It was known as "The Brothers" and its origins had been innocent enough. Johnny, a layabout, liked to be around show business people; so did a group of his thick-ear mates.

They took to frequenting the pubs and little clubs where comics and singers were to be found. If ever an entertainer found himself in trouble with an aggressive or overenthusiastic member of the public, "The Brothers" would move in to the entertainer's assistance. At first they did it for nothing—they'd naturally be offered a drink and a signed picture, but that was the extent of it. But, as things will, it grew from there, fertilized by opportunism and greed and now a great many stars were protected by "The Brothers" whether they wanted to be or not. And they paid for the privilege.

Paid the right kind of money, Johnny would take care of any "problem" from which anyone connected with the business, whom he knew and trusted, might be suffering. Patterson put in a call and made a meet with him for the next day.

Down in Liverpool at the same moment, Tara sat with Bella, who had watched the show with her. Her mind was in a turmoil. While Bella laughed and chatted, reliving the best moment, Tara was working out what she was going to do. She couldn't tell Bella the truth about Patterson. Or that she was inexorably tracking him down like a great beast in his lair. That, her grand design, she could not tell anybody. At the same time, she could not leave Bella at risk. And she was most definitely at risk now that Patterson knew that she was working for her. She had to tell her a lie, which would be as effective as the truth. She turned to her friend.

"Bella, love, I'm afraid I've dropped you in it."

"How d'you mean?" asked Bella, puzzled.

"I've been wondering how to tell you. Smooth Reggie—I found out this afternoon that he's not quite as smooth as we thought he was. Under all that charm there's a vicious streak a foot wide. They say he went in for that particular scam because he hates women. You made a fool of him. And you cost him fifty grand. He's not the type to laugh it off with one of his electric smiles."

Bella tossed back her mantilla of raven's-wing hair from the lovely face: "I'm not frightened of Smooth Reggie."

"But I am," insisted Tara. "I got you into it, it was damned careless of me, and I'm going to see you don't get clobbered for it."

"What are you going to do," asked Bella. "Lock me up in a fortress?"

"I'm going to do better than that," said Tara; "I'm going to bring the fortress to you."

The next day, to his obvious delight, Ben Maitland moved into the flat. There was trouble at first from Aunt Rita. She was just hitting her stride with a thundering denunciation of troilism when Ben whispered in her ear. She shut up abruptly, moved with surprising nimbleness to her room, podgy arms outstretched and went in. They heard her lock the door.

"What on earth did you say to her?" asked Bella.

"I told her I was here to protect you all against an alcoholic rapist in the district," said Ben. "First he screws you, then he drinks all your booze."

He looked around the living room, which was enclosed on three sides by inch-thick glass walls. One of them overlooked the ripe beauty of the Botanic Garden, the other two looked over lush forest. The flat was the penthouse of a large converted Georgian mansion on the edge of the lavish Nature Reserve. The only entrance to the mansion was through a massive front door with entry phones. In the hall there was a lift.

"Tasty," said Ben, after he'd made a tour of inspection. "Only from now on, nobody gets in through the entry phone—got it? Anyone calls, I'll let them in through the front door."

He'd also noted, with some satisfaction, that one of the glass walls directly overlooked the elegant drive up to the front door.

It happened the next night. They were lying around listening to a space-conscious tape of Jarre Senior, composed on a synthesizer. The girls were curled into cozy, voluminous housecoats so as not to put too much of a strain on Ben. He was the first to hear, over the haze of music, the scrunch of fat tires on the graveled drive. He slid onto his stomach—putting out the lights would have been a dead giveaway—and looked out through one of the glass walls. A stretched black Mercedes with its lights out was crabbing its way up the drive. He gave a finger sign to the girls to lock and bar the door behind him; then, without waiting for the bell to ring, went straight downstairs.

When the bell did ring, he opened the door instantly, gaining a tiny advantage of surprise. At the top of the steps stood Bimbo, one of the woolly-haired Brothers, large, wide and lithe. Bimbo's reflexes were some of the best there were. But that little surprise had got a few hundred thousand neurons firing off in his brain on distracting conjecture. Nevertheless, his big white teeth flashed in an ingratiating smile as he stealthily slid the lead-shot-filled leather sap down his sleeve.

"I'm lookin' for . . ." was about as far as he got before Ben hard-fisted him in the solar plexus, then brought his knee up to meet the rapidly descending face as he doubled up, catapulting him backward down the steps. Then he hauled the inert figure indoors by the ankles, its head bumping on each of the four steps, and closed the door.

Outside in the car his companions could see, in some odd way, that Johnny Evans had paled.

"Scarper!" he yelled to the driver of the big Mercedes.

"What about Bim—?" asked one of the brethren.

"I said scarper," said Johnny.

The big Mercedes squealed away. Why didn't anyone fucking ever fill him in properly, reflected Johnny, bitterly, on exactly what he was dealing with? If they sent you after 00-sodding-7, the least they could do was to tell you. He'd *never* seen Bimbo put away like that.

"I don't want no one never tangling with that geezer again unless we're mob-handed," he told the other subdued figures in the car. "Got it?"

He got no argument.

Inside the flat, Bimbo drooped from a hardback chair. Tara was doing her best to clean him up with a damp flannel. Ben stood over him, incredulous.

"I don't believe it," he said. "He comes along here, all tooled up to do you over, and you're washing his rotten face!"

"I don't want him bleeding on the carpet," answered Tara.

"I wasn't going to do nothing to no one," mumbled Bimbo. Ben let the lead-filled sap swing lightly from his fingers.

"Oh no?" he said. "What was this for, then—stunning blue-bottles?"

He reached over into the top pocket of Bimbo's leather jacket and plucked out a cutthroat razor.

"And what about this? Like to keep yourself well-groomed, do you, sweetheart? Or is it to put the frighteners on girls? Yeah, that would be your speciality, I should think; fighting girls. You're certainly no bloody good at fighting men."

The black eyes stared up at him, brilliant with hate. The mind behind them calculated the odds on a lightning lunge; he'd never met anyone faster than himself before.

"Don't even think of it, Mabel," said Ben, slamming the cosh agonizingly across Bimbo's right biceps, where he knew it would hurt without damaging. Bimbo screamed. Bella rushed across the room.

"No!" she shouted.

Tara grabbed her by the arms and hustled her into the study, also glass-walled, that led off the living room. She closed the door. Through it, they heard Bimbo scream again.

"That's torture!" shouted Bella. "That makes us as bad as he is."

"Ben's just hurting him," said Tara.

"Just hurting . . ." Bella made a lunge for the door. Tara grabbed her and shook her until her hair tumbled all over her face.

"Have you any idea what that man in there would have done to you if Ben hadn't been here?" she yelled. "All Ben is doing is giving him something to remember, so that he won't be around again. A good hiding does something to a bully. He's never quite the same again. That's all Ben's doing."

At least, she hoped to God that's all he was doing. If he was trying to beat out of Bimbo the name of the man who laid the contract, he'd eventually come up with Patterson and no one had to know about Patterson—not yet. Not even Ben.

"I think he's probably had enough," she said, hurriedly. "You stay here."

Bella nodded, chastened.

Tara went swiftly into the living room to hear Ben saying to a terrified-looking Bimbo: "What you've had is nothing. I do that to my poor old Grannie every morning to keep her in shape for the wrestling. Now you go back and tell Smooth Reggie that if we have any more visits from gonks like you, I'll call on him personally. And by the time I've finished with him there'll be nothing smooth about him except the plaster they put him in. Head to toe."

Tara watched the relief flood into Bimbo's incredulous eyes. The blond bastard wasn't going to beat the name of the contractor out of him after all; he already knew it. Only he'd got the wrong one! Tara felt sick at making a fool of Ben in this way. But, then, she'd felt sick many times since she first swore her thorny, unalterable course. She used the antidote now she'd always used: the image of the controlled agony in her father's eyes each time she visited him.

Johnny Evans gave Patterson the bad news and the good news. The bad news was that Evans's boy had been wiped out by an unexpected minder, obviously working for Tara Stewart. The good was that they thought the hit had been ordered by Smooth Reggie and not by Patterson.

Patterson went into his private gym and started punching the heavy bag. It was the only way he'd ever been able to think—on his feet doing something punishing. Unlike that clever bastard Jed Stewart, who'd always worked things out like a computer: fast, accurate, as if he didn't know he was doing it. It was plausible that the Stewart bitch had thought it was Reggie. After all, Bella had made a fair old fool of him and Reggie had his pride. On the other hand, Tara Stewart was her father's daughter, always thinking two moves ahead. Maybe she had arranged it so that Evans's thick-headed thug got the message about her thinking it was Reggie to put him off the scent. He transferred to his moving runway, which enabled him to jog without ever leaving his home. In front of him was a television screen with a picture, in color, of an unwinding, leafy country lane, the sun slatting between the trees. He wouldn't know, he decided, until Tara Stewart's next couple of shows. If they were about people from his old firm, then she was definitely coming for him.

Down in Ainsdale, in her study, that same Saturday morning, Tara was lying on her stomach staring at real countryside through one of her glass walls, the moss-green carpet bringing it indoors so that she felt she was living inside some kind of magic bubble. She, too, was thinking hard. If Patterson had gone to the trouble of sending a carver down to shut Bella up, it meant two things. Firstly, Bella knew something far more important about Patterson than Tara had as yet managed to gentle out of her. Secondly, he was now undoubtedly on the alert and there was no further point in diversions. Her next series of subjects would all be Patterson pensioners. She put a call through to Mail Room Sid to go ahead with setting up "Iron Jack." Meanwhile, a storm cloud was boiling up behind her that she had not foreseen.

There was a sudden pounding of heavy boots through the living room, the door of her study burst open and quickly though the family reflexes moved her, she was too late. They were on her. One had her by the wrists, the other by the ankles and they were swinging her to and fro, the fro being in the direction of the glass wall. The arc of the swing got wider and higher.

"Right, when I say three we both let go," said one of them. "One . . . two . . ."

It was obvious that three was going to come as she was swinging toward the glass and the space beyond it. She screamed.

"You stupid bloody apes! If you don't want me to throw up all over you, put me down!"

Her brothers Len and Corby dropped her unceremoniously on the carpet and grinned down at her. She looked up at the two big brutes they now were and despaired of ever being anything in their eyes other than the surrogate-mother-tomboy who had dominated them and brought them up. She scrambled to her feet.

"Why the hell they keep giving you lot leave, I'll never know," she said. "Why can't they keep you in your cages?"

Then she threw herself into their arms. They corresponded spasmodically. Len's and Corby's letters, written in alternate paragraphs in alternate handwriting, were never likely to be included in any epistolary anthology. Tara got more information from the addresses than she did from anything in them: they always seemed to be somewhere far-flung, usually being fired at while trying to stop other people killing each other. It was, in fact, six months since she had seen them and this was their first sight of the new flat. It was also their first sight of Bella, who had let them in. "Hey! Warra pad!" and "Hey! Warra Judy who opened the door!" they shouted simultaneously.

They were in macho Marine uniform, they were sunburned and roughened and they had the Stewart bones and there was no way that anyone was going to keep Bella out of that study. She smoked through the door in that brunette-style that no blonde, it occurred to Tara, could ever emulate.

"And who," she inquired, "are the Magnificent Seven?"

Len and Corby looked at each other.

"There's only two of us," said Len, simply.

"I *know* . . ." said Bella with a mock-sultry look that made Tara laugh outright. The boys looked deceptively bewildered.

"But I mean," replied Corby, in the same Simple Simon intonation of his brother, "we could rustle up five more of the lads if you're a 'Seven Up' kind of judy."

It was a delayed drop while Bella took on board the fact that these lads were not anything like as simple as they came on. Then she smiled broadly. With a pair like this, there could be jollies ahead in a big way.

"When d'you go back?" asked Tara, in the time-honored insult.

"We've gorra week," said Len. "But look, we don't want you to be lumbered with us . . ."

"I mean, we know you're a career girl and all like that, I mean, we read about you, like."

"Will you just button it for one sec," said Tara. "There are more spare bedrooms in this place than the Y.M.C.A. You won't bother me. If you get in my way, I'll just walk over you, as usual. If you get in Bella's way, I know she'll make her own arrangements . . ."

"Oh, I will, darling, I will!" said Bella.

"If you get in Aunt Rita's way, well, you'll go back to camp two very wide, very flat Marines. She's put on another stone."

"Have you had the floor strengthened?" asked Corby.

"We thought it'd be cheaper to fill her knickers with helium every morning," countered Tara.

Which was to be the last cheerful exchange that weekend, because at that moment Michael's Lagonda sighed up the drive and everyone watched as Michael got out, stuck his hand back in through the driver's window and sounded the horn.

"Sorry, everyone," said Tara, "there's my weekend date. Got to go."

"Have a lovely time, darling," said Bella, pecking her briefly. "I'll look after the boys for you."

"That's what I'm afraid of," replied Tara, as she kissed Len and Corby, picked up her weekend case, which was standing ready, and went.

It wasn't until she got into the car that she registered the strange stiffness there had been about her brothers. And they were a mile down the road before it struck her like a hammer-blow in the stomach what the reason was. They had recognized her "weekend date." She kept forgetting that they were that bit older than she was—she always thought of herself as the eldest. For a year or two they had probably run as junior members of the same boy-pack as Michael and they hadn't forgotten him. Their sister was dating the son of the man who was virtually their father's murderer.

For the moment, Michael and Tara were hooked on lakes and mountains and it had been their intention to spend until Monday morning among the towering crags and mirrored waters of Snow-

donia in Wales. The trip was now totally ruined for Tara. At the
tiny, painted port at the mouth of the River Dovey, Michael pointed
out the 7,000-year-old tree trunks, sticking out of the sand at low
tide, dating from a time when all this was land.

"They say you can hear the tolling of the bells of a sunken city
whenever trouble threatens," he told her.

Tara believed him. She heard them. He pointed out "Arthur's
Chair," the name suggested by the shape of the mountain, Cader
Idris. Her imagination responded momentarily to the folk-mind that
could picture a toweringly gigantic King Arthur sitting in that massive
niche, but it responded more to the legend that anyone who slept the
night on the mountain would awake blind, insane or a poet. Poet . . .
she didn't know. But blind or insane would do to help deflect the
wrath of her brothers when she got home.

There was an easy way out, but she couldn't take it. She could
tell them, simply, that she was going with Michael in order to get
information with which to destroy his father. It would mean letting
them in on her grand design, but there would be no danger in that.
The only reason she hadn't let them in on her plans before was because
she knew they would worry themselves sick about the danger she
was putting herself in. But no, she couldn't just tell them that. It was
a half-truth . . . a quarter-truth; what fraction of the truth was it,
anyway? She didn't know anymore. It didn't matter. The fact was
that she could not allow herself to tell her brothers less than the whole
truth and that included the undeniable truth that she was deeply in
love with Michael.

Like his sense of humor, Michael's sensitivity was not obvious,
but very deep and powerful. He sensed Tara's abstraction, her detachment throughout the whole weekend. But he was too clever to
probe. If it was something on which he could help, she would turn
to him. If it was something he could do nothing about, she would
simply pretend that he was imagining things and burden herself with
the extra strain of putting on a false show.

He delivered her back on Sunday night, having decided to cut
his losses. As she got out of the car and kissed him, her stomach felt
as if she had a buzz saw in it. Inside, her brothers were waiting. Bella's
expected orgiastic weekend had been a fiasco. Len and Corby had
spent the weekend either drunk or getting drunk which, for them,
took a long time. Aunt Rita, her psychic powers developed to a fine
pitch where alcohol was concerned, had divined a binge in progress
and had emerged from her room to take part in it. Normally, finding
Bella alone in the flat with two men, she would have assumed the

worst. Noting, however, that the two men—whom she only pe-
ripherally identified as her nephews—were the worse for drink, she
decided that they couldn't be all bad and that all was probably well,
except with that black-haired Lesbian, probably bisexual, hussy Bella,
who looked stupendously bored. She billowed out of her room, several whiskey bottles assembled about her, and started into her repertoire of mysterious Merseyside jingles:

> One, two, three alera,
> I saw me Auntie Sarah
> Sitting on a bandolera
> Eating Nellie's toffee sticks.

That was her first contribution to what even she could sense
were somewhat funereal festivities. She followed it up with another
of her impenetrably obscure favorites:

> On a mountain
> Stands a lady
> Who she is
> I do not know
> All she wants
> Is gold and silver
> All she wants
> Is a nice shampoo.
> So fall in my very best friend,
> Very best friend,
> Very best friend,
> So fall in my very best friend . . .

That was as far as she got before Corby, in the nicest possible
way, asked her: "Aunt Rita, those songs are terrifically interesting.
Did you know they're all to do with sex and the Devil and black
magic?"

Aunt Rita ceased abruptly and was never known to perform
those particular songs again, thus eroding even further the Liverpudlian oral tradition. In revenge she came about, in ponderous mag-
nificence, like a pre-1914 Dreadnought, to go to the lavatory and
contrived, in passing, to stand on Corby's leg. He thought he'd lost
it. The Marine tradition forbade him to make any sound, but he could
not remember such an outrage to the nerves of his fibula since he fell
off the climbing net during his assault course training.

Tara's homecoming was hideous. The minute she set foot inside the door they pounced on her, vicious with whiskey and disillusionment. She had always been a thing to cherish; their kid sister who became their mother. They had looked up to her in everything. To have caught her in an act of family disloyalty of such staggering dimensions had turned their simple worlds upside down.

Bella, who had listened bewilderedly to some of their wild talk over the weekend and knew how they felt, moved instinctively to Tara's side.

"You're back, then, are you, you treacherous little bitch!" was Corby's opener.

Bella saw Tara wince. She was used to hard language, but never in their lives had either of their brothers used words like that on her.

"This is what you get up to when we're not here to see you, is it?" asked Len. "Toddling along every week like a good little plaster virgin to see Dad rotting away in jail"—Bella blinked in confusion—"then spending the weekends screwing with the son of the fucking shitehawk who put him there!"

"What?" frowned Bella, totally disoriented. She was ignored.

"Writing us dolly little letters all about Dad this and Dad that and Dad says this and Dad says that. I wonder what Dad would say if he knew you had a knife in his back right up to the hilt, you rotten little whore," spat out Corby.

Tara hadn't known that she could hurt so badly. There they were, the pair of them, both grown practically into replicas of Jed and the pain in their eyes now was very close to the pain she never failed to see in his. As she looked into those stricken eyes, all she wanted to do was to fold up tight in some dark corner where they couldn't reach her. But she knew that she was fighting for her emotional life, the family, her whole plan, and that the only way to reach them was to hit back in a way they'd understand—with a violence matching their own.

Her opening salvo was deliberately designed to pick up extra power from the embarrassing presence of Bella.

"Who the hell d'you think you're talking to?" she asked. "This is me, Tara Stewart. It wasn't so long ago I had to teach you to wipe your asses and wash your pricks properly! Who the shit are you to tell me how to run my life? As for Dad, what have you ever done for him? I'll tell you what you did: you ran away. You chickened out and went and buried yourself in all the bull and bawling of the Marines . . ."

"That's a bloody lie!" shouted Len. "We visit him every leave. We write to him all the time . . ."

"If it's the kind of stumbling squitter you write to me, he must get a hell of a charge out of that!" she said, contemptuously. Oh God, she was hurting them! She could see it, these big, vulnerable men, who could take out a machine-gun nest, but didn't know how to match a girl with a lashing tongue.

"At least we didn't go and fuck his worst enemy's son!" shouted Len.

"That'd be a bit difficult, wouldn't it?" Tara answered. "Or have you gone that way in the Marines?"

"Cow!" said Corby.

"You've done bugger-all for Dad," she said. "Nothing that'll get him out of that stinking hole of a prison. Now let me tell you what I've done. I put myself through Night School. I got a job at Alhambra. I conned, I climbed, I clawed, I cheated. I asked for help from Dad's old contacts when I needed it. And I did it all because it was the only way I could think of getting the power to pull Patterson down." She heard Bella gasp. "Yes, that's what it's all about, Bella. Patterson's the man who framed my father. And yes, that is the main reason—because you were his ex-girlfriend—that I hired you. Except now I think I'd have hired you anyway."

The boys had become quiet and rapt during this recital and Tara's voice had become factual rather than aggressive.

"It's the same with Michael Patterson. I would have tried to strike up a relationship with him anyway, in the hope of getting information from him about his father. As it happened, I fell in love with him. I make no apologies for that; no one can control that. Maybe I could have burned it out of me if he'd known what his father had done to mine. But he doesn't know. He hasn't the faintest idea that his father framed Jed. But even though I love him, I'm still using him as a source of info about that bastard Shaun Patterson. Quite frankly my life—through falling in love with Michael—is now a mess. I'm using the man I love to help destroy his own father. But I swore to get Dad out of that jail and that's what I'm going to do. That's the story, take it or leave it."

She stopped abruptly and lowered her gaze to the floor.

There was silence for a moment. Then, simultaneously, Len and Corby moved in on her. She practically disappeared as they sandwiched her between them. "Tar . . ." said Len.

"Aw, Tar . . ." said Corby.

"Do me a favor," Tara asked Bella later. "Keep it all to yourself for now. I'd like to tell the rest of the team in my own time."

Bella nodded.

The new openness between Tara and Bella paid its first dividend the same night. After the boys had left to go back to barracks, Tara and Bella sat up talking long into the night. It had started as Tara was brushing her hair in what Bella called her Snow White bedroom, because it was like something out of a Disney fantasy with its fur-soft white carpet, white woodwork, and its blizzard of rose and pale green wallpapers and textures. Bella had knocked at the door and asked if she could come in.

During the ferocity of the family storm she had witnessed and the incredible history she had heard, she had come closer to Tara than she had been to another woman in her life. Bella was not a woman's woman. She normally needed a man in the room before her lights came on. But she could define the quality she had sensed in Tara from the start. It was her intense realness. It was as if an extra gallon of life had been poured into her. She wanted to talk more. They talked of Paul. Tara and he had not made love since she knew that it was serious between her and Michael. Paul's reproachful brown eyes seemed to imply that he thought it was because the row over the show had changed their relationship. She felt that to let him think that was the kinder course. Bella agreed: a man preferred to think that it was something he'd done that had blown it, rather than another man. Tara and Paul still remained staunch friends and he kept a strong administrative safety net under her during her wilder ventures.

The talk turned to Patterson.

"I'd *never* have guessed he was a criminal," said Bella.

"You wouldn't, love," explained Tara. "He comes from a very old firm; the sort that don't wear badges. Besides, now he's laundered himself and sanitized the loot, he's no different from any other rip-off artist millionaire. He's home and dry without a soul in the world to answer to."

"I don't know if that's exactly true," said Bella.

"What—about him being home and dry?"

"No, about him not having to answer to anyone."

Tara became still: "How d'you mean?"

Bella thought for a moment: "Well, there'd sometimes be a call on his very private line—even I didn't know the number and no one else was allowed to take calls on it. He seemed to know when the calls would be coming through and he got very uptight and paced about beforehand. And if I was in his study when the call came through, he'd send me out. Now what would you have made of that?"

"That some ringmaster was cracking the whip," said Tara, ruminatively. "But who could that be?"

"I was never allowed to get the faintest clue," said Bella. "But I do know he was edgy and irritable for at least the next twelve hours after one of those calls."

"He's got a boss," said Tara decisively. "I've got to find him."

She remembered the phantom in the Security Sheilas pictures. Next day she took the photographs from the locked drawer in her office where she kept them. The figure hadn't appeared in any recent batches. She rang the agency in London to make sure they hadn't missed him. They were sure they hadn't. He hadn't been there. She rang off and stared at the teasing shadows on the glossy prints. She was now convinced, illogically, that what she had here were elusive glimpses of someone to whom Patterson was answerable. If she could find him and enlist him on her side she might be able to take Patterson out with one strike. On the other hand she might make an enemy even more powerful than Patterson. She would face that dilemma when she came to it.

That night she brought the pictures home and pinned them on her bedroom wall. She hoped that one day or night some switch would trip and light up the corner of her mind where something slept.

For the next days she was too busy setting up "Iron Jack" to do anything further about her insight. Iron Jack's trade was with Asian and African families. Mail Room Sid had already done the preliminary work when she called him off the first time. What Iron Jack did was very simple. Most of the newer immigrant families had relatives back in their countries who had been precluded from coming over by the new immigration laws. By laying out a little cash to a lowly but greedy civil servant, Iron Jack had access to the names and addresses of those immigrant families who had applied unsuccessfully to get permission to bring over relatives. Jack was big, dressed respectably and, despite his broken nose, had presence and a good manner. Furthermore, his possession of the information that the family had been through official channels and been turned down gave him credibility. He would call on a rejected family, give them his card, which read, simply, "J.D.C.P. Carter, Home Office, Special Section." He would speak the language which they all understood, the language of "baksheesh." Money that crackled in the hand was worth more than any immigration form that had ever been printed. Kindly let him have £500 per person to be imported and he would see to it that they were on a ship with the correct papers within three months. All this, he would impress upon them, was highly illegal and if any word about it reached the authorities, it would mean jail for everyone. Even to have tried it—and he admitted that the chances of success were only ninety-nine percent—was enough to put them inside.

Iron Jack simply took the money, crossed the family concerned off his list and wiped them from his mind. The relatives never arrived. The telephone number on his card was a ceased line and the address was that of a defunct Methodist church at Edgehill. There was no one the cheated family dare complain to, since they were taking part in an illegal enterprise in the first place.

All this Mail Room Sid and Jean Soong had already researched and verified. The problem was to find an immigrant family that was willing to cooperate in baiting the trap for Iron Jack. Most recent immigrant families had something to hide, and even if they hadn't, were possessed of a fear of the media, of anything that would make them stand out and draw attention to themselves. Which was where Tara played the card from the pack she had drawn from the Mail Room, which she had known she was going to need one day.

Jean Soong, Tara knew, was a member of the comical-sounding Chi Kung Thong, a branch of a Chinese secret society known, equally amusingly to the Western ear, as the Hung Man Wui. "Well, he would, wouldn't he?" had been Tara's first comment about the latter; "I'd piss meself, too."

In the fifties both societies had gone into decline, but with the rise in interest, among people of all beliefs, in various species of mysticism, young Chinese people had reactivated the societies, which had always insisted very strongly on mystical belief and ritual. Members of the Thong were highly regarded as people of respect even by other immigrant communities, who were not Chinese, and it was Jean Soong, looking like a smooth porcelain doll, who had persuaded a West Indian family, who had nothing to fear from the strong light of publicity, to cooperate.

Howard Daley was the head of the family, a strong, handsome Trinidadian. He had heard about Iron Jack. He watched, fascinated, as Pam measured the available light in his tiny shack in Toxteth and decided it was insufficient, also that there was nowhere she could conceal the camera and mikes. It was therefore arranged that the meet between Howard and Iron Jack would be on the Goree Piazza, a stretch of waste ground near the Pier Head on the river, where local legend had it that slaves were once bought and sold. Pam and Harry, the sound man, would be cosily rubbing hips in the canvas-topped truck nearby . . .

Iron Jack was intrigued when he got the invitation. "As a notable member of the local community," it read, "Alhambra Studios is pleased to invite you to a private preview of a program entitled *Liverpool Today—A Living City.*" Some wally in the local media had obviously bought a bum mailing list and he'd been mistaken for a worthy citizen. He went along on the appointed day to this little preview theater under a wine bar in Lord Street. He was looking forward to making a few useful contacts. Contacts, to Iron Jack, were the breath of life and—like all villains—he also yearned for the veneer of respectability.

It was all very tastefully organized, he thought. Cocktails before, in a small, crimson plush anteroom, with a canapé or two. He met a most impressive local industrialist, in the shape of Paul Cranmer, a Professor of Anthropology in the delicious form of Ms. Blond-Hackett, and a visiting computer scientist from Taiwan with a face like an ivory angel, called Jean Soong.

There were a number of other people there—all members of Tara's team—whom he didn't manage to meet. After one or two snorts, which Jack adjudged to be pretty fair, they all trooped into the charming little viewing theater with the big, cinema-type screen. Jack settled down in his comfortable, separately swiveled armchair and prepared to appreciate this tribute to a city which had been good to him. One only had to look at his bank accounts, in various banks and under various names, to see how good.

The show started and he felt the floor had fallen away from beneath him. What he was looking at was a split-screen image. One half was a close shot of himself and the other side was a close shot of Tara Stewart.

"Take a good look at this man," said Tara, "he's a reptile."

Over the image came the titles: *Tara Stewart—Public Eye.* He swiveled his chair around for a straight run at the exit. Standing in front of it was a large, fair-haired man in a blue T-shirt and jeans, who hadn't been at the reception. He had his heavily muscled arms crossed and he didn't look as if he would take kindly to being disturbed.

He turned his chair back again and sat there feeling as if he was having his teeth drilled. She took him to pieces. In some uncanny way she had been there during every second of his negotiations with Howard Daley. She had recorded his every word, caught every expression on his face, trapped every nuance of his foul expertise. Not only that, the rotten cow had cheated. Now he knew why Howard Daley, with his handsome, vulnerable face, had pleaded so hard—in vain—for the price to be brought down. Now he knew why, on one occasion, he had even brought along his wife and children, all with huge, doe eyes that belonged on a face from a greetings card, to add their pleas. She'd got the passing over of the two thousand pounds in notes. The camera had practically licked his face as he counted every single one of them, down to the last fiver. She'd got the false telephone number, the false address.

Just when he thought it couldn't get worse, it got worse. She started to bring ghosts from his past to the screen. People he had cozened and defrauded in the past. All with sums of money to quote, all with stories to tell—of relatives overjoyed by the letters of hope they had received from their families and their bitter anguish when they were told it had all been an expensive lie. Some even told of family members on both sides of the ocean sickening and slowly dying from the shock and disappointment meted out to them by this man. The final shot was of a screenful of silent, still, pathetic figures on the Goree Piazza, getting smaller and smaller as the camera tracked away from them.

As always, guided by the two lawyers who now worked permanently on the show, Tara had guarded her back against possible charges of being an accessory after the fact in that she had failed to hand over evidence of a felony to the police. She could plead, this time with truth, that it had been entrapment, that Howard Daley had no relatives he wished to bring over, that the two thousand pounds had been provided by Alhambra, that she hadn't got a viable case to bring straight to the police. But she had brought Iron Jack's criminality to light, she had traced most of the witnesses; it was now up to them to lay their hands on him and make their own case.

The screen faded to black and Iron Jack sat there feeling as if all his strength had drained away through the soles of his feet. To his astonishment, everyone got up and left without a word. Last to go was the big fellow at the exit. As he left, he said, "I'll be just outside, turd."

There was a pause, then the door opened again and Tara Stewart walked in. Her beauty was terrifying. This must be how those whatsits . . . avenging angels looked, he thought. She sat down calmly next to him and gazed at him with eyes clear as mountain springs, the whites of them very white.

"He's right," she said, levelly, "you are a turd. You're going to go inside for a long time . . ."

"You creeping, conniving cow!" he spat out. Christ, he was glad now he'd helped to stitch up her old man.

"You've got one slim chance," she said.

"Oh yes?" he answered with bitter cynicism. "What would that be, then?"

"Me," she said.

"*You*?!"

"Let me put it this way, turd," she explained, in her sweetest lilt, "the police can either see the show within the next hour, or they can see it when everyone else does when it goes out in a week's time. In which case you'll have seven day's start on the posse."

"And what do I have to do to get the jump on the law?"

"It's very simple, really. You leave yourself with eating and running money. The rest you've got stashed away—yeah, we know the banks and the names—the rest you divide up among the people you took it from."

"I should bleeding cocoa!" said Iron Jack. "I'd rather do my porridge and have the money to come out to."

"Ah!" said Tara. "Good thinking, but there's a bit of a snag there."

"Oh, yes?" said Iron Jack, unimpressed.

"Yeah," said Tara, the blue starting to drift disconcertingly into her eyes. "I just don't think you'd be coming out, not alive, that is. You see, you'll be going to Walton to do your time, which is where my old man is. He's in a state now where he could bite the head off an alligator. Just before you went in, I'd tell him how you helped to fit him up."

Iron Jack visibly jumped. How in God's name did she know?

"I had nothing to do with that!" he cried.

"Yes, you did," said Tara, steadily. "I know all about planting the computer on him and I can prove it. Jed's got nothing to lose in there. All I've got to do is tell him and you're dead."

The sweat started to stand out on Iron Jack's forehead. His bottle started to go. This girl was iced steel, and Christ what an organization she must have behind her!

Tara heard the whine start to creep into his voice, despite his efforts to keep it sounding sarcastically businesslike.

"Let me get this straight," he said, "I give the money back. In return I get seven days' start on the scuffers."

"That's right."

"What if I don't get away with it? What if they still finally pick me up and stuff me into Walton?"

"I still don't say anything to my father about you."

He looked around the room.

"Isn't it fucking marvelous!" he said to the world at large.

Tara sensed that he was about to capitulate. It was time to apply the last turn of the screw.

"There's just one last thing," she said.

"Oh?" replied Iron Jack, fearfully.

"I want to know who hired you for the fit-up of my father."

Oh, Christ, it got worse by the minute!

"I can't do that," he cried. "You know I can't!"

"I don't know nothing," said Tara. "I'm just asking. I can't see where you've got much choice." She tapped the telephone next to her on the producer's central console. "One call from me to the Old Bill, inviting them to a film show right this minute, and your nightmare starts rolling. Who was it?"

Iron Jack remained silent, the sweat running down his face. He thought of running for it, but he knew he had no chance against the blond bomber by the door. Tara picked up the telephone and started to dial.

"It was Les Meacher," he blurted. "He asked me for a couple of gofers—one to plant the computer on your old man's manor, the other to stuff a couple of sackful's of cash in his pigshit. I handled the cash drop myself. I got Tommy-The-Roofer to take care of the computer."

Tara knew he was telling the truth. On the surface, Les Meacher was the supplier of industrial tools and equipment his file at Somerset House claimed him to be. In reality, he was the primary source of criminal technology. The gadget which had originally helped Tara to break into Alhambra three years ago had been one of Meacher's, secondhand. If you wanted to open up a security van like a sardine can, Meacher was the obvious man to go to. There was another thing. Meacher and her father had always hated each other. Something about a girl.

"But Meacher's not a planner," objected Tara. "He's a top technician, but he couldn't think up and put together a job like the Mersey Tunnel party. Who was the boss man?"

"I don't know," said Iron Jack, desperately, "God's teeth I don't! I mean we can all have our guesses, but we can't prove nothing. You know how the big boys break these jobs down—smaller and smaller units, all of them knowing their own bit, none of them having the full picture."

She knew he was telling the truth.

"All right," she said, dismissively. "Your seven days' jump on the law starts now. *After* you've given us the cash to pay back the families you robbed."

Iron Jack's features went into spasm. She handed him over to Ben and switched off the built-in mike in her briefcase. She felt a sense of increasing achievement. Meacher was, criminally speaking, a man of substance. She was breaking through to the heavyweights. Meacher wouldn't have agreed to be one of the poor bloody infantry. He'd have wanted to know who the man was he was working for and how good he was. He'd have wanted to meet him. With Meacher she was beginning to breathe down Patterson's neck. The trouble was she couldn't think of a way of leaning on him. There seemed to be no way of catching him at his trade as she had with the others. She paced, long-legged, across her apricot office carpet, chewing pencils as if they were licorice sticks. People approached her at their peril.

Tara wasn't the only one wearing out her carpet. Shaun Patterson was getting his exercise, too. There could no longer be any doubt. First Tommy, then Iron Jack, both instrumental in the framing of Jed Stewart. Then hiring Bella Cranmer. Anticipating and preempting his Johnny Evans strike. She was coming for him and she was formidable, just like her bloody old man. It was time he stepped up his counterattack. He'd done a lot of quiet thinking, the way Jed had taught him. She was striking at him through crime. He would strike at her through her trade—show business. He knew enough people in it.

One of the people he knew was Trudy Shepherd, a very bright, senior and powerful executive with another television company. She had clout throughout the network. She also produced herself: drama specializing in crime and the low life. Her interest to him was that she had just done a play on the Great Mersey Tunnel Robbery. In it, the character obviously representing Jed Stewart had been portrayed as a bungling, bumbling idiot. He knew that Tara must have seen it and that she must be furious. He found himself sitting, through delicately applied leverage, next to Ms. Shepherd at a lunch in honor of one of the sixteen or seventeen members of the Attenborough family currently gracing British screens. She had attractive, slightly prune-like eyes and the beginnings of a moustache of the same shade. She was flattered to find herself sitting next to the great philanthropist. He had thought out his pitch and it was a good one.

"Did you see the last Tara Stewart show?" he asked.

Trudy Shepherd, in a neutral tone, said she had.

"I don't know why you two don't get together," he said.

"In what way?"

"Well, you both deal with the underside of the world—only you make it all up and she does it for real. I don't know how much you could help her, but I'm damn sure she could help you. The stories she must have—the ones she can't use for legal reasons. Think how frustrating that must be for her. But if she could see them done as fiction, well it'd be some consolation and it could give you some damn good plays. And I'll tell you something else—to have Tara Stewart's name on the credits as an adviser or consultant or something would lend an air of authenticity to the whole thing that your stuff, if you'll forgive me, hasn't got at the moment. People know you've made it all up. With Tara Stewart on the credits they'd never be sure. Of course, I know nothing about the game, I could be talking off the top of my hat, but it's an idea I've had buzzing around in my head—I'm always sticking my nose into other people's business—and when I heard I was going to meet you today I thought I might as well let it loose."

Patterson had always had a good insight into human nature and he had judged his sell with precision. It had just the right pinch of frankness to be hurtful and just the right dose of new thinking to be inspirational. Like many great criminals, he'd have done pretty well in any other business he'd chosen to take up. He could see he'd reached Trudy Shepherd's snapping little brain cells. Now all he had to do was pray that he was right in assuming that Tara Stewart would have made a point of watching the play about the Mersey Tunnel robbery— as he had himself—and would have seen her father portrayed as an imbecile.

The call came through the next day—from Trudy Shepherd's right-hand man, Jonathan Berystede, the kind of square-jawed Saxon who got her hormones hopping. For his part he found fragrant elves of the Tara species equally toothsome. He had had more than one abortive crack at her at the functions to which television constantly treated itself as a kind of collective security blanket.

"Tara," the light, golden voice said, "Trudy Shepherd would like a word with you."

Patterson had scored maximum points: Tara was still seething over the ridiculing of her father.

"Look," she said, "I know you're after my body. What's she after?"

"Your talent," he said.

"Tell her to get stuffed," said Tara.

"For God's sake!" said Berystede, "you haven't even met her!"

"And if I never meet her it'll be too soon for me," declared Tara. "I don't like what I hear about her, I don't like what I read about her, and I don't like the stuff she's responsible for."

"What's wrong with it?"

"It's crap. And it's dishonest crap. The working class is always the winner, whereas the truth is it's always the loser. Villains and thieves are funny, jolly fellows, who don't do any harm to anyone but each other, which is also crap. People get hit on the head with a crunch that'd turn them into vegetables and get up and dance away. She's a talentless cow with a cheap mind, who uses people who have got talent to sell a fucking lie. Well, she's not using me."

At the other end, Trudy Shepherd put down the extension on which she'd been listening, one of her cute little tricks. She looked at Berystede without speaking. Berystede knew it was going to be a lousy day.

As Patterson was well aware, Trudy Shepherd had a big say on the powerful committee which did the horse-trading by which companies took each other's programs on the network. The only way a program could get a full network showing was if every company agreed to put it out on the same night at the same time. At the committee's next meeting, Trudy Shepherd managed to interfere with her company's treatment of Tara's program. The show was too strong for her to block it altogether, but she succeeded in having her company put it out in a different time slot to everyone else. This effectively prevented it from delivering the sum total of its viewers all in the same hour, which was what was needed for a big rating. The result was the show slipped in the charts. The same happened with the next show. And the next. Non-analytical chart slaves started to murmur that Tara Stewart had shot her bolt. Her novelty had worn off. Even intelligent people, who knew the mathematical reason why, couldn't help being affected by the malaise that starts to drift about a show that no longer commands the heights in the charts, even though it may be getting just as many viewers as ever. Its impact in the newspapers started to fall, too, since it didn't get reviewed in them all on the same day.

Advertisers started to complain that their commercials were being fragmented. It was a self-accelerating process. The Tara Stewart program began to look like a sick show. The acid indigestion from which Shaun Patterson had begun to suffer started to subside. It looked as if Tara Stewart was not going to be around much longer. She couldn't sleep. She could see the great Dream fading away. She knew she was being undermined, but she couldn't identify the tunneler. All she could do was guess.

The week after the show had slipped for the fifth time, Trudy Shepherd and Tara met at a party at the Park Lane Hilton in London, given by Cyril Goldstein to the whole industry, to celebrate the launching of Alhambra all those years ago when people predicted that television would go the way of the perpetual match and the runless nylon.

"Miss Stewart!" smiled Trudy, prune-eyes juicy with malice. "How well you're looking . . . considering. Tell me, have you met any talentless cows with cheap minds recently?"

It was a self-indulgently delicious gloat which was to cost her dear. Tara had only suspected before. Now she knew. Three days later, Trudy Shepherd came in to her spacious, rubber-planted office to find her files broken open and all her most sensitive and confidential correspondence and memoranda missing. The security men had neither seen nor heard a thing. She was distraught. The things that were in those files! Four days later a large packet was delivered by the Post Office. She was overjoyed to find that it contained her missing papers, every last one of them. A closer look showed her that they were, in fact, only photocopies of the original documents. The only clue was a piece of white paper with a curious shape drawn on it. It was finally identified by a researcher with a geographic turn of mind as the outline of a small island off the coast of Scotland. The island was called Taransay.

At the next meeting of the Network Committee, Trudy Shepherd used no arts against Tara's program. The show resumed its rightful place in the Top Ten. Tara had no further trouble from Ms. Shepherd.

For this caper, which had been criminal, she had used none of her associates; not even the Mail Room mob. For this she had called in a discreet mercenary from The Mystery.

Meanwhile, Tara had not ceased chomping away at the problem of how to get to Les Meacher. Each morning, Elsie, the cleaning lady, patiently lifted the chewed-up pencils from the carpet and took them home to Salford, where she displayed them in a jar, like cut flowers, to her disbelieving neighbors, as relics of the blessed Tara Stewart. Les Meacher was a block. Unless she could get past him, she could never put her case together. Worse, she could never construct the trap that was going to send Shaun Patterson down into hell's fires.

It was Mail Room Sid who cracked it. He came in one day with his intimidating features tortured into the excruciating grimace that told his friends he was smiling.

"Tar!" he said, excitedly, "Tar! I've cut it! Les Meacher's tooling up for a job!"

She jumped out of her steel and leather chair and hugged him: "Where? When? What?"

"Give us a kiss," he challenged her.

She kissed that mashed-up visage.

"If you're kidding me," she warned, "I'll straighten that face of yours out . . . slowly."

"Tug Beckett's going into the Lanson Jaffey bullion vaults in Manchester," he said, triumphantly.

Tara never asked Sid where he got his information from, but he was uncanny. Better, even, than her Mystery sources. She was sure it had something to do with his primeval upheaval of a face. It obviously made people feel you couldn't talk to it about anything but villainy.

Tara instantly called a conference. After the excitement at Sid's news had rippled around, she cooled it.

"We've got a snag here," she said. "In the first place, there's no way we can rig a setup which would allow us to film and mike a crime like that. And in the second place, if we did let a job like that go through without warning the scuffers, we really would be in the shit."

"Yeah, we've got away with it so far," said Terry, her wild, cherry-red T-shirt driving Sid to a frenzy as she thrashed about in her chair—she was a girl who couldn't keep still—"but they'd regard that as a dead stuffing liberty."

There was a moment's pause and then Suzy's precision-cut, sexy tones rang out. "My father once got wind that the Reds were going to bug our Embassy in Moscow while it was being redecorated. Détente was at a very delicate stage and nobody wanted any unpleasantness. So every day the wide-trousers would come in and cut channels in the plaster, pop in the bugs, replaster and go away with their great, square, rather sweet biscuit-box faces smiling like pillar-box slits. And every night, Daddy would have British workmen cut out the plaster, remove the bugs and replaster all over again. The result was the Russians thought they had us bugged up to the eyebrows in every conceivable room, but couldn't understand why they never heard a solitary word."

"Suzy," said Tara, "you tell great stories, but what's it got to do . . ."

"No, I get it," said Terry, her T-shirt in turmoil, "every night when Meacher's finished working on his gadget, we nip in, have a dekko at it . . ."

"I film it and take some stills," said Pam, "and record its progress . . ."

"And then, when we can see it's all finished and they're ready to roll," said Ben, "we . . ."

"Nip in and nick it," croaked Sid, wriggling in an ecstasy of joy. "I can find out exactly when they mean to hit the vaults and we can snogget Meacher's gear the night before."

"That way," said Jean Soong, "with the kind of equipment we've got now, we should be able to record the horrible bloody uproar that follows."

Tara looked around at the semicircle of her team, all as crooked as corkscrews, but on the side of the angels.

"I've turned you into a right load of villains," she said, admiringly.

"Don't be so big-headed, darling," said Suzy.

At eleven o'clock every night Les Meacher finished in his workshop in a back street in Kensington, Liverpool, where, not so long ago, there had been a cow byre, with the cows grazing in nearby Wavertree Park and the milk distributed by pony and trap, a milk churn and a ladle. He was working flat out. At two in the morning the Tara Stewart team went in and inspected his work while Pam filmed it. It seemed to be a combination of a thermic lance and a ferocious-looking drill, made of the hardest material, pound for pound, in the world—carbon fiber, identified by Suzy, who had, among other things, a degree in metallurgy. They cataloged the achievements of Les Meacher's expertise day by day. They watched it creep gradually toward completion, Suzy's admiration quite frank and unbounded.

"If this man chose to go straight I could rustle up a half million of venture capital from the City to back him, before you could blink," she said.

"There wouldn't be the same job satisfaction in it for him, love," explained Tara.

Finally, as far as they could understand it, it was ready. There was a pause of a week. Nothing more was done to the equipment. Sid had his oversized ears cocked like radar dishes. Harry, the sound man, experimented with taking vibrations, set up by conversations inside the workshop, from the panes of its two windows. The results were not half as encouraging as fiction about this particular form of eavesdropping had led him to believe. Pam shook her immaculate, geometrically cut red hair, which contrasted so sharply with her disreputable jeans and green-sheep sweater, and prayed that the storm, when it did break, would erupt outside the workshop, where the ultra-sensitive film, which she had helped the manufacturers, over the last three years, to develop, could pick it up with available light.

"Where the blue-sprayed bollocks are they?" she asked the patron saint of cameramen frustratedly as they all waited, fingers on the triggers at Alhambra.

One Thursday evening Sid, looking even more like a crumpled ball of papier mâché than usual, exploded into Tara's office.

"It's tomorrow!" he yelled. "They're going to give themselves the whole weekend to screw themselves in from the empty shop next door."

"We lift the gear tonight," said Tara.

Two o'clock in the morning, they backed the old canvas-topped truck against the workshop doors. Terry unlocked them as if they'd been sealed with marzipan. With Ben Maitland at one end, everyone else at the other, they lifted Les Meacher's laboriously wrought and brilliant contraption into the back of the truck and drove off into the night, leaving one cylinder of methane and one of oxygen, the spare bits for the drill, and the pressurized canisters of lubricant which were to be used to keep the bits cool.

The next day, for nobody would agree to be left out of this, they parked two old canvas-topped trucks within spitting distance of the workshop, with everyone crowded in. They arrived just before dark. They waited for an hour, giggling and speculating on possible scenarios, like schoolkids. As the last of the light seeped from the sky a truck much larger than either of theirs arrived and backed up to the doors of the workshop under the glare of the neon lights outside. Four men, plus Les Meacher, got out, unlocked the workshop and went in. There was a stunned pause of perhaps five seconds, while Sid stuffed a scarf in his mouth to plug the threatened Krakatoa of his laughter. Five seconds later there was the sound as of a naked man who had unexpectedly lowered himself heavily on to a barbed-wire armchair. The voice was that of Les Meacher. Over and around, however, echoed the voices of the other four. They were the voices of men who were not best pleased. To the joy of Tara's team, the extreme displeasure of Les Meacher's partners could not be confined within the walls of the workshop. All five of them spilled out into the little approach roadway right into the Tara Squadron's field of fire.

"What d'you farting well mean, it's been nicked?"

This from a big man in a navy blue polo-necked sweater.

"Nicked? Nicked? How can it have been fugging well nicked?" This from a slight, wiry slip of a man. "Who'd want to bloody nick bloody that?"

"Look, it's not bloody there and it sodding was this after-sod-ding-noon!" yelled Meacher, his sparse, sandy hair standing up as if he'd had an electric shock—which, indeed, he had. "Con-sodding-clusion: it's been nicked!"

On the floor of one of the soft-topped trucks Sid rolled in a balled agony of suppressed laughter. Pam turned film and Harry angled his directional mikes and watched his green, illuminated needles.

"Names!" whispered Tara to herself. "Let's have some names!"

They obliged almost instantly in the shape of Tug Beckett, a stocky, graying bull, also in a dark, polo-necked sweater: "And how, exactly, do you suggest we get inside the Lanson Jaffey vault, bloody mastermind?"

"Listen," said Meacher, "you came to me, remember. The great Tug Beckett had to come to me. You couldn't open a bloody sardine can on your own! I made you the tools for the job. What am I supposed to do, hire a police escort to make sure some thick-headed tea leaf doesn't nick something he doesn't understand for the scrap metal value?"

"He's just learning," choked Mail Room Sid in the van, "it's a bloody jungle out there!" He went purple in the face as Jean Soong clamped a delicate, but educated, arm across his windpipe to hold in his laughter.

The show itself took a new departure.

"This week," said Tara, in a shimmering green Bill Oldfield dress which left one shoulder bare, "we're going to deal with the artisans, the craftsmen of crime, who make the tools that the thieves and robbers use. They're getting more sophisticated and crafty all the time; they keep up with all the latest developments, get all the electronics magazines and such-like as soon as they come out. They really know their stuff. For instance, what would you say this was for?"

Les Meacher spilled his can of lager as he sat in front of his set at home and watched his brainchild being wheeled into the full glare of the spotlights on a trolley.

"Looks like something out of a James Bond, doesn't it? What's it for, you may well ask. Well, it's not for putting up the kitchen shelves, is it? No, it's for cutting and burning a way through eight or ten inches of metal plate—the sort of stuff that nasty, suspicious bank managers and bullion dealers put around our valuables to keep little prying hands off them. I'd like to show you the work that goes into this kind of gismo. This one was built by a man called Les Meacher and every night when he'd toddled off home we used to creep in like leprechauns to see how he'd got on."

She took the viewers on a fascinating Cook's tour of his very professional workshop and showed them how the work had progressed painstakingly day by day. What she did not tell them was the particular job the machine was intended for, nor did she mention

Meacher's connection with Tug Beckett. It looked as if all she'd shown was all she'd got. She was going to play Meacher like a salmon.

The next day when he showed up at Reception, steam coming from every orifice, she gave instructions for him to be shown straight to her office. Ben was lounging in a corner chair as Meacher motored in on full throttle. There were no preliminaries.

"I'm having you, little smartass, for criminal libel," said Meacher, instantly.

"Oh, yes?" replied Tara, calmly. "Like a cup of tea?"

"No, I would not like a bloody cup of tea—did you hear what I said?"

"Yes, I did," said Tara with a charming smile, "and I'd be really knocked out to hear how you're going to do that?"

"You've got nothing on me, nothing. That whole bloody program was innuendo. That tool I'd built was for use in industry."

"Oh yes?" said Tara. "Wouldn't care to tell us the name of the manufacturer who was going to use it, would you?"

"No, I wouldn't; it's none of your bloody business."

"Ever seen this before?" asked Tara, handing him across a sheet of paper. Meacher took it and his stomach twanged like a banjo. It was a ground plan of the Lanson Jaffey vault. It had been thoughtfully acquired by Sid, using methods she had understood but thought it best not to inquire into too closely.

"Never seen it before in my life," he said, handing it back. "You won't find my fingerprints on that."

"We will now," said Tara, with one of her most dazzling smiles. Meacher went to make a grab for it. Tarzan, in the corner, lazily uncrossed his right leg from his left and rearranged them the other way around. Meacher subsided.

"Let's just have a dekko in the Viewing Room," said Tara.

Ben rose to his feet, but Tara gave him the high-sign that she didn't think he'd be needed. Nevertheless, a couple of minutes later, he posted himself outside. Preparation was his religion.

In the Viewing Room, Tara showed an increasingly ashen-faced Meacher the bits that she had cut out of the program. The row with Tug Beckett outside the workshop. The precise mention, loud and clear, of the Lanson Jaffey vaults. The taunt from Meacher to Tug Beckett about how he needed Meacher to get into them.

Tara cut the film and turned on the lights.

"That's conspiracy, Mr. Meacher," she said. "That's ten to fourteen in anybody's book."

"What do you want from me?" asked Meacher, looking, in his

worn tweed jacket and woolen tie, more like a taggle-haired artist than a criminal.

"I want the name of the man who asked you to frame my father," she answered.

"You know I can't do that," said Meacher, his craftsman's hands trembling. His eyes roved around the coral fabrics and chestnut wood of the Viewing Theater almost appreciatively in an absent sort of way.

"You've got no choice," said Tara. "I've got you bang to rights."

He paused a long time, as if measuring things in his mind as he would a length of steel.

"What happens if I do tell you?" he asked.

"Then all that stuff you've just seen will be burned in front of your eyes and the sound tapes destroyed as well." After they'd all been copied, just in case of slipups, she told herself.

"And the police will never get to hear of Lanson Jaffey—none of it?"

"None of it." He knew at once he could believe her:

"It was Tug Beckett," said Meacher. "The man you saw me with in the film. He asked me to fit up your father. There was five grand in it for me if I managed to fix it up and my face smashed in if I didn't."

"And where did his orders come from?" The flawless gray eyes never left his face.

"I don't know. Honest to God, I don't. And I'll tell you something. You won't find out from Beckett." He tapped his head. "He's thick. I'll bet he'll refuse even to come along and see your film. All he knows is muscle. He doesn't have enough up top to tell him he's in danger, except in an animal sort of way. You'll never get him inside this studio."

"Where do I find him?" asked Tara.

"He runs a club down Upper Parliament Street in the 'Pool. It's called The Screw. He's got a muscle mob down there. Smashing in doors is more his line. I don't know who gave him the idea about the bullion vaults." Neither do I, mused Tara.

When Meacher had gone, Tara rang The Screw. She got straight through to Tug Beckett:

"This is Tara Stewart," she said, "I've got something you'd be interested in."

"The only thing you've got that I'd be interested in," he said, in a Bootle accent one could have cut with a butter pat, "you're sitting on."

"How about bullion vaults?" she asked.

There was a profound silence at the end of the line.

"How about somebody nicking the little screwdriver you were going to open it up with?" she continued. "How about sitting on your big fat ass for ten years for conspiracy?"

What Meacher had called Tug Beckett's animal feeling for danger was right. He had hairs standing on end all over his body. He also had a pain in the head from trying to work out what to do about it.

"Why don't you come in to Alhambra and we'll have a little talk about it," she suggested. Which is when Tug had his Great Thought and his headache vanished on the spot.

"No," he said, "why don't you come down here and we can have a little talk about it?"

It was a long time since he'd beat up on a judy. This one deserved it, telling the mugs things they had no right to know on her show.

"I'll call you," said Tara.

"We'll need to be mob-handed," said Ben, "seeing as he will be—and I'll need a plan of the entrances and exits to the club."

Tara grinned.

"Stuntmen!" she said. "Won't make a move without using their brains. As for the mob-handed question, I'm about to ring Len and Corby, see when their next weekend pass is—and a few of their mates. And for the plan of the club, we have Sid and Terry and Jean. Anything they can't get a plan of isn't worth having!"

Her brothers had leave coming in five days. Ben and the Mail Room gang made their preparations. Bella and Suzy asked their current boyfriends to take them to the club, saying they'd heard it was fun. Their real object was to reconnoiter the interior. It turned out to be a surprisingly luxurious establishment, considering its location and its owner, with opulent royal blue carpet, gleaming, brass-trimmed glass tables, well-designed red leather bar seats, and extremely comfortable club armchairs. There was even a small stage. Tara made a mental note to try to trace the real owner. What had been described to her did not sound like Tug Beckett.

While Tara was making her preparations, two hundred and eighty miles away Shaun Patterson was making his. He had, of course, watched the Meacher program. The bitch was confusing the issue by inserting irrelevant crooks between the significant ones, but the latter were beginning to look like a dotted line, building up dot by dot toward a target on a computer screen. He was still sure he was on the right lines, making his counterattack through his show-business contacts, despite the fact that two attempts had failed.

He had just, in fact, had an insight which had dazzled him with its obviousness. It had occurred to him as he was unveiling a plaque commemorating his donation of a new wing to a hospital in Chester and he had cherished it to his bosom all the way back down the motorway to Eaton Square. He was going to turn her own weapon on herself.

Why was Tara Stewart such a formidable enemy? Because she had understood and now commanded the massive power of television to her will. Television had made her and provided her with her weapon. It was now about to unmake her and destroy her for ever—and in particularly humiliating circumstances. Why did people adore her? Because she was on the side of the angels. She was fighting the good fight. She was putting away or exposing criminals whom even the police had not been able to touch because she wasn't bound by the same rules. She was a modern Ivanhoe, Galahad, Robin Hood. She was an electronic "Saint." And all the time, what people didn't know was that her father was in jail for one of the crimes of the century. That she came from a criminal family whose record went back generations. What a fool he'd been to waste that information on Cyril Goldstein, that sophisticate of sophisticates, who knew it anyway. It was the ordinary public who would be shocked by feeling they'd been made fools of. They'd made Tara Stewart. They'd damn sure unmake her.

He spent considerable time considering which method of revelation would have the most impact. Newspapers? He knew all the gossip columnists. No, much better—for his sense of irony, for the fact that he'd be able to watch her suffer, and for the instant, irreparable damage it would cause her—that it should happen on television. Richard Malcolm was a chat show host who spoke a strange mixture of North and South and consequently sounded as if he were talking through a mouthful of mud. He had a plump face like an uncooked bun with two currants jammed in for eyes and a nose like a potato. But he sweated, and the British public take to performers who sweat. They mistake it for sincerity. He was also spiteful in a schoolmarmish way and Patterson felt he was just the man to squeeze the last drop of humiliation out of a revelation which would, anyway, make the show one of the best he had ever had.

Patterson knew Richard Malcolm. He invited him to dinner at the Garrick, then swept him off back to Eaton Square for a late-night brandy. Malcolm, who'd been trying to divine the point of Patterson's wooing of him, sat on the edge of his Louis Quinze *fauteuil* wondering wildly if Patterson were going to offer to fund a satellite television station of which he, Richard Malcolm, would be the godlike head. He was, therefore, a mite disappointed to discover that his host wished to talk about another television performer, especially one who annoyed him intensely. She annoyed him, firstly because she pulled in roughly twice his audience and secondly because she had never made any effort to lose her native accent and it had made no difference to her success. While he, on the other hand, had done his damnedest to lose his, failed and was now stranded on a phonetic mudbank for every impressionist in the business to snipe at.

His disappointment drifted gradually away when he perceived the direction in which Patterson was steering. It appeared that he was very concerned about the maintenance of standards in television. Caesar's wife was mentioned. It was important that people should be what they appeared to be. It was not right that the public should be gulled.

"Quite," was the only comment that seemed to be called for at this stage.

"For instance, it has come to my attention"—Old Patters was getting a bit pompous, wasn't he? He was usually a bit racier a stylist than this; but the next phrase made Malcolm sit up—"that this Tara Stewart's father is a jailbird. In fact, he pulled off the crime of the century—the Mersey Tunnel robbery. Seventeen million pounds. I wonder if Miss Stewart has got any of *that?*"

"Good God!" exclaimed Malcolm. He took a steadying pull at his brandy.

"This information only came into my hands, purely by chance, the other day and I've had a devil of a time wondering what to do with it," said Patterson, studying his companion carefully. "Should I go to the I.B.A., d'you suppose?"

"Oh, I shouldn't be too hasty" said Malcolm, being far too hasty himself. "One never knows how that lot are going to react, nor what they think is important." He steadied himself down a gear, blinked his minuscule eyes, reaching for his statesmanlike look and managing to look like a constipated koala bear. "No, I believe that this kind of thing is best dealt with by the medium itself. It should clean up its own Augean stables. No . . . I hope I'm not being too precipitate here; I could, of course, be in danger of damaging myself. But I would be prepared to have Miss Stewart on my show and challenge her with the facts. I'd have to have my researchers check them, of course."

"Of course."

"It's not that I doubt your word . . ."

"I realize that, my dear chap . . ."

"But one must be professional about these things."

"I quite understand. But isn't there a danger of your inquiries alerting her to your interest in her?"

Richard Malcolm smiled indulgently: "None whatsoever. My people are the most discreet in the business. They could take your scalp off and you'd have no idea until you went to comb your hair."

Richard Malcolm had made the underestimation of his life. Tara Stewart already had him under surveillance before he'd even started his inquiries. He showed up on the photographs sent in by Security Sheilas, keeping its vigil on Shaun Patterson's visitors.

"Who d'you suppose that is?" she asked Suzy.

"It's that lumpen wally Richard Malcolm," said Suzy crisply. "There's no mistaking that nose—like a child's first effort at modeling in clay. Where was it taken? Why are you interested?"

"Oh, just a thought," said Tara.

It was getting harder and harder for her to keep her team in the dark about her grand design. It made her feel rotten, as if she were somehow cheating on them. They were all so loyal and willing and enthusiastic. And all this time she'd been holding out on them. She felt she couldn't keep it up much longer.

"All the same," she said to Suzy, "get the team on to him. If he shows up down here I want to know."

Tug Beckett wasn't the only one with animal instincts.

That Friday Len, Corby and six large, solid Marines in prime condition and civilian clothes arrived at Tara's and quickly got their sleeping bags billeted neatly in appropriate areas of the huge flat. Primed by Les and Corby, they all insisted on giving Aunt Rita a hug and a kiss, brushing her flailing custard bags aside and leaving her gasping for suitable biblical condemnations. She realized herself that "Gadarene swine" was totally inappropriate and reeled off back to her bedroom with, if anything, the beginnings of a hugely fat smile.

Sid arrived that evening with what one of the Marines, Blocko, described as "a map of the camp." They were inclined at first to take the piss out of Sid, with his outrageous clothes and haircut. When they studied his map of the club, its entrances and exits meticulously marked, their attitude signally changed. They treated him as one pro treats another.

Ben arrived. He and the Marine contingent gave each other a swift, searching glance and were well satisfied with what they saw.

Tara rang Tug Beckett.

"Unless you've changed your molecule-sized mind," she said, "I think it's time for that talk."

"Whenever you like, tart-face," replied Beckett.

"I'll drop in Saturday night," she told him. "Better pack a toothbrush and a change of underpants—if you ever do change them."

"Get stuffed!" said Beckett and put the telephone down.

"He always was noted for his rapier-like wit," Tara told Ben, who'd been listening. "Will he be getting reinforcements in, d'you think?"

"No," said Ben, "He's mob-handed there all the time. He's got more muscle around him than the organizer of Mr. Universe. Besides, he's just stupid enough to think you'll be coming alone."

It therefore came as something of a surprise to the management when Tara presented herself in the discreetly glowing red and amber reception area of the club. She wore a batwing-sleeved soft black cotton shirtdress, well above her knees, cinched in with a soft, pleated scarlet leather belt the color of her lips, tights to match both and black high-heeled ankle boots, and she was accompanied by this blond giant, wearing a blue T-shirt and jeans, who looked as if he could walk through walls. It was a carefully thought-out surprise. Ben was impressive enough to be plausible as Tara's sole escort. But not too worrying, in that the odds against him if it came to a rumble were about fifteen to one. If anything, it relaxed the more thoughtful members of the heavy mob more than if she'd suspiciously walked into the lion's den alone.

One of the minders walked forward—black suit, white shirt, black tie, shoulders that looked as if he'd left the coat hanger in his jacket.

"Nobody gets in here without a tie," he grunted to Ben.

"Yours'll do fine," said Ben, ripping it from the gorilla's neck with a movement so fast the eye could hardly follow it.

"Why you—"

The rest of what the gorilla intended to say can only be conjecture since, as he drew his fist back, Ben tapped him smartly across the Adam's apple and he lay on the floor wondering whether he'd manage to get any last words out before he died. While Tara absently checked her lipstick, Ben stepped over him to speak to the eatable strawberry blonde at the desk. She looked on him with some favor and shook her head almost imperceptibly as a second heavy started to move in on Ben.

"Miss Tara Stewart to see Mr. Beckett," he said, with such a sweet smile, showing such teeth, that she felt like taking all her clothes off. Instead, she said, "Mr. Beckett's expecting her" and picked up a telephone. "Miss Stewart's here," she said into it.

She turned to Tara: "You can go in, Miss Stewart. The door at the end of the bar. Mike will show you."

The Neolithic specimen who had been about to chance his arm at Ben until strawberry top stopped him, came forward. Ben went with Tara.

"I'm sorry," said Strawberry, "just Miss Stewart."

"Whither she goeth, etcetera, sweetheart," replied Ben.

Strawberry shrugged her beautiful shoulders with a faint smile and nodded to Mike. Mike led them to a mahogany-paneled door at the end of the bar. The clientele seemed to be a good sort. Pinstripes and pretty girls doing the modest local equivalent of going to Harlem in diamonds and pearls.

Behind the door was a tastefully furnished office, all buttoned leather, paneling, good woods and some not half bad pictures, all of which had obviously been put together by someone else, plus a number of hideous objects which Tug Beckett had equally obviously provided for himself: miniature armored knights that turned out to be cigarette lighters; red, white and blue enameled cannon that fired out cigarettes to one's guests; pen jars that played the overture from *Carmen*.

Tug Beckett rose from behind a massive partners' desk with the obligatory green-shaded converted oil lamp throwing its soft glow. He looked as if he could tow the Queen Elizabeth into port single-handed. Ben, however, noted the little bulge in the region of his diaphragm. Beckett was wearing cloth carpet slippers. In fact his sole concession to club owner's dress was a black tweed jacket over his black polo-necked sweater. He didn't like the look of Ben one little bit. He motioned Mike to stay.

"Miss Stewart!" he said, with unexpected bonhomie.

He came around the desk, put a chunky left arm along her shoulder and shook her hand in his massive paw, squeezing it mercilessly. Pain, he had found, was always a good intimidating start. Tara, in agony, planted her slim high heel just where his toes were attached to his foot and transferred all her weight to it. Nothing was said by either of them, but Beckett's eyes howled in anguish like a Francis Bacon scream and he let go of her hand. He was dealing with a street fighter, by God! She looked like something from a child's picture book and she was a bloody street fighter! He was going to have to re-think his whole strategy here and that didn't come easily to him. He was beginning to get the pain in the head again.

His plan had been very simple. Its essence had been physical intimidation. It worked with most men: his whole life proved it. It certainly worked with every woman. With them it wasn't just the pain, it was the thought of their faces and bodies being smashed up; they had a different feeling about it. So he was just going to rough this cheeky tart up and that would be that. But now he didn't think it would be; not with this one. He'd better find out exactly what she'd got.

"You've got nut'n on me," was his notion of approaching the subject by indirection. By the time Tara had finished telling him exactly what she had got on him, even quoting his own words from the scene outside the workshop, he had perceptibly lost a great deal of color from his brick-textured face.

"And it's no good doing anything to me," she finished, "because that film is locked up in the vaults at Alhambra Studios and if anything happens to me, I've left orders that it's to go on screen tomorrow night. In fact it's going to go on anyway unless I get a little piece of information from you."

"Oh yes?" asked Beckett, trying to keep cool, "and what would that be?"

"Who told you to frame my father, Jed Stewart?"

Oh, Christ, this was Jed Stewart's kid! He was in more trouble than he'd known. Jed Stewart was the only man he'd ever been frightened of in his life; that was why he'd agreed to help put him away. If this judy were anything like her father—and she seemed to be—oh, God Almighty! He tried to assume a mantle of calm, which his churning insides certainly did not feel.

"I'll tell you what we're going to do," he said. "We're all going to go on a little trip to Alhambra Studios in Manchester. You're going to give the old saliva to whoever's there about how you want to work on the film over the weekend. You take the film away and we have a nice little bonfire."

"Don't be thicker than you have to be," said Tara. "What makes you think I'll do that?"

Beckett picked up the internal telephone, buzzed. This was where the good old intimidation came in.

"Harry, come in, will you?"

Harry came in, same size and mold as Mike and the other one who was still choking in the men's lavatory.

"Harry," said Beckett, "who lives with this Miss Tara Stewart judy here?"

"Her mate, Bella, and her piss-artist old Auntie Rita," said Harry.

"Take a couple of the lads, Harry, and go and pick 'em up," said Tug Beckett. "We might need them to answer for tarty Tara's good behavior."

"Right, guv'nor," said Harry, turning to go. He never saw the punch that removed him from the cares of this world for fifty-five minutes.

Ben, ever a quick thinker, had seen it as his first priority to cut down Harry before he could either execute Beckett's order or pass it on. In return he had had to suffer a punch from behind in the kidneys from Mike, which brought him to his knees, but not before an elbow to Mike's gut had brought him to his. Tara, meanwhile, had picked up the tasteful desk lamp and smashed it over Tug Beckett's head.

Beckett pressed his panic button under the desk at almost the precise instant that Ben blew the Marine P.T.I. whistle.

Beckett's heavy cavalry poured in from doors at either end of the room. Ben, who had put Tug Beckett temporarily *hors de combat* with one jab in the area around the diaphragm he had selected earlier and was now clinically demolishing Mike, went down under a torrent of bodies. Almost simultaneously they were taken in the rear by five Marines in anonymous sweaters, led by Len, who had crashed through a door strategically selected by Sid. A second detachment, led by Corby, came crashing through the wide windows of Beckett's office, taking the frames with them.

Numerically speaking, Beckett's forces had a superiority of four. It was not enough. They were big men, but easy pickings and unequal fights had made them no match for young men who spent every day of their lives pushing themselves to the limit. The battle spilled out into the club, on to the stage, into the tiny restaurant, around and about the bar. Girls stood on chairs and screamed, loving it, lashing out indiscriminately with their handbags at anything that came within range. One or two of the Hooray Henries escorting them, remembering the boxing trophies of their schooldays, saw a chance of glory in plunging in, only to reel out again ninety seconds later, looking as if they'd been in some dreadful accident with a hay baler.

Tara had a hatred of physical violence, which she never allowed for an instant to show—had, in fact, trained herself not to show. Her brothers had always been her muscles and she had the same kind of confidence in them that kids had in Superman. For when they were not there, they had trained her rigorously to look after herself and nobody had ever tangled with Tara a second time as she had passed through the growing pains of childhood viciousness. But tonight's violence was necessary. Her brothers would sort out Tug Beckett and she would be one step nearer to plucking her father out of that dreadful hell's cavern where he was gradually losing his reason.

She had seen Tug Beckett go down like a sack of meal from Ben's first punch and then, in the mêlée, she had lost sight of him.

Since the whole point had been to pressurize Beckett into revealing the next link in the chain Shaun Patterson had so patiently woven around her father, it was important to keep an eye on him. She moved among the flying fists and hurtling bodies, looking for him. He was nowhere to be seen. She went on to the dimly lit little stage, with its shadows in the folds of the back curtains. Several bodies were in a state of war there; she wanted to see if he were one of them. He was not.

Without warning a hand clamped itself across her mouth and she was dragged back behind the curtains surrounding the stage. Instinctively, she let herself go without resistance, throwing her assailant off balance. Then she bent, twisted like a cat, grabbed a rough tweed coat and sent Tug Beckett hurtling with a hip throw. He had evidently never needed to learn how to fall. He fell badly and she heard the bone in his thigh go as he hit the floor. The dull snap, accompanied by Beckett's scream, sickened and unnerved her. She ran to the Ladies, stood for a moment with her back to the door. Then she splashed water on her face. She was patting it dry when she saw, in the mirror, the handle of the door start slowly to turn behind her. Utterly irrationally she ran into one of the cubicles and locked the door. She stood, listening, her legs trembling. She heard a sound which she recognized instantly as a dreadful sound, a sound of nightmare and disgust. It was a dragging sound, a sliding sound, as of some repellent snake. It reminded her of a production of *Treasure Island* she had seen as a child. The actor who had played Long John Silver had invented a bit of business whereby he didn't stump along on his wooden leg; he dragged it behind him.

The dragging stopped. She held her breath. No more sound. She slid slowly down the wall of the cubicle until she could look through the space underneath it. She peered fearfully through the gap. There, grinning horribly at her, his bad and filthy teeth bared, was Tug Beckett, lying upon the floor, as she was. His head was bleeding and his right trouser leg was soaked with blood. There was the irregular sharp bump of a compound fracture, the broken bone pushing out the material of the trousers about seven inches above the knee.

"Ah, there you are, little judy," he said. "I couldn't clock you anywheres out there, so I used me nut—some people think I haven't got much up there, but I'm like a dog; I think with me guts. Where would you go to get out of it all, I asked meself. Oh, I know you started it, but I also know you're a right little Lady Muck and the minute the action started, you wouldn't want to know."

She swung her handbag through the gap under the door and caught him full in his noisome mouth. It started to bleed.

"You'll pay for that, pale little tart-face," he said. "You were going to pay anyway, but you'll pay extra for that!"

He reached into a pocket and brought out a flick-knife. He touched the button and a five-inch blade, sharp at the sides as well as the point, hissed out. He made a swipe at her under the door with the knife, in a hand which was also bloody, but she shrank back and he missed. He started to drag himself upright, using a radiator fixed to the wall and a towel dispenser, grabbing the loop of the towel and hanging his armpit over it to give him support.

He started to kick at the door with his good leg, which sounded as if it had a diver's boot on it, so thunderous was its percussion. The flimsy lock on the inside of Tara's cubicle began to give. Tara knew that, even crippled as he was, once he got her trapped in that cubicle, with the knife and the sheer bulk of him, her expertise would not help her. She had to get out. Desperately, she struggled with the lock. It had buckled and jammed under his assaults on the door, which he continued, the sheer reverberating volume of sound against the marbled walls stunning and confusing her. The door shivered and gave way a little more under each kick. Panic finally gave her the strength to wrench the loosened lock-plate from the door. She pulled it open and hurtled out, shouting with relief. She shouted too soon.

Somehow, with a bellow of pain, Beckett shot out his broken leg sufficiently far to trip her, and as she went sprawling he let go of the towel and fell on top of her. She was crushed, winded, his right arm was barred across her throat, his left, which she was attempting to lock, pressed the knife steadily down toward her right eye. She could see the lights bouncing in little stars from its point as it pressed inexorably nearer. Just as she knew she was going to be unable to complete the lock on his arm, that the knife was going to be pressed home, something happened that she did not, at first, understand.

She glimpsed a swift flash of an elegant male shoe, then Beckett went limp, the knife falling from his hand, just missing her face, his great square body rolling off her. Then she was picked up, only half conscious, and carried out of the room, along a corridor, and through a door that led, blessedly, out into the fresh air. She was being carried toward a large car, gleaming in the shadows. There didn't seem at first glance to be anyone in the driving seat. Yet she was loaded gently into the rear, with its smell of fresh leather, her carrier got in beside her and the Rolls-Royce moved silently off and the street lights were flashing by. Her senses returned to her as the oxygen, cut off by

Beckett's choking arm, irrigated her brain. She turned to look at the savior next to her.

It was Jason Planter.

"What the bloody hell!" she exclaimed.

"I'm glad to hear your language hasn't improved," he answered, with his flashing grin; "it wouldn't be you without the combination of the angel's face and the docker's vocabulary. I've just been reading a book about Clark Gable and Carole Lombard. She was just the same. When she really let go . . ."

"Listen," said Tara, "never mind about Carole Lombard, whoever she was, this is twice you've done a turn for me. Once on the motorway when you spooned me off the road . . ."

"Don't let's talk about that," said Jason, a spasm crossing his face as the painful recollection stabbed him.

"And now this," Tara added. Her mind had suddenly gone into turbulence. She had just realized why she had thought at first that there was no driver in the front. The driver was Jason's man Bowman. His matt black face had merged into the shadows, as had his black sweater. The shadows . . . a spectral face that reflected no light . . . a night-face. The phantom in the Security Sheilas pictures! That had been the connection that had lain dormant in her mind, eluding her. The face at which the photographs only hinted was unmistakably Bowman's face. Therefore Bowman was Patterson's master? No, that didn't make sense. Bowman was Jason's servant. It followed that if anyone were Patterson's master, it was Jason. Jason! The man to whom she now twice owed her life. He had a habit of appearing at crises in her life: the crash, the hospital, the cornerstone lunch with Cyril Goldstein; tonight. But then she'd had that odd "fated" feeling about him since they first locked eyes: that needn't be sinister—quite the reverse. The reel of argument and counterpoint flashed forward through her head.

"What were you doing in that place, anyway?" she asked.

"You don't understand the problems of boredom," said Jason. "You with your ego-fulfilling job; you can't possibly relate to the ennui, the constant search for something to divert one . . ."

The telltale crinkle at the corner of the brilliantly dark eye would have given it away even if his syntax hadn't.

"Bullshit," she said, promptly. "You never stop. If you're not making the lives of the poor buggers who run your estate a misery you're risking your neck on the Cresta Run or riding some poor little polo pony into the ground."

"Mere time-fillers," he answered. "A chap has to do something."

"Bollocks!" said Tara. "What about all this high-powered, low-profile business stuff, then? The stuff I was going to be ever such a help with as your assistant?"

"Join me and you'll find out," he offered.

"Nothing doing," she said. "Come on, what were you really doing at The Screw tonight?"

"Very well, then; I happen to like it. It's civilized—God knows how with that management! It's got a chef there who actually does know that food isn't just something you stick through a hole in your face at regular intervals. And it's the one place in that district, if I haven't got Bowman with me, where they look after my car. You can come out knowing it's not going to look like the aftermath of street fighting somewhere in the Middle East."

"But why go there at all?" asked Tara. "I mean, it's a pretty grotty neighborhood and you can just get on the shuttle to London if you're looking for night life."

"I'm a Liverpudlian," said Planter. "If I want to eat out in my own confounded city, what's it to you?"

"Don't get aereated."

"I am not in the least aereated and if it comes to that, what were you doing there and why did you bring the S.A.S. with you?"

"It was to do with a program," said Tara. "We thought it might get hairy."

"You thought right," he said. "What was it all about—that thug who runs the place, Beckett?"

"Professional secret," said Tara.

"All right, be like that," he said. "See if I care." His smile flashed in his deep, new tan.

Tara's face became serious.

"I haven't really thanked you," she said. "He was going to kill me, you know."

"I know," said Planter, a new hint of gravity in his face.

"Thanks, Jason," she said, simply.

She smiled and then started to tremble, uncontrollably. He cradled her to him. He smelled delicious. It was the smell of warm man, cashmere, money and taste. Am I a gold digger? I ask myself, she asked herself in one of her buck-toothed voices. She was a self-starter, she was positive, aggressive, confident, self-sufficient and afraid of no one; but God it was good to be next to something as disgracefully masculine and dreadfully protective as Jason Planter. There were questions to be answered between them, but just now she wanted to luxuriate in the moment.

"Where are we going?" she asked, dreamily.

"I keep a little suite in the Adelphi," he said. "We can stop off and call your private army from there, tell them you're all right."

At the Adelphi, he was treated with as much deference as if he were in his own home. His suite was still as it had been originally designed: in the spirit of Hepplewhite, pale blue and ivory, with masterly cornices and pilasters, fragile paneling. Entrance hall, sitting room, bedroom, palatial bath-dressing room, kitchenette—it was a small domain that stood outside of time. It was a sensation that Jason Planter often gave her, too. It was as if he inhabited a dimension perhaps a millimeter removed from everyone else.

She telephoned The Screw; they'd been going spare looking for her. She told Len briefly what had happened and assured him that she was all right.

"It's all quiet here," said Len. "We're just patching each other up—the opposition as well; they don't know a thing about First Aid. They're not bad lads, but we beat the tar out of them. The only thing is whatsisname, Tug Beckett—he's disappeared."

"What?! Where did he go? How?"

Jason paused in the act of opening a bottle of champagne, which was one of a number in a small fridge in the kitchenette, struck by the tone of her voice.

"Dunno. When it was all over, we looked around for him and he just wasn't there."

"Oh, great!" exclaimed Tara. "Well, listen, have a scout round the neighborhood. He had a broken leg—really bad—he couldn't have gone far."

"Will do. Are you going home?"

"Yes. See you later." She put down the telephone.

"It's Tug Beckett," she said. "Disappeared."

"He'll turn up again," said Jason. "Men like Beckett can't stay out of sight for long."

The exchange with Len had brought her back to earth. It was time to try and get those questions answered.

"Where does Bowman go when you use this pad?" she asked casually, as an ice-breaker.

"Back to the house," he said, "why?"

"Just curiosity," she answered. "He gets about a bit, doesn't he. I've been in London a couple of times the last few months and both times I've seen Bowman."

"Oh? Where?" asked Jason.

"I think it was in Belgravia."

"Ah!" said Jason, "He'd be going to see Patterson for me."

Her pulse leaped. Then she realized something was wrong. If he were really Patterson's boss, he'd hardly have blurted out the name just like that. Or would he? Maybe he was going to confess, tell her he knew all about her vendetta and her whole story.

"Who's Patterson?" she asked, as carelessly as she could manage.

"Partner in a charity of mine called BLADE," said Jason. "Boring man, but I stiff him for a lot of money for BLADE."

"Blade?"

"Black People's Aid, Development and Education."

It came both as a disappointment and a relief. She realized she'd been mentally holding her breath. And yet she still couldn't let it go. Her intuition insisted that there was something. There was a tension in him.

"I hadn't seen you quite like that," she probed. "The great philanthropist."

"There's a lot of guilt in it," he answered, abruptly. "We Planters made our money out of slaves."

He turned away to attend to the champagne. Tara saw that there was suddenly sweat on his brow. She mightn't have got it quite right, but she'd hit a nerve somewhere.

"What's Patterson guilty about, then?" she prodded.

"God knows. Everything, judging by the money he gives away."

His continuing struggle with the champagne was uncharacteristic. He was a man whom physical things obeyed. He was hiding from her. He looked as if he were suddenly in the grip of a waking nightmare. She felt a pig; but she had to be merciless.

"Is that all you're guilty about—slaves?" she pressed. She reminded herself of a remorseless priest.

"It's not just guilt," he answered, his voice strained. "It's fear."

She saw his hands shake. He was undoubtedly on the rack of some anguish which he couldn't control. Her instinct was to soothe him, but she sensed in him a need to confide: she had to exploit it.

"What are you afraid of?" she prompted him. "Bad things you've done?"

His reply took her totally by surprise. He started to recite as if in a dream: "After my father died I was looking in an old sea chest full of family papers. I found a letter from my great-great-grandfather Tobias. It was to his lawyer. He said he'd had seven children by a beautiful black mistress in Sierra Leone. Three of the children were black. Four were white. The white ones were to be brought up with his legitimate children. They were never to be told of their black mother. 'I will list the names of these white-skinned children on the next page,' he wrote. There was no next page. I scrutinized every last sheet of paper in that chest. I scrabbled ridiculously in every crack in the wood. I've looked a hundred times since. Nothing. My great-grandfather could have been one of those children by the African woman." His eyes burned. "Don't you see? If he was, the black gene could be in me! Suppose it is in me. Suppose I married and it sprang out and my wife were confronted by a black child, found out she'd married some sort of freak half-caste."

"Some girls wouldn't think it any big deal," said Tara.

She wanted now to comfort him. He looked as if every nerve in his body were twitching. A thread of sweat trickled from his dense hairline.

"I would," he insisted. "I do. It's the not knowing that's worst. There's not a day in my life that I don't wake up and look straight at my fingernails, imagining I can see a purple tinge underneath. I know it's wrong, intolerant . . . obsessive. I can't help it. It's me. And there's the horrible dream . . . it's all mixed up with that."

"What dream?" she asked. She saw him visibly tighten his ropes.

"No, I'd no right to unload on you like that," he said. "What the hell was I thinking of? Please be kind and forget the whole nonsense. Here, let's have some champagne."

His hands still shook as he poured it. She was horrified and guilty at the misery she had unleashed. She moved close to him.

She took the bottle from his right hand and the glass from his left and put them down. Then she folded her arms around him and laid her head against his chest.

"Look," she said, "I know there's some smartass proverb that says never save anyone's life because then you become responsible for them for ever after. Well, like all smartass proverbs, it's wrong. I'm an authority after tonight and I can tell you what really happens when someone saves your life. You love them. Oh . . . not the way it sounds. Not in any way it usually means. You don't want them to be responsible for you. You want to guard them. They become, like, family and if there's anything you can do for them, like, *anything* . . . you'll do it."

She felt him relax as she talked, his muscles softening against her. She pushed on.

"I don't really know what's wrong—not properly—and you don't have to tell me. But I don't think there's anything you need that I can't give you. All you've got to do is ask."

He put his hand under her chin and tilted her face gently toward his. If that proud, commanding face could ever look vulnerable, it looked it now. She felt a terrible responsibility.

"I want to sleep," he said simply, "and I don't want to dream. And if I do dream, I want someone with me. That's all I want. Do you understand me, Tara? That is all I want."

She put out a hand and stroked his face.

They slept naked in the big swansdown bed. He buried his face in the hollow between her neck and her shoulder and gave a huge sigh, as if he had come home from a long journey, and he went to sleep like a child. She wondered what Michael's reaction would be if he could see her now; whether he would understand the sense of pride the regular, untroubled breathing of this hard-bodied male creature gave her.

The nightmare struck at three o'clock. Tara, sleeping lightly, had expected something of the kind; she didn't quite know why. She was on him in a flash, quenching his screams with her mouth, stroking his quivering flanks as if he were a frightened horse until slowly, slowly, his nerves responded, were tranquilized and then, inevitably, aroused again in a different way. They lay on their sides, muscle-ribbed stomach to glossy, smooth, firm one. She was relaxed and open and as juicy as a peach, and as he slid into her, hard and educated, it didn't even occur to her to think of the rightness or the wrongness of what she was doing. She simply moaned like a lioness at the sleepy sweetness of it, taken at precisely the right moment. And that moment, as she had felt earlier, was somehow out of time.

9

Tug Beckett had disappeared. Ben, Tara's brothers and her friends and contacts had been looking for him all night. It was Jean Soong, later in the morning, at the office, who came up with the answer. Beckett was known to be friendly with the Chi Kung Thong, she said. He was probably holed up in the impenetrable tangle of interlocking basements and false walls under the streets surrounding Great George Square, which had been vital to the Thong's survival during the opium wars of the 1890s, but were now used mainly as sanctuary for fugitives—from whatever pursuers—whom the Thong happened to like.

"Can you find him?" asked Tara.

"I can't even try," said Jean. "I can't go against the Thong. But he's got to come out. As soon as he does, I'll know."

Tara was frustrated. She was pretty sure that Beckett was the last link in the chain that led to Patterson. She was almost glad, for the moment, to have other things to think about. Suzy had picked up on one of Richard Malcolm's·researchers. She had known where to find him because one of Mail Room Sid's contacts had seen him sniffing around Tara's old neighborhood and he had stuck out like a striped banana. His name was Peter Rick, he was about twenty-six, and Sid had followed him. Suzy met him in a wine bar near the elegant Exchange Flags concourse where slaves were once bought and sold. Suzy had legs which to glance at once was to lose all sense of self-discipline. Peter Rick had looked idly down the bar from his Ploughman's Lunch just as Suzy crossed them and been instantly landed, gasping, on the bank.

"I've ordered a bottle," he shouted down the bar with a smile, "and I'm afraid it's proving too much for me." He had a pleasant, cultured voice and a well-cut tweed jacket. "I wondered if you'd care to help me out?"

"Now that," answered Suzy "rather depends on the label."

Peter Rick brought his lunch and the bottle down the bar to her and they spent an extremely pleasant hour. Suzy, one of the great fun liars of her era, told him in intimate detail about her chic little antique shop, and Peter Rick, mesmerized by the delicate, diamond-cut face, told her how he was one of a team who were out to help Richard Malcolm to do a sensational live interview with the great Tara Stewart. It had to be live, he explained—Suzy had bought the second bottle and had one glass out of it—because if it were recorded for later transmission, Tara Stewart would probably have it blocked. Did Suzy know, asked Peter—his face considerably slacker than it had been an hour ago—who Tara Stewart's father was? . . .

That afternoon's conference in Tara's office was spectacular even by its own exciting standards. Tara summoned her entire staff, including secretaries. She invited Paul. She did not invite Cyril Goldstein. She considered she owed him a private explanation. She was in her old working rig of jeans and bomber jacket. She laid out her grand design before them. She told them who her father was—the Mail Room Mafia already knew, naturally—and what had happened to him and what she had been working toward doing about it. There was a profound silence as they took in the size and audacity of the task this slender girl had conceived.

"I'm really sorry not to have told everyone before," she went on. "There's not one of you I wouldn't trust with my life, but I just didn't dare risk a leak. Well, now Shaun Patterson has obviously worked it out anyway. Next week he plans to have Richard Malcolm take me to pieces, live, on his show. Blood sport. The Great Defender of the Right and the Good turns out to be the daughter of the greatest criminal of the century. Roll up, roll up, watch Tara Stewart destroyed before your very eyes. So what am I going to do about it? I could always refuse to do the interview, of course. But then Patterson could arrange for the newspapers to find out that I had refused—and why. Which would be even worse. So what am I going to do about it?"

There was silence. Sid's face looked, more than it usually did, as if he was in pain. Then the man who knew her best, the man who'd taught her, spoke quietly: "You're going to pull the rug from under him. You're going to tell them first. On your next show."

She ran to him and reached up to put her arms around his neck.

"Oh, Paul, I hoped you were going to say that!" she cried.

"Why wouldn't I?" he demanded, brown eyes twinkling.

"Well, you're my Head of Department, you could have considered it an improper use of the show, you could have said I had no business from the beginning using a great public medium just to help my own father, you could have said I conned you . . ."

"Yes, I could," answered Paul, "I could have said all that and, as a matter of record, I think it's all true. But the fact remains that a public confession, like that, in front of two-thirds of the country, the way you'll do it—what a show! I'm just a corrupt, venal, amoral purveyor of bread and circuses to the public; what other choice can I make!" And I love you, he thought, and I want you to win and, by God, anything I can do to help you win, I will do. Everybody cheered.

Now she had to go and see Cyril Goldstein.

Walking in to see Cyril G., she understood for the first time the quality that had always eluded her about his office. It was the room of a philosopher, not of a tycoon. She refused all offers of tea, coffee, cakes, biscuits.

"I've got a personal confession to make," she began.

"If it's about your father, I've known forever," he said. "What's it got to do with me? You want to discuss the theological stain of the sins of the father, go and see a rabbi. Myself, I'm in television."

"It's about an enemy of mine and my father's," she said.

"I know who your enemy is," he said.

"You can't!" exclaimed Tara.

"Shaun Patterson?" asked Cyril G.

Tara sat quietly, composing her scattered wits for a long moment. Then she told him the whole story and what she proposed to do. He heard her out in silence. When she'd finished, he gazed at her steadily for what seemed an age.

"You are, without doubt, the most exciting kid I have ever met in my life. Since I've known you, you've given me nothing but near-heart failure, turmoil, carnage with the network and the I.B.A., and writs flying about like seagulls around a trawler. But you've given me *television!* My God, when I think of some of the pap and the crap I have to put out and then I think of the Life you've put on my screens!"

He paused, got up and started to pace.

"This, mind you, is different. This is a question of morality. Oh, the hell with it, who am I kidding—I'm just a sentimentalist who likes to see the goodies beat the baddies. This is the goodies versus the baddies and the goodies have got to win. If needs be, I'll put a tank on the lawn of the I.B.A. while you grind your enemies into breadcrumbs."

Tara planted a smacking great kiss on Cyril's astonished round face and belted out of the door. Then she drove off to see her father on her regular visit and she talked to him very intensely. His face was like an outcrop of granite when she started. By the time she'd finished it was as if the sun had thrown a brief shaft of light across the crevices and cracks.

Richard Malcolm sat in his overheated London flat—strange that it should be overheated since he sweated so easily—settled his comfortably rounded hips into his chintzy armchair and gently stroked a leaf of one of his rubber plants while scanning his clipboard with his notes on it for the Tara Stewart interview. The interview was tomorrow night and he was just waiting to see Tara Stewart's latest show tonight in case there were any points he might be able to pick up and incorporate into what was undoubtedly going to be the biggest demolition job since they knocked down the walls of Jericho.

Richard Malcolm always had a tape running through his head on which he played to himself a selection of scenes from an extensive repertoire, ranging from what he was going to get up to next time with his newest friend to a rerun of an argument he had just lost in which, this time, crushingly, he won it, to the maximum humiliation of his opponent. The tape that was running at the moment was a preview of how he saw the confrontation with Tara Stewart going. After a preliminary interview with a pop star, who'd claimed that he was now definitely off the Valium and back into singing just slightly off the note, the main bout of the evening was about to start.

Tara Stewart, on his mental tape, sashayed on, in one of those soft, body-clinging dresses of hers, looking bloody devastating. Fine. That was fine. The more splendid the monument, the more impressive its fall. He was already seated in the chair that favored his better side. He rose, in a very gentlemanly fashion, remembering to suck in the stomach, to greet her. "Ladies and gentlemen, Miss Tara Stewart . . . blah, blah, blah . . . All know what Miss Stewart does . . . national institution, blah blah . . . In case there should be one recluse somewhere who is unaware of the contribution Miss Stewart has made to the cleaning up of our society . . . blah, blah." Show some clips of her more spectacular unveiling of crooks and gangsters. Miss Stewart now lulled into a perilous sense of security. First salvo. Watch her little antennae quiver.

"Miss Stewart, would you say that your personal involvement with crime was rather closer than most people realize?"

The innocent, singsong voice: "Well, since I'm dealing with it all the time, I'd think most people would imagine it must be pretty close, like."

"No, that's not exactly what I meant, Miss Stewart. What I was wondering was whether there was any criminality closer to home . . ."

"I don't think I'm with you." The long black eyelashes flicker, the gray eyes suddenly darken. The hook is in and she feels it. She knows that he knows. Hopes against hope that she's wrong, but, at base, sees the big black cloud closing in.

"Well, I mean," he continues, urbanely, "lots of ordinary people have had brushes with the law—motoring offenses, parking, dear old aunties walking out of stores with half the lingerie department concealed, unpaid-for, about their person" (titter from audience, quick, knowing acknowledgment thereof from him) "you know the kind of thing I'm getting at."

"I suppose we've all been a bit naughty at some time or other." Was her face beginning to sweat, very lightly?

"It's just that you seem so very knowing about villains, Tara—if I may call you Tara . . ."

"Why not? If I can call you Richard."

"Of course you may. Let nobody say that ours" (winning smile to audience) "is not a cozy little program. But to return to our sheep, as the French say. Why they say it, I don't understand. But, then, there's a lot I don't understand about the French." Round of applause. Never fails. Sweat on Miss Stewart's face thickening nicely. Sadistic bastard, she's probably thinking: all the better; she might lose her cool.

"I'm sorry," she says, "I've lost the track. But I think you were asking me about how widespread contempt for the law has become in our society . . ." Oh, no you don't, missy, you're not haring off down that track. He'd better put in his Sunday punch before she took control and ran away with him as she very well might.

"No, I wasn't talking about that at all, Miss Stewart. You look so lovely tonight, I suppose I'd forgotten what it was I really wanted to ask you about. Is it true, Tara Stewart, that your father is Jed Stewart, mastermind of the Mersey Tunnel robbery in which he got away with seventeen million pounds of little people's money? And is it also true that none of that money has ever been recovered?"

Gasps from the audience. Close on Tara Stewart. Every nuance of her thought processes being picked up by the cameras. His bosses swinging from the chandeliers as they watch the major threat to their ratings going down before his guns . . .

His reverie was interrupted by the run-up to Tara's show tonight. The continuity announcer was banging the drum; there'd be four minutes of commercials and then she'd be on. He heaved himself to his feet, fixed himself a Rob Roy and settled down again, the glass glowing by his side. He was glowing, also.

Five minutes later, the Rob Roy was staining his fake Aubusson a rich burgundy and he was reflecting on the transitory nature of human happiness. This time it was a real tape he was watching, not the one in his head. Tara had never looked more stunning. She had on one of those slithery dresses that showed the perfect slide of her shoulders and swerve of her hips. Like her eyes, one couldn't quite define the precise gray-blue color. Her hair glittered like a fall of gold. Her expression was a mixture of defiance and vulnerability. She used no preamble. The instant the camera was on her, she opened up.

"It suddenly hit me," she said, "you don't know about me. I didn't think it mattered, but it's been pointed out to me by someone I respect, that it does. I'm always on about crime—right? Exposing it and trying to help ordinary folk fight back against it. What you don't know is that I'm from a criminal family myself. D'you know who my father is? He's Jed Stewart, master criminal of the century— so they say. He's the man who's supposed to have got away with seventeen million pounds from the Mersey Tunnel job. You've all seen enough cruddy films on T.V. to laugh when I say I think he was framed, but it doesn't matter. He didn't do that one, but he did do a lot of others before he went straight and that's how I come to know so much about villains. When my old man found out how my mother felt about villainy, well . . . that's when he gave it up. And that's why I've dedicated my life to doing what I can to make up for the rotten things I know my father did before he went straight."

Richard Malcolm had one of his hot flushes. Then he went deathly cold. Then he crumpled up every sheet of paper on the clip board on his lap, poured himself another Rob Roy and telephoned the number of his personal assistant. Naturally, the cunning little bastard had the Ansafone on, didn't he? Probably pushed the answer switch one microsecond before he, Malcolm, had dialed the number. Not that there was anything Roger could do, but he could *be* there, godammit, to give him a battering post to flog at and rail and cry to and whinge at while he watched his definitive program of the year go down the slimy tubes!

What was he going to do for a program tomorrow night when that bitch of bitches had just pulled the plug on him tonight? What made it worse was that he had only himself to blame. Roger, who was hunchy about these things, had told him not to mess with Tara Stewart.

"What d'you mean?" he had asked, outraged. "You think I can't handle her?"

And Roger, now he thought of it, had said something interesting.

"I just think she's bigger than what she does," he said.

Watching his flat screen the size of his drawing room wall in Belgravia, Shaun Patterson cursed with the orotund inventiveness that springs only from a Merseyside training.

Watching in the Viewing Room at Alhambra, Tara, Paul, Ben, the Mail Room gang, Suzy, all her team, held their breath and knew that it was good. It was one of those gambles that could have fallen embarrassingly flat on its face. As it was, it took you between wind and water with its frankness and Tara grew in stature. Before the show was half over, the switchboard was jammed with calls from viewers. Eighty-five percent of them were congratulatory. Ten percent said they would never watch the show again ("I'll give them two weeks," said Paul), and the remaining five percent, as usual, detailed, before they were unplugged, precisely why they were the only male beings on the planet who could satisfy Tara Stewart beyond her wildest fantasies.

Back in his flat in Earl's Court in London, while the Australians performed their nightly ritual of "parking a tiger" or "smiling a technicolored smile" in front of his flat, which meant throwing up most of the Foster's beer they had ingested during the evening all over his front steps, Richard Malcolm, pro that he was, was desperately rewriting tomorrow night's show. He was trying to find a flaw in the Stewart diamond.

Tara Stewart was not just good; she was formidable. It was not coincidence that she had made her preemptive strike tonight. It meant that she had built up resources which had enabled her to penetrate his operation. That was impressive. He suddenly went cold as he wondered what she might have on him. He knew that tomorrow night he was going to be in the fight of his life.

He refilled his shattered Rob Roy and wiped the sweat from behind his ears. He might have felt better had he known he had an unexpected ally working for him even at that moment. Malcolm operated from the B.B.C. Television Center in Shepherd's Bush in London. Tara, her own program already in the can, had come up to London that day to avoid a rush on the morrow. She was staying in Blake's, the discreet show-business hotel behind Drayton Gardens in Kensington.

Michael had come to her there to give her dinner in probably the only dining room in London, with its clever complex of strategically placed smoked glass and artfully sited spotlights, where one could both see what one was eating and not be painfully on show. All that could be seen were reflections. Of the people themselves, when one came to look, there was no sign.

"I want you to go easy on Richard Malcolm tomorrow," Michael was saying. He had his glasses off and he looked like a young Robert Redford.

"You what?" she asked, incredulously.

"I know you've got him cold and I know he meant to shoot you out of the sky, but you've taken care of that and to give him a hard time now would only be vengeful."

"You bet your little tweed hat it would!" replied Tara. "People have got to learn not to take liberties with me. Listen, what's Malcolm to you?"

"Nothing. I just thought . . ."

"Michael . . ."

"I just don't want to see you appear malicious."

"Mike, don't bullshit me. Who asked you a favor?"

He was stubbornly silent, angry that she wouldn't grant him his request automatically. For her part, she didn't need an answer. She knew. It was Michael's father, Shaun Patterson, who had put Richard Malcolm up to his hatchet job. It was Shaun Patterson whom Malcolm was going to blame when she chopped him into pieces. And Malcolm *was* vengeful. He would see that Shaun Patterson suffered for getting him into this. The puzzle was to know what he had on Patterson with which to make him suffer. The rest of her dinner was uncharacteristically silent. Not because she was sulking, although he might have been; but because she was rethinking her tactics for tomorrow night.

When she had learned what Malcolm intended to do to her, she had set in motion two lines of action. The first was to prepare her own preemptive strike. The second was to put Suzy, Bella, Ben and the Mail Room Mafia, including Jean and her computer, plus a very private detective into finding out everything they could about Mr. Malcolm, right down to his black nylon bikini underpants. She had the dossier upstairs.

She didn't underestimate Malcolm. It had been her plan, although he was the interviewer, she the subject, to have it all on her own clipboard as she walked on and make a kind of joke of it, only using any of it, or giving him a hint of what was in it, if he looked like getting the better of her despite her initial advantage. Now, like a cloud rolling in the wind, her plan was beginning to change shape. She and Michael did not go to her room after dinner, as he had obviously expected. As his princely back, stiff with mortification, disappeared through the Rolls door his chauffeur held open for him, she felt again the pain of the ambivalent relationship she had with him: ambivalent only on her side; he simply loved her. She was using him, had just done so.

She telephoned Richard Malcolm first thing the next morning. He, with his liver still fighting a gallant rearguard action against the previous evening's Rob Roys, had agreed to have lunch with her at Langan's Brasserie before he'd properly detached his tongue from the roof of his mouth, to which it appeared to have been Velcroed. After half a pint of orange juice and a prairie oyster, which constituted his breakfast, he was beginning to feel decidedly better. He was fast coming to the conclusion, in fact, that her invitation had been a sign of weakness. That for some reason, although she had car-bombed him over the rooftops the previous night, she was still afraid of him and of their encounter this evening.

She was twenty minutes late at Langan's. He had expected ten. Peter Langan had already had a go at him about being stood up *again,* which didn't happen to be true, but how did one argue with a man who might just bite you on the knee for fun? Malcolm reckoned he had lost the first round. He had to forgive her everything, though, when she did arrive, wearing a glittering gold skullcap the same color as her hair, which streamed down beneath it, and a gossamer chain-mail gold dress blown together by leprechauns, and he knew that every man in the room and at least five of the women would have given a great deal to be in his place.

"Like a drink?" she asked, as she was seated, by Langan himself.

"Well, I'm not sure . . ." he began, taking full cognizance of the intelligence of those incredible eyes; he might need all his wits here.

"He'll have a Bellini," she told the waiter, "and so will I."

She doesn't sound like a frightened girl to me, thought Malcolm.

They clinked their glasses together and wished each other health. What variety was she wishing him, he wondered.

When the menu came, he got two. One in a leather cover from the management and the other, in cardboard, from Tara. He studied, pleasurably, the first—he liked his food—and then glanced at the cardboard file Tara had handed him.

"What's this?" he inquired, amused, the Bellini laving his throat, the envy of the glances radiating from all corners laving his ego.

"Why not have a look?" suggested Tara, in her most innocent lilt.

Malcolm took a peek and the sun went in. He groped for his Bellini.

Inside the folder there was a file on him that would have done justice to MI5. As his slightly protruding eyes raced through it, his face turned the color of his Bellini.

"What . . . what's this?" he stammered.

"I would have thought you'd remember most of it," she said.

"I deny every word of it, naturally," he said. "Anyway, what's it for? You've already won. What d'you need that stuff for?"

"Well, I'll tell you," she said. "I had it in reserve just in case you decided to be naughty in some other way on the show."

"You were going to hit me with that stuff?" he asked, incredulously.

"If necessary."

My God, he thought, this girl is a worse swine than I am!

"Well, I'm not going to get up to any tricks," he said, as levelly as he could, "so you can put it away."

"That's how I thought this discussion was going to end . . . at first," said Tara. "But then I had a better idea. You see, I know it was Shaun Patterson who put you up to doing the hatchet job on me. And after I'd exploded you, it was also Shaun Patterson who arranged for someone to ask me to give you an easy ride tonight. I want to know what it is with you two. What's the connection?"

"There isn't one!" protested Malcolm. "He's into show business, that's all. We've met at one or two charity functions."

"I don't think so," Tara contradicted. "I think that he accepts that he got you into this and if I crucify you tonight you're going to blame him and you're going to want to make him suffer in return, because that's the sort of person you are."

"I am not!" The indignation of Richard Malcolm's reply would have convinced a cynic with a heart of stone, but it had no effect on Tara.

"There's no need to get your black bikini in a twist," she started.

He visibly jumped in his chair. She even knew what sort of underpants he wore!

"Now, as I was saying, if you can make Patterson suffer, you must have something on him. And I want to know what it is."

"Even if I did have something on Patterson, which I haven't, why the interest in him?" he countered.

"Because he set me up for you. Now come on, let's stop farting about, Malcolm, Either let's have it or I'll blow you out of the water tonight."

There was a pause while they ordered. Malcolm felt about as much like eating as swallowing swords, but he ordered some Dublin Bay prawns to have something to do with his hands. Tara, her healthy young appetite snarling, started with half a dozen oysters, followed by a big, juicy tournedos.

Richard Malcolm cracked and fiddled with his prawns: "I could just cancel you tonight—get someone else instead of you," he said.

"Oh dear, what a fuss in the newspapers!" exclaimed Tara. She tapped the file. "And this would somehow get to them as well."

Malcolm hesitated, then conceded defeat.

"I don't know what it means, but I know that Patterson's hiding someone in his flat," he said.

"*Hiding* someone?"

"There's a small suite attached to his butler's. That flat's like a maze. Patterson had left me on my own for a minute and I was looking for a loo."

A likely tale, thought Tara. No wonder Malcolm had that prod-nose.

"Anyway, I went into this room and there was this chap, sitting there on the bed like the Rock of Gibraltar, one leg in plaster, all strung up. He looked shocked. Just then, the butler chap came in and hustled me out before I could get a word in. Later, Patterson told me some cock and bull story about an old retainer fallen on hard times. Old retainer! He looked like something you swing on the end of a crane to knock buildings down."

Which, thought Tara, was exactly what Tug Beckett did look like. After the battle at The Screw they had scoured the local hospitals for Beckett, but he had vanished. Now she knew where. She knew something else, too. That Patterson had worked out that she must have a detective agency watching the house and had bought them. How else could a man, looking like Tug and with a broken leg, have got into Patterson's flat without the agency seeing him and sending her a picture. She made a mental note to keep the agency on the payroll, so as not to alert Patterson to the fact that she knew they'd been corrupted, but to hire another one to do the real work. Meanwhile, there was Malcolm. She mustn't let him see how helpful he'd been.

"And that's what you've got on Patterson," she said, scornfully.

"You didn't see Patterson's face," replied Richard Malcolm.

The Richard Malcolm show that evening was pure froth. Two old mates, sparky characters, bouncing off each other. Tara got the first bounce in:

"You've had your nose fixed, haven't you, Richard?"

"Had my nose done! Do you mind! This is the very nose I was born with."

"No, it used to be all twisted to one side. Now it's straight."

"Miss Stewart, we are not here tonight to discuss the angle of my nose. I want to talk to you about your meteoric rise in television. How does a beautiful girl like you . . ."

"Well, if it's not your nose, it's your face, then. They've left your nose alone and tilted the rest of your face to match it . . ."

Up in London, in the opulent Sahara of Eaton Square, Shaun Patterson watched the show with a great sense of relief. In his bed along the corridor, Tug Beckett peered past his jacked-up leg at his T.V. screen and felt the same. Neither would have been anything like so happy had they known what was formulating, even then, behind that lovely face.

"He's well known, darling, as the biggest snob and climber since that chap, whatsisname, who went up the Himalayas because there was an Earl in the party."

It was Bella speaking and it was Tara's Monday morning conference. The conferences had taken on a different tone of late. First they would discuss what crook was the target for the next show. Then they would turn to the much more fascinating subject of Tara's grand design, of which they were all now a part.

"Didn't I tell you that you were going to need me?" demanded Suzy, triumphantly. They were discussing Shaun Patterson and the whereabouts of Tug Beckett. "He's made for me. I could wrap him around my little . . ."

"Steady, Suzy," Ben interrupted.

The problem under examination was, quite simply, how to kidnap Tug Beckett from Shaun Patterson's flat. Michael Patterson was no problem; he was in Marbella where his father had big property interests. That left Shaun Patterson himself and his "minder," the butler. Bella volunteered to pick up the latter at his favorite pub in Sloane Square—"he always fancied me"—make a steady out of him, then keep him dangling until the right time. Suzy volunteered to ensnare Shaun Patterson.

She scooped him up at Ascot on King George and Queen Elizabeth's Diamond Stakes Day. He was a keen racegoer, owned three horses himself but, in Suzy's words, "knew nobody." His horses ran as well as they could, given their bloodlines, his trainer tolerated him because he was a millionaire and never interfered, and the jockeys who rode for him were very jolly and nice, the way they'd be to the stable lads. Suzy managed to have him knock her binocular case off her shoulder while she was talking to Ben and Crystal Brenn in the unsaddling enclosure. As he picked them up and handed them back, his too-proper hat in the other hand, he was lost. Suzy, with her delicate strength, always looked her best against other gleaming thoroughbreds, fresh turf and jockey's flaring silks. He offered to buy her a drink. She thanked him, but said she was expected in the Duke of Abergavenny's private box with its private lift—perhaps he'd care to come? Patterson finally got his feet untangled and followed her. Before she'd finished, she'd introduced him to Captain The Hon. Nicholas Beaumont, Clerk of the Course; to the Queen's Representative, Colonel Bengough; she'd even taken him, Holy of Holies, into the suite from which Racecourse Security Services operated the photo finish. By the time he drove her back to the Knightsbridge flat of her cousin, soon to be a lady-in-waiting to the Princess of Wales, he was besotted.

Two weeks later, both Bella and Suzy said it was a "go." Whenever the second team wanted to move in and snatch Beckett, they could make sure that both Patterson and his "butler" were out of the way. Bella even guaranteed to have the butler so pissed by the time they left the flat that, even if he remembered to turn on the alarms, she would have no difficulty in turning them off again.

The next night, Bella led a reeling "minder" out of the flat in Eaton Square and deftly flipped back the security switches to "off" as she did so.

Patterson was already out, swaying around the illuminated night-landing pad of Annabel's dance floor safely in the slim, calculating arms of Suzy.

Ten minutes after Bella's departure, a smart private ambulance, of American design, drew up in front of the annex to the Patterson flat. Ben Maitland and three other stout lads, whose feats would not have been unknown to movie buffs, went in through the front door, which had been conveniently left open by Bella. They gave a polite "good evening" to Tug Beckett, slapped a strip of adhesive tape across his mouth, fastened, similarly, his wrists and his one mobile ankle to a trolley to which they transferred him, and wheeled him out to the ambulance. As they drove off down the King's Road, they were professionally proud to note there wasn't a bruise on him.

Some hours later Beckett's situation was not quite as comfortable. His leg was still being professionally cared-for by Ben, who knew about such matters. But he was in Tara's flat in Liverpool and there was this gigantic lunatic of a woman who came in, periodically, to belabor him with pillowy bags—they'd slyly told her he was a Mormon—and Tara Stewart and her friend Ben had been hinting that this was just playtime. The serious business started later. It came, in due course, in the shape of Ben popping in now and then and tidying his bad leg ever so slightly out of its true position. Beckett's complaints were long, loud and on many layered levels of obscenity. When Ben had finished, Tara would come in and remind him of what the courts would do to him if he fell into their hands. She would then round off her little homily with a graphic presentation of what Jed Stewart would do to him when Beckett joined him in Walton Gaol.

Beckett was as tough as an old saddle, but the treatment had the terrible quality of remorselessness. They put a quartz clock by the side of his bed and they never varied the time of their visits by so much as five seconds. He knew, with a terrible inevitability, the precise moment when the treatment was about to start again. In addition, Ben hurt him just that measured little bit more each time he gently moved his leg about. He took to bringing Bella with him. She would sit, with her madonna face, watching him squeal like a child and the hurt to his ego was almost worse than that to his leg. Above all, he sensed a quality of mercilessness in these people that froze his marrow. They all knew precisely what kind of foulness Tug Beckett had been guilty of for most of his adult life and there was a terrible absence of pity in their faces.

In the end, he told them what they wanted to know, spilled it into Tara's tape recorder with such a rapid fluency, finally, that they had to ask him to slow down. This time, too, they added the refinement of a hand-held camera, operated by Ben, sound-synchronized, that stayed in close shot on Beckett's face the whole time he was speaking.

Beckett had been the prime carpenter in the framing of Jed Stewart. He had briefed Les Meacher, the engineering genius, who had briefed Iron Jack, the immigration trickster, who had briefed Tom "The Roofer" Lane. He had received his own instructions directly from Shaun Patterson. Tara leaned back in her chair and closed her eyes. The most overpowering sensation of relief and happiness swept over her. Her long and labyrinthine odyssey was over. She had rescued her beloved father.

It was her tiredness talking. She had reached only the beginning of the final complexities of the maze.

They began almost immediately. As she'd known, the minute Patterson came home and found Beckett gone he would know she had him and he would send his wolves howling northward. Which was what, after losing fifteen minutes of precious time in furniture-smashing, butler-beating and obscenities, plus a further half hour rounding up a team through a proxy—he couldn't reveal his own face—he did. A convoy of cars containing twelve men went arrowing up the M1 toward Liverpool.

Just under four hours later, they drew up outside the wooded isolation of Tara's flat on the edge of the forest. This was going to be one of their easier little earners. Ben Maitland, however, had not been exactly idle himself. He'd been in touch with a bunch of Northern lads, who ran a firm called "Rentathug" supplying T.V. and movie companies with the bodies for riot scenes, Hell's Angels beating up old ladies, bar brawls, ugly picketing—anything that required a few faces that only their mothers could love.

The first of Patterson's men, dressed as a policeman, to ring the bell, got a smash in the face with a squelchy bag from the fattest woman he had ever seen and a glimpse of a distressingly large blond geezer behind her. As the rest of the team started to climb out of their cars, Rentathug, whom Ben had had waiting in nicely heated, lager-equipped coaches hidden in the trees, started to stroll out into the open. They came from every direction, seemingly dozens of them. They didn't say anything, but they were wearing the kind of rough gear they used for the movies and they didn't look as if they were out to catch the poetic beauty of the dawn. Furthermore, there didn't seem to be any end to them. Every time you thought that must be the last of them, another one stepped out through the bushes or from behind a tree and started to stroll about in that horribly casual way. Had only Patterson's men known, there wasn't one of them who could fight his way through a wet Kleenex—it was their faces that were their fortunes. But Patterson's men didn't know and they looked around them, looked at each other and by common and silent consent got back into their motor cars and drove away into the faintly blushing sky.

"Who?" roared Mulcahy.

"Tara Stewart, Chief," said Inspector Donaldson. "She says no one else will do."

Detective Chief Superintendent Mulcahy had four years to go to retirement. He'd had the whisper that he'd make Commander within six months. That would make a hell of a difference to his pension. He could send the fifth kid to university like the other four, maybe get a bigger dinghy. At this stage in his career, the last person in the world he wanted to hear from was Tara Stewart.

Like everyone in the country, he had followed her extraordinary

progress. Unlike everyone else—barring her immediate associates—
he had a pretty good idea of what she was up to. And he was buggered
if he was going to have his biggest and most prestigious case fucked
up by a monomaniacal father-lover. What was more, he bloody resented her, anyway. The newspapers had had a field day, watching
him plod laboriously in her footsteps, trying to catch the villains she
had apparently delivered to him on a plate. Except that she hadn't,
had she? He was bloody sure she'd made deals with some of them.
And he had a pretty good idea why. It was to do with what she was
up to.

Mulcahy was a slow thinker, but sure, and over the years it had
come to him that the Mersey Tunnel job and its mistakes—well, it
just wasn't Jed Stewart's handwriting at all. There was something
wrong with the whole thing. He knew in his heart it must have been
a fit-up. He justified it to himself that if Jed Stewart was rotting his
life away in jail for something he hadn't done, he was paying for all
the thieving he *had* done for which he hadn't been caught. Yet he
didn't feel good in his stomach about it. It was the reason why he
hadn't ever hauled Tara Stewart in and questioned her about her show,
her sources of information and her technical infringements of the law.
Now she had come looking for him. He didn't like it. But he couldn't
refuse to see her.

"Send the bitch in," he said, easing his trousers up around his
by now Falstaffian belly. "Then stay."

Donaldson returned with Tara. She looks like the Angel Ga-
briel's bloody twin sister, thought Mulcahy as she walked gracefully
over to his desk in this full-skirted crimson velvet coat with her hair
like a golden tapestry against it.

"Hello, fat gut," she said. "Still doing the 'before' ads for Weight
Watchers?"

He was suddenly sorry he'd asked Donaldson to stay.

"What do you want?" he asked.

"I'd like to treat you to what's known in the trade as a little
audio-visual demonstration," she said. She then played him the three
sound tapes of the confessions of Tom Lane, Iron Jack and Les Meacher,
ending with the film of Tug Beckett on a little portable screen she
had brought with her.

Mulcahy could never go pale, but his normally high, purplish
color subsided to a pale mottled pink as Tara built up her formidable
case. He wasn't sure how much of it would be admissable in a court
of law, but the material was trouble with a capital T; there was no
doubt about that. It wasn't going to go away, there was a case to be
answered here. He decided, without much hope, to try bluff.

"They could be anyone's voices," he said.

"And I suppose Tug Beckett's face could be anyone's face," she said.

"There's no proof that what Beckett's saying goes with his face," said Mulcahy, "I hear you show people can do great things with lip-synchronization these days. There's not a judge in this country that would admit a word of all that as evidence."

"What you know about the law you could write on your belly button," said Tara, "if you could find it these days. I don't know how you sleep at night, Mulcahy, but if you don't already use them, I'd get some pills if I were you. You're going to need them."

Mulcahy's color started to rise again with his Cork temper.

"You listen to me, you little Liverpudlian cow-pat," he roared, "I don't give a sod if your father did the Mersey Tunnel job or not. He did a hell of a lot of other things I could never nail him for, so if he's inside for something he didn't do, that's something that ed-ucated little farts like what you seem to have become—that's what they call poetic justice. Now get out of my bloody office and stay out!"

"Thank you, Detective Chief Superintendent Mulcahy and In-spector Donaldson," said Tara, enunciating very clearly. "That's what I came for."

She pressed the switch on her ingenious little briefcase and went like a slim and sudden breeze.

Mulcahy frowned heavily as he rose from his complaining chair.

"What did she mean by that last bit?" he queried Donaldson.

"I think she had a tape recorder in her briefcase," said Donaldson.

Mulcahy sat down again slowly and his complexion started to go up again quickly.

Tara relaxed back into her Jaguar, next to the powerful presence of Ben, his hands making the steering wheel look like a toy, and felt well satisfied. She had stirred up Pat Mulcahy like a vat of fermenting prune juice. He would currently be rocketing off in all directions at once and activity, preferably uncoordinated and random, was pre-cisely what she wanted at this moment. In physics, someone had told her, you could now have effects without causes, but only if you got everything all churned up first.

Her next call was on Sir Jonathan, her father's "brief," the best criminal lawyer in the business. His office was in Lancaster, a county town which made most others in England look "nouveau." It had the kind of class that only eleven hundred years of uninterrupted serenity and prosperity, undisturbed by developers, can confer.

Tara had never been to his office before, but she immediately appreciated the artistry of the ambience he had created for himself.

The deep blue velvet curtains, framing the luxuriantly silver head; the Savile Row shoulders resting against the unusually high-backed Captain's leather chair, an indescribable color of polished old ship's timbers; the leather-skivered desk with just the right number of pink-ribbon-tied briefs strewn across it.

As she came in, graceful as a mist moving up-river, he rose.

"How's everyone's favorite mouthpiece, then?" she asked.

"Don't you try your black arts on me, you little hussy," he smiled, with the crinkle-cornered eyes that had been the downfall of many a susceptible and potentially hostile female witness. "I've been wondering when you'd realize you needed me."

"What makes you think I need you now?" she asked.

First of all he had sat her down by his log fire, in a superbly comfortable chair, and surrounded her with coffee and coconut biscuits—how the blazes had he remembered those from her childhood? Then, with his superbly precise mind and articulation, he had economically outlined to her her grand design and her progression through it, ending at the point she had currently reached. Her delectable mouth dropped open.

"How the heck did you work all that out?" she demanded.

"Remember, I know your father and his mind, which means— in your case—that I know yours, too. I've followed your every move— through your programs. I would guess that you have admissions regarding the framing of your father from Tom Lane, Iron Jack, Les Meacher and Tug Beckett—on tape. I would surmise you have been to see that great tub of lard, Mulcahy, who has denigrated your findings and declined to take any action. You are tempted to take, shall we say, unconventional further actions, but you have come to me to see if you can proceed respectably instead."

Tara's tempting mouth dropped even further.

"You," she said, "are bloody miraculous!"

"Not so," said Sir Jonathan. "I am merely your interpreter. You've actually done it all. First of all, let me say that the case you've assembled is formidable and I doubt if anyone else could have put it together. However, it is not yet impregnable. Tapes can be tampered with."

"But what if the people who made the tapes go into the witness box and verify them as genuine?"

"In the first place, they could renege and refuse to substantiate them. And even if they agree, they're all criminals. A clever counsel would discredit them or, at the very least, throw doubt on their testimony."

"Then I've got nothing!" said Tara, despairingly.

"On the contrary, you've got everything. All you need is the linchpin. The one witness who slots in and makes the whole edifice of your case bomb-proof."

"Who in God's name is that?"

"The eye witness. The man who picked out your father as the man who suborned him. The computer expert."

Tara floundered: "I never thought of him . . . Where do I start?"

Sir Jonathan swung gently to and fro in his Captain's chair, violinist's fingers tip to precise tip.

"In all cases of cardinal or prodigious larceny there is one party that is commonly overlooked," he said, "and that is the insurance company, which stood the final loss. Should a crime of that scale not be solved, the police have lost nothing but a quantum of their reputation. It hurts momentarily but, like all hurts, it disappears with time. The injury suffered by the insurance company does not, however, dissipate with the years. It is a concrete and tangible loss, which will not go away. My advice to you would be to go and see whomever at the company concerned, which happens to be the Royal Liver, has the case on his file. Test his reactions. I will come with you if you like. But my assessment, without flattery, is that you need no assistance from me. Perhaps at a later stage, yes. Presently, no."

As Tara was shown into the office of Herbert Thynne at the Royal Liver building, overlooking the moving panorama of the River Mersey, her heart sank. Herbert Thynne uncoiled himself from his scraunchy, deprived-looking chair, five feet six inches of string with knots in it here and there to indicate human characteristics. His most noticeable feature was a pair of spectacles so big and so powerful that it might be thought he could look clear through his window into the heart of Prague. Her depression deepened when he spoke.

"Miss Stewart, won't you sit down?" He sounded like Woody Allen with a bad case of stage fright attempting a thin gruel of a Scottish accent.

"I've inherited this file from my predecessor," he went on.

Terrific, thought Tara despondently, there's nothing like taking over somebody else's cold potato to make you really enthusiastic. His next remark made her feel as if the sun had suddenly come out: "I think it's been misjudged, mishandled and mismanaged."

She made to intervene in agreement, but the weedy voice, with the strong mind behind it, did not wish to give way.

"The case against your father was too neat, fastidious, watertight. Forgive me for saying so, Miss Stewart, but it was not in the least typical of your father. He came from a long line of prime and accomplished crooks . . ."

"He'd given it up!" protested Tara.

"Hear me out," continued Thynne. "I'm a criminologist. I've made a study of The Mystery and its traditions. We are asked to believe that your father broke four of the cardinal rules he must have taken in with his mother's milk. Firstly, he retained some of the proceeds of the crime immediately; quite lunatic. Secondly, he retained one of the tools of the crime—the computer, which he didn't even need. Thirdly, he compounded both mistakes by keeping them on his own property. And fourthly, dealing with a forced accomplice—the computer expert—he made no attempt to disguise his appearance. Indeed, he almost made himself a caricature of himself."

He continued to talk, carefully treading along a line in the pattern of his carpet.

"I've been following the line of thought in your show. Many of the criminals you've exposed have been friends and confederates of your father's erstwhile partner Shaun Patterson, formerly known as Sean Pattison, with the Gaelic spelling and an 'i' not 'er,' " he said.

"Just a flaming minute," said Tara, her eyes dancing, "how old are you?"

"Twenty-seven," said Thynne. "Intellectually speaking, in my prime."

"That's as may be," answered Tara, "but how do you know who Patterson's confederates are, were or have been?"

"I told you, I'm a criminologist," said the thin, unshakable Scottish voice. "I read files, court reports, police dossiers, diaries. I can practically tell you who picked whose pocket on the Pier Head on June 4, 1978."

"Oh, yes?"

"And I can tell you one thing," he took out a large pipe, which made his face look even smaller, "there's one person my predecessor didn't even think about in connection with this case."

"Who's that?"

"The man I mentioned. The computer expert."

The man Sir Jonathan mentioned, too, Tara reflected.

"His name's John Balham. I don't know if you've taken any interest in him yourself?" he inquired, drily.

For once, Tara was stranded without a reply. The truth was, she hadn't. Yet he'd been the Crown's principal witness as to identification. How could she have been so thick? She supposed it was because he wasn't a criminal. He'd been blackmailed into it and she therefore thought of him as a victim rather than an adversary. It was still a tenable point of view—but what a vital victim! The one person in the whole case who had actually seen her father. *Seen* him!

Thynne was talking again, the smoke from a Highland moor on fire billowing from his pipe.

"The police gave him immunity from prosecution in return for his evidence: that means they also gave him protection—new name, new location, new life."

"But how the hell," she demanded, "do I find him?"

"He lives somewhere in Spain," said Thynne, crisply. "On the Costa del Sol."

That evening, Tara telephoned Michael in Marbella. She found he'd left for Madrid. It would be three or four days before he was back in England. And in any case she suddenly had something else to think about. Something that demonstrated to her just how powerful Patterson's connections were.

It started with a telephone call to her at the office. It was from a Mr. Dubrown, who was something very exalted in the Ministry of Defense. He'd like to talk to her, he said, about an idea of the Minister's. It might come to nothing, but, on the other hand, it might be that she could be of considerable help to the Army and to the Government. He would be in the North on other business the day after tomorrow; would she care to have lunch with him? He suggested the Moss Nook near Manchester Airport, which he admitted would be convenient for him and which Tara happened to like very much anyway. She said yes.

Mr. Dubrown turned out to be expensively suited with clipped silver hair and moustache—military—and eyes like chips of pale blue ice. His baby-pink complexion went well with the crimson walls and his stick matched the Methodist chapel wood which had been used to convert the place from two adjoining houses. As he worked his way steadily through the "menu gastronomique" and Tara had a simple veal with beetroot mustard, he talked in telegraphic bursts about the Minister's idea.

It was absurd. How would she like to make a series of training films, teaching troops how to avoid entrapment by foreign agents while on service abroad? After all, she obviously knew all the techniques. Why not put them at the service of her country? Tara waited until she had sipped her wine.

"Mr. Dubrown," she said, "you know damn well that there are people in the Ministry of Defense who know more about entrapment than a trawler fleet. Now, I don't know about you, but I haven't got all day. What did you really come up here to talk to me about?"

He put down his fork.

"I'd heard you were no fool . . ." he started.

"You should have listened, then," Tara interrupted. "Now no more bloody soft soap, if you don't mind. Get on with it."

Dubrown, who hadn't been talked to like this since he was a subaltern at Sandhurst, flushed an even richer shade of pink.

"Very well, then." He was going to enjoy this now. "You have two brothers in the Marines, I believe."

"You know I have."

"There is evidence," said Dubrown, with relish, "that they have been engaged in practices which could result in their being severely punished, dismissed from the Service with ignominy—and probably ruined for the rest of their lives."

The lift went zooming down in Tara's stomach as it always did when she thought her brothers were in danger, but she pretended nonchalance.

"Oh yes?" she answered. "And what practices would those be, then?"

"Homosexual incest," snapped Dubrown.

She laughed out loud in feigned relief.

"I thought it was something really serious," she said, "like peeing in the sergeant's helmet "

Inside, she was pale. She could see a fit-up when it came along. It was really very neat. There need be no corroborative witnesses who would have to incriminate themselves, only people who said they'd seen it.

"I really wouldn't laugh if I were you, Miss Stewart," said Dubrown. "Not if you love your brothers. The Services are, in a sense, the *custos morum* of the nation. I'm so sorry, I keep forgetting you have no Latin." It was the third time he'd deliberately hit her with a Latin tag. "It means 'moral guardians.' " We have to set an example."

Tara pasted on one of her sweetest smiles.

"Mr. Dubrown," she said, "you are a pig-nosed little turd and if I had my way I'd push your stick up your ass and tickle your nostrils with it. But I can see I'm going to have to do some filthy little deal with you, which you probably can't put into Latin. What is it, spawn-face?"

Dubrown had now gone pale with rage. But he had discipline. He waited until he had controlled himself.

"You are currently engaged in a vendetta against a certain person," he said. "Should you make one more move in his direction, I shall see to it that the action against your brothers will be implemented. That is all."

He threw down some money and rose, tapping her famous briefcase, which she had beside her.

"And I shouldn't bother to check that," he smirked. "If you'll notice, I put mine beside it. And mine contains a rather powerful magnet."

He was not bluffing. Her tapes were blank.

Tara was in mortal distress. She was staked out, unable to move. Save her father, destroy her brothers. Protect her brothers, condemn her father to living death. And just when she felt she might be beginning to break through. The shadows gathered under her eyes. She had no color underneath her skin. Cyril Goldstein had noticed. He had taken her to lunch at The Club.

"You don't have to tell me what's wrong," he said, "but you must tell me if there's anything I can do."

"Cyril," she said, "you're the sweetest man on earth, which is why there's nothing you can do for me in this."

"Don't underestimate me," he said. "I'm not so sweet."

"There's nothing, Cyril."

"Is it your enemy?"

"I don't even want to tell you that."

"It's that bad . . ." He knew what bad was. He'd been through the course. "Let me tell you," he said, taking her hand, "bad usually wins. But not with you. I'm a bit of a prophet. I know some things."

On the way out they passed Jason Planter, sitting alone at his usual table. He scrutinized her face, kissed her hand with great grace, but said nothing. Jason, she realized, knew when words were useless, but Christ she must look terrible for him to have picked up her vibrations so quickly.

As she got into Cyril's Rolls outside, he said, "I promise you, you'll be laughing at whatever it is in six months' time."

He'd got it right. And sooner than he knew. For the first time, Tara learned what a tremendous team had accreted around her. She had, of course, told them at the very next conference. "I'd appreciate your ideas," she'd said, "but, look, it's my problem and it always has been my problem. Don't let it take you away from your own work."

They had sat dumbly, stricken by the enormity of the choice with which Tara had been presented. They could see that the family involvement had induced an atypical paralysis in Tara's mental reflexes. They had gone away a very subdued crew. That had been a fortnight ago. There was another full conference to discuss program matters that afternoon. Present were Ben, Suzy, Bella, Mail Room Sid and his Mafia, Terry and the porcelain-pretty Miss Soong.

"Who wants to tell it?" asked Suzy, before Tara could even open the meeting.

"Well, seeing as how you're the only one here what's had a proper education," said Ben, "I think you should do the rabbiting."

Suzy, knowing that a blow from her handbag would only damage the handbag, contented herself with the closest she could get to a look of contempt for the man who, last night, had introduced her to a variation that had made even her noisy.

"Well," she said, "I've been doing a bit of nosing around among Daddy's M.O.D. contacts in London—I'm owed a few favors and I didn't want to know anything frightfully sensitive; simply what Mr. Dubrown's career prospects are and where he liked to eat most of all. I've discovered that he's quite a high flyer, that he's married to an Earl's daughter and that his favorite London restaurant is Trinny's in Mayfair. You know, it's sort of St. Trinian's, like School Dinners in Baker Street, where all the waitresses dress up in gym slips and black stockings. Well, it happens to belong to a chum I was at school with so I've got a job there starting next week. It'll mean London expenses, of course, but I do look rather luscious in black stockings, and . . ."

Tara listened, entranced, as her team outlined the campaign. Then they all took off like a flock of starlings, to London. Suzy went to Trinny's for a few tips, Jean Soong went to Gerrard Street in Soho for something she wouldn't specify, Ben went first to Moss Bros. and then to Harrod's car hire department, Sid to one or two estate agents.

A couple of evenings later, fatigued from a day spent beating off his Master's more manic ideas, Dubrown sauntered into his favorite fun restaurant where one could eat good food while at the same time re-creating some of the more nostalgic scenarios of one's youth. They had a new girl, he noticed, a most round and delicately modeled creature, with a back-of-the-knee in those black stockings that really . . . and oh, how straight she'd got that perfect circlet of the tops of them! Most splendid of all, she appeared to be serving his table! This, he promised himself, was going to be a night to remember. He never made himself a more impregnable promise in his life.

Suzy had arranged things so that she served Mr. Dubrown his dinner. Even had the not-too-swift-acting opiate supplied by Jean

Soong not been so subtle, the sight of Suzy's cute little bottom in the school knickers, wiggling to and fro around his table, would have been more than enough to distract Dubrown from any variation in the flavor of his Shepherd's Pie. Together with the carafe of house claret—damn good value, he always thought—it was more than enough to have his nose drooping into the custard by the time his treacle pudding came.

Samantha, Suzy's friend, owner of the restaurant, came hurrying over.

"For Christ's sake get him out of here," she ground out between her teeth; "you didn't tell me he was going to have a heart attack!"

"He hasn't had a heart attack, Sammy, darling," whispered Suzy. "He's just gone bye-byes."

She wiggled innocently to the door and signaled. Ben, looking spectacular in a pale gray chauffeur's uniform, complete with cap, came in, crossed to the table.

"Governor's had a hard day," he said.

He plucked Dubrown from his chair as if he were a baby and carried him out as neatly as a roll of carpet.

"Sorry about this, miss," he said as he left, touching his cap to Suzy, who maintained her composure with difficulty. Then he loaded Dubrown gently into the Rolls outside and sighed softly into the night.

When Dubrown woke up, apart from a slight headache he felt very comfortable. There was something very supportive, he felt, about the bed, although something rather strange about the room. It was not, he felt, in the best of taste, with its frills and laces and folderols. He went to scratch a slight tickle on his nose and discovered that he was unable to do so. Further investigation revealed a dazzling blonde on his left-hand side, a dazzling brunette on his right-hand side, and the fact that he was stark bollock naked. His difficulty in scratching his nose, he discovered, as well as the singular comfort of the bed, was explained by the fact that he seemed to be inextricably knitted up and interlaced in the polished limbs of the blonde on the left and the brunette on the right. They were also stark naked. If he was going to scratch anything, he quickly appreciated, it was not going to be his nose.

A large, fair man came from behind the curtains at the window with an expensive camera and fired off a shot before Dubrown could open his mouth in protest. When he did open his mouth, very widely indeed, the blonde popped her right breast in it. The camera flashed again. When she removed her breast and he was able to shout, his expression looked curiously orgasmic, which he realized an instant after the camera had already caught it. Furious, he shut his mouth, when he immediately looked sated. The camera caught that, too. The great thing about these birds, thought Ben, as he clipped off the shots, was their sense of humor. The things they did to Dubrown! They were not only lubricious; they made him look ridiculous. And the intelligence with which they always left his face in camera.

When they finally released him at a signal from Ben, he came off the bed at Ben like a missile, was caught with as sweet a right cross as you'd see in a day's march and went back to sleep again. Ben straightened him out on his back and lovingly laid on his chest one shot he'd taken with a Polaroid. On the back, he pasted a slip of paper given to him by Suzy, who *had* done her Latin.

It read *Quo fas et gloria ducunt,* meaning whither duty and glory lead. Underneath the maxim was written: "Fas is the blonde, Gloria the brunette, and we all know who Ducunt is. I'm sure you'll keep my brothers just as safe as I'll keep your pictures."

Two days later, she got a call from Dubrown, asking for a meeting. Same time, same place. She had Ben drive her there, not knowing what backup Dubrown might bring with him. He came alone. She had rarely seen such a change in a man. Where, before, he had been all Establishment crispness and contempt, he was now a twitching bundle of uncertainties. It was as if he had to think before deciding which foot to put in front of the other. He had the same kind of shadows under his eyes as had stained Tara's these past weeks. Her first instinct was pity, but she rigidly suppressed it. This was the man who had been quite prepared to trample her brothers into the shit.

"I'm in the devil of a fix," he said, as he settled down against the Methodist carpentry and the complexion-enhancing walls.

"Not necessarily," replied Tara. "Those pictures stay in a safety box so long as my boys are all right."

"But the point is," he said, his color coming and going like a neon sign, "Patterson has something on me, too."

"What?" she asked.

"Well, I'm hardly likely to tell you that!" he protested.

"I don't see that you've got any choice," said Tara, flatly.

With the honesty of desperation, he blurted it out. "I pushed a Ministry of Defense contract in the direction of one of his companies. For money. He has documentary evidence."

"But he can't reveal that without incriminating himself," said Tara.

"Yes, he can. The whole thing was done through one of his subordinates. His name doesn't come into it."

Yes, that sounded like Patterson.

"What are you asking me to do?" she asked. "Give you permission to smash my brothers to save your career?"

"Don't know what to do," answered Dubrown. "Not a strong man. Put on a good front. Got a wife I love and she's fond of me. Children off our hands, thank God! But I can't land Elspeth with a crashed-out disgrace of a husband right at the end. I don't know. Just don't know what to do."

His knuckles were bluey-white as he grasped the arms of his chair.

It was her mother's name, Tara realized later, that got to her subconsciously; Elspeth. It abruptly brought home to her that behind this pompous—weak, she now realized, not ruthless—prick of a man there was a woman, who was liable to suffer in a way she didn't deserve. And besides, she told herself, there was—she didn't know how yet—an advantage to be had out of it. But she had to be assertive about it.

"I tell you what you do," she said, the old gray-blues mesmerizing him, "you take premature retirement—you can't have more than a couple of years to go, anyway—it can't affect your pension that much. And then you come and work for me as a researcher."

"Wha—'

"With your pension and your salary you'd be a bloody sight better off than you've ever been in your life. Patterson would have no further hold on you." Nor, she considered, would Dubrown have any further power over her brothers. But she'd still have the photographs on him.

"Researcher?" he asked. "What would I have to do?"

More than you actually think, for me, sunshine, she thought, but what she actually said was: "Just gathering and organizing facts—the kind of thing you've been doing all your life."

"I could still be in trouble retrospectively over that defense contract," he said, gnawing a much-gnawed lip.

"Where's it kept?" she asked.

"In the files of Yleef Exports, in Liverpool."

As Ben drove her home, Tara was whistling softly. The devil's in a woman that whistles, Ben remembered. He added his own rider: devils were fallen angels. But did they fall or were they pushed?

When Patterson heard that Dubrown had retired and that that bitch Tara Stewart had hired him, his fury would have registered on a seismic needle. Three more glass tables were reduced to tumbled shards. He telephoned the first gofer he could think of, who happened to be a small-eyed pinhead called Marksten, and instructed him to get to the offices of Yleef Exports down in Liverpool and bring him the file marked Dubrown. The size of Marksten's head was a true reflection of his brainpower and he genuinely expected to be congratulated when he returned from Liverpool in a Superman-type flash and told an empurpled Patterson that the Dubrown file had disappeared.

"I don't *know* whereabouts in Spain," squeaked Herbert Thynne, his pipe infringing all known anti-pollution laws. Tara was back in his office. "I've got a theory it's somewhere on the Costa del Sol. I've been there seven times. On holidays, mind—the company think I'm barking up the wrong tree. I've spent a lot of time in all the resorts and up in the mountains, the villages. I've never laid eyes on John Balham there. It doesn't surprise me; he's not likely to be wearing a name tag. There are a lot of people on the coast there"—he spread out a series of pictures of a chubby, intelligent young face on the desk—"and he's liable to have changed a lot since these were taken. He could have gone bald, grown a beard, put on weight—anything."

"How are these things managed?" asked Tara. "New identities, all that?"

"That's what I asked Mulcahy years ago," said Thynne. "He told me to sod off."

"Mulcahy!" cried Tara and was gone, golden hair streaming after her.

She drove from the riverfront to the Bridewell, Liverpool's Lubjanka, where Mulcahy had his headquarters. She asked the desk sergeant politely if she could see him.

"After last time, you've got about as much chance of that as Everton winning the cup again," he answered.

"Like to bet on that, wack?" asked Tara. The desk sergeant shrugged and went through on the telephone.

"Tara Stewart here to see you, Chief," he said.

There was a jungle roar from the other end of the telephone and a crash as the receiver went down.

"He says no," said the sergeant, economically.

"Put us through again," asked Tara with a Liverpool wink that meant fun. "You don't have to get involved."

The sergeant studied her solemnly and redialed the internal number while Tara got her recorder, which she'd already primed in the car outside, out of her briefcase. When Mulcahy answered, the sergeant simply handed her the telephone and she played back the bit where Mulcahy said he didn't care if Jed Stewart's conviction was the biggest miscarriage of justice on earth, so long as he was inside for something, or words to that effect. There was a kind of explosion, then a door nearly came off its hinges somewhere in the bowels of the building and Mulcahy's voice bawled, "Send the little sod in!"

As Tara entered Mulcahy's office, he grabbed her tape recorder, ripped out the tape, threw it on the floor and jumped on it with his full nineteen stones.

"That takes care of that," he said, with considerable satisfaction.

"Not really," said Tara, sweetly. "That was only a copy."

She thought she was going to lose Mulcahy there and then. By his color, either he was going to have a stroke or the top of his head had to come off. Neither happened, because he had the arteries of an elephant.

"What the almighty fuck do you want now, you straw-haired leprechaun's bastard?" he roared.

"Well," said Tara, in her most innocent local intonation, "when you give a supergrass a new identity—like, for instance, John Balham"—it must have needed a titanic jolt of nervous electricity to raise that bulk half an inch out of its chair, she speculated—"how d'you go about it, like?"

Chief Superintendent Mulcahy looked long at Tara. Like many people, he had been slow to realize that it took some little time to get the full strength of her. He had, also, an awful idea that he hadn't had the full, full strength of her yet.

"Why don't you go and stick your head up a gorilla's ass," he said, "that is, if the gorilla doesn't object."

"Are you volunteering?" asked Tara, on her way out.

She went a little dejectedly to her car. A black youth of fourteen or fifteen, in T-shirt and ragged-bottom jeans, was leaning against the wall.

"Hi, Tar," he said. "Saw your motor. You been having aggravation with the scuffers?"

It was Sylvester Manders Blain, son of one of the immigrant families she'd helped against Iron Jack.

"You could say that, Syl," she said. "They won't tell me something I need to know."

"Any Woodentop in particular?" he asked.

"That bladder Mulcahy," she said, bitterly.

"Yeah, he's a bastard," said Sylvester, casually. "Be seeing you, Tar." He moved off.

"Yeah, great, Syl," answered Tara. She climbed into the XJS and drove off, despondent.

That night, Chief Superintendent Mulcahy's select little cul-de-sac in the suburb of Knotty Ash had a very jolly street party. The only singular circumstance was that none of the residents had been invited. At eleven o'clock a festive swarm of some two hundred merrily disposed West Indians and Africans poured into the street, complete with three steel bands. They damaged no property, they interfered with no cars. They danced and cheered and sang light-hearted calypsos and—apart from the fact that one couldn't hear one's television or one's record-player—it was really rather pleasant. For the first hour, that is. True, there was one calypso that did not seem quite so sunny as the rest. To the quick ears that managed to pick it up, it sounded—sung to the rhythm of "Zambesi"—remarkably like:

> Mulcahy, Mulcahy, he gotta belly
> Like a pregnant pig.
> Mulcahy, Mulcahy, who ever think
> A maggot get so big?

During the second hour, the catchy tune was joined by a second one which seemed to go something like:

> Superintendent, he a big man
> He gotta face like a fryin' pan.
> When he go to the zoo one day
> It was the animals who have to pay.

Inside the house, Mulcahy was taking the kind of flak from his small, ferocious wife that usually comes from a helicopter gunship. He was also fielding calls from his neighbors, telling him, superfluously, that he was a policeman and why the hell didn't he do something about it.

He reviewed his options. He couldn't get the revelers on riotous behavior; they were behaving very well. Insulting behavior—yes; but then the words of the songs would be quoted in court and he could just see the field day the media would have with that. Obstruction, possibly, but it was a cul-de-sac, no through road; and none of the neighbors had shown any inclination to want to go out. Trust them! They'd complain all right, but there wasn't one of the bloody hypocrites who wanted to miss a minute of it. What infuriated him most of all was that the situation wasn't even within his jurisdiction. His nick was downtown. Out here, it was the responsibility of the local station. Finally, he decided that the lowest-profiled solution was Nuisance. He got three of the neighbors to make an official complaint to the local station and backed it up with a call himself. "But softly, softly, eh, Jack?" he pleaded with the local Superintendent. "You can see it's a bit . . . like . . . sensitive."

In the event, softly, softly it was. Two young bobbies came along in a Panda car; the singers, the bands and dancers smiled and bowed to them and melted away into the night, singing softly as they went. On the midnight air drifted softly back the strains of "Mulcahy, Mulcahy . . ."

The next night there were four hundred of them. They packed Mulcahy's cul-de-sac to overflowing and spilled out into the surrounding roads and crescents; and there were four steel bands. There were also a number of new calypsos. They had got less refined. The first one Mulcahy heard was:

> There was a hippopotamus called Mulcahy;
> He hadn't seen his thing since 1923
> When he went pee-pee it was a hoot
> It ended up all over his boots.

The third night a carnival procession formed in Upper Parliament Street and wound its way through the inner city out to the suburbs. It must have been twelve hundred strong. There were ten steel bands. There were disco dancers. There were huge, garishly painted papier-mâché figures, some of them representing Detective Chief Superintendent Mulcahy and none of them neglecting his belly. The calypsos were getting cruder all the time. The latest one ran:

> Mulcahy was a man with a great big tum
> But it wasn't half as big as his bum
> When he hit the thunder box you shouldn't be near
> It wasn't for women and children to hear.

That evening, the *Liverpool Echo* had already picked up and printed the happenings of the night before, headlining the story "Mulcahy's Serenade." Thus alerted, television was out in force, covering the jollifications from their start right out to their finish, where they engulfed the whole of Mulcahy's neighborhood. The local police chief did not interfere. The atmosphere was good-natured, if loud; there were twelve hundred of them and he wasn't going to put his pension on the line by sparking off a riot by overreacting. Which was precisely what he told Mulcahy when the latter rang up to ask him, with the maximum profanity, what he proposed to do about the situation.

The same night one of Mulcahy's telephone calls was from a young West Indian voice. There was no introduction. It said, simply, "Hey, man, why don't you wise up. Tell Tara Stewart what she want to know."

Next morning, Mulcahy rang Tara. "I can have you for this, you know," he said.

"What are you talking about?" asked Tara.

"You bloody know," said Mulcahy. "The nig-nogs serenade."

Tara had seen it on local television news. She laughed.

"Oh, that!" she said. "I thought some of those figures were very good of you—a bit flattering, actually."

"I know you're behind it," roared Mulcahy.

"Don't be bloody daft!"

"I had a call last night from some young West Indian kid. He mentioned your name." And it hit her. Sylvester Manders Blain, the kid outside the Bridewell! Now there was a kid who was going places. And she suddenly felt a warm flush of gratitude for Sylvester and all of the people who were, in their own way, saying thank you to her.

"It had nothing to do with me, fat-guts," she said, "so go and soak your nut in goose-grease and stop wasting my time."

"It'll do you no good, you know," he said. "You can bring the whole of Jamaica over, I'll tell you nothing."

But the next night it was two thousand merrymakers and the fetish-figures were bigger and the calypsos were ruder and it was on national television and in all the newspapers next day, complete with pictures, and although nobody could fathom what was behind it, everybody still remembered the Toxteth riots, which were not at all merry, and Mulcahy got a call from the Chief Constable. The Chief Constable said he didn't know what it was all about and he didn't want to know what it was all about, but unless a stop was put to it and sharpish, he, personally, would take it very hard. Mulcahy picked up the telephone and put a call through to Tara.

"You want Special Branch, Section D," he said, "and the best of British bloody luck with them! And I'm just warning you, from now on, you put one foot wrong on my manor, you overstay your parking meter by thirty seconds, I'll throw the book at you so hard, it'll take your bloody head off!"

"Gerroff, Mick," she said. "You can't even read the book."

That evening, she cruised around Sylvester's patch in her XJS, which was as well known in Liverpool by that time as the Liver Bird on the waterfront. She found Sylvester on Brownlow Hill, unscrewing a parking meter. She pulled in. He swiftly concealed the screwdriver.

"Sylvester . . ." she said, in a certain tone of voice.

"I wasn't doing nothing, Tar, honest!" he lied, earnestly. "I just wanted to know how it works."

"Syl," she said, "there's a basic rule in life: never try to bullshit a bullshitter. But that's not what I came to say. I came to say 'Ta very much.' "

"Don't know what you're talking about," said Sylvester, sheepishly.

"And something else. How old are you now?"

"Fourteen, getting on fifteen."

"When you leave school," she said, "come and see me. You keep your nose clean, I'll have a job for you."

His face lit up like a Liverpool sunset, which was locally defined as Birkenhead on fire. She made to drive off. He stuck his head down to her window.

"Tar," he asked eagerly, "did it work?"

"Did what work?" she asked, straight-faced.

"Right," he answered.

"And I'll take the screwdriver," she said. He put it into her hand without a word and she drove off.

Tara and Dubrown were in their by now customary cozy corner in the Moss Nook. He was working out his notice with the Ministry. Meanwhile, he had signed his contract of employment, postdated, with Alhambra. He looked much better. Like a man who had entered into a new golden phase of his life. At least, he had done until Tara had given him, prematurely, his first assignment.

"But I can't do that!" he protested, his hand quivering as he got the fork to his mouth. "I haven't even left yet."

"It'll be a lot easier before you leave than afterward," Tara reassured him.

"Besides," he said, "Special Branch has got nothing to do with us. I've got no entrance into that lot."

"Oh, come on," she said. "I know what's what. All you lot in the Civil Service—in the what-d'you-call-it, the 'First Division'—you all have your little clubs and cliques, a word here, a word there."

"But that's the Home Office," he persisted. "My ground is Ministry of Defense."

"You can't tell me you're all in watertight compartments," Tara insisted. "You're in each other's pockets. People know people, men have obligations, call in favors, ask for favors. My God, you were going to screw my brothers for Patterson and he's not even in 'the club!' "

He had the good grace to look shamefaced.

"That was different," he said. "My whole life was at stake."

"It's still at stake," said Tara, brutally. "If you can't pull this off, you're no good to me and you can regard our arrangements as shredded paper."

She was sorry to see the gray tints creep back into his cheeks, but if it was a choice between her father and anyone else in the world, there really was no choice. Dubrown read her implacable eyes.

"I'll do what I can," he mumbled.

"Not what you can," she said. "What you have to."

Tara realized that the conflict between her loyalty to her father and her attitude to the rest of the world crystallized in its most acute form in her relationship with Michael Patterson. When she had learned that John Balham was somewhere on the Costa del Sol and that that was where Michael was, did the flush of love that flooded her at the image of him precede the thought that he could somehow be useful to her, or was it the other way round? It shuttled through her mind as she waited to meet Michael at Manchester's Ringway Airport, to where he had cabled her he was flying back. And it was at Ringway that Tara had one of the most bizarre experiences of her life. It was triggered by the mounting alarm and excoriating anger of Shaun Patterson.

In a different situation, his state of mind when he found Tara had turned Dubrown around could have been called paranoid. There was this inexorable, merciless, dazzlingly inventive and unpredictable blond sorceress tracking him down, countering his every move against her, seeming almost to know in advance what he was going to do and seemingly possessed of resources far beyond anything he had dreamed she could command. And she was closing, closing; nearer all the time. Patterson had been used, in his young manhood in The Mystery, to commanding and controlling his world. He had despised the "mugs" and the "marks," the centuries-old phrases by which The Mystery described the rest of the population—low-level fodder to be exploited. That attitude had only been reinforced by his rise to formidably affluent respectability. He controlled his world now in a big way, on many levels, and his weapons were all the sweeter to him for being as near as damn it legal. He knew his state was not one of paranoia, however, because he recognized that there was a perfectly rational explanation for what was happening to him. Tara Stewart was Jed Stewart's daughter and somewhere in Shakespeare there was this phrase about one man's genius overtopping another's just by a random gift of Nature. Well, that's how it had been with Jed Stewart and him. And it was beginning to look as though that's how it was with Jed Stewart's daughter and him. He had one consolation to cling to: he remembered that's how it had been with Caesar and Cassius. And it was Caesar who'd ended up sliced.

When he'd heard from Michael that he was coming back from Spain via Manchester he knew perfectly well why. His son was still in the web of the enchantress. He had an irrational feeling that if he could be there and break that web before she could weave it even more securely around him, he would not only free Michael, he would somehow break the ascendancy she seemed to be gaining over himself.

Seeing Patterson suddenly at the exit from Customs, Tara felt as if someone had dealt her a blow between the eyes. He was so like her father. The same flat, hard maleness; the shapely head; the dangerous eyes; and the seamed and dimpled rock of the face. They could have been brothers. She knew in a vague, instinctual way why Patterson was there and she noted that he had not come without allies. With him was one of the most breathtakingly beautiful girls Tara had ever seen. Tall, black-haired, translucently green-eyed, and a mouth to tempt a monk. Tara hadn't enough masculinity in her to be able to judge another woman's chemistry, but if it was anything near her looks, there was trouble here. Michael loved her, yes, indeed: but there was only so much competing female clout a man could be expected to take. This girl was meant to take Michael from her.

Almost without thinking, she did the one thing Shaun Patterson had not anticipated. He expected her to be there, of course he did. But he didn't envisage her coming within a mile of him. His hatred of her had blinded him to the fact that war had never been officially declared between them. Their savage conflict had been subterranean. They hadn't even met since she was a child—a fact which his familiarity with her face on television had blurred. The tacitly accepted scenario, so far as anyone knew, was that he and Jed Stewart had pulled the Mersey Tunnel job together, that Jed had been careless and got caught and that Sean, now Shaun, had got away with it. That was the story Patterson had sold to Michael and she, for her purposes, had gone along with it. They were both, as it were, ancestrally related in the criminal arts and would therefore be expected to have a familial feeling toward each other. This was the equation which Tara's brain, working many times more quickly than any computer faced with the same input, came up with.

"Shaun!" she said, as she bounced up to him and the girl from their blind side, deliberately chosen. "What a surprise! God, it must be how long? Michael's always talking about you." She gave the green-eyed goddess the kind of girly smile that said I know you're gorgeous, but that's no reason we shouldn't be friends.

Patterson, for a moment, was routed, the center of his mental forces smashed by Tara's totally unorthodox cavalry charge. His face showed something very like panic, which was not lost on his companion. Sensing just how hard a man Patterson, a new conquest of hers, was, she was interested in any girl who could throw him into such evident confusion. In the next instant, she recognized her from television. So it wasn't lighting that gave her those eyes . . .

Patterson was recovering—and doing it well.

"Taransay!" he cried, embracing her; "I don't know why you let them call you Tara. Taransay suits you so well. My God, will you look at you. Last time I saw you in the flesh, as they say, you looked like a boy!"

He was pouring on the charm like golden syrup. He turned to his companion.

"You've seen Tara Stewart on the box," he said. "She's the biggest thing in television."

"Yes, I recognized you," said green eyes, with a flashing smile.

"And this," said Patterson, taking green eyes proprietorially by the elbow, "is Donna Calvesi. Originally from Italy, lived over here since she was three. She's a model."

"I thought I knew your face," said Tara, lying. The girl would undoubtedly go to the top of her tree, but she hadn't taken off yet. All it needed was one good cover. "Great to meet you," she said. "I *love* that jacket."

"It's St. Laurent," said Donna. She hugged it. "I got it whole-sale!" she confessed.

The public address system crackled and there was an announcement that Michael's plane was going to be forty-five minutes late. Patterson knew it was just about the worst thing that could have happened, because he could already sense what Tara's move was going to be. She was going to make friends with Donna, the classic maneuver to dilute competition. He tried to take the play away from her by monopolizing the chat, keeping it on the old days, holding Tara's attention and leaving Donna on the sidelines. It worked for perhaps ten minutes and then Tara quite simply hauled Donna into the conversation, turned on the girl talk and left Patterson gasping on the bank like a stranded salmon. Steadily, to his fury, the girls got cozy; hair texture, eye makeup, that lipstick you could only get in France, what did you say the name of that blusher was? Moving on to career decisions and the people who got in the way, the frustrations, men. Tara contrived to make it abundantly obvious that Michael was hers without ever actually uttering a straight word about the situation. She rounded off by telling Donna that she had a perfect screen face and that she'd like to introduce her to one or two people in Alhambra, to see if they might have anything to suggest for her. "If you're interested, that is."

"If I'm interested!" exclaimed Donna.

When Michael finally arrived, Donna allowed herself no more than the regulation lighting up of the eyes at his obvious attractiveness and he clinched Tara to him as if there was no tomorrow.

Patterson's face, unwatched by the others, had turned to stone. He had decided he was going to have to kill her.

11

ichael had just asked Tara to marry him. They were lying in bed together in the Fairy Bedroom in her home. The curtains were undrawn, a moon as big as a cartwheel was irradiating the room in silver through the glass wall, the sky was fired with stars, and she and Michael were gently pulsating toward a second bout of lovemaking. At another time, another place—strange how that feeling permeated her life—the proposal would have cloaked what was already near-perfection in magic. It was, in fact, something she had been dreading for weeks, ever since he had come back from Spain.

With Beckett tucked away in the Lancashire dales where Patterson wouldn't find him—and Beckett knew it was very much in his own interest that Patterson shouldn't—and Dubrown working on the whereabouts of John Balham, Tara felt that she was nearing the end of her long odyssey; she was getting very close, with luck, to exposing Patterson. But the closer she got, the more acute became her terror at what it was going to do to her relationship with Michael. At night, on her own, she would often utter a little involuntary groan as the thought jumped into her mind, just before she fell asleep, of the perfidy with which she was increasingly treating him. In her most ruthlessly lucid moments, she knew that her bond with Michael was doomed and she ranted at the unfairness of things, that to correct a great wrong she had to poison a great love. Sometimes Bella, in the next bedroom, would hear her sobbing in the night and would come in to try to comfort her. But she found her always inconsolable.

"Michael's a good man," Bella would insist. "He'll be horrified by what his father did, he'll be on your side."

"Yes," Tara would sob, "but he is his father and he loves him, I know he does. There's that and then there's how I've used him. It . . . I mean . . . it may all come out right and proper if some professor, some moral philosophy expert worked it out and balanced it up, but . . . oh, you know what I mean . . ."

Puzzled now by her silence, Michael leaned up on an elbow and gazed at her, the moonlight glittering on his blue, blue eyes.

"I said I want, more than anything else in the world, to marry you," he repeated.

She groped for words, any words: "And so do I, love, oh so do I. But I can't. Not just yet."

"What?!" he asked, incredulously. During the last few weeks they had lived in Tara's flat during the week and in his cottage outside Chester at the weekends. They had *been* married, for God's sake, in all but name. He kept Aunt Rita supplied with "Old Antiquary" and ruinously expensive boxes of truffles, and she condoned the fact that he was a lecherous limb and emissary of the devil, although often fetching him a buffet across the earhole if she imagined he'd been peeping at her through the bathroom keyhole, as she frequently did.

"What I mean is," wriggled Tara, calling desperately on all her inventiveness, "I'm afraid of it . . . I'm . . . I dunno, I'm just windy about it, like."

She was deliberately turning on the Liverpool tap rather strongish in the hope of sounding—even to someone who knew her so well—a bit dim.

"Afraid about what, for God's sake?"

"Well, it's just that I've gabbed on about it, like, to girlfriends who've been married and they say it can change things."

"What things?"

"Well, they say the mystery and that goes out of it all, like, and it's slippers and umbrellas and washing machines, sort of thing."

"I've never owned a pair of slippers or a damned umbrella in my life," shouted Michael. "Why should I be suddenly knee-deep in them the minute I get married? And as for washing machines, we've already got one each, anyway, mine in the country, yours here. Anyway, what a damned ridiculous conversation about washing machines."

"You're taking me too literally," she protested. "What these women tell me is that it's like, well . . . the bloom goes off."

"Oh, sod your women and their bloom!" he cried. "I'm going back to the cottage."

But it wasn't the cottage he went back to. The blood pumped up by his fury didn't go to his head, it went down below and before he knew it he was sunk fathoms-deep into the mysteries of her body and she seemed to have found a new way to revolve her apple-sweet buttocks. She had saved the situation for now; but she knew there must come a reckoning.

Tara's program was now a national institution, rivalling even the big soap operas in its audience-pulling power. It had the extraordinary credentials of being the one program since television's inception to be seen, beyond argument, to be providing a genuine public service. It was absolutely obligatory viewing for the police, much as some constabulary philosophers might deplore her methods, and for the criminal classes. *The Sunday Times* produced statistics showing that burglaries between nine and ten on a Wednesday evening were down by 93 percent, because all the burglars were at home, waiting to see if they had to hit the trail if they happened to be this week's victim. Tara herself, besides being the anchor-woman and producer of the show, frequently took part in the stratagem set up to trap the crook of the week. With the aid of the makeup department she demonstrated an uncanny flair for impenetrable disguises and was nicknamed by some of the press the "Blond Pimpernel."

One thing she did not do was ever to pick on a member of the authentic Mystery. She could not have justified their immunity on any moral grounds. But she had good reasons of her own. Firstly, she had been born into it and she simply couldn't bring herself to act against it. Secondly, they were the aristocrats of crime, with certain standards; they took only from those who could well afford it. Thirdly, she still knew many of them—and especially their children of her own age, who had all been toddlers together. And fourthly, they were always ready to use their special skills on her behalf against her enemies, whenever she asked them. She realized that, morally speaking, she was probably an inexcusable mess. Pragmatically speaking, however, she functioned as a highly valuable member of society.

Inevitably, she had become a celebrity in her own right and every chat show host clamored for her as a guest. Her beauty, her quaint voice, her unique job and success at it, and her wit all made her a natural choice.

Magazines of all kinds ran features on her. She got used to newspapers telephoning or ringing her doorbell at all hours. Dempster and Hickey constantly speculated about her sex life, but the ingenuity she put into her shows she used in her private life, too. Her smoke-screens and diversions were brilliant; their ploys for penetrating them were not far behind. She enjoyed the game. So that when the entry-phone at her flat went on the Saturday morning after her discussion with Michael about marriage and a voice said "Electoral Register," she grinned to herself and replied "Oh, yes?"

"Beg pardon?" said the voice, a little bewilderedly.

"What d'you want?"

"We're compiling a new—"

"Never mind the story, what d'you want?" she repeated.

"How many people are there in your flat?"

"At the moment—one. Me." It was true. Aunt Rita had hit a critical shortage of supplies to see her over the weekend and Bella had just run her to the shops.

"No, I don't mean now, I mean generally," said the voice, a hint of exasperation creeping into it.

Tara sighed.

"You'd better come up," she said.

She pressed the button and heard the front door open and the lift start up. It opened straight into the hall and as it did so Tara had hastily to revise her not altogether stilled suspicions. For out stepped an owl-spectacled little man in a raincoat that looked as if it had been crushed into a ball in his pocket before he put it on and a scarf that could only have been knitted from the combings from a Shetland pony. The sight of the genuine Tara Stewart, in the flesh, in a soft woolen pale lemon housecoat, with her hair a little vulnerably mussed, seemed to trigger off a latent stammer in him.

"Goo . . . goo . . ."

"Good morning," said Tara. "Take the weight off your feet."

He sat gingerly on the edge of a chair.

"M-may I s-say how very m-much I enj . . . j . . ."

"That's very kind of you," said Tara. "Now what was it you wanted to know?"

"W-well, it really b-boils down to th-this. How m-many p-people were under the r-roof last night."

A slow grin spread across Tara's face.

"I've been asked that question before," she said. "It really means how many people were in my bed last night and what were their names."

"I b-beg your p-p-pardon?"

"*Express, Mirror, Star* or *Sun?*" she asked.

He took off his owl spectacles. He looked much younger and tougher without them. He grinned back.

"You really are as good as they say," he admitted. "*Mirror.* John Bates."

"Newsdesk or Peter Tory?" she asked, naming the *Mirror*'s current gossip columnist.

"Well, really, I'm just a stringer," said Bates, "practically a freelance."

"So you just thought you might drop on an exclusive here and make a name for yourself," she said.

"Something like that." He roamed across the room. "Hey, you're pretty isolated here," he said, looking out of the glass wall of the

sitting room to the magnificent brooding greens of the National Park
beyond.

"It gives me peace and quiet," she said, amicably, "unless I'm
bothered by people like you. Can I get you some coffee? You're not
going to get anything else. My private life's my own and I'm pretty
good at keeping it that way."

"No thanks, no coffee," he said. "The girl who lives with you,
the one who just drove off with the fat lady—incidentally, I didn't
think she was ever going to get her into that car . . ."

"You leave Rita alone," said Tara. "She'd make five of you."

"You're dead right there," said Bates.

En route to the shops in Bella's Maestro, Aunt Rita had started
to fidget.

"That fellow-me-lad we saw in the trees back there," she said.

"I didn't see anyone," said Bella.

"Yes, well that's the difference between thee and me," said Aunt
Rita, already lapsing into the biblical. "He was of the unclean. I could
sense it."

"The what?"

"First off, he was astride a bloody great motorbike—chariot of
the devil—but he looked as if he should have been handing out books
at the local library."

"Well, maybe that's his release," explained Bella. "He's acting
out a fantasy of some kind."

"He's tainted, I tell you. He's of the kingdom of Moloch,"
ranted Aunt Rita. "He had an assignation with that Jezebel niece of
mine, Taransay Stewart! Turn back! Turn back!"

"Oh, Rita, don't be a bore," said Bella, impatiently, driving
straight on.

At the flat, Bates was saying, "But to get back to the girl who
lives with you."

"Well, what about her?" asked Tara. Then, slowly, "Oh no . . .
not that old chestnut! You can't be serious."

"No, nothing like that," he said. "I was just wondering if she
was driving your aunt into town."

"What's that got to do with you?" asked Tara. "Listen, what
is all this? How d'you know she's my aunt, anyway?"

"Oh, I know a lot about you," said Bates. "I do my research."

In the car, Bella felt that she was being attacked by a giant
jelly from outer space, could hardly think straight, let alone drive
straight.

"Rita, will you for God's sake, stop it! You'll have us off the road!" A truck gusted past, blaring its horn as it swerved to avoid the crazily erratic car.

"Turn back! Turn back!" yelled Aunt Rita. "The devil is loose! I smell his sulphurous mischief!"

"You'll be smelling ether and hospital smells if you don't let go of this bloody wheel!" screamed Bella. "Let go, you great fat freak!"

"Turn back!" roared Aunt Rita.

"Look," Tara was telling Bates. "You don't want any coffee, there's no story here and I've got things to do. I hope you don't mind, but I'd rather have your space than your company."

The man was starting to give her the creeps. For one thing, he'd put his owl glasses back on. So he did need them, after all. Yet they changed his whole personality. He became slightly weird. She turned abruptly away, dismissing him. A black cloud rolled across the sky, turning, momentarily, the glass of the wall through which she was looking into a mirror. With a spasm in her stomach like a knife thrust she saw in the reflection Bates, behind her, pull from his pocket a thin cord and stretch it between his hands. As he came for her, she picked up, on reflex, a heavy lamp by the side of her and turned, swinging blindly. With luck, she could have got him on the head. Hitting out without time to judge it, she caught him only on the side of the neck. Still, it was enough to knock him sideways, stunned. As she made to run past him, he was still quick enough to stretch out a foot and trip her. She went down and he lurched toward her, the cord taut between his hands.

On the road, Aunt Rita, by sheer power and weight, had squeezed Bella, like a rubber doll, into a corner of the driver's side that she shouldn't logically have been able to fit into and had command of the wheel with a hand the size of a Christmas ham. She was throwing the car all over the road.

"Back! Back!" she cried. "For the gates of hell shall not prevail against us!"

"All right!" shouted Bella. "For Christ's sake! Leave go. I'll take you back!"

She screamed as a bus driver, handling his huge machine like a Nelson Picquet, managed to miss them by a coat of paint. Rita let go of the wheel, Bella brought the car to a stop, took out a handkerchief and wiped her face with a shaking hand.

"Well, don't just sit there!" bellowed Aunt Rita. "Get bloody motoring!"

Bella turned the car around in a screaming arc and started back to the flat.

As Bates had bent his knees toward the sprawled Tara, she had doubled her legs, let his stomach come within range and then kicked out with both feet, sending him clasped-up and gasping against a sofa. It should have been enough. But it was the point at which she realized she was up against a professional. His muscles absorbed the impact and his mind buffered the pain and he got up and came after her again. She was on her feet and already on her way to the front door. He caught her just as she had her hand on the door catch. He wasted no time trying to tear her hand away from the door, but flung the cord around her neck. Tara knew from her brothers, whose training she had been relying on from the start, that his next move would be the knee in the small of the back, arching her into a death crescent where applied mathematics would make it impossible for her to respond in any way.

In the instant of time available to her, she lashed backward with her right foot, bending her knee with precision as her brothers had taught her, and caught him full in the testicles.

Professional though he might have been, he could not stifle the howl of agony as he sank to his knees, the cord sliding from around her throat. Even in his convulsion, however, he still had the presence of mind to crawl between her and the front door and clamp his arms around her legs. She kneed him in the face, hearing the crunch of cartilage, and broke away toward the bathroom. He came after her, unable yet to stand, like some monstrous, anguished crab, and she felt, fleetingly, his nails on her ankle as she opened the bathroom door, got inside and slammed it.

On the road, Aunt Rita was flogging Bella with a jellified bag, urging her to greater and greater acceleration.

"The devil," she intoned, "is not to be caught by laggards, sloths and drones! Even now he and that Jezebel could be working their carnal profanities in the face of the Lord!"

Bella said nothing, simply kept her foot hard down, her eyes on the road and her sanity in a little plastic bag she always reserved for such occasions in a corner of her mind.

He was crashing against the door. The lock was only a bathroom lock, not intended to be proof against homicidal determination. Too late, Tara realized that she had made the wrong decision, the same mistake she'd made with Tug Beckett in The Screw. The last place she should have fled was a small room with nowhere else to go where he could cut off any possible escape simply by staying between her and the door. Remorselessly, methodically, came the thud of his heel against the point where the lock was. The securing screws inside were already starting to spring and start from their lodgings. The first one burst loose from its bedding and fell, tinkling, on to the marble floor. It would get quicker from now on. The second one was starting to give way.

On the road, Bella drove like a maniac who still had some measure of control—a kind of parallel to the man Bates inside Tara's flat. She was somehow thrashed onward by the equal and contagious mania of Aunt Rita who, satisfied by the skill and speed of Bella's driving, now seemed to be reciting from the Apocalypse:

"And the Angel thrust his sharp sickle into the earth and gathered the vineyard of the earth, and cast it into the great press of the wrath of God," she chanted. "And the press was trodden without the city and blood came out of the press, up to the horses's bridles for a thousand and six hundred furlongs."

"Will you for Christ's sake shut up!" screeched Bella. "If we're going to keep this car on the road, shut up, shut up, shut up!"

Aunt Rita said nothing, but relapsed into obedient silence, although her feet beat a tattoo on the car's carpeted floor.

In the flat, in the bathroom, on the lock, the last screw was giving way. Tara watched it, fascinated, as in slow-motion playback, as it reluctantly gave way its hold, thousandths of a millimeter at a time, and finally relinquished its grip, its note as it hit the floor sounding like the great bell Tom. The door opened slowly and Bates appeared around the edge of it, goggling. She was not entirely unprepared. She had a tin of hair spray, which she immediately spewed at his eyes. The bastard was wearing those glasses. It blinded him, but only until he took off the opaque-sprayed lenses, which he did instantly, knocking the spray out of her hand at the same time. It distracted him from her other hand, which was also holding a spray can, this one of pressurized toilet water with which she now blasted him straight into his unprotected eyes. The aerosol carrier, mixed with the spirit base of the fragrance, blinded him again. It was to no avail.

He gasped in pain, kept his eyes open just a diabolical slit and came on, his arms and hands a barrier against which she could strike at no vulnerable part. She reached for the shower attachment in the bath and struck at him with its heavy nozzle. He deflected the blow with a forearm, threw his weight at her, knocked her backward into the bath and knelt over her. She had nowhere else to go. She watched, mesmerized, as, again in slow motion, he took the cord from his pocket. He slid it around her throat. She pressed her chin desperately into her chest, but she could feel the cord, as he tightened it, beginning to force its way through.

Then there were noises outside and Aunt Rita ballooned into the room, reached out for Bates with arms like elephant legs, plucked him up from behind, seemingly by the armpits, and banged him face-first against the bathroom wall until he was still. Somewhere else in her mind, Tara could hear Bella's voice on the telephone, talking to the police. Then she allowed herself the luxury of fainting.

Tara stayed in shock far longer than anyone would have expected a tough girl like her to do. The police, anxious for her statement, were obliged to wait, on her doctor's advice. She refused to go to hospital, but remained in bed at home, where she could operate. She wasn't in shock at all. She was at her tricks. First of all, she gathered from Bella what Bates's story was. He had fallen in love with her on the television screen; it had become an obsession; he had tracked her down and gone to worship her in person and when she had reacted badly, he had panicked. He was touching, the way he told it.

He was Mr. Clean. He had no record, had never been in trouble before, had never even been done for a parking offense. Naturally, thought Tara. His business was killing people for money; he couldn't afford any other vices.

She called Sir Jonathan. She had a deal to propose to the police. If she were allowed an interview with Bates before the trial, she thought she could persuade him to plead guilty to intent to commit grievous bodily harm. They wanted to charge him with attempted murder, to which he was resolutely pleading "Not Guilty" and he had a good story. He'd probably get a suspended sentence on condition he took psychiatric treatment. At least, if they agreed to go with Tara, they'd get him put away.

In view of her unique position—while reserving their right to disapprove of some of her methods the police regarded her as almost another arm of the law—and in relief at her coming out of shock, they granted her the interview, which took place in a remand cell at Walton four days later. One of the conditions was that there were to be no witnesses.

As she walked into Bates's cell, unaccompanied, carrying her briefcase, Bates, lounging insolently on his bed, stiffened and swung to his feet.

"What do you want?" he asked, flatly, no ironic reaction in his morally inadequate mind to the fact that, if he'd had his way, Tara would be dead and buried. All she represented to him was a job gone wrong and self-reproach that he'd underestimated her.

"I've got a deal to offer, you sick, flat-faced bastard," she said, amiably. Without his glasses, which had been smashed in his first collision with the bathroom wall in the grip of Aunt Rita, his face *was* flat.

"What deal?"

"Plead guilty to intent to commit G.B.H., I won't have to go into the witness box, you'll get three to five, less if you're lucky."

"No chance," he said. "I've got a great story. I was in love with you. Infatuated. They've probably told you. No, I'll stay with their attempted murder charge and plead Not Guilty."

"Oh dear," Tara sighed. "That means I'll have to go into the witness box."

"So? You can only tell them what happened—that I suddenly attacked you. I'll tell them why: I'm a shy, disturbed lad, who panicked."

"That's only if I tell them the truth," said Tara. "I wouldn't tell them the truth."

"You what?" he gaped, a new dimension of depravity opening up to him in which ordinary, honest folk lied.

"I would tell them that from the minute you walked in you very coolly told me that you were a thief, who intended to rob my flat, but that you liked a bit of spice to go with your robberies, so you were going to rape me first and then strangle me before stripping the flat. I would tell them you said you'd done it before, a number of times, and you were so good at it that you'd never even come under suspicion."

"That's a total, fucking lie," he shouted.

"Yes, isn't it," grinned Tara, "but it wouldn't half finish you. They'd put you inside and burn the file."

"You'd never get away with it," he raved. "You can't lie like that in court and get away with it!"

"Oh, be your age!" said Tara. "Even villains get away with it. I'm a pillar of virtue, remember, defender of the people. Think how much easier it is for me!"

He paced the cell like a small, wiry animal, looking for a mental out. He couldn't find one. Finally, he turned to Tara: "So your deal is I plead guilty to a lesser charge and do a stretch and you don't give any evidence at all."

She could see she'd got him going.

"That's the first part of the deal," she said, blandly.

"What?"

"There's a second part. I want to know the name of the man who paid you to kill me."

The shock on his face showed that he had believed up to this point she knew nothing about the real facts. It took him some time to collect his thoughts. At last the message penetrated. She really was a pro. As hard and as ruthless, probably, as he was himself. He'd been paid to do a simple killing; not to tangle with anything like this. Yet still he tried to prevaricate.

"You know I can't tell you that," he said. "He finds out, that means he just pays someone else to wipe me."

"Not if you're in prison," said Tara.

"Oh, come on! Do us a favor! What difference does that make?"

"True. Very true," said Tara, sadly. "So we'll have to do this the other way around. I'll tell you who it was. All you have to do is tell me whether I'm right. It was Shaun Patterson, wasn't it?"

She could see the blood drain down to his toes.

"You know I can't tell you that," he answered. "Have a bleeding heart!" He sat abruptly on his bunk.

"That's all I am," said Tara, "One great big, bleeding heart. And I'm fan-bloody-tastic in the witness box. Was it?"

She raised and sharpened her voice, standing over him. He winced, sensing the hate in it.

"Was it Shaun Patterson who paid you to kill me? Was it?"

Still he couldn't bring himself to utter.

"Fine. Have it your way." She turned to go, as if she'd tired of a game against a stupid opponent.

"Yes," he shouted. "Yes, yes, yes!"

"Yes what?" she demanded.

"Yes, it was Shaun Patterson who paid me to kill you."

"There . . . that wasn't hard now, was it?" she asked, in a deadly, nanny-like tone. She de-activated her briefcase and left.

Five minutes after she got back home, Ben arrived. He was carrying the traveling roll in which he seemed to be able to pack all his worldly needs.

"Where's my room?" he inquired, briskly.

"Your what?"

"I'm moving in," he explained, simply. "From now on, Snow White, I'm going to stick to you as close as wallpaper. Day and night."

"Oh no, you're bloody not," said Aunt Rita, who had just appeared in the hallway behind Tara. She stood, arms akimbo, blocking the way into the living room. Ben put down his bag, placed a hand under each of her upholstered elbows and lifted her gently sideways out of the way. As she rose slowly into the air, like a balloon taking off, her face displayed a prodigious astonishment. On being put down again she looked at Ben with awe, turned and paddled to her room. She never interfered with him again.

"Ben . . ." started Tara, warningly.

"I know, I know," said Ben, putting up a big, hard hand. "Strictly business. But Patterson has tried once, and now he's shown his hand he won't stop there. The game's really on now. He knows it's either you or him and he's going to try to make sure it's not him."

"I know that, too," said Tara. "And thanks, Ben."

She looked at the handsome face with its blond's tan, the extraordinary blue eyes. "It's not that I actually find you repulsive, you know," she smiled.

"No," he said, softly.

They had both long come to terms with the complex bar to a physical relationship between them, yet just to see him, touch him, sit next to him gave her a warm glow that was not entirely confined to her heart and head. They broke away from each other.

"We've got everything now except Balham," said Tara. "If we can only locate him, somehow find a flaw in his identification of my old man, we can clinch it."

"Patterson'll be looking for him, too," Ben pointed out. "How's Dubrown coming along?"

At that moment, Dubrown was sweating like a bull. It had taken him six weeks and cost him five pounds in weight and the experience of a lifetime cruising the corridors of power to get into the office in which he was now sitting. He was calling in a very heavy favor. One which he was owed by the man sitting across the desk from him who, as an old schoolfriend, had never expected to have to repay it. He recognized the justice of the situation, but there was more to life than justice, dammit, and he would never have imagined that Dubrown . . . And he wouldn't even explain why he wanted it. However, he congratulated himself that he had stage-managed the thing rather well. As Dubrown had entered his office, which his assistant had timed, as instructed, to the second, he had simulated a start of surprise and hastily slipped the piece of paper, which he was holding, underneath his blotter. He now rose.

"Dubrown," he said, "I'm going to the lavatory. When I get back, I expect to find you gone. And I never expect to see you again."

He put out no hand to shake and did not look back as he went out. Dubrown lifted the blotter and plucked the sheet of paper from beneath it. On it was printed John Balham's new identity and his present whereabouts.

"Marbella!" Sid exploded. "But Bella told us weeks ago that Patterson had a lot of bricks and mortar out there. He must have a lot of contacts—stands to reason. How do we know he hasn't already found John Balham and straightened him?"

"I agree," said Ben.

It was Tara's usual weekly conference except that, instead of being held in her office at Alhambra, it was taking place in the living room of her flat. Sitting on the chairs and sofas, sprawled on the moss-green carpet, looking—with the background of massed acres of forest—as if they were holding a meeting in a glade, were Tara, Bella, Ben, Suzy, Mail Room Sid, Terry and Jean Soong. Tara had just told them that Dubrown had come through with the information they needed and there had been an explosion of excitement.

"I don't think so," said Tara. "Patterson's got nothing to fear from John Balham. It was Balham's positive identification that put my father away, remember."

"That's true," Suzy put in, "but I think Sid's right. Patterson must realize now that we'll be looking for Balham to try and crack his identification. If he gets to him first, I'd say it was exit Mr. Balham."

"So what are you thinking of doing?" asked Jean Soong.

"I'm going to take a unit out to Marbella and interview Mr. Balham," said Tara.

"You'll never get out there without Patterson finding out where you've gone and sussing something," said Sid. "Stands to common sense he's bound to be having you watched."

"I'll have a convincing personal, private reason for going out there," answered Tara. "The crew can go separately. Meanwhile, I want you lot to take those tape recordings I've got and get video to go with them. We've already got Tug Beckett. The others are in the same jail as my Dad—Walton."

"Tara, we'll never get permission," said Suzy, "from the authorities."

"Not if you tell the authorities the truth, no. But you won't tell them the truth, will you? Look, you may find it funny, but we're an Establishment show. We're on the side of the righteous, as Aunt Rita would say. There'll be no trouble getting in—I'll pull a few strings. After that, you're on your own. If you get any aggro from the targets, threaten them with shopping them to my Dad like I did. That'll do it. The crew can take the tiny little Jap cameras—they don't alarm anybody—and you just get those statements on vision, that's all! Listen, why did I hire you, anyway? Because you're the biggest bunch of rogues and liars outside of the House of Commons! You can do it!"

There was a laugh, interrupted by Ben.

"There's just one thing," he said quietly. "I come to Marbella, too."

There was a murmur of assent and Tara paused. "But not on the same plane," she said.

As the meeting broke up, Tara knew she was facing three confrontations she'd rather have avoided—with Paul Cranmer, with Cyril Goldstein and with Michael Patterson. The last was going to be the most hideous of all because it involved the ultimate deception of him.

The first two she managed to concertina into one. She asked for a joint meeting with Cyril Goldstein and Paul Cranmer. It was held in Cyril G.'s opulently monastic office. She wore no makeup except eye shadow and her most severely functional gray-blue leather suit. Her hair was pulled back. She looked sensational.

"I need permission . . ." she began.

"You've never asked permission for anything before, why start now?" asked Cyril G.

"Because what I'm at is heavily personal and I think you've a right to know."

"We're present at an historic occasion," exclaimed Paul, ironically.

There was nothing for it, Tara decided, but to start at Day One or, rather, Night One, of her grand design, when she broke into the building and hid Paul's *Rape of a City* and go right through to where she was now, on the trail of John Balham.

She held them spellbound. When she finished, there was a silence, stunned on Paul's part. Then Cyril spoke.

"So what do you want from us?" he asked. "Applause? You've got it. But I must tell you—bighead that I am—that some of it I already suspected."

"Well, I didn't suspect a bloody thing!" exclaimed Paul. "What on earth can you want from us that you couldn't do yourself with your own little finger?"

"I want the go-ahead to take a team to Marbella to put the finishing touch to an operation which is purely personal and I thought it was time I declared my interest. I feel bad about keeping you in the dark so long," she confessed.

"In the first place," said Cyril, "as I told you, I haven't been quite as much in the dark as you thought. And in the second place, I don't agree that it's a purely personal issue. If you are right, there is a catastrophic miscarriage of justice here and a terrible crime. It's a sort of murder of the spirit. That is of public concern. Furthermore, if you want my opinion as an old showman, if you really pull it together and bring it off, I'd say it was hell-of-a-good-television. If he were to ask me, I would strongly advise your Head of Department to authorize the budget for the Marbella adventure and argue with me about it afterward. How d'you feel about that, Paul?" he asked, turning toward him.

"I was thinking of authorizing a reconnaissance-and-shoot to Marbella on this project," said Paul, straight-faced. "What do you think?"

"You know how I hate these fishing expeditions," answered Cyril, equally straight-faced, "especially when they just happen conveniently to be to glamorous foreign resorts. But on this occasion . . . well, I suppose it's more promising than most. You've got it."

God, they were such honeys, thought Tara. You'd think they'd invented the word "supportive."

She walked out of Cyril G.'s office on winged feet. She came crashing to earth when she remembered that she still had her third confrontation to come. Her date with Michael Patterson that evening. She knew that, in looking after his father's interests in Marbella, Michael had found it convenient to buy a pad over there. She also knew that the one way she could get to Marbella without arousing Patterson's suspicions would be to go with Michael. Patterson would be so furious about this evidence of her developing relationship with his son that it would blind him to any other reason she might have for going there.

But that meant deceiving Michael, too. It meant doing the acting bit she did so well, she mused bitterly. So that when he picked her up for dinner that night, she had somehow willed away the glow that normally warmed the smooth ivory of her skin and beneath her eyes was a blue shadow she didn't get out of any makeup bottle. And over dinner at The Sanctuary, deep in the protective folds of Cheshire, an inn where they were to spend a weekend of November outdoors and log-warmed indoors, the blue eyes darkened with concern behind the glasses and he asked the inevitable question: "Are you all right?"

"I'm fine, love," she said. "You know how it is. Sometimes you just feel completely sold out. I feel like shutting myself in a box and hiding."

"You need to get away," he said, with the decisiveness she was cynically counting on. "Take a week off; two weeks. A month. They can't refuse you—you've hardly had a break since I met you. Look,

I've got to go back to Spain on business. You know I've got a pad in Marbella. It's marvelous there just now. Seventy in the shade, blue skies day after day, beauty that has to be seen to be believed. Come and stretch out. You'd fill up with energy!"

She allowed herself, treacherous bitch that she was, she felt, to be talked into coming and staying with him for two weeks. Only the memory of her latest visit to her father, the light now so obviously fading from his eyes, put back the iron into her resolve.

Michael's pad was a penthouse in La Alcazaba, which was like saying to a Marbellan that one had a piece of paradise. Set off the road that hissed like an arrow along the coast all the way from Malaga to Cadiz, with the lion's roar of the Sierras on one side and tranquil blue mother Mediterranean on the other, dazzling white domes and turrets and minarets were cut out of a stainless cobalt sky, surrounding a kind of Garden of Allah. There were streams and diamond-spraying waterfalls and fountains, surrounded by explosive banks of tropical flowers of colors she had seen only on canvas. Impossible lilacs, throbbing crimsons, slashing scarlets and aquamarines and golds, agapanthus bursting like foaming blue fireworks, tamed by homelier flowers like white Michaelmas daisies and roses and marguerites. And everywhere avenues of tall palms, sudden eruptions of small ones breaking out of the ground. Over everything was the haunting scent of the tiny white trumpets of Night Lady, still hanging in the air from its musky opening of the previous evening. And flowing everywhere, forming its base, flawless emerald lawns that looked as if they had laid and been nurtured there for a thousand years. She remembered reading somewhere the Moorish proverb: that one built not with stone alone, but also with sky and water and flowers.

Tara was a Liverpudlian, with all the innate sophistication that implied: she was also famous. But this place brought home to her the fact that this was the first time she had ever been abroad. Even the light, the minute you stepped off the plane into it, changed your appearance instantly—skin tone, eyes; everything. For two days they didn't move out of Michael's penthouse, with its white marble, white columns, white rugs, its warmly hugging blue swimming pool, indoors, but open to the sky and its surrounding terraces, seducing one never to go outdoors. Whether it was the sorcery of the place itself or the effect, as Michael claimed, of the flooding sun on some gland— the "pineal," was it?—they spent most of the time locked together, or playfully preparing to be locked together—to "dock" as space-buff Michael called it—or resting afterward. On the first afternoon they put on oxygen tanks and went underwater in the swimming pool, to simulate the sensation of making love in space. Tara found it a bit disappointing: she missed the element of weight. "Bit like eating candy floss," she said.

It was in the middle of the second night that she found herself suddenly awake, reminding herself of why she'd come here. She told herself there was nothing she could do until morning, when Michael had a business meeting, but she couldn't rest. She fidgeted and sweated. She felt as if there were an itch in the muscles of her legs, which she couldn't reach. In the end, she slid out of bed and walked to the second bathroom, barefoot and silent on the marble floor. She rang Ben from the bathroom. He was staying at an apartment at the Puente Romano three minutes away. From the way he answered the telephone, she knew he'd been awake, too.

"Where the hell have you been?" he asked, "I've been going spare!"

"I'm sorry," she said. "I'll see you at ten-thirty this morning."

"I'll pick you up," said Ben.

"No, better if I come to you," she said. She hung up, flushed the cistern as camouflage just in case, went out; and lost her breath. Michael was standing outside.

"I woke up and missed you," he said. "Who was that?" He scratched his head sleepily.

"I couldn't find my watch," she lied. "I asked the operator the time. I didn't use the bedroom telephone in case I woke you."

"Oh," he said. He stumbled past her into the bathroom. A minute later he fell back into bed, cuddled her and went instantly back to sleep, his arms around her. She had never felt such a shit in her life.

The next morning, after Michael had left for his business meeting in Malaga, Tara put on a simple short sleeved khaki cotton dress and sandals and screwed her hair back tight in an effort at low profiling. Even so, her beauty attracted every dark eye on her short walk to the dazzling modern Spanish village that was Puente Romano.

"I've got news," said Ben, the instant they met. "Shaun Patterson's here."

"What?"

"Either it's coincidence or he's had a hint of where Balham may be and he hasn't bought your cover that you're just over here on a trip with Michael."

"I keep underestimating that bastard," said Tara.

"Don't worry," said Ben, "I've got him covered. I've done a

lot of movies out here. Patterson's staying at the Los Monteros. The head concierge there is an old mate of mine. He's keeping me posted on his movements."

Ben had hired a Range Rover—"the only thing to drive out here if you can't get hold of a Centurion tank"—with cow-catchers on the front and back. They drove the ninety seconds down the dusty back road from La Alcazaba to the Puerto Banus. Her first sight of the port, created by the genius of one man—José Banus—stunned Tara, despite the growing paddling of anxiety in her stomach. It was almost too pretty, in the subtlety of its multi-levelled, eye-deceiving design, like a tumble of white-iced tiered cakes in a blue window, a profusion of restaurants and glittering shops fighting the cascading crimson bougainvillea and pink geraniums for every inch of space. Along and around the snaking quay the yachts of seemingly every rich part-time sailor in the world jostled and tinkled. "If Banus hadn't built it, Hollyood would have invented it," said Ben. This, according to Dubrown, was where John Balham was. To be accurate, this was where his main boutique—he had four—was located. His name was now Peter Rodriguez. He had done well in his new life.

Ben parked the Land Rover outside the gold-glinting, bronze-windowed "Su Casa" and they went in. Señor Rodriguez wasn't there. He was at his branch just off the Orange Square in the old town. As they drove off, neither Ben nor Tara noticed the little Seat, the Spanish form of the Fiat, which had followed them from the Puente Romano and which now tucked discreetly in behind them again.

They parked in a side street outside the Orange Square, adopting the practical local expedient of shunting backward and forward until enough space had been made. They walked through the Square. Tara mistook the golden globes glowing in the trees for lights. It was Ben who explained that they were oranges, ripening nicely in time for December. Still neither of them noticed the Seat, which parked a little way down the street, where a bicycle had pulled out.

The shop was just as stylish as that on the Puerto Banus. Peter Rodriguez had well-oiled, curly black hair, a plump, olive-smooth face, a bandit's moustache and a comfortable paunch. He wore a beautifully cut beige suit, blue shirt and white tie. He was pouring out a flood of Andalucian Spanish to an assistant as they went in. Tara began to think Dubrown had got it wrong. Rodriguez turned and stared at her.

"Can I help you?" he asked, in what most people would have taken for fairly heavily Spanish-accented English. But Tara's heart leaped as her ear picked up the underlying melody of her native city.

"You can, Mr. Balham," she said. "In fact, I need your help really, really badly."

He paled slightly.

"I don't know what you're talking about," he said, his natural accent now much stronger, "but whatever it is, we'd better discuss it in the cafe next door."

As they sat down with their coffee, it was Balham who opened fire.

"Look," he said, "I know you. You're Tara Stewart. They put your program out regularly on Gibraltar T.V. We get it here. You can only want to talk about the Mersey Tunnel job. Well, you already admitted on your show that your father did that. You know the police gave me immunity and set me up nicely here. My wife couldn't stand it here so she went back home and married an accountant, but I'm married now to a lovely Spanish girl, we've got two fat kids; I hope you're not going to blow all that."

Tara covered him solemnly with the translucent gray eyes in which the cobalt sky was reflected.

"I'm hoping," she said slowly, "that by the time I've finished you'll want to blow it yourself."

She went on to give the most compellingly lucid, heart-bending performance of her career. Both men were riveted. Ben's attention wandered only once. It was toward the end, when he saw a lank-haired man getting into a Seat which he seemed vaguely to have seen a couple of times earlier that morning and drive off. He came back to the conversation to hear Tara saying, "Listen, all I'm asking is that you come and look at a man. You don't even have to come to England to do it; he's here now. You could see him without him seeing you. What have you got to lose?"

It was the following day. Patterson was sitting in Don Leone's on the Puerto Banus. Ben's concierge friend had told him he had booked there for lunch. He was under the royal yellow canopy, center table, against the flower-wreathed pillar. He couldn't have been more conspicuous if he'd been standing on his head on the table. Donna was with him. The combination of the table, Donna with her eyes like emeralds against her tan, and his own hard good looks, gave him what he loved: the attention and envy of the less fortunate. He was wearing a tailored safari jacket—the favorite gear of her father—reflected Tara, bitterly, and dark glasses.

She parked the car at the edge of the quay, miraculously finding a space directly opposite Don Leone's. The inevitable soft-topped truck, with Pam in her hideout, was parked just a couple of cars in front. It had been there since early morning, to make sure. Tara turned to Balham, next to her in the unobtrusive saloon they had substituted for the Land Rover.

"Take a good look," she said. "Is that the man? The one by the . . ."

"I know which one you mean," said Balham. "He's older, of course, but he hasn't changed much. I don't understand—if they've let him out early, what's all the fuss about? Out is out. Funny, I was right about the mole."

"What mole?" asked Tara, sharply.

"Under certain lights you could see a sort of extra darkness under the hair—under the hairline at the temple. I wondered if there was a mole there. Now his hair's receded at the temples, you can see it—look!"

"Watching him now," asked Tara, her heart beating increasingly faster, "would you say he was left- or right-handed?"

"Well, he's right-handed, isn't he," said Balham, glancing at her as if she were a bit of an idiot. "Anyone can see that."

"Think hard," said Tara. "Was the man who blackmailed you all those years ago left-handed or right-handed?"

"Don't have to think," said Balham, "he was right-handed, definitely, same as now."

"How can you be so sure?" asked Tara.

Again, Balham looked at her as if she were a bit stupid, but had to be humored.

"He used to do a trick," he explained, "to show off his reflexes. You put four coins on the back of your hand. Right? Then you flip them up in the air and catch them, one by one, with the same hand, before any of them hit the floor. He was fantastically quick. He always used his right hand—like he did for everything else. He was right-handed."

"My father's left-handed," said Tara triumphantly. "They thrashed him for it at school, but no one was ever able to change him. And he hasn't got any mole on his temple."

Their view was momentarily obscured by a huge wine truck, maneuvering into a position from which it could make a delivery to Da Paolo's next door. It reversed a little way toward them. Then it kept coming, swerving slightly sideways, moving very slowly, its engine revving slowly and thunderously.

"He's coming into us!" shouted Balham.

The next second, the truck's huge bumpers had made contact with the little saloon and started to shove it inexorably toward the edge of the quay. Tara screamed, Balham yelled, standing on the brakes. The clientele of Don Leone's, from whom the whole drama was obscured by the bulk of the truck, ate and drank and shrieked and chatted, as usual.

Just before the car went over the edge, Ben wrenched open a rear door and squeezed in. One huge fist had put to sleep the lank-haired man in the Seat, three cars behind, on the way. Ben settled himself in the back of the car and spoke very rapidly, but very coolly and clearly.

"When we hit the water, do nothing," he said. "Don't try to open the doors, you won't be able to. Stay cool, let the water rise inside the car. As it reaches your chin, take a deep breath. When it reaches the roof, the water pressures outside and inside will be equal, you'll be able to open the doors as easily as if you were in the fresh air. It's a doddle. I've done it a hundred times for movie stunts. Just keep cool."

Such was the man's presence that they obeyed him to the letter. As the green, moted water closed over them, they sat still and it all happened as Ben had said. When the water hit the roof, the doors opened easily; but Tara's seat belt, snaking in the water, tangled around and trapped her. Ben turned back and wrestled with it. In the end, he tore the belt from its mooring by brute force. Freed, she shot to the surface, following Balham.

Ben turned to eel out of the rear door. But the hammer-strap on the leg of his jeans snagged on the torn mooring of the seat belt. Desperately, he tried to reach it, but his size, in the confined space, was against him. He tugged, but the tough denim wouldn't give way and he was now weak. Finally, he unzipped his jeans. He got halfway out of them. He'd used up too much of his oxygen freeing Tara. When she dived down to see what had happened to him she found that he'd died with a smile on his face, as if amused at being caught with his trousers down. She had the unique experience of wanting to sob, but being unable to do so, as she swam underwater with Balham, past the prow of the unattended yacht next to where the car went down. As she heaved herself on to the quay, still screened by the parked cars from all the beautiful people in the restaurants, that's when she started to sob. She and Balham climbed over the side of the canvas-covered truck to join Pam, who simply opened her arms. Tara fell into them.

"Ben's dead," she said.

Balham peered through the spy-hole in the canvas. The table where Patterson had been sitting was empty. The truck was moving swiftly off, its number plate totally obscured by mud, no markings on its sides. Pam rocked Tara gently.

"I know it's no consolation now," she said, "but it will be later— I got the whole murderous thing." She tapped her camera: "In here."

"That bastard tried to kill us!" said Balham, as they drove off toward the crew's quarters at the Andalucia Plaza, five minutes away.

"What bastard?" asked Tara, her sobs subsiding as her sharp intelligence clicked into action.

"Well, it wasn't your father, was it?" he exclaimed.

After that it was easy. One could hardly stop Balham talking. Left-handed, right-handed, mole, no mole, mistaken identity, wanted to retract, would stand up in any court in the land and retract his identification. Look on this picture and on this. Photographs of the two men as they were fourteen years ago. All meticulously shot by Pam and recorded by the sound crew. The makeup girl made no attempt to embellish Tara's red-rimmed eyes as she questioned him. It was the final knot in Patterson's noose.

As Balham finished, they switched on Radio Marbella. The evening news carried a story about a man found drowned in the Puerto Banus. No further details. Don't worry Ben, swore Tara, her heart cracking at the thought that she'd never given that gallant blue and gold god what he'd really wanted, we'll nail that multi-damned fucker now. Balham telephoned his Spanish wife and asked her to collect him. He told her they would be spending some time with her relatives in the mountains behind Mijas.

All Tara wanted to do now was to get back to La Alcazaba, collect her passport and get out of Spain. Pam and the crew wanted to go with her as a protective posse, but she begged them to stay and see that Ben's body got home to England. She took a taxi to La Alcazaba, the precious can of that afternoon's tape clutched under her arm. Michael was home when she arrived. He took one look at her red-rimmed eyes:

"What . . . ?" he began. The telephone interrupted him. His father's voice rasped ferociously at the other end.

"Is that cow there?"

Frantically, Tara signaled "No!"

Michael's voice came out of the deep freeze: "If you're referring to Tara Stewart, no she's not."

"If the bitch turns up, let me know."

"Unless you stop talking about her as if she's one of your Torre-molinos tarts," said Michael, "I'll tell you damn all."

"Ah, what's the use!" said the voice on the other end, its viciousness a surprise even to Michael. "Trust me to have a pansy for a son!" The click of the telephone hanging up was a whiplash.

"What's all that about?" asked Michael bewildered.

"I can't tell you now, Michael," said Tara. "I think it's probably the end of it for you and me. But I can't tell you anything more. Family comes first, we both know that. That's what will probably kill us. When you find out what I've done to you, you'll understand, but you won't forgive. Just accept my oath that it didn't start like that. Now would you please drive me to Malaga airport, I have to get back to England."

Michael knew his Tara. There had been that tone in her voice which meant that she had slammed down the steel door between the outside world and whatever was going on inside her head. To try and break through it was hopeless. He drove her to Malaga airport and kissed her goodbye at the passport desks. It was a kiss that took him by surprise with a depth he couldn't define at the time. He finally analyzed it, in the middle of the night, as a kind of loving despair.

There was a lank-haired man with a livid bruise on his jaw some way behind Tara and Michael in the passport queue, whose facial discoloration seemed to disconcert the passport officers. They told him, in the uncompromising Spanish fashion, to wait, while the appropriate arm of the law-enforcement agencies was called to examine him more closely. On the flight across, Tara had three whiskies, which she very rarely drank. The stewardesses, who recognized her, also registered the symptoms of deep human distress and did not bother her in any way.

She came out of Customs at Manchester in a daze. All she carried was one flight bag and the can of tape under her arm. All she wanted was home, a familiar scent, a familiar face. She ran headfirst, in a sense, into all three.

"Whoa! Whoa!" he said, as she collided, eyes down, with the familiar scent of Jason Planter's gold velvet waistcoat which, typically, he was wearing with a mutedly spectacular tweed suit. He soothed her as he would a runaway horse. "Where d'you think you're going?" he asked.

"Home," she said, on the verge of whiskey-numbed tears. He snapped his fingers at his porter, who added her flight bag to the neat pile of Jason's fashionably anonymous baggage, New York stickers on it, on his trolley. She resisted dumbly and fiercely the puzzled porter's attempt to take the tape reel. They went out into the nipping autumn air to his red Lamborghini, which had magically appeared, a garage attendant at the wheel, at the exit doors. Jason tipped the man and settled her down in the warm, deep–mined luxury of her seat. The car grumbled suavely off and almost, it seemed, within a gear change they were away from the lighted doll's house of the airport and out on the open road.

The unaccustomed Scotch was having its effect and it was not for some minutes after the event that Tara noticed that they had missed the turnoff to Liverpool.

"Hey," she asked, drowsily, "are you getting addle-nutted in your old age?"

"You said 'home,' " he smiled, without taking his eyes off the road they were devouring. "You didn't specify yours or mine. You look to me as if you need taking care of, so we're going to mine."

She relaxed into her snug seat, in the warmth, content, for an interval, not to have to think about anything. The thinking would come back when the pain came back.

They rumbled up the drive to the manor house, the headlights picking out the immaculate box hedges, the Norman tower. Bowman came immediately out into the courtyard as the engine apologized to a stop and carried her flight bag inside. The tape reel she kept still clutched tightly to her.

In the drawing room, Jason made her comfortable on the big Ottoman sofa in front of a great, chuckling log fire. He had the trick of making her feel safe. Ben had had it and so did Paul. He took the coffee from Bowman at the door and brought it over to the fire himself.

"Here," he said, pouring it black and handing it to her, "this is what you need. What's the phrase—'it'll warm the cockles of your heart?' Drink it while it's hot."

She gulped it gratefully; the whiskey had dehydrated her. She started to talk, finding an infinite relief as it poured out: Balham and the truck and Ben and Patterson and the tape. Jason listened, fascinated. All Patterson had been able to tell him, belatedly, on the telephone earlier, was the plane she was on, which had given him just enough time to get some baggage organized and get out to the airport in a guise that looked convincing.

"That goon!" he said aloud. "That all-thumbs idiot!"

Tara's survival instinct switched on like a thermostat, sending out adrenalin which counteracted, temporarily, the hypnotic effect of the five non-lethal Mogadon he had put in her coffee. All the doors opened at once.

"You *are* Patterson's boss!" she cried.

"Of course I am," Planter grinned. "I own him! You were on the right track that night at the Adelphi."

"Until you blinded me with all that crap about your great-great-grandfather."

"It wasn't crap, it was all true. It was just that my little seizure came at a rather convenient time for me. Provided me with a shield against those searchlight eyes of yours. Incidentally, I thought you might like to know, I've decided I definitely have got a touch of the tarbrush—the dream I keep having: it's obviously a race memory. Poetic justice, really. It's comforting to have accepted it."

"The hell with all that," she said, "it's you and Patterson I can't stomach. You and that filth. Why?"

He looked at her bewildered face.

"The 'old' money was finally running out," he explained, patiently. "I had to show initiative. Crime seemed to be best suited to my needs, my temperament and the state of the modern world. I had to choose my associates carefully, of course; breeding still counts, you know, even in piracy. After all, my family were looting the world while the forebears of most of today's criminals were still picking pockets.

"Ideally, I would have liked your father as my running mate but I learned that he'd turned middle class. So I made contact with his former partner, Pattison, alias Patterson. I put up the seed money for the Mersey Tunnel operation, you know. My share of Patterson's roll-over profits are keeping me nicely in my old age. I'm still an active 'angel,' too, as you might say. I provided the development money, for instance, for that wonderful vault-busting machine of Mr. Les Meacher. You ruined that particular enterprise."

"That first time," said Tara, "when you were in front of me on the motorway—that was no coincidence."

"Of course not, sweet Tara. I'd heard on my grapevine that Jed Stewart's daughter had borrowed a little device that neutralized security systems. I became interested. The daughter of Jed Stewart going into business for herself!"

"My father would eat you alive," said Tara, her limbs becoming curiously heavy.

"That may well be true," admitted Planter. "But, then, his pedigree in piracy is as good as mine. And so is yours. And having watched you operate—admittedly on the other side of the fence—these last few years, I ache with the knowledge of possibilities." The black eyes were lustrous with enthusiasm. "Tara, my dear, won't you join me in taking crime, elegantly, with inspiration and artistry, into the twenty-first century, while the constabulary are still rooted in the first half of the twentieth? We would physically injure no one. We wouldn't even possess a peashooter. I'm already the king of computer crime—which is what your father would have been. It's what I've had in mind for us ever since I met you. We would live a life of sophisticated pillage which, given the time, I could probably even justify morally. What do you say?"

The man's magnetism, his fanaticism, given her drug-impaired state of mind, swept through her. For a space, it all seemed to make exciting sense. Then: "What about my father?" she asked.

Jason rose and paced carefully to and fro in front of the fire.

"Ah, well, there we have it," he said. "If you bring Patterson down in order to free your father, then I inevitably go down with Patterson."

"Then down with Patterson you bloody go," said Tara, finding she had to force the words out, her arms and legs feeling as if they had diver's weights attached to them. Despite her drowsiness, there was a quality of finality and a force of will behind her words that Planter couldn't mistake. Ah well, that was that. Pity.

He had it worked out. All the ruthless unsentimentality of his line stood behind him. He would drive her home now. There he would transfer her to her XJS. He would leave a half-finished bottle of Scotch, naturally without his fingerprints on it, on the passenger seat, together with a half-empty bottle of barbiturates, ditto. He would leave also a picture of Ben Maitland, which had appeared in that evening's *Echo,* illustrating a brief account of his mysterious death, a locally loved lad. Conclusion unavoidable.

His back to her, he cracked open the barbiturate capsules and emptied the powder into a three-quarters full tumbler of whiskey. Tara watched his back dimly, sleep beginning to overpower her. He turned to her with the lethal glass.

"Here you are, my dear. Sip it slowly"—he didn't want her to be sick—"we'll talk about it again in the morning. The important thing for you now is rest."

God, what a waste! he thought. Real, unmistakable quality here, little enough of it left in the world; he'd preserved it twice and now he was blotting it out. She put her lips to the proffered glass obediently. A voice spoke behind him.

"I'm sorry, sir. I can't permit you to do that."

Planter whirled to see Bowman standing, arms respectfully by his side.

"What the devil, Bowman?" he demanded.

"One of her first shows, sir," said Bowman, in his finest style. "A young couple, sir, she got their money back from a person called Iron Jack. The young wife in the case was a niece of mine."

Planter's hand strayed toward the drawer of an occasional table to the left of the Ottoman. Bowman raised his right hand, which proved to be holding an old-fashioned nine-millimeter Walther automatic, and shot Planter, with great precision, through the right shoulder. He bent down swiftly to his stricken master, instinctively scooping up the spilled glass first, but dropping his butlerian intonations in favor of his native Liverpool:

"Sorry, Mr. Planter," he said, "but I did owe her one. Don't worry; I'll get you to old Charlie, the quack; he'll fix you up without no nosy-parkering. Then I think it's the Caribbean for you, don't you?"

"Fuck you, Bowman," said Planter, swearing for the first time in his manservant's memory.

"Likewise, wacker," answered Bowman, without malice.

Tara, to whom it had all been a dream, was already asleep.

A month later, Shaun Patterson, back in London, was distracted from his obsessive search for Tara—a call from Planter had told him she was still alive—by an invitation to a prestigious little première at the 20th Century-Fox preview theater in Golden Square, Soho. It was to have first sight of a documentary to do with World Wild Life and the gilt-embossed card indicated the presence of a Highness or two. It also indicated that a donation would not be turned away. Come to that, he thought, maybe it was about time he did something really big for World Wild Life. Perhaps that would finally tilt the knighthood toward him, which had been a curiously long time coming for a philanthropist on his scale. There might be a chance of bumping into His Nibs and having a word about it— these preview theaters were, after all, tiny.

His card said seven o'clock, but when he got there, at six fifty-five, the film had already started. He stumbled in the dark to his seat in the front row, aided by a very classy young girl, but barracked by "tuts" and sighs from behind.

By the time he'd got his temper back and put on his glasses, he was relieved to see that all he had missed were the opening credits. It was the last relaxation he was to feel for the next fifty minutes. The riveting first shot was of the car being pushed into the water by the truck, intercut with shots of himself and Donna in Don Leone's, pinning down their precise proximity to the disaster. Tara, looking dreadful, then appeared in close shot and declared her interest.

"A friend of mine drowned in that car," she said, briefly. "In fact, this whole thing's very personal. Keep watching."

The movie then went into flashback on the Mersey Tunnel rob-

bery with contemporary footage of John Balham, after the trial, con-
fiming his crucial identification of Jed Stewart. Patterson, his eyes
accustomed now to the light, looked around. At the one exit, his
eyes caught the flash of uniform buttons. His eyes were dragged com-
pulsively back to the screen, his gut plunging.

Tara had asked Paul, still the best editor in the business, to put
it together. He had done it in Cyril G.'s mansion in Hoylake in the
private, fully professional editing suite which was the only rich man's
toy with which Cyril indulged himself. It was with him that Tara
had been hiding since she woke up on the Planter sofa, covered by
a duvet, with a splitting head and nightmarish memories. Paul had
rebuilt the apparently overwhelming case against Jed Stewart and
then, with Tara's material from Tom Lane the roofing cowboy, Iron
Jack the immigrant exploiter, Les Meacher the tool-maker, Tug Beckett the bank breaker, Bates the hit-man and Mulcahy, he lucidly and
inexorably demolished it, showing it to have been an elaborate and
vicious frame. He then, equally lucidly, reaffixed the guilt, both for
the frame and the robbery, to Patterson, ending with the ultimate,
damning contribution of Balham, interviewed by a red-eyed Tara.

Nobody had seen Patterson, in the dark, come in. Nobody saw
him as they left. He sat there, immobile, until everyone had gone.
Then he turned to meet the large, polite men standing by the exit.
And standing next to them, like a blond avenging angel, the gunsmoke in her eyes, was Tara.

"I heard you were looking for me," she said.

His reflexes were nearly as fast as they'd ever been and he floored
her with a brutal backhander before the big men could move to
restrain him. But the press photographer whom Tara had suggested
might care to stay behind in the background after the show had reflexes
that were just as fast and his flash blazed at the precise moment Patterson's hand struck Tara's face. She gazed up at Patterson from the
floor, blood trickling from the corner of her mouth as he was led away,
too proud to struggle, maintaining a level flow of gutter obscenities.

Two weeks afterward, she telephoned Michael. The only sound
he made was when he replaced the receiver. She thought she had no
tears left—and she was prepared for it, too—but that night she wept
as if she were the first woman who had ever cried.

Six months later, she wept again, this time for pure joy, as Jed
Stewart walked out of Walton Gaol to meet her. The light was back
behind his eyes like sunshine through crystal. Father and daughter
hugged as if they meant to kill each other. It would be pleasant to
record that on the way out he crossed paths with Shaun Patterson

going in, but the law isn't as tidy as that. Patterson did go in, finally, but only after his lawyers had run out of tricks.

The insurance company, in the small but formidable person of Herbert Thynne, tried for a legal first by taking suit against the Patterson Foundation for recovery of the original seventeen million on which its fortunes were based. Michael Patterson fought them ferociously. Given how much the lawyers are making out of it, nothing is likely to be decided for a very long while.

Tara and Michael Patterson have taken to using the same restaurant, same time, same day every week, different corners of the room. Neither has caught the other looking yet.

With grateful acknowledgments for much help from:

Ex-Commander X.
Ex-Det. Chief Supt. R.
Ex-Supt. T.
Det. Chief Insp. M.
Ex-Det. Insp. K.
Det. Sgt. W.
Det. Sgt. B.
Det. Sgt. B. T.
Det. Sgt. L.
Det. Sgt. P.
Det. Sgt. A.
Det. Sgt. A. N.
Mr. D. L. M. R. W.
Mr. Simon Randall
The Departments of Sociology, the Universities of Liverpool and
Salford.

Also various houseguests of Her Majesty, including Billy, John,
Lem, Scrubsy, Denny, Roy, Arthur, Jinnsy, Rol, Parkie, Worm, Pan,
Roley, Whitey, and Pearl.

Also all the marvelous colleagues I've worked with in television. They
know who they are.